THE
SILVERBLOOD
PROMISE

THE
SILVERBLOOD PROMISE

The Last Legacy
BOOK ONE

James Logan

TOR

TOR PUBLISHING GROUP
NEW YORK

THE SILVERBLOOD PROMISE

Copyright © 2024 by James Logan

A Tor Book
Published by Tom Doherty Associates / Tor Publishing Group
120 Broadway
New York, NY 10271

www.tor-forge.com

Tor® is a registered trademark of Macmillan Publishing Group, LLC.

The Library of Congress Cataloging-in-Publication Data
is available upon request.

ISBN 978-1-250-34580-6 (trade paperback)
ISBN 978-1-250-36053-3 (hardcover)
ISBN 978-1-250-34581-3 (ebook)

Our books may be purchased in bulk for promotional, educational, or business
use. Please contact your local bookseller or the Macmillan Corporate and
Premium Sales Department at 1-800-221-7945, extension 5442, or by email at
MacmillanSpecialMarkets@macmillan.com.

Originally published in Great Britain by Quercus / Hachette U.K.

First U.S. Edition: 2024

Printed in the United States of America

0 9 8 7 6 5 4 3 2 1

For Emma, always

1

THE LADY OF LAST CHANCES

The tavern was called the Pathfinder's Gambit, though its patrons referred to it as "the Armpit," or simply just "the Pit," on account of its stale odor and the fact that its interior rarely saw sunlight. The Pit had a particular reputation for violence, and tonight had proven no exception. The evening's current tally stood at three assaults (two stabbings and an attempted strangulation), two brawls, and—so far, at least—just the one death. Still, the night was young, the drink was flowing, and half the card games taking place in the tavern's smoke-filled common room were rigged. It was only a matter of time before someone else took a blade between the ribs.

Could be me if I'm not careful, Lukan Gardova mused, eyeing the small pile of coins he'd won over the past half hour. The Pit's one saving grace was that it was an excellent place to win a bit of silver, and it was for this reason that Lukan found himself sitting at a table with several companions of dubious virtue, drinking gin of dubious quality, and holding two cards of dubious value. *Peasant of Crowns and a Priest of Blades,* he thought, studying the faded illustrations. *Bloody hells.* It was a miserable hand, but that didn't matter. In rummijake you played your opponents first and your cards second.

"I'll raise," the sharp-featured man to Lukan's left finally declared, after squinting at his cards for what seemed like an eternity. "Three coppers." He scratched at his straggly beard. "No, *four* coppers." He nudged the coins toward the center of the table, only to pause and glance at his cards again. "No, wait . . ."

"You know," Lukan said amiably, "entire wars have been fought in the time you've been staring at those cards."

The man glared at him, dark eyes glinting with a base cunning that hadn't yet manifested in his cardplay. "I'm trying to think."

"I suspect that's the problem."

The man muttered an insult under his breath as he turned back to his cards. Lukan took a swallow of gin to hide his smile. He'd seen this man's type many times before: the small-time rogue who owed too much money to the wrong people and thought that gambling would be a good way to raise the necessary funds. It might have been, had he been a good player. But he wasn't.

"Five coppers," the rogue grunted, pushing his coins into the growing pile at the center of the table.

Lukan studied his own cards again, just for show. The only question in his mind was by how much to raise the bet. *Eight coppers should do it. Hells, may as well make it a silver—*

Shouting interrupted his thoughts and he glanced toward the bar, where a familiar scene was playing out: two adventuring companies squaring up to each other, the crews trading insults while their captains exchanged glares. Steel glinted in the candlelight as blades were drawn, a hush falling across the tavern as games and conversations were abandoned. The taller of the two captains, a woman who wore a wide-brimmed hat tilted at a jaunty angle, said something that Lukan didn't catch. Her opposite number blinked in surprise, his face—already flushed with drink—reddening even further. Then he bellowed a laugh and held out his hand, which the woman gripped in her own. Blades were returned to their sheaths as the two crews exchanged smiles instead of blows, and a cheer rose to the rafters as the red-faced captain called for a round of drinks.

Lukan wasn't surprised by how quickly the threat of violence had faded; he'd seen this sort of scene play out a dozen times in the three weeks he'd been in Torlaine. Tensions ran high among the adventuring crews who made a living scavenging Phaeron relics from the Grey Lands, a couple of leagues to the north. This sort of behavior was just their way of blowing off steam after surviving the dangers of that shadow-haunted landscape. For those who returned, at least.

How did it come to this? he asked himself, his gaze passing over the adventurers and opportunists who packed the tavern. *How did I end up in this den of rogues at the edge of the world?*

He knew the answer all too well.

Agreeing to a duel with the heir of one of the most powerful families in the Old Empire had been a bad mistake. *But not nearly so much as winning it.* Memories pressed in—a cry of rage, the flash of steel, and blood spilling across pink cherry blossoms . . .

No, he thought, forcing the images aside. *Not here. Not now.* Such thoughts would only spark the old anger, and then he would think of *her,* and—

"Who's taking their time now?"

It was the woman sitting to his right who had spoken. Another adventurer, judging by the sword strapped to her back and the old leather armor she wore. By Lukan's reckoning she had so far made at least three bluffs and had downed twice that many shots of vodka. She sank another one now, mouth curling in what might have been amusement. The scar that split her lips made it hard to tell.

Lukan glanced at his own cards again but found that his enthusiasm for the game had faded. He almost folded his hand there and then, only for the rogue's coins to glint seductively. *Might as well see this through.*

"I raise," he said, plucking a silver coin from his pouch and dropping it onto the coppers in the center of the table. The rogue hissed through his teeth and threw down his cards even though it wasn't his turn. The adventurer did likewise, albeit with more dignity. That just left the well-dressed stranger sitting opposite Lukan, whose subtle plays had revealed him as a cut above the others. His clothes were more refined too. Dust clung to his velvet jacket, and his silken shirt was badly creased, but there was no mistaking the fine tailoring. Nor was it possible to ignore the way his emerald ring flashed when it caught the candlelight. In the gloom of the tavern, the man might have been mistaken for one of the few treasure hunters lucky enough to find their fortune out in the Grey Lands, or even one of the moneylenders who financed the adventuring companies.

Lukan knew better.

"Well, isn't this a conundrum," the man said with a smirk that carried more than a hint of the aristocracy. "What's a fellow to do . . ."

"A fellow could lay down his cards."

"Oh, I think not," the man replied, drumming his fingers on the table. "That would be so dreadfully dull. Besides"—his ring gleamed as he gestured at the pile of coins—"there's too much of my money in there for me to walk away."

Too much of your family's money, you mean. Lukan could see the man for who he was: a child of privilege, a spoiled dandy, who had taken it upon himself to gamble away a sliver of his family's fortune. *And why not,* Lukan thought, his gaze flitting to the two heavyset men watching from a nearby table, *when you can just have your hired muscle retrieve it for you afterward.* They were the only reason the dandy wasn't lying dead in a gutter, his corpse stripped of valuables. What he was even doing in Torlaine Lukan could only guess. Perhaps he was intending to take a short trip into the Grey Lands and poke around some of the ruins, or try to catch a glimpse of a gloomfiend. Something to boast about to his friends over a brandy or two in the smoking rooms of Amberlé, or Seldarine, or wherever the hells he was from. *Well, whatever his plans are, I'll ensure his purse is that little bit lighter.*

"What say we liven things up a little?" the dandy said, producing a gold ducat and sliding it into the middle of the table with deliberate slowness. Lukan heard the rogue's sharp intake of breath to his left; no doubt that coin alone was more than enough to pay off his debts. Its value far exceeded the assembled pile of copper and silver. *Which makes it more trouble than it's worth.* Lukan made to toss his cards away, only to pause as the dandy reached for his glass of wine.

A flash of white.

Well, well. That changes things. Lukan considered his options. He could still back out and walk away, but what he'd just seen now made that option harder to bear. Sometimes you owed it to yourself to do what was necessary, not what was easy.

Especially when some arsehole was cheating you at cards.

"So what's it to be?" the dandy asked, smirking as he toyed with his ring.

Lukan laid his cards down on the table.

"Pity," the man said, reaching out to gather his winnings. "I was hoping the two of us might go another round—"

"The three of us, you mean."

The dandy hesitated, hand outstretched. "I beg your pardon?"

"The three of us," Lukan repeated. "You, me . . . and the Lady of Last Chances you've got tucked up your right sleeve."

The words hung in the air between them.

"You dare accuse me?" the dandy said, with an edge to his voice that might have sounded threatening if used by someone else. "Do you have any idea who I am?"

"A dead man if you've cheated us," the adventurer replied.

"Enough!" the dandy snapped, rising from his chair. "I don't answer to gutter scum like you—" He gasped as the rogue hauled him back down. "Get off me, you filth—" He fell silent as the man pressed a dagger against his throat.

"You don't have to answer to *them*," the rogue said, nodding at Lukan and the adventurer, "but you'll damned well answer to me."

He's not much of a cardplayer, Lukan thought, *but he knows how to handle a blade. And make a threat.*

As the dandy squealed for help, his guards decided they should probably intervene—after all, neither of them was going to get paid if their employer was busy choking on his own blood. They rose from their table, hands reaching for their weapons.

"One more step and I'll open his throat," the rogue announced, the cold gleam in his eyes more convincing than any bluff he'd made at cards.

"Do as he says," the dandy squeaked.

The two guards traded glances and remained still.

"Now," the rogue said to the dandy, "let's see about this lady friend of yours, shall we?" He nodded at the adventurer, who slid her fingers under the man's lacy cuff and withdrew a dog-eared card that bore a depiction of a woman with her arms spread wide, a wry smile on her lips.

"Well, would you look at that," the rogue said, applying more pressure with his blade.

"P-please," the dandy stuttered, his earlier bravado leaking out of him along with the blood now trickling down his neck. "I-I can explain—"

"Not without a tongue you can't," the rogue snarled. He rose to his feet, dragging the dandy up with him, and glanced around the tavern, clearly sensing the opportunity to make a statement. "No one crosses Galthan Adris and lives," he said loudly, drawing nothing more than a handful of stares and a snigger.

"Idiot," the adventurer muttered.

"The hells did you say?" the rogue demanded, clearly ruffled that his grand announcement hadn't had the effect he'd desired. Sensing that his captor's attention was elsewhere, the dandy chose that moment to try to struggle free.

"Stay still, you dog," the rogue hissed, a rather unfair request to put to someone whose tongue you'd threatened to remove. As the two men struggled, the rogue's foot slipped in a puddle of stale beer, and he fell, dragging his opponent down with him. A ragged cheer rose from the handful of patrons who had been watching the little drama unfold, causing others to turn and stare.

"A fight!" someone shouted, quite unnecessarily, and suddenly everyone in the tavern was crowding around the two figures flailing at each other on the floor. The dandy's two guards strode over to the struggling pair and tried to separate them, while the crowd shouted insults. Someone hurled a bowl of soup, which struck one of the guards on the shoulder and exploded all over the side of his face. The guard spun round, eyes blazing as he wiped the soup from his beard. "Who the hells did that?" he bellowed. The crowd's laughter quieted as the guard drew his sword.

Time to get out of here.

Lukan opened his money pouch and swept the pile of coins—including the dandy's gold ducat—inside. As he pulled the drawstrings he caught the adventurer looking at him, one eyebrow raised. "I won the hand," Lukan said. "The pot's mine."

"You folded."

"So did you."

"He cheated us both."

True enough. Lukan dug a silver coin out of his pouch and flicked it to the adventurer. "If we're being fair," he said, "we ought to give our friend down there his share."

"I don't think he's in a position to accept it," the adventurer replied, pocketing the coin. "Do you?"

"No," Lukan replied, watching as the rogue snarled in his frustrated attempts at opening the dandy's throat. "I don't think he is." While the soup-drenched guard continued to bellow at the increasingly unruly crowd, his comrade was trying his best to stop their young charge from meeting a messy end on the tavern floor. He grabbed hold of the rogue's jerkin, only to lose his footing and fall back against a table, spilling beer everywhere.

Another cheer rose to the rafters.

"Good luck," the mercenary said, lips curling in what might have been a smile.

"You too."

With those words Lukan slipped through the crowd and out of the tavern.

———

Cold air slapped him as he stepped outside.

For a moment he stood still, savoring the sudden quiet, the coolness of the night against his skin. *Seems autumn comes early this far north.* He would have to purchase a new coat; the one he wore was a patched-up relic from his days at the Academy of

Parva, and its sentimental value did little to keep out the chill. *Still*, he thought, resting his hand on the coin purse at his belt, *at least I can afford something decent.* Shouting sounded from the tavern behind him, and he wondered whether the rogue had managed to open the dandy's throat, or whether the young man's guards had succeeded in beating him into submission. He couldn't say he cared either way. The world wouldn't miss either of them.

Lukan set off down the street, the breeze tugging at his collar and ruffling his blond hair. His father claimed that the winds that blew in from the Grey Lands weren't natural, that they were the result of powerful sorcery that had obliterated the Phaeron civilization a thousand years ago—distant echoes of an event lost to history. Whatever the truth, there was certainly nothing natural about the scent the wind carried, which was vaguely sulfurous, yet ultimately unfamiliar. *The dying breath of a lost empire*, his father had once called it. He winced at the memory. It was going to be one of *those* nights, when the past wouldn't stay where it belonged. At least he still had that bottle of gin back at his room in the flophouse. *If it hasn't already been stolen.*

Even at this time of night, Torlaine's main thoroughfare was busy. Adventurers smoked cigarillos on street corners, courtesans prowled beneath the red glow of bawdy-house lanterns, and dealers hawked illegal narcotics from shadowed doorways. Burning torches did little to drive back the darkness, which was probably for the best, since the gloom did much to conceal the worst of the town's blemishes—the crumbling stonework, rotting timbers, and cracked paving stones. Plenty of fortunes had been made in Torlaine, but little of that money stayed for long. The lenders who financed the expeditions into the Grey Lands all kept their wealth in Amberlé, many leagues to the south, while the few adventurers who managed to make some coin tended to blow their money in classier surroundings. In the sort of refined places where Lukan once drank and dined.

Before I threw everything away.

There it was again: the old anger stirring inside him. He breathed deeply, forced it back down. Only alcohol would temper its bite and soften its claws. It would probably take all the gin he had left, and no doubt he'd be good for nothing the next morning. Still, there was little in this dismal place worth waking up for anyway. *Perhaps I should join one of the companies, head out into the Grey Lands. Try and find my own fortune—*

Lukan snapped into awareness, suddenly alert.

Someone's following me.

He couldn't say how he knew. It was a vague feeling, a sense that he'd honed during his years on the road. When you slept in the kind of places that Lukan did, bedding down every night half expecting to be woken by a blade pressing against your throat, you gained a feel for these sorts of things. He swore under his breath, resisting the urge to glance over his shoulder.

"Gloomfiend talons!" a hustler cried, stepping into Lukan's path as she waved what looked like a stuffed dog's paw bound with leather.

"Out of my way," he replied, stepping round her.

"Just three coppers for a claw from the fearsome beast!"

Lukan turned back. "Let me see that."

The woman grinned with stained teeth as she waved the fake at him. He ignored it as he stared over her shoulder.

There.

A cloaked figure ducked into the shadows, about twenty yards away. *One of the dandy's guards?* No, they were both big men, and the glimpse he'd had of his pursuer suggested that this person was smaller. *Maybe someone from the tavern who saw me leave with a bag of coin and fancied taking it for themselves. They're welcome to try.*

"Well?" the hustler demanded.

"Looks like things are about to get interesting," Lukan replied, leaving her cursing after him as he walked away. He considered his options as he carried on down the thoroughfare, careful to keep a casual pace. His instinct was to confront his pursuer, but he couldn't be sure if they were alone. Lukan fancied himself against any opponent when it came to blades, but if he faced multiple adversaries it would be a short fight, and likely one that wouldn't end in his favor. Ducking into a tavern or bawdy house might buy him a little time but could also leave him cornered. His room at the flophouse offered no sanctuary—he doubted the door would stand up to a strong sneeze, never mind an intruder's shoulder. *Which leaves just one option . . .*

Lukan ducked into the nearest alley and broke into a run, one arm stretched before him as if to ward off the darkness. A half-shuttered lantern glowed ahead of him, revealing a tangle of pathways. He veered right, leaping over a slumped body that might have been a corpse. The path split again and this time he went left, turning almost sideways to squeeze through a narrow walkway so dark he could barely see his own hand before his face. Something snagged his foot but he managed to kick it loose. Lukan listened for sounds of pursuit but all he could hear was his own ragged breathing. He twisted into another passage and grinned when he saw light up ahead. With a little luck he'd emerge onto a side street that led back to the thoroughfare, where he could blend into the crowds. He'd be back at the flophouse in no time, toasting his escape with that bottle of gin while his pursuer blundered around in the dark.

Smiling at the thought, Lukan burst out of the alley . . . and froze.

Three men glanced up from where they sat around a brazier, flames throwing their shadows against the walls of the small yard.

A dead end.

"Apologies," Lukan managed, noting the hostility in their eyes. "Wrong turn."

The men exchanged grins and rose to their feet, hefting an assortment of weapons. Lukan spun round, only to find a fourth figure blocking his retreat. The man leered as he slapped a cudgel against his palm.

Oh, wonderful . . .

Lukan turned back to the three men, regretting his decision to leave his sword under the floorboards at the flophouse. He only had his dirk, while the bearded man he took to be the leader of this sorry band wielded an old sword. Its blade was notched and spotted with rust, but the tip looked sharp.

"Hand it over," the leader said, pointing at Lukan's coin pouch.

"Someone's following me," Lukan replied, glancing over his shoulder to check the position of the thug behind him. "Help me scare them off and half of *this*"—he patted his coin pouch—"is yours."

"Piss on that. Easier to kill you and take the whole lot."

A fair point. "And get between a Bloodless and their prize?" Lukan asked, thinking quickly. "I'd be careful about that if I were you."

The leader's eyes widened at the mention of the Old Empire's most feared assassin cabal.

"Drem," one of the other men whispered, a note of anxiety in his voice. "I heard tales o' them. They say that they don't bleed, that when you cut them only ash spills out—"

"Quiet," Drem snapped. "We've all heard the stories, you idiot. Nothing but tavern talk." He snapped his fingers at Lukan. "Hand it over."

"Fine," Lukan replied, untying the pouch. "Have it your way."

Drem grinned and held out his hand. He was still smiling as Lukan hurled the pouch into his face. The man gave a choked cry and stumbled backward. Lukan drew his dirk and spun round, thrusting instinctively as the thug behind him raised his cudgel to strike. The man blinked in surprise as Lukan's blade punched into his throat, his weapon falling from nerveless fingers. Lukan pulled his dirk free in a spray of blood and shoved the man away. He whirled round, teeth bared, blade raised . . .

And was sent reeling by a vicious blow to his jaw.

He staggered, the world pitching around him, the brazier's flames streaking across his blurred vision. Somehow he kept his balance, and lashed out with his dirk as he backed away. *Forget the pouch.* There was little choice now but to make a run for it—

His feet tangled with those of the dying thug, who lay gurgling behind him.

Lukan fell and hit the ground hard, blade tumbling from his grip. Blood roared in his ears, the coppery taste of it on his tongue. He gritted his teeth, tried to rise—only for a booted foot to force him back down, crushing the air from his lungs. Strong hands clamped round his arms, pinning him down. He snarled, tried to struggle free.

Cold steel pressed against his throat.

Lukan blinked to clear his vision.

Drem stood over him. The man's sword arm trembled with suppressed rage, each little twitch causing the tip of his blade to rasp against Lukan's skin.

"That," Drem hissed through split lips, "was a mistake."

Lukan felt inclined to agree. He spat blood, wincing at the pain in his jaw—not broken at least, but that was little comfort. *To think it ends like this, dying in some back alley at the hands of a second-rate cutpurse. Still, perhaps it's the least I deserve.*

"Get him up," Drem barked, withdrawing his sword.

The two men hauled Lukan to his feet. The world seemed to tilt around him.

"You killed Rass," Drem continued, gesturing at the dead man, whose wet, ragged breathing had now ceased. "For that, I'll make sure your own death is slow and—" He jolted, eyes widening. Slowly he sank to one knee.

"Drem?" one of the other men said, frowning. "You all right?"

His leader's only response was a hiss of breath as he toppled forward, revealing the hilt of a throwing knife lodged in his back. Lukan glanced up to see a shadowed figure crouched on the far wall. Firelight gleamed on steel as they drew another blade.

"Lady's blood," one of the men swore, letting go of Lukan's arm. The other followed suit.

The figure dropped silently from the wall.

"Run!" one of the thugs blurted.

Lukan couldn't have said it better himself—with his head still swimming, he was in no condition for a fight. As the two men fled into the alley, he snatched up his coin pouch and made to follow, only to pause as he glanced at the knife protruding from Drem's back. *It can't be.* His eyes widened as his vision cleared, revealing a carved ivory hilt. *I know that weapon . . .*

"You held that knife once," the newcomer said as they approached. "Do you remember?"

That voice. Rich and throaty, with the hint of a Talassian accent. A voice he hadn't heard in years and hadn't thought he'd ever hear again. A voice that by turns used to praise and scold him, though mostly the latter as childhood years gave way to adolescence.

"I remember," he replied, recalling the feel of the ivory against his palm, the gleam of the blade in the sunlight. "My hands were smaller then."

"And mine had fewer wrinkles." The figure pulled the blade from Drem's back and wiped it on the dead man's shirt.

"They still know how to throw a knife, though."

"Fortunately for you."

"I thought I had a thief or two after me. If I'd known it was you, then none of this would have happened." He gestured at the body of the man he'd killed. "I wouldn't have had to do . . . *that.*"

"If you'd remembered half the things I taught you," the hooded figure replied, picking up Lukan's dirk and tossing it to him, "you wouldn't have needed me to rescue you."

Lukan caught the blade. "If you had greeted me like a *normal* person, you wouldn't have had to." He wiped the dirk on Drem's shirt. "What's with the literal cloak and dagger, anyway?"

"I wanted to see how you'd react." The hood tilted. "To see how you handled yourself. To see whether you were still the young man I remembered."

"And?"

"Well, you still have a knack for getting into trouble." The figure pulled back their hood, revealing a woman's face with sharp lines and olive skin. Her dark eyes narrowed as she regarded him. Time's passage had left its mark on her features—the crinkles around her eyes, the strands of silver in her raven-black hair, tied back as always—yet her frown was just the same. "And your foot-work seems rusty."

Lukan smiled. "Always the hard taskmaster."

The woman returned the smile, and the years fell away from her face. "It's so good to see you, Lukan."

"You too, Shafia. I never thought I'd see you again, not after . . ." He made a vague gesture. "Well, after what happened. What are you doing here, anyway? You're not working for my father any-more? I *told* you that your talents were wasted on him. Pretty sure I told him that too . . ."

He trailed off at the look of pain that flashed across the woman's face.

"Shafia? Is something—"

"Not here," she replied, glancing around. "Do you know some-where we can talk?"

"I've got a room at a flophouse."

"Perfect."

"Trust me, it's not. It smells like something died under the floorboards, and—"

"Lukan," Shafia said, wearily raising a hand. "This is urgent. Just lead the way."

2

A CHEAPER KIND OF PROMISE

"Well," Shafia said, standing in the doorway and glancing around the room. "This is . . ."

"A shithole?" Lukan suggested, placing a lighted candle into the lantern that hung from a crossbeam. The lantern swung as he let go, casting a wan light over the cracked plaster of the walls.

"I was going to be charitable . . ."

"That's most unlike you."

". . . and say *cozy*."

"Seems you've become more generous with age." Lukan lit two more candles on the table at the center of the room, the flames flickering in the draft that whistled through the broken window. "I'd offer to take your coat," he added, blowing out the taper and setting it down, "but you probably want to keep it on. I can, however, offer you a drink."

"How kind," Shafia replied, closing the door behind her. "I'll have a glass of Parvan Red, '17 vintage."

"Will a '19 do if I can't find the '17?" Lukan retrieved the bottle that stood on a nightstand by the bed, along with two dirty glasses. "All I've got is gin. It's not Parvan Silver, but it'll warm you up."

"That'll do."

He poured two measures and handed one to Shafia. They regarded each other in the dim light. Lukan raised his glass.

"To . . ."

"Finding you alive," Shafia said with a half smile. "And as trouble-prone as ever."

"To trouble, and to your tongue," Lukan replied, grinning in return. "Sharp as always."

They clinked glasses and drank.

"You're right," Shafia said, grimacing as she swallowed. "That's nothing like Parvan Silver."

"It becomes bearable around the fourth or fifth glass." Lukan raised the bottle. "Another?"

"Lady's mercy, yes."

He refilled their glasses and they sat at the table.

"So how did you find me?" Lukan asked.

"With some difficulty. You're not an easy man to find."

"I tend to keep moving, don't stay in any one place too long. Figured that way I could keep outrunning the past." He managed a smile as he tipped his glass toward Shafia. "Guess I was wrong."

"You can't escape the past, Lukan. It's our lifelong companion, always at our side."

"You and your Talassian sayings. Some things never change."

"No," Shafia replied, giving him an appraising look. "They don't."

"You've not answered my question."

"I still have contacts in every city across the Old Empire."

"Ah, of course. Your old intelligence network. So you've been keeping tabs on me?"

"As best I could, ever since you left the Academy."

"You mean after the Academy expelled me for killing Giorgio Castori."

"I see the years haven't lessened your anger."

"Damn right they haven't," Lukan replied, his voice hardening. "It was an accident. I won the duel. He attacked me when my back was turned, and . . ." He sighed, waved his own words away. "Never mind. You know what happened. And you know I'm right."

"I know," Shafia said, "but I was hoping that—"

"I'd got over it? That I'd made peace with having my whole life ruined?"

"Something like that, yes." The woman was silent for a moment.

"I thought that . . . How many years has it been since we last saw each other—six?"

"More than seven."

"I had hoped that maybe you'd been able to move on." She paused again, as if choosing her words carefully. "And that maybe you'd managed to forgive your father—"

"*Forgive* him? After he accepted the Academy's decision without challenging it?"

"Lukan, let's not—"

"After he groveled at the feet of the Castoris and gave away what was left of our family fortune as compensation? *Compensation*, for pity's sake. Giorgio Castori attacked *me*, and yet I'm the one who's branded a murderer and disowned by my own father—"

"*Lukan*."

He flinched as Shafia's voice cracked like a whip, her fierce glare rendering him silent, as it had so many times in his younger years. "Enough," she said firmly, her expression softening. "I'm on your side. I always have been."

"I know. I'm . . . I'm sorry." He ground his teeth, feeling foolish—no wiser than the man he'd been when last they'd met. "It's just . . ."

"Those events still cut deeply."

"Exactly. And try as I might, I just can't . . ." He shook his head, waved as if to dismiss the thought. *If only it was that easy.* "Forget it. You were saying?"

"I was saying that after you left the Academy I did my best to follow your movements. You disappeared from time to time, of course, but generally I had a reasonable idea of where you might be."

"And you did all this at my father's request?"

"I acted on my own volition."

"Of course you did," Lukan replied sourly, knocking back his gin. "Silly of me to think the honorable Lord Gardova would care about whether his only child was still breathing." He refilled his glass. "How is the old man, anyway? Still busy with all his scrolls and Phaeron relics, no doubt—"

"He's dead, Lukan."

The words stole the breath from Lukan's lungs, a strange numbness spreading through him as his mind reeled. *Dead.* "I . . ." he began, then fell silent, his lips trying to form words even though he had no idea what he was trying to say. *Lady's mercy.* "How . . . how did it happen?"

Shafia glanced away, and Lukan felt a stab of unease. He'd never known her to hesitate or show reluctance. In his mind, she was still his father's stern-faced steward, the woman who had first taught him how to hold a blade, who had practically raised him after his mother had died when he was still a child. When she looked back at him now, her expression was pained.

"Your father was murdered."

"Murdered?" he echoed. "But . . ." He took a breath, tried to compose himself. *Murdered. Lady's blood . . .* He reached for his glass, vaguely aware that his hand was shaking. Shafia caught his wrist and gently pushed his hand back down.

"You need to hear what I have to say," she said firmly. "With a clear head."

"Then tell me what happened," he replied, clenching his fist until his knuckles turned white. "Tell me everything."

"I wasn't there when it happened." A flicker of anger passed across Shafia's face. "This was a little over a month ago now—"

"A month?" *He's been dead all this time and I didn't even know.*

"I wish I could have reached you sooner but, as I said, you're not an easy man to find."

Lukan barely heard her. "Go on," he murmured.

"I was returning from an errand," Shafia continued. "I arrived back at the estate not long after midnight. Everything seemed normal—the guards were on duty, there was no sense of anything out of place. I left my horse in the stables, entered the house and . . ." She trailed off, her jaw tightening. "I went upstairs. At the top of the staircase I found Jhosem, one of the guards, lying on the landing. He was dead. Someone had opened his throat—from

behind, far as I could tell. He hadn't even drawn his sword. I ran
to your father's bedroom, but he wasn't there."

"Of course he wasn't," Lukan said, managing a bitter laugh.
"He lived in his damned study."

"Which is where I looked next. I found him"—Shafia paused,
swallowing—"on the floor, covered in blood."

Lukan's stomach lurched. "Dead?"

She nodded. "He . . . had been stabbed several times. There
was nothing I could do."

Lukan sat back, scarcely able to believe what he'd heard. But he
knew Shafia spoke the truth—she'd served his father for twenty
years; her loyalty was unquestionable. Besides, her anger—and
the guilt she felt at not having been there—were etched into every
line of her face. "Who did this, Shafia?" he asked eventually.
"Hells, do you think the Castoris—"

"No," she said firmly, shaking her head. "This has nothing to
do with them. Nothing to do with you, or what you did to Giorgio
Castori."

"How can you be sure?"

"Well, I can't . . . It's just a feeling. I think they would have left
a sign—something subtle just to let us know it was them. But we
found nothing. Besides, they've never shown much interest in your
father—their grudge was always with you."

"Thanks for reminding me." The bitterness of his tone masked
the relief he felt. As wide as the chasm between him and his father
had grown, he would never have forgiven himself if his past actions had led to his father's death. "If the Castoris didn't murder
my father," he said, "then who did?"

"I have no idea," Shafia admitted. "But whoever did it was
looking for something—they'd turned your father's study upside
down. There were papers and documents everywhere, though
whether they found what they were looking for I couldn't say."

"But there was nothing *in* his study," Lukan replied. "Nothing
worth stealing, anyway. It was just a mess of old antiques and books

and scrolls about whatever he was currently obsessed with. You know how he was—myths and legends, the Phaeron and the Faceless, all that nonsense. No wonder the rest of the aristocracy looked down on us. First my grandfather gambles away our fortune, then his son becomes a recluse obsessed with dead civilizations and demons out of children's stories." He shook his head. "Just as well I turned out all right, isn't it?"

"Lukan."

"Don't *Lukan* me," he replied, but without conviction. His mind was spinning, though whether from the drink or from Shafia's revelations he couldn't say. Both, probably. Still, if ever there was a time for a clear head, it was now. "I'm sorry," he said, raising a hand. "That was . . . *unbecoming* of me, as Father would say."

"It was." Shafia gave him a hint of a smile.

"Tell me I'm wrong, though."

Her smile faded. "You're not. Your father's study was as you remember."

"So it was an opportunist then? A thief hunting for anything valuable."

"That's what I thought at first, but nothing of value was taken. You know your mother's sapphire necklace, the one your father always kept on the marble bust on the landing? That was untouched, though the killer must have walked right past it to get to your father's study." Shafia shook her head. "This was no common thief."

"So what were they looking for?"

"I was wondering whether your father may have stumbled across something in his research. His interest in the Phaeron—"

"Obsession, you mean," Lukan said bitterly. "Phaeron this, Phaeron that . . . Honestly, it's all he ever talked about. He was more interested in them than his own family."

"I won't defend your father's flaws as a parent," Shafia replied, "but it was this obsession that made him such an expert."

"Try telling that to the Academy—they rejected his papers about a dozen times—"

"Lukan, please."

"Sorry. You were saying . . ."

"I'm just wondering whether your father uncovered information—a secret, perhaps—that his murderer wanted to protect."

"About the Phaeron?" Lukan shook his head. "They disappeared a thousand years ago, what could he have possibly learned about them that would give someone reason to kill him? No, there must have been another motive."

"Perhaps you're right," Shafia said, drumming her fingers on the table. "Regardless, we do have one lead." She reached into a pocket and withdrew a folded piece of paper. "I found this with your father's body." She held it out. "He must have still been alive when his attacker left."

Lukan took the paper, his throat suddenly dry. It was creased and worn, presumably from the weeks it had spent nestled in Shafia's pocket. He unfolded it, trepidation gnawing at him as he stared at the bloodstains on the lower half of the page. His eyes moved to the three words scrawled in the center in red ink. *No,* he realized, his eyes widening. *Written in blood. My father's blood.* He took a breath, glanced at Shafia, who remained silent, her expression grim. Lukan looked back at the page, tried to concentrate on the words.

Lukan   Saphrona   Zandrusa

He lowered the paper, the sight of his father's handwriting and the weight of the revelations conspiring to make him feel dizzy.

"Take your time," Shafia said gently.

Lukan nodded and took a swallow of gin, looking at the paper again as the liquid burned the back of his throat. He stared at the words, his father's final desperate act, written even as his life slipped away. He read them once, twice, three times, mouthing them silently.

The meaning of the first word, his own name, was clear enough—obviously his father had intended this message for him. The second word, *Saphrona,* could only mean the city of the same name that stood at the southern tip of the Old Empire, a city that he'd heard much about but never seen with his own eyes. The last word—*Zandrusa*—was unfamiliar. He murmured the word as he racked his mind, trying to recall any mention of it. Nothing, not even the faintest glimmer of recognition. He looked up, met Shafia's eyes. "You have any idea what Zandrusa is?"

The woman smiled faintly. "I was hoping you might be able to tell me."

"It doesn't mean anything to you?"

"Never heard it before. My initial thought was that it might be the identity of your father's murderer, or some sort of clue, but . . ." She shrugged. "If it's a name, it's not one I'm familiar with."

Lukan glanced back at the paper. "What about Saphrona? Did my father have some sort of interests there?"

"None that I'm aware of."

"This doesn't make any sense." Lukan set the paper down.

"One thing is clear," Shafia said. "Your father used his final moments to write that message. He wanted you to have it. So, it must be important."

"But we don't even know what in the hells it means."

"Then you must go to Saphrona and find out."

"Go to . . ." Lukan stared at her, incredulous. "I can't just . . . Saphrona is hundreds of leagues to the south." He shook his head. "No, I need to get back to Parva. With my father dead . . ." He trailed off, eyes widening as a realization struck him. *With my father dead, I'm now Lord Gardova.* The thought left a bitter taste. "I need to go home," he continued. "There must be affairs that need attention. The estate—"

"Is all taken care of," Shafia cut in smoothly. "Your father's will named me as custodian until such time as you can return and take up your new responsibilities. Let me take care of things for the time being."

"But . . . are you sure?"

"Lukan, you know how little interest your father took in domestic matters. He may have been lord of the manor, but we both know who looked after the estate's affairs."

"I know, but . . . I mean, after all these years, isn't there somewhere else you'd rather be, something else you'd rather be doing? Because I wouldn't hold it against you if you wanted to leave—"

"Lukan . . ."

"You don't owe me anything, Shafia, you know that? If anything I owe *you* for all the times you put up with my bullsh—"

"*Lukan*," she repeated, her voice snapping the way it used to whenever she chastised him during his swordplay lessons. "Believe me when I say that there's nothing I would rather be doing than helping you." She raised a finger. "And if you ask me if I'm sure one more time, I'll throw that gin in your face."

"You wouldn't," he replied, but picked up his glass just in case. "Seriously though, Shafia, I'm grateful for everything you've done for my family. Both now and over the years. My father should've given you a damned medal."

"He gave me something far more valuable than that."

"Oh?"

"Purpose." Shafia leaned forward, hands clasped. "When your father took me into his service, I was lost. I'd dedicated my entire life to the Parvan crown. Spycraft was all I knew. So when that ended . . . I didn't know what to do. I had nothing. No friends, no family. No future. I was left wondering if the sacrifices I'd made had been worth it. But then your father made me his steward and invited me into his family. He gave me fresh purpose and for that I will always be grateful. Now that Conrad— now that your father's gone, I can no longer help him." Her jaw tightened. "But I *can* help his son." She met his gaze. "If he'll have me."

Lukan could only stare back at her. He'd never heard Shafia talk at such length and with such vulnerability. *She needs this,* he realized. *And I need her if I'm going to make any sense of this mess.* "He will," he replied, raising his glass. "Always."

Shafia smiled, the tension melting from her face as she raised her own glass and clinked it against his. "In that case," she said, taking a sip of her drink, "my first piece of advice to you, as your steward, is to heed your father's words." She indicated the paper with its bloody scrawl. "I don't know what Conrad was thinking in his final moments, but it was clearly important to him that you go to Saphrona and seek out this *Zandrusa*, whoever—or whatever—that is. So, honor his dying wish. I know you and your father weren't on good terms these last few years, but you owe him this. For the love he bore you and the love I know you still bear him. Despite everything."

"Despite everything," Lukan echoed softly, as grief, anger, and regret warred in his head. "I wanted to go home," he continued, staring at his glass. It helped to have something to focus on. "I thought of it so many times. Seeing the old house, seeing my father, apologizing for . . ." He met Shafia's gaze. "I wanted to apologize. For what I did, for what I said. I hated the rift that had grown between us."

"I know your father felt the same."

"I always told myself the time wasn't right. I always found an excuse . . ." He shook his head. "And now it's too late."

"No it isn't," Shafia replied firmly. "This is how you can make things up to him. Carry out his final wish."

Lukan picked up the piece of paper, scanned the words again. *Zandrusa.* Perhaps the word was a clue that would reveal his father's killer, or maybe it was something else entirely. Either way, the answer to the mystery was in Saphrona. He folded the paper up, slipped it into a pocket. *So be it.*

"I'll go," Lukan said, meeting Shafia's eyes.

"Swear it. Make a goldenblood promise."

"I only have silver," he replied, sliding a ring off his finger and holding it up to the candlelight.

Shafia curled her lip. "A cheaper metal cheapens the oath."

"This was my mother's ring. My father gave it to me after she passed."

"Then it is more than enough." She drew the diamond-shaped

throwing knife and handed it to him hilt-first. "Swear a silverblood promise, then."

Lukan took the blade, placed the tip against his palm. He hesitated, feeling suddenly dizzy, light-headed from the rush of emotions that still coursed through him. Anger, regret, both wrapped around a thorny knot of grief whose barbs he was only now starting to feel. *My father's dead and I don't know who killed him, or why.* He sucked in a breath, feeling a sudden pressure settling over him. *But I need to find out. I have to.* With that admission the pressure eased, to be replaced with something he hadn't felt in years.

Purpose.

Seven years of running from the past, but no more. He grimaced as he drew the blade lightly across his left palm, drawing blood. He placed his ring in the middle of his palm and closed his hand into a fist. "I swear a silverblood promise," he intoned, holding Shafia's gaze, "to carry out my father's final wish. I'll go to Saphrona. I'll find his murderer and bring them to justice. So be it."

"So be it," Shafia echoed.

Lukan handed the blade back and stared at his bloody palm. *Might have cut that a little too deep.* "I don't suppose you have a—"

The woman tossed a clean handkerchief at him.

"The quickest way to Saphrona is by sea," she said. "Take a horse south to Deladrin—it should only take you a few days. There you can find a ship."

"A ship? That'll be expensive."

"Which is why you'll need this."

Shafia reached into a pocket and withdrew an envelope sealed by a stamp of green wax bearing two stylized Bs. "A letter of credit from the Brandt and Balinor Banking House in Parva," she said, in response to his inquiring look. "Signed by me in my role as custodian and executor of your estate. If you visit their branch in Deladrin you can exchange it for two ducats from your father's—from *your* account. It'll be enough to cover the cost of your passage, and whatever supplies you might need. I wish I could have given you more, but . . . well, your family's fortune isn't what it was."

Don't I just know it. "Thank you," Lukan replied as he took the envelope. "For this and everything else."

"Always." Shafia rose from the table.

"You're leaving?"

"I have lodgings on the other side of town that are a little more . . . *refined*." She smiled. "I can hear a glass of decent red wine calling my name, and I fully intend to drink it while taking a hot bath."

"But we've got so much to catch up on," Lukan said, wincing as he pressed the handkerchief to his bloody palm. "And you need to tell me what you know of Saphrona—" He was cut short by Shafia producing a tattered, dog-eared booklet and tossing it onto the table. "What's this?" he asked, peering at the faded title on the cover.

"*A Gentleman's Guide to Saphrona,*" Shafia intoned, "by Velleras Gellame: traveler, philosopher, and poet."

"Sounds like a buffoon."

"Oh, he is. Happy reading."

"Wait, there must be more you can tell me. Didn't you visit Saphrona in your spying days?"

"Sadly not. Though the sun would have made a nice change from the endless rain in Seldarine." She cocked an eyebrow. "Anyway, you're the one with the Academy education. Surely there were lessons in the Old Empire's history and geography."

"I'm sure there were."

"But you didn't attend any of them?"

"Of course not. What do you take me for? Anyway, if it's any consolation, I *did* put your lessons in unarmed combat to good use in several tavern brawls."

"It isn't," Shafia replied, though not without the hint of a smile. She nodded at the booklet. "I can't tell you anything more than what's in there, so be sure to read it. Gellame will give you a good sense of Saphrona, if you can stand his flowery language." She frowned. "There *was* one thing . . . No, never mind."

"Tell me."

"No, it . . . it was a story a fellow agent told me many years ago. But we were drinking and I was as sure then as I am now that he was pulling my leg. Something about a gigantic . . ." She waved her words away. "It was a jest, as I said, and he'd die laughing if he knew I'd taken it seriously. Forget it. Gellame doesn't mention it, so it's almost certainly nonsense."

"And if it's not?"

"You can tell me all about it." Shafia moved toward the door.

"Perhaps tomorrow we could . . ."

"I'll be gone with the dawn, whereas you, I suspect, will not be awake before noon."

Lukan grinned. "You know me too well."

"I have to," she replied dryly. "After all, you're my employer now."

"I hope I'm paying you enough."

"Oh, I'd say there's room for improvement." She smiled, a glint in her dark eyes, before her expression became serious again. "Good luck, Lukan. And be careful—you're a threat to whoever murdered your father, and that makes you a target if they discover your purpose in Saphrona. Travel under a false name, trust no one, and keep your wits about you. I'll see you in Parva when you return."

"*If* I return." Lukan rose and embraced his former tutor—something that years ago he would never have imagined doing, yet now felt entirely natural. Shafia tensed, as if caught off guard, then folded her arms round him.

"Your father did love you, Lukan," she said as they stepped apart. "Despite everything that happened between you. Never forget that."

"I'll try not to."

"Get some rest. You've got a long trip ahead of you."

With those words she was gone, the door creaking as it shut behind her. Lukan sat back down at the table and studied the piece of paper again, imagining his father's hand pressed against it as he scribbled these final, desperate words, his last act an attempt to communicate with the son he'd been estranged from for so long. *What mystery have you left for me, Father?* He let the paper fall from his fingers and reached for the bottle, pouring the last of the gin into his glass. *I should say something. Toast the old man on his way.* Yet no words would come.

He drank anyway, his thoughts turning to the journey that lay ahead, and to the destination that awaited at the end of it. *Saphrona.* While he knew precious little about the city, he knew its location well enough from the hours he'd spent staring at the map pinned to his father's study wall. Saphrona perched on the most southerly tip of the Old Empire, looking across the Scepter Sea to Zar-Ghosa, the northernmost of the Southern Queendoms. *Didn't they fight a war or two against each other?* Perhaps he should have bothered to attend more of those history lectures. He'd seen an oil painting once—*Dusk Falls upon Saphrona,* goodness knows why the title had lodged in his mind—and retained a vague impression of the sun sinking below bronze domes and red-tiled roofs, and of lengthening shadows cast across courtyards filled with fountains and orange trees. How true to life it had been he could only guess; those old masters had certainly been known to exaggerate beauty and grandeur. *No doubt I'll find out soon enough.*

How soon was another question entirely. Even by ship it would surely take weeks to reach Saphrona. Then again, he knew nothing about ships; the only nautical experience he had was rowing a boat around the lake in Parva's Ducal Park, swigging wine and trying to topple his equally drunk friends into the placid waters. He smiled at the memory, which flitted away as other questions crowded in. *How hot will it be that far south?* After all, Saphrona wasn't far from the Southern Queendoms and their great deserts. *But it'll be nearly autumn, won't it, so perhaps not so warm.* He downed the rest of his drink. The questions could wait. Right now, the night was still young, and—he patted his coin purse, which tinkled reassuringly—he had plenty of coin to get into some trouble with. Not the blades-stabbing-at-your-face kind of trouble, but something—anything—to distract him from the guilt and grief that had lodged next to his heart.

Tomorrow would take care of itself.

3

THE MOTHER OF CITIES

A sharp rap at his cabin door jolted Lukan from sleep.

"Go away," he said—or tried to say. His tongue was gummed to the top of his mouth. He worked it free, grimacing at the sour aftertaste. *Another rum-filled night.* There had been plenty of those during the second week of his voyage. The ship's captain—a jovial bear of a man by the name of Graziano Grabulli—had taken to inviting Lukan to his cabin each night for a glass or two (or several) of rum. Like most men from the Talassian Isles, he liked to talk, mostly about himself and his various exploits and escapades—of which there were many. Lukan felt inclined to believe some of them (such as the captain's encounter with a black shark; the man had the teeth marks on his forearm to prove it) but was sure that others (like his claim to have seen the fabled ghost ship the *Pride of Prince Relair*) were little more than tall tales. Still, a lack of truthfulness was to be expected from a man who had—courtesy of the Tamberlin Trading Company—a brand on his left wrist that marked him out as a former pirate. Fortunately Grabulli was even more generous with his rum than he was with his lies.

A second knock at the door, slower and more deliberate.

"Piss off," Lukan shouted. He shifted in his hammock, not enjoying the way his stomach lurched. An ache was slowly building at his temples.

The door creaked open.

Lady's mercy.

He opened his eyes, squinting against the sunlight that poured in through the solitary porthole, illuminating the tiny cabin that had been his home for the past two weeks. Grabulli had promised him quarters fit for a king, but the cabin was barely fit for the rats that lurked in its corners. Lukan had seen bigger broom cupboards. Cleaner ones too.

He blinked at the figure standing in the doorway, recognizing the slight figure of the ship's cabin girl.

"Thought I told you to get lost," he said.

The girl shrugged and made an *I didn't hear you* gesture.

"Yeah, you did. You might be mute, but I know you're not deaf."

The girl ignored him and moved to his dresser, which along with a stool was the cabin's only furniture. She picked up a dagger that Lukan had won from one of the crew, in the early days of the voyage before they had started refusing to play with him, and turned it over in her hands, staring at the garnet set in its pommel.

"Put that down."

The girl obliged, placing the dagger back down on the dresser with exaggerated care.

"You've got some nerve, kid, I'll give you that. What the hells do you want?"

The girl made a shape with her hands: thumbs pressed together, fingers steepled. *Captain.*

"Grabulli? What about him?"

She pointed at Lukan—*you*—and formed a beak with her right hand, opening and closing it. *Talk.*

"What, *now*?" Lukan winced as he rubbed a thumb against his right temple; his headache was growing worse, and the girl wasn't helping. "Tell him I'll be up in a bit . . . it's too damned early."

The girl traced a circle in the air, then held up nine fingers. *Ninth hour of the day.*

"Yeah, well that's early for me."

She made a cutting gesture. *Now.*

Lukan swore under his breath. "Fine, have it your way. Tell the bastard—uh, tell the *captain*—that I'll be up shortly."

The girl nodded and turned back to the dresser, a smile playing across her lips.

Lukan raised a finger. "Don't you even *think* about—"

She snatched the dagger and darted through the door.

"You cheeky little . . ." Lukan managed to get one foot out of the hammock, only for his left leg to get tangled up as he tried to lunge forward. The room flipped and suddenly he was lying on his back, the hammock swinging above him as the patter of the girl's feet disappeared down the passage. He tried to rise, only to abandon the attempt when the rum in his stomach gurgled a warning that it was considering making a swift, explosive exit. With a groan, Lukan sank back down to the floor and closed his eyes.

Grabulli could wait a little longer.

————

"Ah, friend Lekaan!" Grabulli called from where he stood at the *Sunfish*'s prow, butchering the pronunciation of Lukan's name in his usual fashion. The captain was unmistakable in the red velvet coat that he claimed had been a gift from some prince or other, though Lukan suspected—judging by the faded stains and poor quality of the lacework—he'd actually picked it up at a flea market in some far-flung port. "So good of you to join us. A beautiful day, no?"

Perhaps, if you're not hungover. As it was, the sun was a little too bright, the blue sky a little too vibrant. Still, the breeze that slapped at Lukan and ruffled his hair was proving effective at driving away his headache. He gave a lazy wave in response and picked his way across the deck, doing his best to avoid the crew as they hauled on ropes and called to each other in their peculiar singsong dialect that seemed comprised almost entirely of insults. The sailors of the *Sunfish* were a creative bunch when it came to invective, as they'd demonstrated when Lukan fleeced them at cards. He glanced around but didn't see any sign of the cabin girl. No doubt she would reappear later—without the dagger, of course. *Not that it matters,* Lukan thought as he climbed the steps to the prow. *Damned garnet was fake anyway . . .*

"The morning's sun to you, friend Lekaan," Grabulli said, grinning through his black snarl of a beard.

"And the evening's stars for yourself," Lukan replied, completing the traditional Talassian greeting as he joined the older man at the railing. He still wasn't sure when it was that he'd revealed his true identity to Grabulli—no doubt it had been during one of their late-night drinking sessions, the rum loosening his tongue and lowering his guard. Perhaps that's what Grabulli had intended all along, his own tall tales merely serving as cover while the liquor did its work. *Or maybe all the liquor is making me paranoid.*

"You seem thoughtful," Grabulli said, slapping the back of his left hand against Lukan's chest. "And even paler than usual." He frowned. "You are well, yes?"

"I'm fine."

"Come, tell me what's on your mind."

I've told you too much already. "I'm just wondering what's so important that you woke me up at this ungodly hour."

The captain grinned and gestured at the horizon. "See for yourself."

Lukan shielded his eyes against the sun and squinted at the expanse of ocean. Not just ocean, he realized—in the distance were the dark shapes of mountains.

"Land, friend Lekaan!" Grabulli clapped Lukan's shoulder. "We'll dock in Saphrona within the hour. And we've arrived two days ahead of schedule, just as I promised you."

"You said three days."

"I must beg your forgiveness, but I said two."

"You said three and then banged the bottle of rum on the table three times, just in case I didn't quite get your point. And then shouted it again when I didn't look convinced."

"Two days, three days . . ." Grabulli puffed out his cheeks and shrugged. "What does it matter? There's hardly any difference, no?"

Lukan smiled as he imagined the captain taking the same approach with customs officials. *No wonder the Tamberlin Trading*

Company left their mark on him. "You," he said, turning his gaze back to the horizon, "are a scoundrel."

Grabulli barked a laugh. "Now *that* is something I can agree with!"

———————

As the *Sunfish*'s captain prowled the deck, barking orders to his crew as they began final preparations for making port, Lukan remained at the prow and watched the distant mountains draw closer. A half hour passed before he finally caught sight of Saphrona's famous Phaeron landmark. The tower rose from the sea in the middle of Saphrona's bay, a dark edifice constructed from the mysterious black material that the Phaeron had used in all their architecture.

As the *Sunfish* drew closer, Lukan had to crane his neck to take in the tower's full height, which must have exceeded two hundred feet. Its surfaces seemed smooth as glass, save for the uppermost stories, which had splayed outward like black, broken fingers, as if something within had exploded.

"The Ebon Hand," Lukan murmured. "It's more impressive than I imagined."

"Best behave yourself in Saphrona, friend Lekaan." Grabulli spat over the railing. "You don't want to end up in that place."

"What do you mean?"

The captain pointed. "See for yourself."

As the *Sunfish* sailed past the tower, Lukan saw several rowing boats bobbing beside a ramshackle wooden jetty. Two figures in uniforms of black trimmed with silver were dragging a third figure between them—a man in a rough-spun tunic, his hands bound. He struggled as they climbed a flight of steps that rose from the end of the jetty, leading to an arched doorway. The man threw back his head, mouth wide, but his scream didn't reach the *Sunfish* as he was dragged inside the tower. Lukan's gaze moved to the banner that hung above the entrance, crossed silver keys on a black background.

"Whose symbol is that?" he asked.

"The Saphronan Inquisition," Grabulli replied, his expression darkening. "Protectors of law and order in this fair city, or so they would have you believe." He spat over the side again. "You do *not* want to tangle with them, friend Lekaan."

"I don't plan to. So they use the Ebon Hand as a prison?"

"Just so. And a nasty one it is, too. The stories I've heard . . ." The Talassian shook his head. "Anyway," he continued, his grin returning as he gestured to the approaching city. "Behold the Jewel of the South, the Mother of Cities!"

Lukan turned his attention back to Saphrona. The city sprawled across the crescent-shaped bay and the foothills of the mountains beyond, a hazy tapestry of red-tiled roofs and countless bronze domes gleaming in the morning sunlight. Grabulli pointed to the largest dome, near the center of the city.

"The Lady's House," he said, adopting a tone of mock reverence. "Where the Lady of Seven Shadows judges us all." He belched. "If you believe that sort of thing."

"You're not one of the faithful, then? Color me shocked."

"I believe in the strength of steel, friend Lekaan! In the color of courage, in the—"

"Language of lies?"

Grabulli punched his arm, a little harder than necessary. "Just so! You're a smart boy."

Lukan winced as the liquor in his stomach churned another warning. *Not so smart.* "What's that place?" he asked, pointing to a grand, turreted building that crowned a promontory at the eastern end of the bay, looming imposingly over the city.

"That's the ducal palace atop Borja's Bluff," the captain replied. "But the Duke rules Saphrona in name only. You see those towers?" He pointed to seven stone towers rising from the foothills of the mountains behind the city. "They belong to the Silken Septet—the most powerful merchant princes. The Septet dominate the Gilded Council, which is the true political power in Saphrona."

"So I've read," Lukan replied, recalling Velleras Gellame's *Gentleman's Guide to Saphrona.* He'd managed to read nearly two-thirds of the booklet before hurling it across his cabin after one flowery metaphor too many, and had no intention of picking it up again. Grabulli was still talking, but Lukan wasn't listening, staring instead at Saphrona's sprawling expanse. Somewhere in there lay the answer to the question of who, or what, Zandrusa was. *And why my father wrote that name in his own blood.*

"You have gone quiet, friend Lekaan," Grabulli said, scratching at his black beard. "You are lost for words, I think."

"It's an impressive sight," Lukan admitted.

Velleras Gellame claimed that Saphrona was the greatest center of commerce in the Old Empire, and, while the buffoon had written his treatise nearly fifty years prior, the number of vessels crowding the waters of the bay suggested his claim still rang true. As they drew closer to the city's docks, Lukan saw trade ships from various cities of the Old Empire—Deladrin, where he himself had sailed from, Tamberlin, and even distant Korslakov. There were also dhows from the Southern Queendoms, most of which bore the flag of Zar-Ghosa, three silver circles on a pale blue background. He even caught a glimpse of a sleek, crimson-sailed vessel from one of the ports of the Mourning Sea, its black, lacquered hull bearing intricate carvings. Countless flags and banners rippled in the breeze as gulls wheeled overhead.

"I don't think I've ever seen so many ships," Lukan said.

"I have," Grabulli replied nonchalantly. "Though half of them were on fire. Including my own." He shrugged. "No doubt most of these are here for the celebrations. Just like us, eh?"

"What celebrations?"

The man threw him a sharp look. "The Grand Restoration, of course." His dark eyes narrowed at Lukan's blank expression. "The symbolic exchange of the Silver Spear . . . Truly, you don't know of what I speak?"

Lukan grinned. "I don't have a clue."

"Then what brings you to Saphrona, friend Lekaan?"

"Personal business," he replied, determined not to give anything else away. "But I never say no to a good knees-up. What are we celebrating?"

"You surely know of the great war between Saphrona and Zar-Ghosa, yes?"

"Uh, vaguely . . ."

"A naval conflict like nothing the world has ever seen!" the captain continued, quickly warming to his subject. "Hundreds of ships destroyed, thousands of gallant sailors lost on both sides! And then, during what promised to be the decisive battle—"

"The Corsair Lord of the Shattered Isles arrived with his fleet, hoping to kill two enemies with one stone," Lukan said, recalling one of the few lectures he'd bothered attending at the Academy. "And so the Saphronans and Zar-Ghosans joined forces to defeat the corsairs. An act that ended the war."

"And forged a newfound peace between the cities that has lasted forty years," Grabulli finished, making a sweeping gesture. "A grand story, don't you think?"

"Very," Lukan agreed. "And so these celebrations . . . they're to mark the anniversary of the war's end?"

"Just so. And to mark the renewal of friendship between the cities."

"Right. You said something about a spear?"

"The Silver Spear!" Grabulli's eyes lit up. "A Phaeron weapon of savage beauty that once belonged to the Corsair Lord himself, and which he wielded in the final battle. The Zar-Ghosan admiral is said to have offered the spear to his Saphronan counterpart at the battle's end as a gesture of comradeship, and so the two cities have exchanged it every decade since, when they renew their vow of peace. This time it's Saphrona's turn to host the celebration, hence . . ." He gestured to the multitude of ships in the bay.

"So the spear is handed over, someone makes a speech, and then everyone gets drunk?"

"Just so, friend Lekaan! The ceremony is in a few days. Enough time for you to conclude your business and join the party, eh?"

"Perhaps."

Grabulli coughed into his fist. "Ah, speaking of business . . ." He turned and snapped his fingers. The *Sunfish*'s quartermaster joined them at the railing, the jaunty angle of her three-cornered hat completely at odds with the scowl on her face. She held a sack, the bottom of which was stained with what could have been wine, but Lukan suspected was something else entirely. Two other crew members—hulking brutes who looked like they'd seen their fair share of tavern fights—stood behind her, eyes alert, postures tense. As if expecting trouble.

"What's this, Grabulli?" Lukan asked warily, wishing he'd buckled his sword on before staggering out of his cabin.

"We need to discuss the matter of payment, friend Lekaan. As you can see, I have delivered you to Saphrona, safe and sound."

"You'll get your seven silvers. I gave you my word."

"Yes, well . . ." The captain grinned wide, gold tooth flashing. "The price just went up."

"We agreed on seven silvers," Lukan replied, his tone hardening. "We *shook* on seven silvers, though of course I should have known that means little to a pirate."

One of the sailors stepped forward, only to freeze as Grabulli raised a hand. "We also agreed," the captain said, "that you would keep your hands off the cargo in my hold. And yet, just the other day, Sandria here noticed that a crate had been tampered with, and that it seemed to contain a little less tobacco than when we left Deladrin."

"A *lot* less," the quartermaster put in, speaking around her scowl.

"So you see," Grabulli continued, spreading his hands, "we have something of a problem."

"No problem," Lukan replied, with a sigh. He'd snuck into the hold in search of a bottle of something, *anything* that was better than the coarse rum he'd been drinking. Instead he'd found a cache of Purple Dragon, premium Parvan pipeweed, and . . . well. One cheeky smoke had turned into several dozen. "What can I say?" he continued, offering Grabulli a rueful smile. "I guess I just fancied a taste of home."

The captain frowned. "You said you were from a town near Deladrin."

"Ah . . ."

"You stole from us," Sandria hissed, her scowl deepening.

"Lady's mercy, you're *pirates*."

"Careful, friend Lekaan," Grabulli warned, with no trace of his usual humor.

"All right," Lukan said, raising his hands. "I'm sorry. I shouldn't have taken the pipeweed. Let me make amends. I'll pay for the amount I took."

"Fourteen silvers."

Lukan blinked. "I . . . *What*?"

"Fourteen silvers," the captain repeated. "The price of your voyage just doubled, friend Lekaan."

"I don't have that sort of money."

"We both know that's not true."

"Been spying on me in my cabin, Grabulli?"

The man's grin returned, flashing gold. "There's no secrets aboard my ship."

"And if I refuse to pay?"

"We'll toss you over the side. Nothing personal, of course."

"Of course." Lukan glanced at the distant waterfront. *Not so distant now . . .* "Doesn't seem too bad," he said, with more bravado than he felt. "I can swim that."

"You think, eh?" Grabulli snapped his fingers again.

Sandria reached into her sack and pulled out a hunk of raw meat, blood oozing between her fingers. She stepped up to the rail and hurled it out across the water. The meat struck the waves with barely a splash. A moment later a mottled, sandy-colored snout broke the surface, and Lukan caught a glimpse of a black eye and a grinning maw of needlelike teeth, ringed by a peculiar, loose fold of skin that almost had the appearance of a mane.

The creature disappeared back beneath the waves, taking the meat with it.

"Lion shark," Grabulli said, a glint in his eye. "The bay is full of them. Must be the guts from the fisheries that attracts them, though no doubt the Kindred sometimes throw them a tastier morsel."

"The Kindred?"

"The criminal underworld of Saphrona." Grabulli clapped Lukan on the back. "You still fancy a swim, friend Lekaan?"

"Not as much as I fancy keeping all my limbs."

"Ha! Then fourteen silvers seems like a fair price for that privilege, no?"

"Fine," Lukan said, meeting the captain's gaze. "Fourteen silvers and you forget all about me. If anyone asks the name of the passenger you picked up in Deladrin, you tell them he was called . . . Dubois. Bastien Dubois." He held out his hand. "Do we have a deal?"

"I don't know, friend Lekaan," Grabulli mused, tugging at his black beard. "I am renowned for my long memory."

"Enough bullshit," Lukan replied, with far more conviction than he felt. "If you try to screw me any further I'll take my chances with the sharks."

Grabulli and Sandria exchanged a look. One of the brutes behind them cracked his tattooed knuckles.

For a moment Lukan thought he'd pushed it too far.

Then Grabulli laughed and seized his hand, crushing it in an iron grip as he shook vigorously. "Welcome to Saphrona, Master Dubois."

4

A FLEA IN THE FLEA MARKET

A traveler's first impression of Saphrona, so Velleras Gellame's treatise began, *is of a beguiling and graceful maiden, her perfume one of jasmine and honeysuckle, her laughter the sound of distant bells.*

Lukan was starting to suspect that Gellame had sunk one too many brandies. *Or perhaps he just arrived by a different entrance.* Either way, Lukan's first impression of Saphrona was proving to be rather different. There was nothing beguiling about watching two tattooed sailors beating each other bloody while their comrades shouted encouragement, nothing graceful about sweat-slicked dockworkers unloading barrels under the gaze of thin-lipped customs officers. Nor did the air smell of jasmine and honeysuckle so much as rotting fish, woodsmoke, and fresh shit. As for the sound of distant bells . . . no doubt they were lost beneath the cacophony of shouting and laughter, the barking of dogs, and the creaking of the dockside winches.

As Lukan stood there, the sights and sounds of an unfamiliar city crashing over him, he felt the enormity of his task settle on his shoulders like a dead weight. With it came the fear that had shadowed his every step since he'd left Torlaine, whispering to him that this was a fool's errand, that the meaning of *Zandrusa* would remain a mystery. That the justice he'd promised his father would remain unserved, a shadow that would always hang over him. *As if I've not got enough of those already.* Lukan glanced at the sea, eyes searching for the rowing boat that had dropped him off at the waterfront. He was half minded to call it back, but it was already out of earshot, well on its way to where the *Sunfish* was anchored in the bay. There was nothing for it but to press on and hope for the best.

He turned back to the bustling quayside and adjusted his knapsack. *I'm coming for you, Zandrusa,* he thought, taking a deep breath as he started forward. *Whoever or whatever you are.*

A short time later Lukan was staring into the jaws of a gigantic monster.

He'd heard tell of it, of course—along with the Ebon Hand it was one of Saphrona's most famous landmarks—but the third-hand anecdotes and references in countless plays and songs failed to do the real thing justice. Decades—*centuries,* perhaps—of sunlight had bleached the skull almost a perfect white, though that did little to diminish the threat it exuded. Darkness pooled in its tear-shaped eye sockets, while the horns that rose above them appeared wickedly sharp. The teeth that lined the elongated jaw—all as long as swords, save the fangs at the front that were even longer—cast jagged shadows across the road below. What manner of beast the skull had belonged to, or why it now hung suspended above the waterfront's main gate, was a mystery that not even Velleras Gellame (who never missed a chance to boast about his intellect) could unravel. The chronicler had nonetheless described the skull as one of the most outlandish things he'd ever seen, and Lukan couldn't help but agree.

He joined the stream of people and wagons that was passing through the gates beneath the skull's sightless gaze. A couple of guards stood in the shadow of the arch, leaning on their halberds as they watched the endless procession, cigarillos dangling from their lips. Now and then they'd pull someone aside and ask a few questions, or stop a wagon and have a half-hearted poke around in the back, though mostly they seemed content to stand and smoke. Lukan glanced up as he passed beneath the great skull, staring into the black depths and wondering what sort of mind had once lived within. *Something ancient, intangible . . .*

"Hey you, get a move on," one of the guards called, exhaling smoke from her nostrils as she gave Lukan a hard stare. He hadn't even realized he'd stopped. *Last thing I need is to be drawing attention.* He made a gesture of apology and walked through the gateway to the wide avenue beyond.

The Southern Boneway was aptly named. Huge bones rose from both sides of the avenue at regular intervals, presumably belonging to the same creature whose skull hung above the gate. *Ribs, judging by their curves.* They stood between the stone buildings, rising above the red-tiled roofs and curving out over the avenue to form archways. *Lady's mercy, that creature must have been gigantic.* Beggars sat at the graffiti-covered bases of the bones, withered hands pleading with the torrent of humanity that flowed by. The air was thick with dust, the heat intense even though it wasn't even noon.

According to Velleras Gellame there were four Boneways in the city, one at each compass point, and all led to the same place: the Plaza of Silver and Spice, which lay at the center of Saphrona. If Gellame was to be believed, the plaza was a huge market and the beating heart of the city, where, the chronicler claimed, *anything can be bought, be that a glittering jewel, a whispered word, or even someone's death.* It was the second of those things that had drawn Lukan's attention. If by "a whispered word" Gellame meant information, then the plaza was the best place to begin his search. He'd assumed at first that Zandrusa was the name of his father's murderer—in his moments of grief he had whispered the word over and over again, feeling it cut a little deeper each time.

Yet he'd come to realize that the name might belong to someone else entirely—a friend of his father's, or some sort of associate. Someone who might know who the actual murderer was. Then again, perhaps *Zandrusa* didn't refer to a person at all, but a place, or even an object. Speculation was pointless; he could only hope the truth awaited him somewhere in the Plaza of Silver and Spice. *I'll ask around, see what I can find out,* he decided, as he passed beneath one of the looming rib bones. *And then I'll find a decent taverna and see if the local red wine is really as good as Velleras Gellame claims it is.*

By the time Lukan reached the Plaza of Silver and Spice, his shirt was damp, his throat was dry, and—after he'd stepped in a second pile of horseshit—his good humor had mostly evaporated. *You'd never guess winter was only a few weeks away.* Sweat trickled down his back as he stood between the towering bones that marked the plaza's entrance. He stared at the hundreds of stalls and pavilions beyond, at the torrent of people flowing between them, and felt his enthusiasm for his task fading as well. *Lady's mercy, where to even begin.*

With a sigh, Lukan walked into the plaza, though it felt to him as if he was drawn in the same way the tide pulled shells into its embrace. A thousand voices rose and fell like the ceaseless roar of the ocean as he was swept into a wave of humanity and borne along by its ebb and flow. Faces flashed past—people from the Old Empire, the Southern Queendoms, and beyond, their needs and desires bringing them together and creating a restless energy that Lukan felt he could reach out and touch. The various stalls with their silken awnings passed by in a blur of color, piled high with an endless array of items from across the Old Empire. There were furs, blades, and extravagant clocks from Korslakov, medicines and fine jewelry from Seldarine, and strange wooden charms from Volstav, where long-dead gods still held sway. There were Phaeron trinkets too, allegedly from the Grey Lands, though most of them were undoubtedly fake. He lingered for a moment at a stall selling bottles of Parvan Red, accepting a thimble of wine from the smiling vendor—a little taste of home in this chaotic, unfamiliar place.

As Lukan moved deeper into the market, he found himself looking upon jade figurines, crumbling scrolls, and wax-sealed jars of spices, among countless other trinkets from the far-flung corners of the world. Merchants stood behind their stalls, fanning themselves and swatting at flies as they called out their wares.

"Spectral silk! Spun by the ghost spiders of Liang-Ti . . ."

"Zar-Ghosan ivory, banded with blooded gold . . ."

"Perfumes from the ports of the Mourning Sea—now *you* can smell like the gods themselves . . ."

"Sea snake, hot and spicy—one copper a slice."

It was that last call that caught Lukan's attention, not least because his stomach chose that moment to rumble in protest. Save for some crumbling ship's biscuits, which he'd had to pick a weevil out of, he'd not eaten all morning. He fought his way through the crowd to the stall in question, where the vendor—a man with brown skin and long locs falling down his back—was laying out one of the aforementioned sea snakes on the stained board before him.

"Copper a slice," the man repeated cheerfully, snatching up a cleaver.

The snake's scales bore a rippling pattern of black, white, and emerald—far more striking than the dull-colored lake eels Lukan remembered from childhood. It was much larger as well, sporting a striped dorsal frill that ran the length of its sleek body. Glassy black eyes stared up at him, its open jaws revealing needlelike fangs.

"Never seen one of these beasts before?" the vendor asked, glancing up and cracking a grin.

"There's a lot in this city I've not seen before."

"Well," the man continued, raising his cleaver, "they don't call it the City of Splendor for nothing." He severed the snake's head with a powerful stroke and tossed it into a bucket behind him, scattering the flies that hovered at its edges.

"How does it taste?" Lukan asked, peering at the pale flesh beneath the scales.

"Why not try it and see?"

"Perhaps I don't like surprises."

The man laughed. "Then you're in the wrong city, friend."

You don't say. "I'll take a slice," he replied, placing a copper coin on the stall. The vendor turned to a nearby skillet where several skewers of sea snake hissed and crackled over glowing coals. He picked one up and squeezed a slice of lemon over it before dusting the meat with a pinch of ocher-colored spice. "Enjoy," he said, offering the skewer to Lukan.

Lukan eased a piece of meat off the skewer and popped it into his mouth. Unfamiliar tastes blossomed on his tongue, accompanied by a subtle heat. Juice exploded from the meat, which was surprisingly tender. He swallowed. "That's good," he said, licking spice from his lips. "Very good."

The man grinned as he pocketed the copper. "I'm glad you think so, my friend. Blessings of the day to you."

"And you."

Lukan made to turn away, only to pause. "I don't suppose . . . Does the word *Zandrusa* mean anything to you?"

The man frowned, cleaver raised above the sea snake. "Zandrusa . . ." He shook his head. "I can't say it does. Why, what does it mean?"

Lukan sighed. "I wish I knew."

———

He asked the same question a hundred times over the next two hours, and every time received a similar response—a blank look, a shrug, a murmured apology. Some of the merchants dismissed his question out of hand, false smiles sliding from their faces when they realized he wasn't looking to buy whatever they were selling. They waved him away with sharp gestures and muttered curses. One particularly irate jeweler even threatened to call the guards. *Zandrusa be damned*, Lukan thought, as he beat a hasty retreat, *I need to get away from this*. He shouldered his way through the crowd, ignoring the glares and heedless of the direction he was heading in, wanting only to escape this mad labyrinth of commerce and greed.

Instead he found himself at the center of the plaza, where a bronze statue of the Lady of Seven Shadows towered over the surrounding stalls and pavilions. The Lady, according to holy scripture, was the goddess who held back the seven shadows, or sins, that would otherwise corrupt humanity (a sacrifice, Her priests claimed, that should be repaid with unswerving devotion—not to mention generous temple donations). Lukan had never had much faith in the Lady—and, as far as he could tell, the feeling was mutual—but he was happy to offer up a murmur of thanks if the goddess could grant him a moment of respite.

As he climbed the steps carved into the plinth, stepping into the statue's shadow, he recalled a passage from Velleras Gellame's guide: *Though there are countless statues and temples dedicated to She Who Walks with Shadows, the truth is that coin is the only true god in Saphrona.* Lukan's experience so far had done little to disabuse him of that notion, though he couldn't deny that the goddess cut an impressive figure, Her pose one of defiance as She held the leash of the seven snarling hounds that surrounded her. Her left hand was held out before Her, palm raised, a reminder of the debt that humanity owed for Her protection. *Not that anyone here seems to be taking any notice.* If the goddess could see through the veil that concealed her features, Lukan suspected She wouldn't be pleased with what She saw.

With a sigh he unslung his pack and sat down next to one of the hounds, teeth bared as it strained against its leash. "So which one of them are you?" Lukan murmured, placing a hand against the creature's muscular flank, the bronze warm against his skin. "Avarice? Deceit? I'll bet you feel right at home in this place."

He looked out over the chaos of the plaza, a sense of hopelessness stealing over him. *I'm chasing a whisper. An echo.* "Why did you send me here, Father?" he murmured, fishing the note out of his pocket and staring at the bloody scrawl. *Lukan. Saphrona. Zandrusa.* He'd read those words so many times now that he could see them when he closed his eyes, yet still he found himself studying them as if they held some hidden meaning—

Lukan tensed, a vague sense of unease at the edges of his mind— the same sensation he had felt in Torlaine. *I'm being watched.* He folded the paper up and casually slipped it into his pocket, his eyes sweeping over the marketplace.

A rustle of cloth sounded behind him, so faint he almost missed it.

Lukan twisted round.

A small figure crouched behind him, snapping back the bony arm that had been reaching for his knapsack. The boy spun on his heel, darting away.

Lukan lunged and grasped the child's wrist, hauling him back.

"Let *go* of me," the boy demanded, scowling as he tried to pull himself free.

"Calm down . . ."

The boy snarled and lashed out with his free arm, but Lukan batted the blow aside. "I'm not going to ask again," he warned, tightening his grip on the street urchin's wrist. Defiance gleamed in the boy's brown eyes. *No,* Lukan realized as he held the kid's gaze. *Her eyes.* Despite the dark hair that was chopped short, it was definitely a girl standing before him. She wore a tattered linen shirt that hung from her bony frame, and sackcloth britches tied with hemp rope. Smears of dirt and small scars marked her olive skin, clear signs of a life lived on the streets. She couldn't have been more than ten or eleven.

"The hells you staring at?" the girl demanded, trying to twist free again. "Let *go.*"

"Or you'll what?"

"I'll . . . I'll scream." She thrust her chin out at him.

"Go ahead. You think anyone is listening?" He gestured at the plaza, where people continued about their business, no one sparing them so much as a glance. "I'll bet no one cares what happens to a street rat like you, am I right?"

The girl glared at him.

"Or maybe they do. Maybe you've sifted through their pockets before. Maybe they'd like to see some justice done." He made a show of looking around. "I'm sure I saw a guard pass by just a moment ago . . ."

"No," the girl replied, a sudden resignation in her voice that sounded too old to come from someone so young. When he looked back at her Lukan could see the fear blooming in her eyes. "Please . . . don't. Don't hand me in."

It was only then that Lukan realized the girl was missing the little finger from her left hand. "What happens the next time you get caught by the guards?" he asked. "Will they take your whole hand?"

The girl glared at him again, some of her defiance returning. "What do you want?"

The question caught him off guard. He'd been prepared to let the girl go with nothing more than a warning not to cross his path again, but now he thought about it . . .

"Does the word *Zandrusa* mean anything to you?"

"What?"

"*Zandrusa*. Zan-drew-sa. Have you heard that word before?"

She tilted her head, dark eyes calculating. "Maybe."

"No games," Lukan warned, "or I *will* call the guards."

"All right " She looked away, chewing her lip. "No," she said eventually. "Never heard it before. What does it mean?"

"Forget it, kid, it doesn't matter."

"I know someone who might know."

"Who?"

"If I tell you, will you let me go?"

"I'll do better than that." Lukan reached into a pocket with his free hand and withdrew a copper coin. "Take me to them and I'll give you this."

The girl shook her head. "Not worth my time."

"I'm sorry, I didn't realize gutter rats charged by the hour—"

"I can steal more than that in the blink of an eye," she boasted. "But if you give me a silver . . ."

"A *silver*?" Lukan snorted. "No chance. You're not in a position to argue."

"Neither are you if you're asking me for help."

She had him there. *The girl's sharp.*

"How do I know if this person of yours can help me?"

"You don't."

"Not good enough."

The girl sighed. "Look, he . . . knows things. Lots of things. He's blind, but he sees things no one else does."

"That sounds dangerously like horseshit to me."

"It's true," she insisted. "I'll prove it."

Lukan took a slow breath. *The state of this . . . I'm arguing with a street rat about whether a blind man can help me when I don't even know what I'm looking for. Still, what choice do I have?* "Fine," he said. "But I'm not giving you a silver. You can have three coppers."

"Four, and I want two up front."

Lady's mercy. Lukan had to bite his tongue so as not to smile. "What's your name, kid?"

"Flea."

"Flea? Don't you have a real name?"

"It's *Flea*," she said, her gaze hardening. "What's yours?"

"Lukan," he replied, before realizing his mistake.

"Huh. So you gonna give me those coppers?"

"Fine," Lukan said, trying not to smile at her boldness. "Four coppers if you take me to this blind man of yours. *One* up front. Deal?"

The girl grinned. "Deal."

Lukan released his grip on her wrist and pressed the copper coin into her hand—the same hand that just moments ago had been trying to steal from him. He half expected her to dart away, playing him for the fool he suspected he was, but instead Flea pocketed the coin and nodded. "Follow me," she said, moving past him and descending the stone steps two at a time.

Wondering what he'd got himself into, Lukan picked up his knapsack and followed.

5

A Story for a Story

The taverna had seen better days. *Possibly better decades,* Lukan thought as his eyes moved over the crumbling brick and warped timber of the building, which stood in one corner of the Plaza of Silver and Spice. The building seemed to sag in on itself, as if weighed down by its own memories, while a crooked sign displayed the words BLUE OYSTER in peeling, faded paint. Despite the taverna's proximity to the market, most of its outside tables were empty. Three elderly women sat at one, conversing quietly over steaming teacups, while at another two old men played a game of tiles in companionable silence. Another man sat on his own at a third table, whittling away at a piece of wood. His dark brown skin spoke of Southern Queendoms ancestry, and his greying beard suggested he was well into his middle years. His linen robe was fraying in places, though his carving knife—which he held in firm, steady hands—appeared sharp.

It was this man that Flea approached, Lukan following behind. The man looked up as they neared his table, revealing eyes that were milky white. *Blind,* Lukan thought, *just as Flea said. Let's hope she's right about everything else.*

"Flea," the man said, before the girl had a chance to announce herself. He smiled as he set his piece of wood down, though Lukan noted he still held his blade. "What a nice surprise. It's been a while since you and I have exchanged stories." He tilted his head. "And you've brought a friend."

"Not a friend," Lukan replied, "so much as someone she tried to pickpocket."

The man clucked his tongue.

"Flea, my girl . . . What have I told you, hmm?"

"Not to get caught when I have my hand in someone's pocket."

"Quite right." He laughed, the sound deep and rich. "So, stranger," he continued, his sightless eyes looking unerringly at Lukan. "My name, which Flea may or may not have told you, is Obassa. Would you do me the courtesy of telling me yours?"

"Bastien Dubois."

"Well met, Master Dubois." A flicker of amusement ghosted across the man's face. "Your accent is that of the Heartlands, am I right?"

Lukan nodded, immediately feeling foolish for doing so. "I was born and raised in Parva."

"Ah, yes . . . A beautiful city. Good wine. I saw it once, many years ago. Before I . . ." He trailed off, gesturing to his eyes.

Lukan hesitated, unsure of how to respond. "I . . . haven't been home in many years."

Obassa smiled. "That makes two of us, my friend. Anyway, to business—because I'm sure you didn't wake up this morning and decide on a whim to visit an old, blind beggar."

You might be old and blind, Lukan thought, *but you're far more than a simple beggar.*

"I'm . . . looking for something."

"Everyone who comes to this city is looking for something, Master Dubois. You'll need to be more specific."

"I'm seeking information. Flea said you could help me, that you're . . ." He trailed off, feeling foolish for a second time. "I don't know, some sort of seer."

"The young are prone to exaggeration."

"So you can't help me?"

"Oh, I didn't say that, Master Dubois. That depends on what information you need."

"Does the word *Zandrusa* mean anything to you?"

"Zandrusa," the man echoed, rolling the word from his tongue as if tasting it. "Now that is a name I've not heard in a long time."

Lukan felt a spark of hope.

"You know Zandrusa?"

"I knew her once, many years ago. A most interesting woman."

So it is a person I'm looking for, Lukan thought, feeling a mixture of relief and elation. "Who is she? I need to talk to her."

"Let's not get ahead of ourselves, Master Dubois." Obassa's lips pursed in a knowing smile. "I will tell you of Zandrusa, but first you must tell me a story."

"A story," Lukan repeated, suddenly wary. "What story?"

"Yours, of course."

"My business is my own. But I have coin."

"I have no need of coin."

"You'll forgive me if I say that your appearance suggests otherwise."

"Looks can be deceiving."

"You don't say. You're certainly no beggar."

"And your name isn't Bastien Dubois."

"As I said," Lukan said stiffly, "my business is my own."

"Then I'll let you be about it. A fine day to you, my friend." Obassa picked up his piece of wood and began whittling again. Lukan swore under his breath and turned away, considering his options. He didn't like either of them. "You're still here," Obassa commented from behind him.

"Is this all an act?" Lukan asked heatedly, wiggling his fingers in front of his face as he turned back to the man. "Are you really blind, or is this just some sort of mummery?"

"No act," Obassa said mildly, pausing in his whittling. "Much to my regret. But I don't need eyes to know that you're there, nor to know what you're thinking."

"And what's that?"

"You're wondering if you should try and sell me a falsehood, an imaginary story, because for some reason you're reluctant to tell me the truth."

"You're no better, trying to convince me you're a beggar."

"I'm not trying to convince you. You've already decided I'm not."

"Enough. I'm done with this bullshit."

"Then I wish you well," Obassa replied, the scrape of his knife resuming. "Until we meet again."

"We won't," Lukan muttered as he turned and walked back toward the bustle of the market.

"Hey." Flea appeared beside him. "You owe me three coppers."

Lukan stopped and pulled the coins from his pocket. "Here," he said, dropping them into the girl's grubby hands. "Thanks for nothing, kid." He grunted in surprise as the girl punched his thigh. "What the hells?"

"Don't blame me," she said indignantly. "It's not my fault you won't tell Obassa your real name."

"No, I guess it's not," Lukan admitted. "But he asks too much."

"It's just what he does. He asks people for their stories, I told him mine. Why won't you tell him yours?"

"Why do you care?"

Flea shrugged her bony shoulders. "I don't. But he said he knew who Zandrusa was."

"He did, but . . ."

"But *what*?"

"I don't trust him. He's not who he pretends to be."

"Neither are you, *Master Dubois*." The girl rolled her eyes. "Why didn't you tell him your real name?"

"Because . . ." He sighed. "Look, it's complicated. I'm here on personal business, and I'm using a pseudonym—"

"A pseudo-what?"

"A fake name."

"Why?"

"Because I don't want to attract any attention, and I'd bet my last copper that *that* man"—he gestured at Obassa—"has links to the criminal underworld in this city."

"You mean the Kindred?"

"Right, and they're the last people I want to tangle with."

The girl grinned and held out her palm. "Your last copper, please."

Lukan frowned at her. "You mean . . ."

"Obassa's not with the Kindred."

"You're sure?" Lukan glanced at the old man. "Because he seems pretty suspicious to me. All that blind-beggar bullsh—"

"I'm sure," the girl cut in, eyes narrowing. "And don't be mean about Obassa, he's my friend." She snapped her fingers. "You owe me a copper."

"It was a figure of speech," Lukan muttered, but he flipped her a copper anyway. *This changes things,* he mused, as Flea snatched the coin from the air. *If Obassa's not Kindred, perhaps there's little harm in talking to him. Not like I've got any other leads.* He wiped sweat from his brow. *Still feels like a risk, though.* He looked at the market and felt the familiar sense of hopelessness as he eyed the countless stalls, the hordes of people shouting and gesticulating. *I could search this place for months and not find any answers. Which only leaves one option.*

He turned and started back toward Obassa.

"Where are you going?" Flea called after him.

"To throw caution to the wind."

———

"Master Dubois," Obassa said, glancing up from his whittling. "You've returned. A change of heart, I wonder?"

"No . . . more a change of perspective."

"I find they often amount to the same thing."

"Look, how about we skip the cheap philosophy and get down to it? I'll tell you who I am and why I'm here, and in return you'll tell me who Zandrusa is and where I can find her. Is that acceptable to you?"

"Perfectly." The man gave that knowing smile again, as if he'd known Lukan would return all along. "Alejo," he said to a young man wiping down a nearby table, "could I trouble you for a pot of black tea? And for my friend here . . ."

"Just water."

As the waiter disappeared back inside the Blue Oyster, Obassa turned his sightless eyes to Flea. "I find myself with a sudden desire for one of Kressa's honey cakes. Perhaps, Flea, you would do me the favor of retrieving one."

The girl pouted. "Kressa's stall is on the far side of the market."

"Then purchase one for yourself as well. Here." The blind man held out a weathered palm containing two copper coins. *Definitely not a beggar,* Lukan thought as the girl snatched the coins and darted away. "Now," Obassa said, gesturing at the bench beside him. "Why don't you take a seat, Master . . . ?"

"Gardova," Lukan replied as he sat down. "Lukan Gardova."

"And what's your story, Master Gardova?"

"Where should I begin?"

"At the beginning, of course."

"Right." Lukan paused as Alejo reappeared with their refreshments, accepting his cup of water with a nod of thanks. "I was born into one of the oldest families in Parva," he continued, once the waiter had left them. "We used to be one of the wealthiest as well, until my grandfather blew most of our fortune on his gambling habits. These days we're little more than minor aristocracy. My father is—*was*—Conrad Gardova. He died recently."

"My condolences."

"Thanks. We . . . didn't have the best relationship. We hadn't talked in many years."

"You were estranged?" Obassa blew gently on his tea.

"Something like that. We were never close, and at eighteen I left home to attend the Academy of Parva, but it didn't work out." *Which is putting it mildly.*

"Academic pursuits are not for everyone," Obassa said charitably.

"True . . . though my expulsion had more to do with the fact that I killed a fellow student."

Obassa raised an eyebrow. "Oh?"

"In self-defense," Lukan added hurriedly. "We fought a duel. I won. He attacked me afterward when I turned my back, and my sword just . . . It was an accident. Anyway, I was expelled from the Academy. That was seven years ago and I've been traveling ever since. Trying to, you know . . . find my place in the world. Most recently I was in Torlaine, near the Grey Lands."

"Is that so? I've heard tales of that place, even all the way down here. They say only the foolish, the deranged, or the desperate venture there." The man smiled thinly. "Which of those are you, I wonder."

Take your pick, Lukan thought.

"While I was there," he continued, "I received word from my father's steward. She told me that my father had been murdered." Even now, it felt strange to say it out loud.

"Murdered? My deepest sympathies, Master Gardova."

"I don't need your sympathies. What I *do* need"—Lukan withdrew the folded note from his pocket—"is an answer to why my father scrawled the word *Zandrusa* on a scrap of paper before he died." He held the note out before realizing his mistake. Even so, the blind man reached out and took the parchment, gently running his fingers over it.

"There are two more words here . . ."

"The first is my name. The second is *Saphrona,* hence why I'm here."

"How curious," Obassa murmured.

"So will you tell me what you know?"

"But of course," the man replied, handing back the note. "That was the deal, after all. A story for a story." He took a sip of tea. "You've arrived in Saphrona at an exciting time, Master Gardova."

"So I gather."

"Forty years since the end of the war." The man shook his head as he set down his cup. "I can scarcely believe it's been so long. I was part of the first wave of Zar-Ghosan immigrants to settle here after the peace treaty was signed. You might think that strange, moving to the very city you'd previously sought to destroy, living among people who had once been your enemies. But there were opportunities to be had, and it was a chance for a new beginning for those of us who had struggled to find a path for ourselves at home. I had been here for maybe a couple of years when Zandrusa arrived."

"She came from Zar-Ghosa?"

Obassa nodded. "Most of my countrymen who made the journey across the sea had an honest trade, while others took a wage working in the silver mines outside the city. Some, however, pursued interests that were not so . . . legitimate. Zandrusa was one of them."

"So she was a criminal?"

"She was a *smuggler,* and a very good one at that. There weren't many of us in those early days and there was still a lot of resentment because of the war. Sometimes it was hard for us immigrants to obtain certain supplies. Zandrusa changed that by smuggling in what we needed—medicines and the like."

"So a smuggler with a heart of gold."

"Oh, make no mistake: Zandrusa mostly moved high-value goods like ivory and silk, but she did what she could to help her countrymen out. She ran her little operation for nearly a decade before winding it up and investing her small fortune in legitimate businesses."

"So she went straight? Why?"

"Who can say?" Obassa replied, spreading his hands. "Perhaps she started to feel the long arm of the law; the Saphronan Inquisition is nothing if not diligent in rooting out those who pursue illegal lines of work."

"So I've seen," Lukan replied, recalling the black-clad inquisitors leading their prisoner into the Ebon Hand.

"Or maybe she just felt it would aid her philanthropic efforts," Obassa continued. "Either way, Zandrusa proved as skilled at investments as she was at smuggling. She became a very wealthy woman, and in Saphrona a wealthy woman is also a powerful woman."

"If that's the case," Lukan countered, "then why does no one here seem to know her name?"

"Because she dropped it when she abandoned her smuggling operation, and now few of us remain who still remember her true birth name. She adopted the name Saïda Jelassi for her new business practices and has gone by that ever since. It was under this name that she eventually achieved what none of us thought possible—a place on the Gilded Council."

Lukan's eyes widened.

"Zandrusa is a merchant prince?"

"The first Zar-Ghosan to hold that honor, if you can call it that. She's held the position for well over a decade now." Obassa tilted his head and grinned. "You seem lost for words, Master Gardova. You're wondering, no doubt, what one of the most powerful women in Saphrona could possibly have to do with your father's death."

"The question had crossed my mind."

The beggar chuckled. "Well, in that matter, I'm afraid I cannot help you."

"I need to talk to Zandrusa. I need to find out what she knows—"

"I'm afraid that's impossible."

"Why?"

"Because she's due to be executed tomorrow morning."

"She's *what*?" Lukan shook his head, his mind reeling. "Why? What for?"

"For the murder of Lord Saviola, a fellow merchant prince. It's been the talk of the city for the past month or so, not to mention casting something of a shadow over the preparations for the Grand Restoration." Obassa took another sip of tea, twisting his lips as if the taste had turned bitter. "Lord Saviola's servants found Zandrusa—Lady Jelassi—standing over their master's body, bloodied dagger in hand." He lowered his cup, one eyebrow moving in the opposite direction. "Or so they say."

"You think she's innocent?"

"Lord Saviola was Zandrusa's closest ally on the Gilded Council. More than that, they were said to be good friends. It seems highly strange to me, Master Gardova. But then what do I know? I'm just—"

"A blind old beggar," Lukan cut in. "Yeah, I get it." He sat back, swore under his breath. *I came all this way for nothing.* "So where is she now? Zandrusa, I mean."

"In the Ebon Hand. And no, they don't permit visitors." Obassa sighed as he rose to his feet, picking up the cane that rested beside him. "The execution will be at the tenth bell tomorrow morning, in the old amphitheater. Flea can take you there, should you wish to attend. If Zandrusa survives, seek me out and we will talk further."

"Hold on," Lukan said as the older man turned away. "What do you mean *if* she survives? I thought you said she was being executed?"

Obassa grinned. "You'll find we do things a little differently in Saphrona, Master Gardova."

6

GARGANTUA

Lukan was no stranger to executions.

He had been eleven when he'd first seen a man die, and, though he'd long forgotten the man's crimes, he could still recall the silver blur of the executioner's blade as it swept down, and the crimson spray that followed. He remembered being surprised by how quickly it had happened, how simple the act of killing was. The executioner—their features concealed behind a golden filigree mask—had picked the head up and held it aloft, striking a series of dramatic poses as the crowd cheered. Lukan had quickly learned that in Parva, the self-proclaimed capital of culture in the Old Empire, even the executions had to be carried out with a sense of theater. None of those he'd seen on his travels had possessed quite the same dramatic flair, leading him to believe that his home city stood apart when it came to making a spectacle of death.

Seems I was wrong, he thought now, as he surveyed the crowded amphitheater.

Several thousand people had come to witness Zandrusa's execution—*possible* execution, he corrected himself—and the sound of their laughter and conversation echoed across the tiers of stone seating and across the hard-packed dirt of the arena's floor. If Lukan hadn't known any better, he would have thought this was some sort of carnival or sporting event. He shifted on the bench, noting that many of the people around him had brought their own cushions to sit on. *Nothing like sitting comfortably while you watch someone die.*

Flea sat beside him, eating some grapes she'd lifted from a stall outside. As Lukan watched, she plucked another grape from the bunch and—taking careful aim—tossed it at a man sitting a few rows in front of them. She snorted as it struck the back of his head, causing him to glance around, eyes narrowed in suspicion. As the man turned away, the girl prepared to throw another.

Lukan caught her wrist. "Don't."

"Why not?"

"Because what did I tell you yesterday, when that innkeeper heard you say his face looked like a . . . what was it—"

"Smacked arse."

"Right. And what did I tell you?"

"Not to upset people and attract attention."

"Exactly." He released her arm. "I don't want to have to remind you again."

The girl rolled her eyes and popped the grape into her mouth. Even so, Lukan found himself wondering—not for the first time—whether he'd made a mistake in accepting her offer of further assistance. He'd thought they would part ways after his meeting with Obassa—after all, Flea had got her coin and he'd obtained the information he sought. Yet the street girl, no doubt sensing the opportunity for some easy money, had suggested she accompany him for a while, and it occurred to Lukan that having someone to show him around Saphrona wouldn't be a bad thing. So after some prolonged negotiating (the girl was stubborn as the hells, to put it mildly) they'd reached an agreement. Only time would tell whether it would prove a mistake on his part; some of the girl's behavior so far had certainly caused him to question his judgment. Still, Flea had at least shown him to a decent inn called the Orange Tree, where he'd slept well and not been robbed in the night, so it hadn't been a bad start.

"Oh, look," the girl said, pointing across the amphitheater to a private enclosure of polished marble and purple velvet drapes. "The merchant princes."

"I see them," Lukan replied, watching as Saphrona's elite citizens sipped from crystal glasses and chatted among themselves as they took their seats. Even from a distance there was no mistaking their silks and jewelry—or their relaxed demeanors. *Zandrusa's former peers arriving to watch her die, and not looking at all concerned by the prospect. Quite the opposite, in fact.*

"It won't be long now," Flea said, popping another grape into her mouth.

Lukan turned his attention to the arena floor.

To the Bone Pit.

The circular stone platform was some forty yards in diameter. A large bronze disc was set at its center, its surface embossed with details that he couldn't make out. Four bones—presumably from the monster whose skull loomed above the waterfront gate—stood at the edge of the platform, one at each compass point. Iron collars and manacles hung from them on chains, dark with rust. *Or blood,* he thought, feeling a flicker of trepidation. *It can't be true,* he thought, recalling what Flea had told him the night before. *It can't be. She's playing me for a fool. Gellame made no mention of a giant—*

"Here they come," Flea said, just as a murmur of excitement rippled around the amphitheater. The gates at the eastern end, away to their right, were slowly opening. A detachment of constables emerged from the darkness beyond, marching out in two columns, their conical bronze helms glinting in the sunlight. Between them shuffled three figures, all dressed in grey, their hands cuffed behind their backs. *The prisoners,* Lukan realized.

The first was a youth, still in his teens. The second was a man of middle years, his beard streaked with grey. *Which can only mean . . .* He eyed the third figure, a tall woman with light brown skin. *That must be Zandrusa.* In contrast to her fellow prisoners, the merchant prince held her shaven head high, her expression impassive. While the two men cowered beneath the roar of the crowd, she seemed to breathe it in and grow in stature. *What connection do you have to my father?* Lukan wondered. He could only hope she lived long enough for him to find out.

As the prisoners and their escort approached the Bone Pit, a second group entered the arena. Seven figures, wearing silk robes of varying colors. Their faces were hidden by extravagant masks, each one a grotesque parody of a human face.

"Who are they?" Lukan asked, having to raise his voice over the noise of the crowd.

"The Keepers of the Seven Shadows," the girl replied, raising an eyebrow. "Don't you know *anything* about Saphrona?"

"That's why I'm paying you." He plucked a grape from the bunch in the girl's lap, ignoring her glare. "So what's their role in this?"

"Each one represents a different shadow," she replied, swatting away his hand as he reached for another. "That's why they all wear different masks."

"So let me guess," Lukan said, squinting at a figure in a crimson robe whose scarlet-colored mask resembled a snarling face with an almost demonic aspect. "That one in red represents Bloodlust, right?"

"Yeah." The girl pointed at each of the figures, ticking them off in turn. "Avarice, Envy, Impurity, Corruption, Defilement, and Deceit."

"They must be sweating in those masks." Lukan's gaze flicked back to the gate as two more figures appeared—a man and a woman, both dark-haired with olive skin, clad in identical outfits of sleeveless leather tunics, black leather trousers, and tall boots. A thin chain dangled between them, connecting a silver band on the man's right wrist to an identical band on the woman's left. Even from a distance there was no mistaking their self-confidence; they strutted across the arena floor as if they owned the place.

"Look, the Constanza twins!" Flea said excitedly, nudging him in the ribs and pointing at the newcomers. "They're gleamers."

"Yeah," Lukan replied, his lip curling in distaste. "I can tell." *I know their kind all too well.*

He ignored Flea's questioning look and watched as the prisoners and their escort of guards reached the stone platform and ascended the steps carved into its side. Suddenly the youth turned and bolted down the steps, twisting away from the guards' desperate attempts to restrain him. He ran back toward the gates with a frenzied energy born of terror, the crowd roaring with excitement at this unexpected development. The seven Keepers parted to let him through; clearly none of them fancied getting their silk robes dirty.

All that now stood between the prisoner and his escape were the two gleamers.

The poor boy doesn't stand a chance, Lukan thought.

The twins shared an amused glance, the chain that bound their wrists slackening as they clasped hands. They pivoted smoothly, the woman taking up position at the front, right arm outstretched, fingers splayed. Her brother stood behind, head bowed as he raised his left arm to the sky.

The prisoner veered to avoid them.

A tremor ran through the man's raised arm and then his entire body was trembling, his teeth gritted from the effort of channeling raw power from beyond the veil of the world. *Here it comes,* Lukan thought. *Any moment now . . .*

A streak of turquoise sorcery shot from the woman's hand, splitting the air with a crack as it lashed out like a whip, striking the fleeing prisoner in the face and sending him sprawling to the ground. The crowd roared. The youth managed to climb to one knee, but fell back into the dirt as the lash hovered over him, tensed as if ready to strike. It was only then that Lukan realized the tip of the lash resembled a snake's head, eyes glowing yellow above bared fangs. *Damned gleamers. Everything's a game to them.*

The prisoner remained on the ground, one arm raised against the hovering lash, until a pair of guards dragged him roughly to his feet. He offered no further resistance as he was marched back toward the Bone Pit. The female gleamer smirked and closed her fist, the turquoise snake dissipating like smoke. She said something over her shoulder to her brother, who nodded and lowered his arm, his posture relaxing as he severed his connection to whatever otherworldly powers he was drawing on. Still holding hands, the twins strolled after the re-formed rank of Keepers, apparently indifferent to the approving roar of the crowd.

Flea turned to him, her eyes wide. "Did you *see* that?"

"I saw it." *And I'll bet it was barely a glimpse of what they can do.*

Perhaps chagrined by their failure to control the prisoners, the guards set about their next task with renewed energy, pushing the three prisoners into position before the bones and fastening the iron collars round their necks and manacles round their wrists. Satisfied they were secure, the guards left the platform. The Constanza twins took up a position about ten yards away, while the seven Keepers stood in a line a short distance behind them. A hush fell over the arena as the purple-robed figure of Corruption stepped forward and raised a conical device to the mouth of her mask, which resembled a smirking face adorned by a crown set at a crooked angle—a nod, perhaps, to the abuses of power that had eventually brought down the Amberléne Empire several centuries before.

"Good citizens of Saphrona," she said, her voice echoing around the arena. "These three prisoners have violated our city's sacred laws. The Lady of Seven Shadows demands justice. Will you bear witness as one of them gives their life to atone for their sins?"

"*We will bear witness,*" the crowd roared as one.

"Then heed the names and crimes of the condemned." The Keeper pointed to the young man. "Gallias Savanos, clerk of the first rank at the Trade Council, has invoked the Sixth Shadow of Corruption. He broke his oath of service and abused his position of authority to steal sensitive information, which he then sold to foreign powers, thus undermining the safety and security of our city. A debt must be paid."

The youth shook his head and tried to speak, but his plea of innocence was lost beneath the roar of the crowd. Corruption handed the speaking horn to Deceit, who wore a yellow robe and a mask featuring a pointed chin and ridiculously long nose, which reminded Lukan of a pantomime villain. The Keeper raised the horn to his lips and pointed at the older man.

"Antillas Karza, customs official, has invoked the Fifth Shadow of Deceit. He falsified hundreds of documents, which allowed the import of illegal narcotics into our city. A debt must be paid."

The man flinched as the crowd roared again, his head bowed.

Bloodlust stepped forward to stand beside Corruption and Deceit, accepting the horn from the latter. He raised the device to the lips of his demonic mask and pointed at Zandrusa.

"Lady Saïda Jelassi, merchant prince and formerly an esteemed member of the Gilded Council, has invoked the First Shadow of Bloodlust," he intoned in a deep voice. "She murdered Lord Saviola, a fellow merchant prince and council member, in cold blood. A debt must be paid."

The crowd had clearly reserved most of their ire for the former merchant prince; the cacophony that followed was almost deafening. If only one of the three prisoners was to die that morning, it was clear who the popular choice was. Zandrusa, for her part, appeared unmoved—unlike her fellow prisoners, she stood up straight, chin raised, face impassive. *A guilty woman accepting her fate?* Lukan wondered. *Or an innocent woman determined to keep her dignity?* If Zandrusa survived what was to come, perhaps he would find out. Yet if she died here, right before his eyes, well . . . that would be the end of everything. Whatever link Zandrusa had to his father would forever remain a mystery. *As will the identity of my father's murderer.* Lukan clenched a fist in frustration. Never before had something so important to him been so completely out of his hands.

"Here come the drummers," Flea said, as twenty men and women—immaculate in outfits of black and gold—filed into the amphitheater in two columns, large drums resting on their hips. They made their way to the Bone Pit and formed a circle around the platform, some of them looking less than delighted to be so close to the prisoners. *I don't blame them,* Lukan thought. *If half of what Flea has said is true, I wouldn't want to be standing there either.*

The crimson-robed figure of Bloodlust stepped forward from the line of Keepers and raised the speaking horn to his mask once again.

"Three debts must be paid," the Keeper intoned. "But only one of the condemned will today be granted the honor of offering their life to the Lady of Seven Shadows. She will decide."

"*She will decide,*" the crowd echoed as Bloodlust rejoined the line of Keepers.

Silence fell, weighed down by a collective anticipation that stole the breath from Lukan's lungs.

For several moments nothing happened.

Then the large bronze seal at the center of the platform began to move, sliding sideways into a hidden recess, revealing the darkness beneath. The low rumble of its movement was drowned out as the crowd began a chant, which rose in volume as the hole—the *pit*—grew steadily wider. As the seal finally disappeared from view, the crowd cheered even louder than before. Lukan felt almost dizzy as he glanced at the prisoners. The youth was gaping at the pit in wide-eyed terror, while the older man's shoulders shook as he sobbed. Zandrusa remained still, staring straight ahead.

Then the drums started—slow at first, like the booming of a huge, unseen clock, counting down the final moments of the prisoners' lives. A hush fell over the crowd as the tempo quickened, until the only sound was the drumbeat echoing around the amphitheater. Each pounding beat drove the anxiety in Lukan's gut a little closer to his throat. Movement caught his eyes: the Constanza twins, adopting the same position they had taken earlier—the sister in front, arm outstretched and fingers spread wide, her brother behind with his left arm raised. Both gleamers ready to unleash their sorcery against . . . what?

Yet Lukan already knew. He'd known from the moment when Flea had told him the night before, even if he'd refused to believe it. Now, as he stared at the prisoners chained around the pit, as his heart pounded in time to the drumbeat—and as he felt a series of subtle tremors in the stone beneath him—he finally admitted what he'd known all along. *Flea wasn't joking. Lady's mercy . . .* He wanted to close his eyes, but instead he stared at the pit, unable to look away.

"Here she comes," Flea shouted.

The monster rose from the darkness, a nightmare slipping into the waking world. To Lukan's eyes it had the look of a worm, though in truth it was as close to a worm as a wolf was to a puppy. He watched, speechless, as the huge creature emerged from the depths of the pit, a primal force that had somehow outlived the age that had witnessed its birth. It moved slowly, its elongated body twisting upward with a languor born from being a predator without equal.

A predator that no longer even needed to hunt.

The drumbeat faltered, then died as the drummers backed away, terror flitting across their faces. A ragged cheer swelled around the amphitheater as the crowd found its voice. The worm's tan-colored body arched in response to the sound, a series of wicked black spines protruding from the carapace along its back. Sand and dirt spilled from the creature's huge tusks as it turned its massive head in different directions. *Trying to pinpoint the sound,* Lukan realized as his initial shock receded. *Damned thing must be blind.*

"Gargantua," Flea shouted, practically bouncing with excitement.

"Gargantua?" he echoed, glancing at the girl.

"That's her name."

"Her? How do you know it's—"

"Just watch!"

The creature—Gargantua—didn't seem to have detected the three potential meals on offer, despite two of them doing their utmost to be noticed. The youth was shaking, lips quivering as he mouthed a frantic prayer, while the older man was busy pissing himself, chest heaving as he gasped lungfuls of air. Zandrusa remained still as a statue, her tensed jaw and flaring nostrils the only sign of the terror she must have felt as she stared up at the worm.

Gargantua snapped forward, quick as a whip, but not down toward one of the prisoners—instead she surged upward.

"Lady's blood," Lukan whispered, half rising. "It's going to escape—"

A muted crack split the air like distant thunder. The worm recoiled as if struck, and a web of turquoise light flickered into existence: a glowing latticework of sorcery, shaped like a dome, that enclosed the entire pit and the three prisoners. After a moment it faded from sight. *The gleamers,* Lukan realized, glancing over to their position. If either of the twins felt any pressure at being the solitary barrier that was preventing the worm escaping and smashing the amphitheater into dust, they certainly weren't showing it. The woman even wore a small smile as her fingers weaved invisible threads in the air. He shook his head in disbelief. *Arrogant bastards.*

"Sit *down,*" Flea said, rolling her eyes as she pulled him back onto the bench.

Perhaps spurred on by the crowd's jeers, Gargantua tried again, this time lunging in a different direction. Once more she recoiled at the sound of distant thunder, the web flickering briefly before fading once more. The creature made three more attempts, each more frenzied than the last.

Each time it was forced back by the gleamers' sorcery.

Seemingly enraged by her failure, Gargantua threw back her head and emitted a bass roar that momentarily drowned out the noise of the crowd, her jaws splaying open like the petals of a flower to reveal a gaping, circular mouth filled with countless rows of needlelike teeth. The creature drew back, preparing for another attempt at the invisible barrier.

Then she paused.

With an agonizing slowness, Gargantua turned toward the youth, who was still sobbing uncontrollably, half suspended in his chains, his knees having given way. The worm tilted her great head, as if listening. *Or sensing the vibrations,* Lukan thought, recalling how some snakes hunted by feeling the movement of their prey. *No wonder Zandrusa is doing her best to remain still.*

The youth looked up, as if realizing for the first time that he was the subject of the worm's attention. *Take him,* Lukan silently urged the creature. He felt a rush of guilt at wishing death on the boy, but Zandrusa *had* to survive, and if that meant the boy had to die in her place then so be it. Yet as he watched the boy quaking before the worm's maw, he couldn't help but feel that nobody deserved an end like this—certainly not for the crime of selling trade secrets.

Perhaps the Lady herself agreed, for the worm swung away from the boy and instead focused on the older man, who started thrashing in his chains, eyes bright with terror.

"Come on," Lukan murmured under his breath, feeling no less guilt at hoping for the man's death. *Put the poor bastard out of his misery and end this charade.* For a moment it seemed the worm might oblige; she leaned in close to the man, who screamed and turned his face away, flailing hopelessly in his chains. Lukan held his breath as the worm drew back, body curling as if readying to strike . . . only to twist round in a languid movement. *No*, Lukan thought, panic rising. *No, no, no.*

He watched helplessly as Gargantua moved toward Zandrusa.

A roar rippled around the arena at this unexpected turn of events. People surged to their feet, cheering. "Take her!" someone screamed, their voice shrill above the din. "Take the prince!" Others took up the chant, which quickly spread through the crowd. *Take the prince! Take the prince! Take the prince!*

Zandrusa remained unmoved. Lukan couldn't help but admire her in that moment, this stranger he didn't even know—a woman who might even be his father's murderer. She didn't scream, didn't flail in her chains, didn't glance up at the sky and plead for divine intervention. Instead she set her jaw and stared defiantly up at the worm as she loomed over her, looking her death in the eye.

The chanting tailed off, the crowd falling into quiet anticipation. Lukan didn't dare to breathe. All of his hopes rested on this moment—on the whims of this ancient creature, who had been tasked with carrying out the will of a god.

It was so absurd he could have laughed.

Gargantua turned her great head from side to side, as if somehow appraising Zandrusa. The merchant prince tensed as the creature leaned toward her, yet still she refused to look away, her expression as firm and unyielding as stone.

The creature drew back, powerful body arching. Preparing to lunge.

Time slowed, leaving Lukan with an image that he knew would always be imprinted on his mind: the spine-laden curve of Gargantua's back as she reared upward, the final defiance of Zandrusa even as the shadow of her death fell upon her. Lukan almost looked away, wanting to ignore the final act of this charade that passed for justice. Instead he kept his eyes on the merchant prince. Whatever the woman's link to his father, he felt an obligation to watch her final moments.

The worm moved with a speed that belied her size, head snapping down, jaws widening to reveal the rows of teeth within . . . only to twist away at the last moment and lunge at the older man instead. He didn't even have time to scream as the creature's jaws ripped him from his chains.

It was over in less than a heartbeat.

Gargantua straightened, a ripple passing down her length as she swallowed the unfortunate prisoner before turning back toward Zandrusa. Yet her task—whether the creature knew it or not—was done. The female gleamer weaved a complex pattern with her fingers, as if plucking a harp, and the cage of turquoise light materialized once more—smaller in radius this time, encompassing just the pit itself. The worm lunged at Zandrusa, who stood on the other side of the sorcerous barrier.

The cage flickered but held.

Gargantua roared as the cage grew smaller, throwing herself against the mesh of sorcery even as she was forced back down into the pit. The woman's smile never faltered, though Lukan noted her brother was sweating freely, teeth bared as his body shook from the energies that were coursing through him.

With a final bellow, Gargantua disappeared. The cage shrank until it covered the pit like a sorcerous spider's web, then descended into the darkness. As the bronze disc slid back into place, the male gleamer fell to one knee, exhausted from his efforts.

It was over.

The yellow-robed figure of Deceit stepped forward and raised the speaking horn. "A debt has been paid," he said, his voice echoing around the amphitheater. This time there was no answering cry from the crowd; it was as if their lust for violence and death had now been sated. "Go with the Lady's grace." The figure lowered the horn and as one the seven Keepers turned, heading for the gates without so much as a glance at the two remaining prisoners. The youth all but collapsed into the arms of the guards as they freed him from his collar and manacles. Zandrusa needed no such assistance.

"What happens to them now?" Lukan asked Flea as the prisoners were led away, Zandrusa staring in the direction of the merchant princes' enclosure.

"They'll be taken back to the Hand," Flea replied. "Then they'll do this all over again."

"Again? When?"

"Ten days from now."

"So Zandrusa will have to face that . . . *thing* again?"

"And the boy too." Flea nodded. "There will be a new prisoner as well, to replace the one that got eaten."

Lukan shook his head. *Lady's blood.* "So it's just a stay of execution then," he said, his relief at Zandrusa's survival fading. "Nothing more than a reprieve."

"A what?"

"Never mind." He rubbed the stubble on his jaw, brow creased in thought. "So they just keep bringing each prisoner back, then? Until the worm finally takes them?"

"Yeah, though people say if you survive seven times the Keepers set you free."

How generous of them. "You ever seen that happen?"

The girl shook her head. "I saw a woman who survived five

times, but the worm ate her the sixth time." She shrugged. "There're stories of prisoners who survived and were released, but they were all a long time ago."

They sat in silence for a while as the people around them headed toward the exits, talking and laughing as if they'd just watched a comedy performance rather than a horrifying execution.

"So," Lukan said eventually, "if Zandrusa has got ten days until she's back down there, that means I've got ten days to try and talk to her."

"*Talk* to her?" Flea said, giving him a withering look. "She's going to be in the *Hand*. It's like . . . one of the most guarded places in the city. You'll never get inside."

Lukan stole one of her grapes and popped it into his mouth. "Let me worry about that."

7

A MATTER OF PERSPECTIVE

"How did you know?"

"Hmm?" Lukan glanced up from the platter of cold meats and cheeses. "Know what?" He worked his tongue around his gums, dislodging a piece of smoked cheese, and took a swallow from his cup—white wine, a little too sweet for his taste. It wasn't even midday but, after the morning's events, he needed a drink and it didn't matter what it was.

"About the Constanza twins being gleamers," Flea continued, picking up a piece of salami and stuffing it into her mouth. "You said you could tell."

Lukan leaned back in his chair, watching the quiet side street and the trickle of people passing by the taverna. "I've seen a few gleamers over the years," he replied, turning back to the platter and selecting a strip of cured ham. "I also knew a couple for a short time. You come to know how to recognize them. What to look for."

Flea blinked. "You've . . . *known* gleamers? But I thought that—"

"They're all demigods who will melt the flesh from your bones if you so much as look at them?" Lukan gave a wan smile, shook his head. "Yeah, they'd love you to think that. But no, they're only human. They eat and drink, complain if they don't get enough sleep . . . Bad losers at cards, too."

"You played *cards* with a gleamer?"

"Both of them, actually. At the same time. It didn't end well."

"What happened?"

"They set the tavern on fire." He raised a hand to forestall the question already forming on the girl's lips. "They were part of an expedition I signed on to, a couple of years back. It's a long story." *And not one with a happy ending.*

"What about the sorcery?" Flea asked, enthusiasm undimmed. "Do you know how they do it? Obassa told me they draw their power from a place that we can't see, but I think he was just trying to trick me."

"No, the old man's right about that," Lukan replied, trying to recall what little he knew about sorcery. "Gleamers draw their power from a place called the Gloaming, a shadowy world that presses up against our own, but never merges with it. It's like if you put oil and water in a bottle. They occupy the same space but are always separate."

"But if we can't see the glowing—"

"Gloaming."

"That's what I said."

"It most assuredly wasn't."

"*It most assuredly wasn't,*" Flea mimicked, rolling her eyes. "Do you always talk like this?"

"Like what?"

"Like a frilly."

"A what? Oh, you mean—"

"A rich person."

Lukan gestured to his travel-worn clothes. "Do I look rich to you?"

"You sound it."

"Well, contrary to your impression—"

"You're doing it again." The girl shoved an olive into her mouth, chewed, and spat out the pip. "So if we can't *see* the Gleaming—"

"*Gloaming,*" Lukan corrected, impatiently. "I already told you . . ." He trailed off as a sly grin worked its way across Flea's face. "Ah. You're messing with me."

"Yep." The girl flicked another olive, which bounced off his chest. "So if we can't see the Gloaming, how do we know it's there?"

"Well, we don't," Lukan replied. "But the gleamers can sense it. I don't know how. More importantly, they can touch it—

they can reach into the Gloaming. That's where they find the glimmer."

"Glimmer?"

"The power they use. It's said to be like flashes of light among all the shadows."

"And that's what they use to do sorcery?"

"Exactly. They pull the glimmer through into our world, and then shape it to their will. But it's impossible for one person to perform both tasks, which is why gleamers always work in pairs, like the Constanza twins. One summons the glimmer and the other shapes it."

"So the man was the summoner," Flea said, brow creasing in thought, "and the woman was the shaper. She shaped the glimmer into the snake, and then the cage."

"Right."

"But *how*? How do they do it?"

"I asked one of the gleamers I knew that very question. Got him drunk one night on some rough whiskey, thought it might loosen his tongue."

"And did it?"

"No, though I always wondered whether his reluctance to talk was because he didn't know the answer himself. He did talk a little about the connection between the summoner and shaper, how they always have to be in physical contact, which is why they hold hands."

"So that's why the Constanza twins wear the chain?"

"Exactly, though apparently a physical connection is not enough on its own—the gleamers also need to share an emotional bond. The stronger the bond, the easier it is for them to summon and shape glimmer, which in turn makes for more powerful sorcery." He shrugged. "So I was told, anyway."

"The Constanza twins are brother and sister," Flea said, eyes narrowing as she followed the logic. "So they must be tight."

"Exactly. That's why they're capable of sorcery powerful enough to control that . . . *thing* from the pit."

"I had a brother once," Flea said, picking up another slice of salami. "Maybe we could have worked sorcery like them."

"You were close?"

"I guess. Matteo used to look after me."

"Where is he now?"

"Gone."

"Oh. I'm sorry."

"It was a few years ago." Flea shrugged. "I can look after myself now."

"Yeah, I noticed." He grinned. "Might need to work on your pickpocketing though."

The girl scowled and threw another olive at him. "One day I'll be as good as Lady Midnight."

"Lady who?"

"Midnight." Her eyes narrowed. "Don't tell me you haven't heard of her."

"I only arrived in the city yesterday, kid. Enlighten me."

Flea stared at him blankly.

"Tell me who she is," he clarified.

"Only the best thief in the whole city," the girl replied, enthusiasm replacing her disgust at Lukan's ignorance. "Her name's Ashra Seramis, but everyone calls her Lady Midnight. She can sneak past any guard and pick any lock, *and*"—the girl leaned forward—"she can walk through walls."

"Impressive."

The girl's eyes narrowed. "Why are you laughing?"

"I'm not." Lukan forced the smile from his face. "It's a good story."

"It's not a story. It's the truth." Flea sat back, glowering at him. "And one day I'm gonna be like her." The girl grabbed some salami and pushed it into her mouth. "Sho do you shink—"

"Don't talk with your mouth full."

Flea rolled her eyes and made a show of chewing, followed by an exaggerated swallow. "So do you think Zandrusa murdered your father?"

Lukan blinked in surprise. "How do you even know about that?"

"I listened to you talking to Obassa."

"But . . . you went to buy those honey cakes." He couldn't help but smile as realization dawned. "You doubled back. Listened in."

"I hid under a table." The girl grinned. "I think Obassa knew I was there."

I'll bet he bloody did. "Why?"

"I wanted to hear your story."

"It's not much of a story. More a cautionary tale." *How to ruin your life in one moment of madness.* He downed what remained of his wine and stood. "Speaking of Obassa, can you take me back to the old rogue? I need to speak to him."

"Do you really think you can get inside the Hand?"

"Maybe. I have an idea." *Or half of one, at least.*

Flea grabbed the last slice of salami and stood. "Follow me."

———

The blind beggar, if indeed that's what he was—and Lukan's doubts had only grown since their meeting the previous day—was not to be found outside the Blue Oyster taverna, but Flea was untroubled. "I know where he'll be," she said with a shrug, leaving Lukan no choice but to follow her out of the plaza and into a tangle of smoke-filled streets lined with workshops.

"This is the Smokes," Flea remarked as they passed a blacksmith hammering at her anvil.

"I'd never have guessed."

The girl gave him a sharp look. "What's that supposed to mean?"

"Nothing, kid." Lukan wrinkled his nose against the stench that emanated from a nearby tannery. "Where are we going, anyway?"

"To the Zar-Ghosan quarter. That's where Obassa will be."

Eventually the air cleared, the sounds of industry faded, and the surrounding buildings took on a different appearance, sporting an abundance of arches and domes, elaborate arabesques and colorful tilework. The people changed too; most of the citizens going about their business had the appearance of the Southern Queendoms. The oldest among them had likely arrived from Zar-Ghosa after the end of the war, but the younger would have been born in Saphrona in the forty years since, sons and daughters of the original immigrants. *Freshly minted citizens of a city that not so long ago was their people's sworn enemy. Funny how times change.*

"There he is," Flea said, interrupting Lukan's thoughts as she pointed to a building that had the look of a coffeehouse. The tables outside were busy with patrons, laughing and talking over steaming mugs. Some smoked from elaborate pipes, the likes of which Lukan had never seen before. It took him a moment to spot Obassa, sitting alone and whittling away at another piece of wood.

"Master Gardova," the Zar-Ghosan said, smiling as they reached his table. He set down his wood and carving knife. "A good day to you."

Lukan's own greeting was still forming on his tongue. *How did he know it was me?* He glanced questioningly at Flea, but the girl just shrugged. "Hey Obassa," she said.

"Ah, Flea. A good day to you as well." His sightless gaze switched back to Lukan. "Welcome to the Zar-Ghosan quarter, Master Gardova. A little slice of my homeland, here across the sea."

"Thanks," Lukan replied, glancing at the other patrons. "It's . . . lively."

Obassa laughed. "It wasn't always so. The Saphronans were very generous, after the war, with all their talk of friendship and opportunity. They were less generous with what they actually offered to those of us who wanted to start a new life here. We were promised a home, but what we got were a few crumbling streets, wedged between the slums of the Splinters and the filth of the Smokes. Those first years were hard, but we endured. And now look." He waved a hand at the bustling street. "We didn't just survive here. We thrived."

"I can see."

"Now I'm content to sit here, sip my tea, and enjoy the fruits of my people's early struggles. A wise man once said that the years of hardship are the sweetest. What do you think of that?"

"I think you just made that up."

Obassa laughed. "Sit," he said, gesturing to the empty stools before him. "Were you at the execution this morning?"

"I was," Lukan replied, taking a seat.

"And did you enjoy the spectacle of the Bone Pit?" There was a knowing twist to the man's lips.

"If by *spectacle* you mean watching grown men piss themselves while some sort of monster decides which prisoner it fancies for breakfast, then no, I can't say I did. What the hells is that creature, anyway?"

"It's justice, Master Gardova. Or so the Saphronan law courts would have you believe. As to your question, I can't give you an answer. No one truly knows what Gargantua is, not even the sharp minds up at our Collegium."

"Perhaps they should ask Zandrusa. She got a pretty close look."

"Yes, I heard our esteemed merchant prince survived her ordeal."

"She did. Seems Gargantua was more in the mood for a sweating customs official with a side order of soiled breeches."

Obassa smiled faintly. "Zandrusa will face the Bone Pit again ten days from now."

"I know. And I need to speak to her before then."

"They'll have already taken her back to the Ebon Hand."

"Then I need to get inside."

"And how do you propose to do that?"

"I was hoping you might be able to help me."

"Is that so?"

"Flea told me you're not part of the Kindred," Lukan said, leaning forward. "But I'd bet my last copper that you've got some sort of game going on, and that you know exactly how I might get inside the Ebon Hand. So tell me. If you want your palm greasing, I can do that too."

"There'll be no need for that," Obassa replied amiably. "I don't need such an incentive. My *game,* as you put it, pays me well enough." He turned his sightless eyes to Flea. "Perhaps, my dear, you could—"

"Uh-uh," Flea interrupted, shaking her head as she sat down beside Lukan. "I'm not fetching you any more honey cakes. Besides, I already know what you're talking about."

"She eavesdropped last time," Lukan said.

"I know." Obassa smiled as he took a sip of tea.

"Of course you do," Lukan muttered.

"So," the old man said, setting his cup down. "You want to get into the Hand. That won't be easy."

"There must be a way."

"Well, you could commit a serious crime. That would do the trick."

"Very funny," Lukan said irritably. "Spare me your wit."

"I'm not joking," Obassa said mildly. "If you were *believed* to have committed a serious enough crime, then no one would question your presence in the Hand. Not if you were being escorted by a constable."

"You mean I could impersonate a prisoner?" Lukan recalled the man he'd seen being dragged into the Ebon Hand by black-uniformed inquisitors. "Could that actually work?"

"You would need to bribe a constable to play along with your ruse and escort you inside—half the constables in this city are on the take, but finding one agreeable to such a risk would be a challenge in itself. Even if you found one, you'd still need the correct paperwork to get inside the Hand. And even if you made it in, you'd still need to get *out,* and that presents its own set of challenges."

"But could it work?" Lukan asked.

"Yes, it could work." Obassa shook his head. "But it almost certainly won't. You'll be caught and sentenced to a decade's hard labor—that's if you're lucky. If you're not—"

"I'll be chained to a stake in the Bone Pit."

"Yes."

"Great." Lukan sighed, drumming his fingers on the tabletop. "There's got to be a way. Got to be something . . ."

"If you're serious—"

"I'm deadly serious."

"Deadly *stupid,* more like," Flea muttered.

"The difference between the two is merely a matter of perspective," Obassa said gently. "But if you *are* serious about this," he continued, eyes on Lukan, "then you should speak to the Scrivener."

"The Scrivener?" Lukan echoed. "Who's that?"

"The best shammer in the city," Flea piped up.

"Shammer?"

"Yeah." Seeing his confused expression, the girl gave him a hopeless look. "Do I have to explain *everything*?"

"A shammer is a forger," Obassa supplied. "A counterfeiter. And as Flea says, the Scrivener is the best in the city—really, such terms don't do her justice. She's more of an artist. A master of her craft, which is the art of deception."

"And you think she can help me?"

"Perhaps. If she's willing. But first you'll need to earn her trust to gain an audience."

"An audience? You make her sound like royalty."

"She practically is. There are few among the Kindred of Saphrona as highly respected."

"Except for Lady Midnight," Flea said, enthused.

"Indeed," Obassa replied, smiling faintly.

"Fine," Lukan said, rising from the table. He'd been hoping to avoid dealing with the Kindred, but it seemed he had no choice. "How do I get an audience with the Scrivener?"

"Go to Salazar's House of Fortune—Flea can show you the way. At the bar, ask for Parvan Silver with a slice of lime—"

"Lime? You drink Parvan Silver with lemon, not lime."

"—and a duskbloom flower."

"Duskbloom? Isn't that plant poisonous?"

"Only the extract, taken from the root. The petals themselves are harmless."

"Right, so . . . I order the gin with the flower—what then?"

"One of the Scrivener's people will make themselves known to you. They'll explain the test you will need to undertake if you wish for an audience."

"Test?" Lukan said warily. "What test?"

"As I told you, you must first earn the Scrivener's trust. No doubt her representative can explain the game much better than I."

"The *game*? What game?"

"Good luck, Master Gardova," Obassa said, picking up his carving knife and resuming his whittling. "You'll most certainly need it."

8

THE ART OF DECEPTION

Salazar's House of Fortune was easily the most impressive gambling den Lukan had ever seen, and he'd seen more than his fair share. Situated just off the Eastern Boneway, in an affluent part of the city known as the Silks, the building dominated one side of a plaza, an impressive vision of cusped arches, sculpted columns, and colorful tilework. Purple banners hung from its upper story, bearing a silver motif of two dice encircled by a snake eating its own tail. Even so, if it weren't for the words *Salazar's House of Fortune* stitched below in flowing script, Lukan might have thought they'd come to the wrong place.

"Looks more like a palace than a gambling den," he remarked, wiping sweat from his brow as they crossed the near-empty plaza, the afternoon sun beating down on them.

"I think it used to be a bathhouse," Flea replied, seemingly unbothered by the heat. She took a bite from the peach she'd lifted from a cart. "Back when the Zar-Ghosans ruled Saphrona."

Lukan had read about that period of the city's history—or rather, he'd read the three lines that Velleras Gellame had dedicated to it in his *Gentleman's Guide to Saphrona*. The Zar-Ghosans, well over two centuries before, had captured Saphrona and ruled for nearly a decade, leaving a clear mark on the city before their rule was overthrown. Lukan had seen numerous signs of Zar-Ghosan architecture as he'd followed Flea through the bustling streets. *Still, nothing as grand as this.*

As they approached the bathhouse-turned-gambling-den, two guards in purple-and-silver livery emerged from the columned entrance, dragging a protesting man behind them.

"I wasn't cheating!" he squealed, trying to dig his heels into the smooth flagstones. "The card—it must have slipped into my sleeve! I don't know how—" His words became a cry as the guards shoved him down the three wide steps. The man staggered, his arms windmilling frantically, only to collapse in a heap on the cobbles. Flea giggled as the man groaned.

"All right," Lukan said, glancing at the girl. "You know what to do?"

"Wait outside until you return."

"And?"

Flea rolled her eyes. "Don't annoy the guards."

"Right. Because I don't—"

"Have a sense of humor, I get it."

"—want the *attention*," Lukan finished, as they halted at the steps and the man lying prostrate before them. "You got that?"

"Yeah, I got it." Flea pulled a face. "You're no fun at all."

"That so? Maybe later I'll tell you a tale or two from my time at the Academy back in Parva. Reckon that might change your mind." He pointed to a nearby fountain. "Wait there. I'll find you when I'm done."

The girl held out a hand, rubbing her thumb and forefinger.

"Later," Lukan said.

Flea started snapping her fingers.

"Lady's mercy . . ." Lukan reached into his coin pouch and flicked her a copper. "There. Now stay out of trouble."

Flea grinned and slunk away.

Lukan stepped around the unfortunate man, who was still groaning, and sprang lightly up the steps. "Good day, gentlemen," he said to the two guards, who eyed him warily.

"First time?" one of them grunted.

"It is."

"Three rules," the man continued. "Number one: No weapons, so hand 'em over." The second guard stepped forward and Lukan obliged by handing him his sword and dirk. "And the dagger in your boot," the first guard said, eyes narrowing as Lukan smiled and offered it up. "Two," he continued, "if you want to fight, you do it outside. Three, no cheating. If you get caught—"

"You get thrown out," Lukan said, gesturing at the man lying on the ground. "I noticed."

The guard scowled. "And banned," he added huffily, rounding on his companion as the other man sniggered. "The hells you laughing about . . ."

Lukan left the two men to their argument, their voices fading as he passed between the columns and entered Salazar's House of Fortune. The marble entrance hall was adorned with more of the purple-and-silver banners, illuminated by intricate brass lanterns. As the smell of incense tickled Lukan's nostrils, he felt as if he were entering a temple rather than a gambling den. *Perhaps I am,* he thought, recalling Velleras Gellame's words. *Coin is the only true god in Saphrona.* Only the faded mosaic beneath his feet—depicting a fountain and a rising plume of water—served as a reminder of the establishment's more respectable past.

An archway at the end of the hall led to what must have once been the bathhouse's changing room, which now served as a bar. Wooden pegs intended for bathrobes now held the travel cloaks of the patrons who sat drinking at the dozen or so tables. Despite it being barely past noon, the ale and liquor were flowing freely as the gamblers either celebrated their good fortune or drowned their sorrows. *The house wins regardless.*

Beyond a row of arches to his left Lukan could see the baths themselves, illuminated by the glow of countless lanterns. Both were rectangular in shape and stretched all the way to the far wall, thirty yards distant. Marble columns, sculpted in the shape of waves, lined them on either side, rising to the vaulted ceiling above. The water that had once filled the baths was long gone, replaced by gaming tables and fortune wheels. At a glance, Lukan estimated that a hundred or more gamblers were seated around the tables, cigarillo smoke curling above their heads. The cavernous space echoed with their laughter and curses, underscored by the unmistakable clink of coin. Lukan was tempted to join them, his hand already straying to the coin pouch at his belt. *A couple of games couldn't hurt* . . . He pushed the thought away, knowing he couldn't let pleasure get in the way of business. Not when every hour might prove crucial. Still, it was with a touch of regret that he turned away from the baths and made his way toward the bar that lined one wall of the former changing room.

The barman—a young man barely out of his teens—looked up as Lukan approached. He wore a purple waistcoat, the snake and dice symbol embroidered in silver thread.

"Good morn—ah, I mean afternoon," the youth said, swallowing nervously. "Um, sir. Can I, ah, get you—"

"A drink, yes," Lukan cut in, reasoning they'd be there until midnight if he didn't. "I'll have a Parvan Silver with a slice of lime and a . . ." He glanced at the only other patron sitting at the bar, a woman aimlessly swilling the dregs of her drink as she stared into space. "Duskbloom flower," he finished, lowering his voice.

"Duskbloom?" the barman squeaked loudly, his eyes widening. *Lady's blood.* "That's right." Lukan nodded, giving the boy a meaningful look.

"But-but sir, aren't . . . aren't duskbloom flowers—"

"Poisonous," the woman drawled, her unfocused stare suddenly fixing on Lukan. "If you've got a death wish, handsome, well . . ." She smiled, though in truth it was more of a grimace. "I'll happily stick a blade in you for a copper or two."

"Much obliged," he replied, "but I think I'll take a slow lingering death by way of marsh flora."

The woman shrugged, turned back to her drink. "Your funeral."

It'll be Obassa's bloody funeral if he's bullshitting me. "So," Lukan said brightly, smiling at the barman as if this weren't already turning into the farce he'd expected it to be. "How about that Parvan Silver with the extra floral ornamentation?"

The youth just stared at him.

"You know what," Lukan said, giving the boy a *thanks for nothing* glare, "I seem to have lost my thirst—"

"Is there a problem, sir?"

Lukan turned to find a waiter standing behind him, bearing a tray of empty glasses. "No," he replied, not wanting to prolong the embarrassment. "No problem at all."

"He—he wanted Parvan Silver," the barman stammered, clearly relieved that the cavalry had arrived. "With—"

"It doesn't matter," Lukan cut in, raising a hand.

"—a duskbloom flower."

Seven bloody shadows . . .

"Is that right," the waiter murmured, raising an eyebrow.

"Look, just forget it," Lukan replied. "I'll be on my way."

"As you wish," the waiter said smoothly. "Or, sir may wish to take a seat while I prepare his gin with duskbloom flower." He smiled. "It is entirely sir's call."

"I . . . guess I'll take the seat."

"Very good, sir."

With a final glance at the barman—whose eyes looked like they might pop out of his head—Lukan made his way to a corner table. His relief that Obassa had not misled him was tempered by the knowledge—or rather his lack of knowledge—of the test, the *game,* still to come. Why the Scrivener would insist on such a ritual was also a mystery to him. *Guess I'll find out soon enough.*

The waiter returned a moment later.

"My thanks," Lukan said, as the man set the glass down in front of him, the purple-grey duskbloom flower resting against its rim. He reached for his coin purse. "How much do I—"

"The gin is on the house, sir," the man replied, inclining his head. "It always is for those on your particular path."

"And what path is that?"

The waiter merely smiled. "I apologize for the earlier confusion," he continued with a glance at the barman, who was struggling to pull the cork from a bottle. "My young colleague is new here, and not yet versed in some of our more subtle conventions."

"Yeah, I noticed." Lukan eyed the drink in front of him. "So what happens now? Do I actually need to drink this?"

"Only if you wish. Either way, you must wait."

"For what?"

"A man will come for you."

"What will he look like?"

"He will know you." The waiter indicated the duskbloom flower.

"And the test?"

"I suggest you drink the gin, sir. Help settle your nerves." With those final words, the waiter moved away. Lukan watched him go, then eyed the flower on the rim of his glass.

Settle my nerves for what?

————

The time passed slowly.

Lukan took the waiter's advice and sipped at his gin, feeling like a fool every time the flower brushed his lips. Not that anyone was paying him the slightest attention; the drinkers around him were either brooding in silence or boasting of their success at the tables. For over an hour he studied the ebb and flow of the room: gamblers returning from the gaming pits and taking the seats of drinkers who were ready to return to the action, dosed on liquid courage. Lukan watched them depart with envy, his desire to play a few hands increasing in direct proportion to his growing boredom. *Another half an hour,* he thought. *Then maybe I'll give this up as a bad job—*

"Good afternoon."

Lukan jolted, glancing up to find a man standing before him. He was clean-shaven and bareheaded, save for a topknot of dark hair. His copper skin spoke of the cities of the Mourning Sea, or lands even farther east, yet his eyes—amber flecked with scarlet—hinted at a different heritage altogether. The man pulled out a chair and sat down.

"I didn't say you could sit," Lukan said sharply, irritated at being caught off guard.

"I never asked," the stranger replied, lips etched in the faint impression of a smile. Such words—spoken by someone else, in a different manner—might have caused Lukan to brace himself for trouble. Yet there was no hint of threat in the man's voice, merely a touch of amusement. Nor was there anything intimidating about his stature; he was of lithe build and shorter than Lukan. Even so, there was a weight to his gaze that warned Lukan to tread carefully.

"You need something?" Lukan asked.

"I could ask you the same question." The man reached across the table and plucked the duskbloom flower from Lukan's empty glass.

"Ah . . ." Lukan glanced around, leaned closer. "So you're the Scrivener's man?"

"I am my own man. But yes, I have the honor to serve the woman you know as the Scrivener. My name is Juro."

Lukan gestured at the flower. "Was that your idea?"

"The duskbloom is a most remarkable plant," Juro replied, twirling the flower between two fingers. "Its petals remain closed during the day, giving it a dry, shriveled appearance. And yet, when dusk draws in . . ." He made a fist with his free hand before splaying his fingers out in mimicry of an opening flower. "The appearance of death is revealed as an illusion, a deception." He lowered the flower. "Just like a forgery."

"Yeah, I get it. Very symbolic." Lukan picked up his glass, drained the dregs of gin. "Perhaps next time you could dispense with the cloak and dagger bullshit and use something less conspicuous. Asking for something like that is about as subtle as a kick in the balls."

"Symbols are important," the man replied, again with the ghost of a smile. "They tell the world what we strive for, what we believe in."

"Like deceit."

"And beauty. Because the most exquisite forgeries are as beautiful as any artwork."

"Yeah, well . . . I need a convincing forgery. Not a piece of art."

"The works my mistress creates are one and the same."

"Then perhaps we can do business."

"Perhaps." The man gave a light shrug. "That depends on whether you seek something worthy of her time and talent—and whether you want it badly enough." He pocketed the flower and sat back, hands clasped on the table. "So, tell me—who are you? And why do you seek my mistress's help?"

"My business is my own."

"Not if you wish to pursue this further," Juro said, steel now mixing with the silk of his voice. "I will speak clearly so we understand one another. My mistress is the best forger in the Old Empire and if you wish to engage her services, you will tell me who you are, what you want, and why you want it. Do not leave anything out." His amber eyes narrowed. "Most importantly, do not lie. I will know if you do."

Lady's blood. Revealing his real name to a member of the Kindred risked drawing the attention of his father's murderer, if the killer moved in similar circles. Revealing his intentions was even more dangerous—all it would take was a whisper in the ear of a constable and he'd be clapped in irons in no time. *Still, what choice do I have?*

"What you tell me will remain confidential," Juro said, sensing Lukan's reluctance. "It will go no further than my lips and my mistress's ears. You have my word."

And the word of a stranger is worth less than dust. "Fine," Lukan sighed. "But the least you can do is buy me another drink."

———

It took him a quarter hour to tell his tale, aided by another glass of gin, which helped to loosen his tongue—though not to the extent that he revealed everything. Juro listened in silence, his expression impassive.

"How curious," he said once Lukan had finished. "My condolences for your loss."

"Yeah, thanks. So you're not going to tell me that I'm crazy for wanting to get inside the Ebon Hand?"

"It's not my place to do so."

"But you think I am."

"Yes."

"Well, you're probably right." The act of explaining his intention to Juro had only served to help Lukan realize how foolish it was. *Obassa was right. This is only going to end with me in chains.* "You know what," he said, rising to his feet, "let's just forget this."

"If it helps," Juro said, leaning forward, "I think my mistress would very much like to speak with you."

Lukan frowned. "Really?"

"Yes. But first you must win her trust. You must prove that you truly desire her help."

"Ah, of course. This test of yours." Lukan drained the last of his gin, reaching a decision as he rolled the liquid on his tongue. He swallowed. "I understand it's some sort of game?"

Juro stood, a faint smile on his lips again. "Follow me, Lukan."

9

THE PYRAMID

Lukan followed Juro through the arches and down the central walkway that ran between the two baths. Gamblers cheered and swore at the tables as stony-faced croupiers dealt cards and spun fortune wheels, while guards lounged against columns, watching for any sign of trouble. Any desire Lukan had to play a few hands had now been replaced by a gnawing anxiety at what test lay ahead of him—a feeling that intensified as Juro led him toward a door set in the far wall.

A guard stood before the door, eyeing them as they approached. Juro showed something to her—Lukan caught a flash of silver in the lantern light—and she gave a respectful nod, turning and pushing the door open for them before standing aside.

"Where are we going?" Lukan asked as he followed Juro into the dimly lit corridor beyond, the sounds of the hall fading to silence as the guard closed the door behind them.

"Patience, Lukan," Juro replied as he led the way. "All will be revealed."

Was that amusement in his voice? Lukan wished he still had the dagger in his boot—or even better, his sword and dirk. *Following a man I barely know into the dark. Great work, Gardova.* The passage turned to the right, candlelight and conversation spilling through a doorway up ahead. He followed Juro into the circular chamber beyond, which still retained some of its former grandeur: faded murals of semi-naked men and women decorated the walls, while an intricate mosaic depicting various aquatic creatures covered the floor. More impressive still were the arches that lined the edges of the hexagonal bath at the room's center, which were artfully carved with swirling arabesques. Lanterns glowed in alcoves, throwing dancing shadows across the stonework and the domed ceiling above. *A private bathroom for the Zar-Ghosan elite,* Lukan thought, as he looked around. *Once, anyway.*

Now it appeared to serve a very different purpose.

A group of people crowded around the edges of the bath, sitting on its raised stone lip or leaning against its arches, whispering to each other as they watched whatever was happening in the depths of the bath itself. Lukan glanced a question at Juro, but all he got in return was that infuriating half smile and a gesture that suggested he should go and see for himself.

Lukan approached the closest side of the bath and peered over the heads of the spectators who sat beneath its arch, his eyes drawn to the spectacle below.

The hexagonal bath, like those in the main bathhouse, had been drained of water. A circular table stood at its center, empty save for an angular object covered by a cloth of purple velvet. Four players sat round the table, all attempting to conceal their unease—with varying levels of success. Two men jested with each other, though their laughter seemed forced, while a third sat with his arms folded, his impassive expression undermined by the sheen of sweat on his brow. The only woman appeared the most relaxed, smoking a cigarillo as she leaned back in her chair, yet Lukan noted the faint tremor in her hand. *What are they so afraid of?* The answer clearly lay beneath the folds of purple velvet, but he couldn't begin to guess what the cloth concealed. *Nothing good, I'll bet.*

A white-gloved attendant wearing a purple waistcoat stood close by. "Ladies and gentlemen," he called, his booming voice echoing around the small chamber. "Final bets, if you please." Lukan noticed another pair of attendants making their way around the arches, nodding politely as they accepted coins and handed out tokens.

"What manner of game is this?" he asked Juro, who stood beside him.

"Usually a painful one."

Well, that explains why they all look nervous. "And the purple cloth?" he prompted. "What's that hiding?"

"See for yourself."

Lukan looked back at the table just as the attendant stepped forward, one white-gloved hand reaching for the cloth. With a flourish that seemed slightly excessive, the man swept the cloth away.

A hush fell across the chamber.

Lukan found himself staring at a black pyramid. The two sides he could see appeared to be formed from single panes of smooth glass, rising to a peak that stood three handspans above the surface of the table.

"What is that?" he whispered.

"Observe," the Scrivener's man replied.

The attendant reached out and pressed a gloved finger to the tip of the pyramid. Nothing happened as he removed his hand and stepped away.

Then a low humming sound broke the silence.

What in the hells . . .

Glowing white lines appeared on the black glass. They pulsed softly, forming a lattice of rows and columns on both visible sides of the pyramid. Each row was formed of equally sized segments; Lukan counted seven in the row at the pyramid's base, six in the row above, and so on all the way up to the single segment that formed the pyramid's apex.

Phaeron, he realized, a knot of anxiety forming in his gut. *It's a bloody Phaeron relic.*

The pyramid suddenly flared with blue and gold light, each individual segment alternating between the two colors, creating an almost hypnotic effect. The display continued for a few moments, intensifying until blue and gold became indecipherable. Then the panes of glass faded to black once again, leaving just the glowing latticework of white lines.

"And now it begins," Juro murmured.

"What begins?"

"Why, the game of course."

"Whenever you're ready, madam," the attendant said, gesturing at the pyramid before stepping away.

Silence fell as the woman leaned forward, cigarillo still smoking in one hand as she studied the pyramid. A long moment passed before she finally reached out and—with only the slightest hesitation—pressed one of the segments on the bottom row.

The entire room seemed to hold its breath.

A faint chime sounded and the segment she'd touched lit up, glowing gold. The woman sat back, taking a relieved drag on her cigarillo as the crowd applauded. A few cheers rang out, presumably from those who had placed bets on her.

"She chose well," Juro observed. "But then the first round is always the easiest, when the odds are at their most favorable."

Play passed to the man sitting to the woman's right, one of the pair who had been jesting just moments before. He wasn't laughing now. He wet his lips nervously as he stared at his side of the pyramid, which displayed the same glowing lattice. Eventually he reached out and touched a segment on the bottom row. This time a dolorous note sounded and the segment glowed blue instead of gold. Horror dawned on the man's face. A murmur passed through the crowd, punctuated by jeers.

"A poor choice," Juro murmured.

The man cried out as fire engulfed his left arm, flames licking hungrily at his clothes. His chair toppled over as he shot to his feet, frantically waving his burning limb. "Water!" he shouted, eyes wide with panic. "Water! Please, someone . . ." He collapsed to the floor, writhing against the stone.

Laughter echoed around the chamber, quickly drowned out as the man began to scream.

"Lady's blood," Lukan swore, glancing at Juro. "Why is no one helping him?"

"Because he doesn't need help."

"He's on *fire*!"

"Is he?"

Lukan looked back at the man, who was thrashing as the flames consumed him. "What in the *hells* are you—"

The fire vanished.

The man continued to scream, rolling around as he desperately tried to douse flames that were no longer there. His movements slowed until he was lying still, his cries giving way to ragged breaths. *He's not even burned,* Lukan realized as more laughter echoed around the chamber. The man sat up slowly, his legs shaking as he climbed to his feet.

"Does the gentleman wish to continue?" the attendant called out. The man hesitated, then righted his chair. A smattering of applause sounded as he took his place at the table. The woman gave him a respectful nod, while one of the other players slapped him on the shoulder. The man flinched.

"The fire wasn't real," Lukan observed.

"No. Merely an illusion."

"So why was he screaming?"

"Because the pain *was*."

"You mean . . . he *felt* that? Those flames?"

"Every moment of it."

Lady's blood. Lukan watched as the game restarted, another player now staring anxiously at the pyramid, fingers twitching as they contemplated their move. "You call this a game? It's more like a form of torture."

Juro shrugged. "As I said, the illusions are harmless."

"It didn't sound harmless."

"The man was unhurt. Players who take on the pyramid never suffer any physical damage, save the odd bump or scrape."

Applause and cheers rang out as the current player selected a golden segment. He sat back, grinning with relief.

"You said *physical* damage," Lukan noted. "Do you mean to say . . ."

"The game's effects on the mind are a different matter entirely,"

Juro conceded. "Experiencing several of the pyramid's illusions in a short space of time is known to have . . . consequences."

"You don't say."

The fourth player contemplated the pyramid, sweating profusely. Someone from the crowd shouted encouragement.

"Silence please," the attendant called.

"The most notable case," Juro whispered, "was a player called Black Rallam. This was, oh . . . more than ten years ago now. Rallam is the only player known to have chosen the blue segment on every single row of the pyramid. Yet he kept going, refusing to quit—apparently he had considerable debts. He won the game, but endured the maximum possible total of seven illusions. It damaged his mind."

"I'll bet it did."

"Once Rallam had recovered from his ordeal, he left Salazar's in good health and high spirits. Later that night he went on a rampage and killed seven people before the city watch managed to subdue him. He went to the Bone Pit, of course. It's said that he painted on the walls of his prison cell with his own blood."

"Painted what?"

"Pyramids. Dozens of pyramids."

Seven shadows. "And you tell me this game is harmless."

"It is. If you know when to quit."

They watched as the fourth player made a successful choice, punching the air as the crowd applauded.

"Now they move to the next level of the pyramid," Juro said, as the woman leaned forward, exhaling a puff of smoke.

"So let me get this straight," Lukan replied, lowering his voice as the attendant called for quiet. "The players take it in turn to pick a segment on their side of the pyramid, starting on the bottom row. Gold is a free pass to the next level, blue means an illusion as a punishment."

"Precisely."

"And how many blues are on each level?"

"Just one. But as you can see, the risk of picking blue increases with each successive level."

"And to win you have to reach the top?"

"Correct."

"What if more than one player makes it?"

"Then the player who selected the fewest blue segments wins."

Lukan paused as the woman touched a segment, which shone gold. "What if you're only halfway up," he said, speaking over the applause, "and everyone else has quit?"

"The last player standing is entitled to resign and will receive the buy-in fees of their fellow players—minus Salazar's cut, of course. That's what most players aim for—to simply outlast their rivals. But to win the jackpot, a player must play every single level."

"Even the top?" Lukan squinted at the pyramid. "The top row's only got one segment."

Juro smiled. "There's no pleasure without at least a little pain."

The attendant called again for silence, and play passed to the man who had already enjoyed a taste of what Phaeron punishment felt like. He didn't look delighted at the prospect of repeating that experience, and Lukan couldn't blame him. The man's hand trembled as he reached out and—face contorted in a grimace—jabbed a segment. He sagged to the table in relief as it glowed gold.

"So this . . . *game* is really a test of endurance," Lukan said.

"And holding one's nerve."

"How often does someone win the jackpot?"

"Very rarely. Most players quit after one or two illusions. It's been nearly three years since someone last won the prize for defeating the pyramid."

"Which is what?"

"A hundred gold ducats."

Lukan whistled. "Impressive."

"Now you see why people are willing to play this game."

"It's not a game. A game is meant to be fun. This is . . . torture."

"It's entertainment."

"Yeah, I'm starting to realize they are one and the same in this city."

Another chime sounded, followed by the usual round of applause.

"You mean for me to play the pyramid," Lukan said. "That's the Scrivener's test."

"It is." No two words had ever sent such a shiver down Lukan's spine. "I will pay your entrance fee."

"Kind of you."

"If you want to meet my mistress, Lukan, you have no choice."

"So this game, if you can call it that—it's run by the Scrivener? Are they"—he gestured at the players below—"also looking to meet her?"

"Oh, no. This game is Salazar's own invention. My mistress merely uses it for her own ends. Most players enter to win the game, and don't have any idea that on occasion one of their opponents may have a different motive."

"But why? Why bother with this charade in the first place?"

"My mistress takes her security and privacy very seriously, not to mention her time. You must earn the right to speak with her. It is a boon not freely granted." Juro tilted his head, his half smile returning. "So, are you prepared to play the game?"

"Yes," Lukan said, dread knotting in his stomach. "I am."

Another dolorous note sounded from below, the crowd drawing a collective breath.

Then the screams began.

10

TWO SIDES OF
THE SAME COIN

"Fire?" Flea said, eyes wide. "He was on *fire*?"

"Uh-huh." Lukan splashed some water from the fountain over his face, then cupped his hands under one of its streams and drank deeply.

"But it wasn't real?"

"No."

"But it felt like it was?"

"So I'm told." He sat down beside her on the edge of the fountain. In his mind's eye he saw the man once again, engulfed in flames, screaming as he thrashed on the floor. "Certainly looked like it."

"And you're going to play this game?" She shook her head slowly. "Are you *mad*?"

Flea's question shook a memory loose in his mind: A single candle throwing shadows across whitewashed walls, their plaster cracked and peeling. Jaques, his friend and reluctant partner in crime at the Academy, pacing back and forth in the light. *A duel*, he said, wringing his hands. Lukan could remember the exact pitch of his voice, its nervous cadence. *Giorgio Castori challenged you to a duel? Tomorrow? And—and you accepted? I . . . I don't . . .* The young man stopped pacing and turned to face him, concern writ large across his plump face. *Lukan, what have you done? Are you mad?* He winced as the memory faded. How he wished he had taken his friend's advice to call the duel off. But he hadn't listened to Jaques then, and he knew—probably against his better judgment—that he wasn't going to listen to Flea now. *You never bloody learn, Gardova.*

"Why are you doing this?"

"Hmm?"

Flea punched his arm. "Are you even listening to me? I said, why are you doing this?"

"You know why. I need the Scrivener's help if I'm going to speak to Zandrusa, and to get an audience with her I need to play this damned game."

"Yeah, I know that—but *why*? You told Obassa you didn't get on with your father. You said you were . . . estrained."

"Estranged." *Seven shadows, this girl doesn't miss a thing.*

"What does that mean?"

"It means we weren't talking to each other. By the end we could barely stand to be in the same room."

"You had an argument?"

Lukan snorted. "Yeah. One or two."

"What about?"

"About . . ." He shook his head, blew out his cheeks. "I don't know. A lot passed between us." *Or maybe not nearly enough.* "It's a long story, kid." He hoped that might deflect her question, but the girl merely stared at him, eyes expectant. *She's stubborn too.* Lukan sighed, ran a hand through his hair. He had no desire to rake over old coals, not when they still smoldered hot, yet it was preferable to worrying about what fate the pyramid might have in store for him. "It started when my mother died. I was eleven at the time."

"What happened?"

"Some sort of fever. I was too young to understand, and when I was older my father refused to talk much about it. But it changed him. He was never the same after she died. He became cold, distant. Practically left me to be raised by the servants—"

"You had servants?"

"Only a couple. A cook to prepare meals and a steward who looked after the estate's affairs. They did their best to look after me. Shufia, the steward, taught me swordplay and how to fight with my fists. Sometimes she let me spar with the guards—"

"You had *guards* as well?"

"Lady's blood, do you want to hear my sob story or not? Yes, we had a few guards." *Though not nearly enough, in the end.*

"But . . ." Flea's eyes narrowed. "Only rich people have guards and servants. You told Obassa your grandfather gambled all your money away."

"He did. My dear old grandfather played hard and fast with our family fortune and managed to lose most of it. These days the only thing we have of value is our name."

"Gardova?" The girl's brow creased. "Why is that valuable?"

"Because our family can trace its lineage all the way back to the founding of Parva. If my father was around, he would talk your ear off about it—how our ancestors played an influential role in the founding of the city, all that sort of thing. We lost most of our standing along with our fortune, but the family name still carried some weight . . . until I ruined it."

"What did you do?"

"That would depend on who you asked. My father would tell you I was a fool who let my pride get in the way of common sense." *Just as he told me.* "I would say that I was defending my honor—my *family's* honor—in the face of constant provocation. I guess you could say the truth is somewhere in the middle."

Flea gave a theatrical groan. "Are you actually going to answer my question?"

Sharp, stubborn, and straight-talking. Lady's mercy, I'm starting to like this kid. "Fine. I killed a man from a family whose wealth and influence far outweighed my own." He managed a wan smile. "In terms of life choices, it's not one I recommend."

"You *killed* someone?"

"Not deliberately."

Flea raised an eyebrow.

"It was an accident." Lukan sighed, the words sounding

just as futile as they had when he'd spoken them at the time, as blood stained the cherry blossoms. *It was an accident, it was an accident* . . .

"Who was he?"

"Giorgio Castori—the eldest son of a powerful family from Vispana. Or was it Virenze? One of the Talassian cities, anyway. In fact, that's a lesson for you, kid: Never mistake a Vispanian for a Virenzian, or the other way round. At best you'll get a glare, at worst a punch in the face."

"Why?"

"Because they've spent the past century trying to kill each other. Lots of bad blood in the Talassian Isles. Mistaking one for the other is likely to be taken as an insult by both parties."

"So how do you tell them apart?"

"You can't, that's the problem. And asking a Talassian which city they're from is almost as bad as guessing and getting it wrong." He gestured dismissively. "Anyway, I digress—"

"You *what*?"

"I'm going off on a tangent."

Flea sighed. "Will you just talk *normal*?"

"Normally," he corrected, regretting his response as Flea's face darkened. "Fine," he continued, raising a placating hand. "What I was saying was that Giorgio Castori and I were at the Academy together." Noting the girl's blank expression, he added, "The Academy of Parva. A university."

"A uni-what?"

"It's like . . . a school for adults. Like the Collegium here."

"So you go there to learn stuff?"

"Right."

"Like what?"

"Like . . . I don't know. History, art, languages . . ."

"Sounds boring."

"It was."

"So why'd you go?"

"Because it was expected of me. If I'd had an older brother or sister, they would have been groomed to become Lord or Lady Gardova and I would have been free to do whatever the hells I wanted. But I was an only child, so I always knew that one day I would take my father's place. Subsequently I was expected to go to the Academy and obtain something resembling an education. But . . . I also went because I hoped that by doing so I'd please my father. Make him proud, even. I thought that if I studied history and natural philosophy—don't bother asking, it doesn't matter what that is—I could maybe close the gap that had grown between us." Lukan sighed. "It might even have worked if I hadn't discovered that I enjoyed gambling, drinking, and fighting a lot more than reading old books."

"So Giorgio Castori was at the Academy too?"

"That's right. Giorgio was a year older than me, and one of the most insufferable, arrogant pricks you're ever likely to meet. We mostly ignored each other for the first two years I was there—I thought he was an arsehole and he thought I was beneath him. Not rich enough to warrant his attention. Anyway, that changed in my third year. I . . . ah, I was . . . Well, there was a girl."

Flea sighed, rolled her eyes. "I knew it."

"You knew what?"

"I knew this was about a girl. There's *always* a girl."

"What do you mean?"

"I used to work the taverns near the docks. You know, pick-pocketing drunks and stuff. There were fights all the time, usually over a girl." She shrugged. "Men are idiots."

"Yeah, can't argue with that."

"What was her name?"

"Amicia." He said the syllables slowly, as if worried they might sting. It was strange to speak her name aloud after all these years. "We had already been together for a year when Giorgio decided that he wanted her for himself—as if she was some sort of prize to be taken." He shook his head, clenched his fist. "The fact that Amicia couldn't stand him didn't seem to bother him. She threw a glass of wine in his face on one occasion and it only seemed to encourage him even more."

Flea grinned. "I like her already."

"You'd get along pretty well, I reckon." *You've certainly got the same spark.* "Anyway, Giorgio was like a dog with a bone. He wouldn't let her go. His interest in Amicia became lust, then infatuation."

"In-fat-u-*what*?"

"He . . . um, really liked her."

"But she liked you instead?"

"Right. And for that Giorgio hated me. The fact that I was his social inferior only made it worse. An animosity—a *hatred*," he clarified, before Flea could interrupt, "grew between us. It started with small things. A few casual insults, the odd prank. But as the months passed it got worse. He tried to get me expelled from the Academy, and when that didn't work he had a couple of toughs give me a beating. But I refused to give in. I rolled with the punches, figuratively and literally—"

"Figura . . ."

"Never mind. What I mean is that I didn't let his bullshit affect me, which only made him hate me even more. Things eventually came to a head one night in a tavern. I don't remember what was said, only that he was drunk and he came at me with his fists. He ended up on his arse in a puddle of stale beer. I don't think he even realized it was Amicia who tripped him. Anyway, that was when he challenged me to a duel. He claimed it was because I'd humiliated him in public, but I knew what it was really about. Everyone knew."

Lukan took a slow breath, the familiar memory rising in his mind—it was polished smooth like a sea-tossed stone, yet it always seemed to cut him nonetheless.

"We fought at dawn the next day with rapiers. Giorgio was his usual smug self. He probably thought I would stand down and forfeit the duel—apparently that was expected of me, due to my inferior social standing."

"But you didn't."

"Damned right I didn't. You have to stand up for yourself, you understand? You can't let someone have their way just because they were born into wealth and privilege. That doesn't make them better than you. So I fought him. Giorgio was a good swordsman, I'll give him that, but I was better. I drew first blood, which was the victory condition we had agreed on."

"So you won?"

"I did." *And I lost everything.* "I left Giorgio on his knees, whimpering like the coward he was. I turned away—"

"And he attacked you," Flea said, eyes shining with excitement. "I remember you telling Obassa."

"That's right. He came at me with a knife. Must have had it in his boot. I spun round, raised my sword . . ." Lukan trailed off, recalling the judder of his wrist as his blade pierced flesh, the look of shock in Giorgio's eyes. *Blood on cherry blossoms.*

"And? What then?"

"He ran straight into it. Took the tip of my rapier right in his throat. And he died. Bled to death right in front of me." Lukan shook his head, forcing the memory away. "Everything changed then."

"Did they put you in prison?"

"No. Dueling is legal in Parva and there were witnesses who testified that I acted in self-defense after Giorgio attacked me. I spent a couple of days in a cell and was then released without charge. The Academy also accepted that I wasn't at fault but expelled me anyway. As for my father . . . the Castori family demanded compensation and the old man gave it to them—paid them off even though the blame lay with their own son." Lukan's knuckles turned white as he gripped the edge of the fountain. "We lost what little remained of our family's fortune, and—so my father said— the honor of our name. I lost my temper and we argued. He told me I was a disgrace as a son, I told him he was a failure as a father. That was the last thing I ever said to him." He shook his head, jaw tightening as he felt a fresh stab of grief. *And now I'll never have the chance to take those words back.*

"What did you do then?"

"I left Parva and never went back. I was angry and the city held too many bad memories. That's what I told myself, anyway. The truth was that I was afraid to go back. I didn't know how to mend things with my father, wasn't sure I could. I guess it was easier to just pretend that our relationship was beyond repair." He shook his head. "I always intended to go home eventually, to try and work things out. But my pride got in the way, and now it's too bloody late—" He checked himself, realizing he was rambling, his voice tight with anger. Still, it felt good to unburden himself, to let some of the bitterness and regret bleed out. It didn't matter that his only listener was a street kid who couldn't possibly relate to his experience. *Then again, I'll bet she's had a far harder time of it than I have.* He felt suddenly foolish. *Here I am, bleating about my problems to a girl who lost her brother and is forced to steal food to survive—*

"What about Amicia? What happened to her?"

If only I knew. How many nights had he lain awake, pondering that very question? *Too many to count.* "I don't know. She refused to talk to me afterward. I tried to find her before I left the city, but . . ." He shook his head, breath escaping as a sigh. "I haven't seen her since."

"Oh."

"Anyway, enough about all that," Lukan said, gesturing dismissively. "Nothing good comes from stirring up the past."

"But you still haven't answered my question," Flea complained.

"What question? I've just told you my bloody life story."

"You *still* haven't told me why you're doing all this for your father even though you hated him."

"I didn't hate him, I— Well, I suppose there were moments when I did, but . . ." Lukan sighed, traced a finger through the water of the fountain. "We had our issues," he continued, unable to keep the regret from his voice. "But despite everything that passed between us, I still loved the old man."

Flea was silent for a moment. "Is that possible?" she asked eventually.

"Is what possible?"

"To love someone but hate them at the same time."

"Sometimes I think they're two sides of the same coin."

The girl kicked her heels against the side of the fountain, her head bowed. "I loved my brother Matteo," she said after a long pause, "but then he left me all alone, and for a long time I hated him." She looked away, but not before Lukan saw the pain in her dark eyes. "And I still do, a little bit. But I miss him as well."

"I understand," Lukan said.

"Really?"

"Of course. That's how I feel about my father. Which is why I need to do this, you understand? I waited too long to try and mend things between us, so this is my one chance to try and put things right. He sent me to Saphrona for a reason, and I need to find out why. I'll do whatever it takes to find out how Zandrusa is connected to his murder, and to find justice for him. It's all I can do."

Flea nodded, her somber expression seeming out of place on such a young face. Then her youthfulness returned as she grinned. "Can I watch you play the game? I want to see you catch fire."

"Thanks for the vote of confidence."

Flea tilted her head. "Do you think you *will* end up on fire?"

A distant bell tolled, echoing across the rooftops.

"I don't know," Lukan replied, rising to his feet. "But it looks like I'm about to find out."

11

A LITTLE SHOW
OF CONFIDENCE

Lukan strode into the pyramid chamber with a fake smile, a forced swagger, and a heart that was threatening to burst from his rib cage. It was the first two things, however, that caused the gathered spectators to raise their eyebrows as they watched him approach the bath. He paused on the top step and made a show of rolling his head and shoulders, as if preparing for a fight. *A bit much, perhaps*. Still, the whispers that passed through the room suggested the action had the desired effect. Several patrons snapped their fingers at the attendants, keen to place bets after his show of bravado. *Just as well they can't hear my pounding heart*. He caught Juro's gaze, and the Scrivener's man gave him a nod, lips curled in a knowing smile.

Lukan stepped lightly down into the bath, feeling the collective gaze of his three fellow players as they watched him. *Good. This little show of confidence is for them, after all*. One of the first things he'd learned about gambling was that a little bravado went a long way. If you could plant a seed of doubt in your opponents' minds, and nurture it with the appropriate words and gestures, you could force them into making mistakes.

The pyramid, of course, was no simple card game, and Lukan's actions would not directly impact his opponents' progress. Yet they were still in competition with each other, and that meant there was an edge to be gained. *But only if I can keep my composure while they lose theirs*.

"Good afternoon," he said breezily as he reached the table,

doing his best not to look at the velvet-covered pyramid. None of the other players replied, though the woman sitting to his left did at least give him a brusque nod. She had the look of a mercenary, or perhaps something even less reputable. Whatever her profession, she clearly knew her way around a fight—a number of nicks and scars marred the brown skin of her arms and shoulders, while the tip of a blade had left its mark down her right cheek and along her jaw. Her dark eyes held his—only for a moment, but long enough for him to glimpse the conviction in them. *This woman won't crack easily.*

Nor would the broad-shouldered man sitting to Lukan's right. Black tattoos swirled across his shaven head in an intricate pattern, revealing him as a corsair of the Shattered Isles. The man's kohl-rimmed eyes regarded Lukan with a contempt that also found expression in his scowl. *A real charmer, this one.*

The final player, sitting opposite him, was more of a mystery. She was slight where the other two were imposing, refined where they were rugged. A silver tiara studded with garnets—*or are those rubies?*—held back silken red hair, while her sharp features possessed more than a hint of the aristocratic. *The mysterious lady in red,* Lukan mused, for in addition to the rubies in her tiara she also wore a large ruby at her throat, and another on a finger, while her fine clothes were in varying shades of crimson. Compared to the other two players, she seemed delicate, almost fragile. Yet when her eyes met Lukan's, he saw resolve in her startling red irises. *That, and something else.* The edges of her scarlet lips teased upward, as if she could sense his thoughts and they amused her.

The attendant gave a polite cough. "If the gentleman would be so kind?"

Lukan realized he'd been staring, mouth slightly open. *Great work, Gardova.* He sat down before he could embarrass himself further, ignoring the snort of derision from the corsair. The cloth-draped pyramid mostly hid the Lady in Red from view, yet he could almost sense her amused smile. *Get a bloody grip,* he told himself as the attendant stepped forward, a pouch of purple velvet in his gloved hands. *The game is all that matters now.*

"My lady," the attendant purred, inclining his head. "Gentlemen. I trust you are familiar with the rules of the game and the terms of victory? Excellent. May I remind you that you may resign at any time, though you will forfeit your entry fee—unless you are the last remaining player, in which case your fee will be returned to you, along with those of your fellow players, minus the house's cut. The jackpot stands at one hundred ducats."

The corsair cracked an ugly grin and smacked a fist into his palm.

"Exciting, isn't it?" Lukan said, eyes on the big man. "Maybe you'll finally be able to buy some decent perfume to mask your stench."

The corsair's expression darkened. "The hells did you just—"

"We now need to decide the order of play," the attendant continued, shooting Lukan a pointed look that said *behave*. "In this pouch are four tokens. Three of them are gold, one is blue. You will choose one each, without looking. Whoever selects the blue token will go first, with play moving to the right." He offered the pouch to the Lady in Red. As she reached out, her sleeve fell back to reveal a tattoo on her wrist, scarlet ink bright against her alabaster skin, forming a symbol that sparked recognition in the depths of Lukan's memory.

"Gold," she announced, holding the token up. Her voice was like smoke against silk, carrying a strong northern accent. *Korslakov*, Lukan thought, *or possibly Volstav. Either way, she's far from home.*

The corsair went next, also selecting a gold token. The mercenary followed, her face remaining impassive as she withdrew the blue token. A round of whispers sounded from the spectators above. The attendant offered Lukan the pouch. "If you please, sir? In the interests of fairness."

Lukan reached into the pouch and withdrew the final gold token.

"Thank you, sir," the attendant said, as Lukan handed it back.

"You will go first, madam," he told the mercenary, "with play passing to the right. I wish you all the best of luck." The man gathered the remaining tokens and stepped away. "Ladies and gentlemen," he called out to the chamber, "final bets, if you please."

"So," Lukan said, grinning as he glanced around at his fellow players. "Who's ready for a little pain?"

The mercenary ignored him; her eyes were closed, lips moving ever so slightly as she mouthed something—a prayer, perhaps—to herself. The Lady in Red merely returned his gaze with those unnerving red eyes, a faint smile on her scarlet lips. The corsair, however, folded his thick arms and leaned forward, just as Lukan knew he would.

"The hells do you know about pain, pretty boy?" he asked, his coarse voice heavy with the accent of the Shattered Isles.

"Plenty. I have a lot of scars."

"Yeah? I don't see 'em."

"No one can." *Giorgio Castori's pale face staring up at me. The woman I love, walking away and telling me not to follow. Blood on cherry blossoms—*

"*This* is a scar," the corsair boasted, pointing to a series of raised lacerations along the length of one forearm. "Death's-head jellyfish." The man then unbuttoned his shirt and pulled it open, revealing a selection of scars that crisscrossed his barrel of a chest. "Knife marks from eleven honor duels. I won them all." He sat back and folded his arms again. "So don't lecture me on pain, boy. I am far more familiar with its taste than you."

"Ladies and *gentlemen,*" the attendant said, giving the pair of them a glare, "the game will now begin." With a deft flick of his wrist, he whipped the velvet cloth from the pyramid. Lukan felt a stab of fear as he looked upon the Phaeron artifact's sleek black surface. He'd initially thought it to be made of polished dark glass, yet the side that faced him bore no reflection, seemingly swallowing the light rather than reflecting it. *I wonder what Father would have made of this.* Conrad Gardova had held the Phaeron in high esteem, claiming that the vanished race had valued wisdom and enlightenment above all else, but Lukan—faced with an object that could make the purest agony a reality—begged to differ.

The attendant touched the top of the pyramid with a gloved finger. The familiar low hum sounded, fading as the glowing lines appeared. Then the light display began, segments flashing blue and gold. Lukan took the opportunity to glance at his opponents, hoping to see signs of the same trepidation that he felt himself.

If any of them were afraid, they didn't show it.

The mercenary eyed the pyramid with a coolness that bordered on disdain. The Lady in Red, by contrast, appeared enraptured, her wide eyes unblinking as if she was hypnotized by the changing colors. The corsair, meanwhile, was glaring daggers at Lukan, his earlier insult clearly not forgotten. *Nor forgiven. So much the better.*

Blue and gold blurred to white, and then the pyramid fell dark once more, leaving just the latticework of white lines. The attendant gave a stiff bow. "Madam," he said to the mercenary, "please proceed when you're ready." With those final words, he withdrew.

A hush fell across the chamber.

The mercenary leaned forward and with a steady hand jabbed one of the segments on her bottom row, the speed of her action bringing a murmur of approval from the audience. Whether she'd chosen that segment in advance or had made a random decision Lukan could only guess, but either way she was rewarded with the glow of gold and the soft chime. Applause sounded from above. The woman sat back, her cool demeanor unchanged.

My turn. Shit.

Lukan managed to keep his smile in place as he eyed the seven segments on the bottom row of his side of the pyramid. There was no way of guessing which segment was the blue one; this was a game of pure chance, so one choice was as good as another. *I've certainly faced worse odds.* Besides, the mercenary's swift action meant that any hesitation from him would look like weakness. *Can't be having that.* He reached out—hand steady despite his pounding heart—and touched the segment third from the left. The pyramid was surprisingly cool to the touch, but Lukan barely noticed; all he registered was the chime of success and the golden glow before his eyes. He sat back, trying to conceal his relief, his gaze finding Juro in the crowd above. The Scrivener's man gave him a subtle nod, lips still quirked in amusement.

"Your turn, sailor boy," Lukan said to the corsair. "Take as much time as . . ."

But the corsair was already reaching out for the pyramid, prompting a murmur from the crowd—clearly the game was unfolding at a greater pace than usual. Lukan couldn't see which segment the man touched, but there was no mistaking the accompanying chime. The corsair leered at him as he sat back, folding his tattooed arms. A few shouts and whistles sounded above the accompanying applause, and Lukan glanced up to see two women and a man who all possessed a similar appearance and bearing to those of the corsair. *His shipmates,* he thought, as one of the women caught his eye and made an obscene gesture. *Just as charming as their comrade.*

A hush of anticipation fell as play passed to the Lady in Red, who appeared to have little regard for the speed of the game so far. A murmur passed through the crowd as the woman remained still, showing no intention of making her move—or of even realizing it was her turn. Someone gave a theatrical boo, causing a ripple of laughter.

"Silence please," the attendant called.

If the woman heard the shout of the attendant and the muttering of the crowd, she gave no sign. Instead she continued to stare intently at the pyramid, an unnerving gleam in her red eyes.

A murmuring began as the spectators grew restless. The attendant held a gloved fist to his mouth and coughed politely. "Madam," he said quietly, "you must make your choice, or else forfeit the competition and your entry fee."

As if she cares about that, Lukan thought. *She's probably lost larger sums down the back of her divan.* The woman was noble-born; he would have bet good coin on it. *After all, takes one to know one.* She was certainly dressed as finely as any aristocrat, and he half expected her to reply with a sharp rebuke befitting her patrician status. He was surprised, then, when the woman merely smiled at the attendant and leaned back in her chair, stretching out her arms like a cat waking from sleep.

"Oh, well," she replied, teeth flashing white behind her scarlet lips. "If I must." She leaned forward and, seemingly without fear or thought, touched a finger to the pyramid. Lukan couldn't see which segment she selected, but her choice was a good one; the chime sounded and she sat back, her expression one of mild amusement. She caught his eye as the applause echoed around the chamber, arching an eyebrow and giving him a coy smile. *It's almost like she's not afraid of the consequences.*

With the first round of the game complete, play moved back to the mercenary—and to the second row of the pyramid. This time the woman wasn't so quick to make a move. She drummed a couple of fingers on the tabletop, the irregular rhythm betraying a nervousness that her expression did not.

"You know," Lukan said, sensing an opportunity to get under the mercenary's skin, "you could always—"

"Shut it," she spat through gritted teeth, her dark eyes not leaving the surface of the pyramid. A moment later she made her choice, with the same result as before. Lukan caught a flash of relief in her eyes as she sat back.

And here we are again.

He clasped his hands and steepled his two index fingers, tapping them against his lips as he examined the pyramid, hoping his false display of nonchalance hid the churning fear that was once more rising inside him. *Only six segments this time,* he told himself. *Five to one. Come on, you'd play those odds any day of the week in rummijake. You've taken far bigger risks.* Yet none of those risks, he had to admit, had carried the prospect of self-inflicted immolation.

"What's the matter, pretty boy?" the corsair sneered. "You look scared."

"Not at all." Lukan leaned forward and made a show of peering at the pyramid. "I'm just trying to remember whether I paid your mother for last night."

As insults went, it was crude and unimaginative—but then so was its recipient. Lukan could see the corsair tense in the corner of his vision, but resisted the urge to look—it wouldn't do to push the man too far. *Not yet, at least.*

"Sir, if you wouldn't mind . . ." The attendant's tone was brisk, and Lukan wasn't sure if he was being reprimanded for his behavior or for the delay in taking his turn. *Probably both.* He eyed the row of six segments, all identical, but one hiding a nasty surprise. *Well, here goes nothing.* He reached out—wincing inwardly at the faint tremor in his hand—and touched the second segment from the right.

A dolorous note sounded, horribly loud in the silence.

Lukan stared in horror at the blue glow. *Oh, shit . . .*

Then the pain started.

12

Just an Illusion

It began in the palm of his right hand; an itch that blossomed into a subtle heat that was not altogether unpleasant—until the first spike of pain, which felt like a hot nail being driven into his palm. Lukan gasped as the heat intensified and flowed into his arm. *Like molten steel in my veins.* He winced as another lance of pain flashed beneath his skin, breath hissing through his gritted teeth. *I can handle this. Just keep it together.* Tears blurred his vision and he blinked them away, glancing down at his arm . . .

There were no flames.

Instead, something was moving beneath his skin.

His resolve crumbled as he saw the bulge, writhing its way up his forearm. The pain came again, more intense than before, and this time he couldn't help but cry out. His arm began to shake uncontrollably as his heart pounded, breath coming in ragged gasps. A fresh jolt of agony drew another cry from his lips, his eyes widening as he realized the bulge was growing larger, his skin whitening as it became stretched.

Lady's mercy, it's coming through—

His skin split open.

Lukan stared in horror as a huge centipede emerged, black segmented body slick with blood. It wound around his arm, countless legs like needles on his flesh. He swiped at it desperately, tried to grasp the creature and rip it from his skin, but his fingers couldn't seem to find purchase on its body. The nightmarish thing squirmed up and across his shoulder. He felt the creature's mandibles tickle his chin as it slid beneath his shirt.

Lukan shot up from his chair and stumbled backward. "No,"

he pleaded, bile rising in his throat as the centipede squirmed down toward his groin. "No no no, please, *please*—"

He fell to the floor, tearing frantically at his clothes, whimpering as he felt the creature's mandibles brush against his balls . . .

He screamed, closing his eyes in anticipation of an explosion of agony.

It never came.

After a few moments he stilled, chest heaving and nostrils flaring, a distant part of his mind aware that he could no longer feel the slick body of the centipede squirming against him—could not, in fact, feel pain in any part of his body. He took a shuddering breath, slowly coming to his senses. *An illusion,* he thought, with relief as sweet as nectar. *It was just an illusion.*

It was then that he became aware of the cold stone floor beneath him, of the sour taste in his mouth—and the laughter echoing around the chamber. He swayed a little as he climbed to his feet, disoriented by the blood rushing to his head. His stomach churned; he thought he might throw up, but mercifully the feeling passed.

"Sir?" the attendant said, stepping toward him. "Do you wish to continue?"

Hells, no. "Yes," he managed to croak.

A few cheers sounded as Lukan returned to the table. He glanced up and met Juro's stare—was there a hint of respect in the man's expression? *I should bloody hope so.* The corsair's three comrades certainly didn't share any such sentiment, as they jeered at him and made more obscene gestures. Lukan would have been happy to reply with a gesture of his own, but didn't trust his hand not to shake if he raised it. He was having trouble just standing up.

"Pathetic," the corsair snarled as Lukan sat down. "You bleat like a scared sheep."

"I imagine you've screwed enough of them to know," Lukan replied.

The Lady in Red gave a throaty chuckle. The mercenary remained silent.

"The hells did you just say?" the man demanded, surging to his feet.

"Gentlemen, *please,*" the attendant said, raising a gloved hand, "we don't tolerate violence here—"

"Shut your fool mouth," the corsair barked, jabbing the air with a ringed finger.

"—and if you continue to behave in such a fashion," the attendant continued, admirably unruffled, "you will be removed from the premises and will forfeit your entry fee."

"That means you don't get it back," Lukan offered.

"I know what it means," the corsair snarled. Lukan smiled at him. *Go on,* he urged. *Hit me.* He could tell the man was thinking about it, clenching his meaty fists, but instead he showed surprising restraint by opting to spit on the floor before sitting back down. *Damn. Still, perhaps it's for the best.* Lukan's body felt numb, his limbs heavy. If it came to a physical confrontation, he doubted he could defend himself, and the last thing he needed was the very real pain of a broken jaw. Even if it meant the corsair being disqualified. *Back to the game, then.*

"Your move, sailor," Lukan said as the corsair studied the pyramid. "Worse odds this time though."

The man gave a disdainful snort. "Every time I attack a ship," he replied, "I face worse odds than this. And I'm still standing." With that he pressed a segment on the second row of the pyramid. His comrades hooted as it shone gold. The corsair sat back and folded his tattooed arms, smirking at Lukan. The Lady in Red also made a successful choice—more quickly this time, and still without any sign of anxiety.

The next round began with the mercenary touching gold as well, though her unsteady hand suggested her nerves were starting to get the better of her.

Lady's blood, Lukan thought as play returned to him. *Here we go again.* His heart, which had only just settled down, started to pound once more. It required all of his discipline to keep his growing fear from showing on his face. *Four to one,* he told himself, eyeing the five segments on the third row. *Still good odds.* The thought wasn't as reassuring as it should have been.

"Not so quick now, eh?" the corsair said, knuckling his jaw. "Something upsetting you?"

"Only your ugly face," Lukan replied, not taking his eyes from the pyramid. *Which one?* he wondered, gazing at each segment as if one might yield some sort of clue. *Just pick one,* he urged himself, yet he couldn't seem to summon the strength to raise his hand—the image of the blue glow was still too fresh in his mind, the sound of the drone still echoing in his head. His stomach churned as he sat frozen in indecision.

"Hey," the corsair called out, gesturing at the attendant, "this is taking too long."

The attendant gave the man a sharp look, yet nonetheless approached the table.

"Sir," he said to Lukan, "I'm afraid I must ask you to—"

"Make my choice," Lukan cut in, waving the man away. "Yeah, I know."

"Hurry up, you son of a whore," someone shouted from the audience. *One of the corsair's friends, no doubt.*

"Silence," the attendant snapped, his patience finally wearing thin.

Lukan could see the corsair grinning in the corner of his eye and resolved not to give him any further satisfaction. He reached out—hand surprisingly steady—and pressed the segment at the center of the row. *Not blue, Lady's mercy not blue . . .*

The golden glow was one of the most welcome things he'd ever seen in his life, and the accompanying chime was music to his ears. He sat back, barely hearing the smattering of applause as he tried to keep his relief from showing. *Still in the game.*

"You play this game like a scared little boy," the corsair said, drawing himself up as play passed to him. "I'll show you how to play like a man." *You do that,* Lukan thought. *Let's see where it gets you.* The corsair moved with the same speed as before, rings gleaming as he reached forward.

His bravado didn't survive contact with the pyramid.

The man's kohl-rimmed eyes widened as the droning note sounded, followed by a murmur of excitement from above.

"Whoops," Lukan said.

The corsair stiffened, powerful muscles tensing. His right hand trembled as he held it up, revealing the large blister that was forming at the center of his palm, his skin turning an unhealthy shade of green. He gritted his teeth as the discoloration moved up his arm, cysts and abscesses forming in its wake. Sweat broke out on his brow, his eyes so wide it seemed they might burst. Within moments his whole arm was a tortured mess of weeping sores and rotting flesh. He rose shakily to his feet, just as a chunk of meat fell from his arm and hit the floor with a wet slap.

"Try not to scream," Lukan said with a grin.

The corsair screamed.

———————

As Lukan watched the corsair's suffering—which he didn't enjoy nearly as much as his grin might have suggested—he hoped the man's first taste of the pyramid's capabilities would prove too much for him. *Some of that bravado has got to be forced, surely.* Yet he suspected it was a fragile hope, and so it proved: once the illusion had faded and the corsair realized that his arm had in fact not disintegrated into a diseased mess, he picked himself up from the ground and returned to the table. *At least the experience has wiped the smirk from his face. Now to strike while the iron's hot . . .*

"A constipated ape," Lukan said airily. "That's what you sounded like. A constipated ape who thought it would be a good idea to slather honey over his cock and stick it in a fire ants' nest."

The corsair tried to smile, but it came out as a grimace. "When we are done here," he replied, words slightly slurred, "I will cut out your tongue, since you seem to like it so much."

"Your mother liked it too, so best not—you'd only disappoint her." Lukan shrugged. "Then again, you grew up to be a murdering, thieving, raping piece of shit, so I imagine she's disappointed enough already—"

The corsair lunged at him, moving with a speed that was all the more impressive given that just moments before he'd been on his knees, body shaking as he retched. Despite the swiftness of the man's attack, Lukan was ready. Instead of trying to block the corsair's punch, he gritted his teeth and rolled with the blow, using the momentum to hurl himself to the floor. He heard the crowd's collective gasp—then nothing but the roaring of blood in his ears as the corsair's powerful hands clamped round his throat.

"Where are your clever words now?" the corsair hissed, his face pressed so close to Lukan's that their noses practically touched. Fury shone in his eyes as he tightened his grip. Lukan pawed hopelessly at the man's hands, darkness pooling at the edges of his vision until all he could see was the corsair's snarling face. *Come on*, he pleaded, a distant part of his mind wondering whether he'd overestimated the efficiency of Salazar's security. Tears blurred his vision, his panic rising as he tried and failed to breathe. *Come on, come on, come on—*

The corsair jolted, eyes widening. The pressure round Lukan's neck eased as the man toppled sideways to reveal two guards, one of them wielding a cudgel that she'd presumably just cracked against the corsair's skull. The attendant stood beside them, his face solemn.

"Took . . . your damned . . . time," Lukan wheezed as he gasped for breath.

"My sincere apologies, sir," the attendant said, as the other guard helped Lukan to his feet. "As I made clear earlier, we don't tolerate violence here—your assailant will of course be disqualified." He nodded at the guards, who dragged the unconscious corsair away to furious insults from the man's watching comrades. One of them leaned over the side of the bath and spat at Lukan, drawing a line across her throat with a finger.

"Do you wish to continue, sir?" the attendant asked. "Given

the circumstances, if you wish to resign I can arrange for your entry fee to be returned."

"That won't be necessary," Lukan replied, wincing as he rubbed his jaw. *Though honestly I'd like nothing more.* He righted his chair and sat back down, to several cheers from the crowd. "Well, this is nice," he said, glancing around the table. "I prefer things to be a little more intimate."

"You and I both," the Lady in Red purred, pursing her scarlet lips as amusement danced in her eyes. Despite his weakened state—not to mention having far more pressing concerns—Lukan felt a thrill at the way she regarded him. *That coy smile . . .* If the circumstances had been different, he would have wasted no time in suggesting they pursue a little *intimacy* in a more private location.

"Your turn, I believe," he said, returning her smile.

"Yes," she replied, unfazed. "It is."

Take as long as you like. Lukan was certainly in no hurry for play to return to him, but, if the Lady in Red could sense his thoughts, she gave them no regard. She hummed softly to herself, tilting her head from side to side, as if she were choosing a bottle of wine—*red wine, I'll bet*—before touching the pyramid.

Gold, again—and the curl in her lower lip that could have been amusement or disappointment. *Or both.*

The mercenary took longer over her decision. Lukan kept quiet—no point trying to wind her up, she was far too cool for that. All he could do was hope she picked blue and couldn't handle the consequences, though the numerous scars she bore suggested she was no stranger to pain. *Still, let's see whether she can handle the sight of a centipede bursting out of her arm.* He grimaced at the thought, the horror still fresh in his mind, and blinked it away. He watched as the mercenary reached out, only to hesitate, her fingers twitching just before the pyramid. *Blue,* Lukan urged silently, as if he could somehow influence the woman's actions. *Pick the blue, pick the blue . . .*

The mercenary picked gold.

Shit. Lukan's fear rose once more and it took all of his resolve to force it back down. *Not a flicker,* he told himself, as he had so many times around the gambling tables back in Parva. *Not so much as a blink of the eye. My face is a mask—*

"You're afraid."

Lukan looked up to find the Lady in Red watching him, the intensity of her gaze at odds with her sultry smile.

"Why do you say that?" he replied, aiming for nonchalance.

"Because you're trying so hard to appear calm. But the fear is taking control, isn't it? Squeezing you." There was no malice in her words, though the simple honesty cut Lukan far more than any gibe or insult. He made to reply, though for once no words came. *It's hard to argue with the truth.*

"You're dreading the sight of the blue glow," she continued. "You can still see it in your mind. The Phaeron held the color blue in contempt, did you know that?"

"No, but I know plenty of other worthless shit about them. Perhaps we could compare notes sometime."

The woman pursed her scarlet lips as she leaned forward, amusement flickering in the red depths of her eyes. "Perhaps," she purred. "Once you've recovered from the exquisite agony they are about to inflict on you. *If you recover.*"

She's playing me at my own game. Lukan returned her smile. "You think I can't handle it?"

"I think you should resign before we find out."

"Honestly," Lukan replied, holding her gaze, "I'd like nothing more. But needs must." *And duty calls.* Drawing a deep breath, he reached out and touched one of the segments on the pyramid's third row.

The blue glow sent ice through his heart.

The Lady in Red sat back, smile still in place, no trace of sympathy in her eyes.

Lukan gasped as his right hand suddenly felt like it was submerged in icy water. The numbing cold swept up his arm, his skin cracking and blackening in its wake. *Frostbite,* he realized, gritting his teeth as it spread across his shoulders and chest. *Just an illusion.* Yet he cried out all the same as the pain moved up his neck and spread over his face, a low moan escaping his chapped lips. *It's not real, it's not real* . . . The thought felt distant, as if his brain were encased in ice. Panic gripped him; he could feel the skin of his face splitting, his cheeks sinking inward. *No, please* . . . He raised a shaking hand and stared in horror as one of his fingers—little more than a blackened stump—cracked off and fell to the floor. Bile surged up his throat.

Lukan toppled from his chair, his body convulsing as he vomited.

Darkness took him a moment later.

13

BAD DREAMS

Blood stained the cherry blossoms, scarlet on pink.

Giorgio Castori lay before him, body splayed like a collapsed marionette, with eyes just as lifeless. His mouth was open, reflecting the surprise he must have felt as Lukan's blade pierced his throat. Blood still flowed from the wound, still dripped from his rapier's tip, each drop echoing in Lukan's ears like the mockery of a heartbeat. His sword suddenly felt very heavy in his hand. When he finally looked up, he found the world unchanged, as if it was indifferent to the unfolding human tragedy. Lukan stared numbly at the cherry trees—still so beautiful amid the ivy-choked ruins—his gaze slowly moving up to the flawless blue sky.

It was a spring day to die for.

And Giorgio Castori had done just that.

Lukan blinked as a scream rent the air. It might have even been his own, he couldn't tell—his mind was reeling as the significance of what had just happened, what he had done, finally struck him like a hammer blow. He staggered, knees suddenly weak, barely aware of his rapier clattering to the cobbles. A young man appeared beside him—Giorgio's second, he realized. The youth had been jesting with Giorgio before the duel, their laughter echoing between the stone columns. Neither of them were laughing now. The boy stared down at his friend's corpse, horror writ large across his pale face. He tried to speak, but no words passed his quivering lips. His hat fell from nerveless fingers.

Lukan flinched as someone touched his shoulder—Jaques, his own second, face flushed as he stammered something, a question in his wide eyes. Lukan didn't hear his friend's words; he stared over the boy's shoulder, his attention on the woman striding toward them, dark hair rippling in the breeze . . .

Amicia.

Lukan pushed Jaques away as she drew closer, tried to voice the words that had been spinning around his own mind ever since Giorgio Castori had slumped to the ground.

It was an accident, I didn't mean to kill him, it was a mistake . . .

Yet the words wouldn't come; they caught in his throat as if unsure of their own validity.

"Lukan?" she asked, eyes widening as she saw the red ruin of Giorgio's neck. "What . . . what have you done?"

Still the words wouldn't come.

Amicia knelt by Giorgio's side, said something to his second; the boy shook his head, tears streaming down his cheeks. How young he suddenly looked. Amicia rose slowly, turned to face Lukan.

His stomach lurched as her hazel eyes met his.

He'd looked into those eyes so many times over the past few months, seen so many things in their depths: amusement, delight, affection . . . perhaps, on occasion, something more. But now he saw something in them he'd never seen before: revulsion.

"I can't believe you've done this." Her voice was barely above a whisper.

"Amicia," he managed, finding his voice at last. "It was an accident—I didn't mean to—"

"What were you thinking!" she yelled, shoving him in the chest. "You . . . you coward!"

When he didn't answer, she turned and strode away.

Lukan watched her go, the silence broken only by the gasping sobs from Giorgio's friend. Lukan felt tears on his own cheeks, though he wasn't sure who they were for.

Petals fluttered around his feet, stirred by the breeze.

Blood on cherry blossoms.

Lukan jolted awake, his heart racing even as the dream—the *nightmare*—faded away, retreating to the deepest recesses of his mind, where he knew it would lurk until it chose to torment him again. He groaned as a headache took its place, the shooting pain triggering a rush of memories: the pyramid, the corsair, the Lady in Red's beguiling smile . . . and the agony. *Lady's mercy, the sheer bloody agony.* Lukan shuddered, remembering the centipede skittering across his skin and his arm blackening with frostbite. He raised his hand, blinking to clear his hazy vision. *I'm unharmed,* he realized, staring at his unblemished skin, all fingers intact. He managed a weak laugh as he let his hand fall.

"You see?" a smooth voice said. "They were merely illusions."

Lukan looked up, taking in his surroundings: a small room, bare walls dimly illuminated by a half-shuttered lantern resting on a table beside his bed. As his eyes adjusted to the gloom, he saw a darkened figure sitting in one corner of the room, just beyond the light's reach.

"Juro?" he croaked, struggling to sit up.

"Relax, Lukan," the Scrivener's man said as he rose and stepped into the light, his customary half smile still in place. "You need to rest. I understand the aftereffects of playing the pyramid can be unpleasant."

"Yeah, I noticed."

"Bad dreams?" Juro asked, filling a clay cup with water from a jug.

"How'd you know?"

"It's a common occurrence. Unconsciousness induced by the pyramid often involves painful or traumatic memories." He offered the cup to Lukan. "Drink this. Should help with the headache."

Lukan grunted his thanks, managing to spill half the cup's contents over himself. The water that did reach his throat tasted like nectar. He took a few more swallows, the pain in his temples already receding.

"Where am I?" he asked, handing the cup back to Juro, who refilled it.

"Still in Salazar's. This is one of several rooms set aside for players who require recuperation after facing the pyramid. I had you brought here after you lost consciousness."

"Kind of you," Lukan said dryly, "though I can't help but feel you're partly responsible for my current state of well-being." He took another sip of water. "Or lack thereof."

Juro arched a fine eyebrow. "You entered the game of your own free will, Lukan. I merely facilitated the process."

"You gave me no choice. Not if I wanted to meet your mistress."

The man shrugged. "You could have walked away."

If only that was true. "So who won the game? Wait, let me guess—that strange woman in red."

"Lady Marni."

"You know her?"

"No, though I found her behavior intriguing, to say the least. I asked around and heard a whisper or two. An interesting woman, by all accounts."

I'll bet. Would have liked the chance to discover that myself. "She had a tattoo on her wrist, looked like a Phaeron glyph . . ."

"Indeed. It seems that Lady Marni is something of a closed book, but she has certain interests that she wears very much on her sleeve. Or beneath it, in this case."

"Get to the point, Juro. I've got enough of a headache as it is."

"The tattoo on her wrist is the symbol of a cult known as the Scarlet Throne."

"The Scarlet Throne," Lukan echoed, his brow creasing in thought. "That's a famous Phaeron relic. A throne forged from an unknown metal."

"Indeed. It seems this cult named themselves for it."

"To what purpose? Who are they?"

"The Scarlet Throne regard the Phaeron as gods and worship them as such. Their membership supposedly includes several powerful figures across the Old Empire—including the Lady Marni."

"Who is she? I thought her accent was Korslakovan . . ."

"Correct. Lady Marni is the daughter of Lord Fyodor Volkov,

the head of the Volkov family—one of the most powerful noble houses in Korslakov."

"Then she's a long way from home," Lukan mused, thinking of that far-flung northern city, nestled between the pine-covered slopes of the Wolfclaw Mountains—another place he knew only from pictures and old anecdotes. "I wonder what brought her so far south . . . And why in the hells did she decide to play the pyramid? She clearly doesn't need the money."

"The Scarlet Throne regard Phaeron artifacts as holy relics. I imagine Lady Marni participated in the game simply for the chance to be close to the pyramid itself. To touch it. To feel its power."

"Seriously? You think she risked unbearable agony just for that?"

"Perhaps the agony was the point. As I said, the Scarlet Throne believe the Phaeron to be gods. Perhaps Lady Marni wanted to feel the touch of one."

That would certainly explain the intensity in her eyes, and her lack of fear. "And did she?"

"No. Her opponent chose blue during the subsequent round and decided not to continue after witnessing a number of insects bursting out of her stomach. Lady Marni withdrew shortly afterward and was declared the victor."

Clearly not that desperate to feel the touch of the divine then. Lukan sat up, grimacing as the weight of his failure settled over him. He'd lost the game, and with it his one chance to meet the Scrivener. *All that pain for nothing.* "Well, I'd say it's been a pleasure, Juro," he said, swinging his legs off the bed, "but it really hasn't."

"You should rest, Lukan," Juro replied. "You ought to be of clear mind when you meet my mistress."

"Your *mistress*? But I didn't win the game."

"I never said anything about winning. I merely said you needed to play the pyramid—which you did." The man rose from his chair. "There is a statue of Ademir the Elder in a small plaza, a few streets west of the amphitheater. Be there at the eleventh bell tonight. Flea can show you the way."

"I'll be there," Lukan replied, frowning as a thought occurred to him. *How the hells does he know about Flea?* "Juro, how do you—"

But the Scrivener's man was gone.

14

AMATEUR DRAMATICS

"A giant centipede?"

"Something like that, yeah."

"And it came out of your *arm*?"

"Burst out, more like." Lukan winced at the memory. *Glistening segments slick with blood.* "Anyway, can we just—"

"What color was it? I saw a red one once in a warehouse near the waterfront . . ."

Lady's mercy. He'd managed to evade Flea's questions in the immediate aftermath of his experience at Salazar's, remaining tight-lipped as they headed back to his room at the inn, where he managed to grab a few hours of sleep. But there was no avoiding them now as they waited beneath the tarnished bronze statue of Ademir the Elder. *Whoever the hells he is. Or was.* He didn't recall any mention of the man in Velleras Gellame's booklet, and when he asked Flea the girl merely shrugged and replied, "Probably some dead frilly." Whatever the man's background, his statue stood at the center of a small plaza that—save for a cat prowling along its western side—they had to themselves. No lights shone in the windows of the closed shops and premises lining the square, though the night's breeze carried sounds of life: distant laughter, a dog barking, and a violin playing an unwitting accompaniment to a lovers' tiff.

". . . did it have a hundred legs?"

"I don't know, kid. I was too busy screaming to count."

"Because it hurt?"

"No, because I was enjoying it tickling my balls."

"Someone's coming."

Lukan looked up, eyes scanning the darkened plaza. "I don't see any—"

"There," Flea whispered, pointing toward a building away to their right. *Damn, the kid's got sharp eyes,* Lukan thought as he spied three figures emerging from an alleyway. He felt a flicker of trepidation as they approached, their movements brisk, faces concealed by hoods. One of the figures trailed a step or two behind the others, and Lukan felt sure it was Juro. *Something about the way he walks . . .*

"Remember what I told you," he whispered.

"That you ruined your life because of a stupid duel?"

"What I told you *literally* just now."

"To keep my mouth shut and let you do the talking?"

"Yes. Can you do that? Please?"

"Maybe."

Lukan suppressed another sigh. *I guess that's the best I can hope for.* He resisted the urge to reach for his sword as the three figures stopped before him. He relaxed as the third figure pulled back his hood and confirmed his earlier suspicion.

"Good evening, Lukan," Juro said, his half smile firmly in place. "And to you, Flea."

"I'd say hello," the girl replied, "but Lukan told me to keep my mouth shut and let him do the talking."

Seven shadows . . .

"That seems like a wise decision." Juro's lip quirked in amusement. "Certainly wiser than most of the decisions he made earlier, to be sure."

Flea giggled. "I heard about the centipede—"

"Yes, well," Lukan interrupted, shooting her a glare. "Perhaps we could get down to business?"

"Of course," Juro replied. "My two companions and I will escort you to my mistress—alone, I must hasten to add."

"Understood." Lukan turned to Flea. "Head back to the inn, I'll see you later."

"I'll wait here," the girl replied, sitting down on the cobbles as if there would be no further argument. Lukan tried anyway.

"Flea, I could be gone some time."

"Are you gonna find your own way home?"

She's got a point. "Fine. Just don't get into trouble."

"And don't follow us," Juro said, still smiling. "Or there will be consequences. Do you understand, Flea?"

The girl shrugged, not at all bothered by the subtle threat. "Sure, whatever."

"Then let's be away." The Scrivener's man pulled up his hood. "Lukan, please follow me." He strode toward the alley.

"Stay here," Lukan murmured to Flea. "I'll try not to be too long."

He walked after Juro, the two other figures falling in behind him. Their presence at his back made him twitchy, a feeling that only grew worse as they entered the darkness of the alley. This time he allowed his hand to stray to the hilt of his sword, his eyes barely able to make out Juro in the gloom ahead. They were a good way down the alley when the Scrivener's man turned to face him.

"My apologies in advance, Lukan."

Lukan tensed, hearing a whisper of movement behind him. *Oh shit—*

A strong arm wrapped round his shoulders, another clamping a damp cloth against his face; he inhaled a lungful of a sharp, acrid stench before he even thought to try to hold his breath. He struggled, trying to shout but managing only a muffled roar as the world tilted around him, his vision blurring.

"Relax, Lukan," Juro said, raising a hand. "If I meant you harm, you'd be dead already."

Well, that's reassuring, Lukan thought, his legs buckling. *You bastard.*

Unconsciousness took him a moment later.

———

He awoke to darkness.

For a few blissful moments Lukan thought he was back in his room at the inn, before his memory roused itself: the plaza, the alley . . . *Juro*. He tried to move, only to realize he was tied to the chair he was sitting on, his wrists bound tightly to the backrest. *Shit*. A coarse material rasped against his skin as he turned his head, reflecting the heat of his own breath—some sort of hood. *That explains the darkness*. Bound and temporarily blinded, Lukan opted to listen instead.

Nothing.

No, wait . . .

Footsteps. Lukan realized they were approaching him barely a moment before the sackcloth was pulled from his head. He looked up to find Juro standing over him, the man's infuriating half smile illuminated by candlelight.

"You and I need to talk," Lukan said, his voice a rasp.

"No, Lukan. You and my *mistress* need to talk." The man stepped away, gesturing at the figure who faced Lukan from the other side of a table that was empty save for a solitary candle. The Scrivener remained silent, her features concealed by a hood, but Lukan could feel the weight of her unseen gaze all the same. He resisted the urge to shift in his chair as she regarded him, the silence growing more oppressive with each passing moment. Eventually his patience snapped.

"You're fond of your cloak-and-dagger bullshit, aren't you?"

Probably not the best thing to say to the one person in this city who could actually help him, but it did at least make him feel a little more at ease. *Always best to be on the front foot.*

The Scrivener's hood tilted a little, though whether in amusement or annoyance he couldn't say.

"Do forgive me, Master Gardova," she replied in a crisp voice that could have cut glass, "but caution and secrecy lend themselves well to the vineyard in which I toil. Still, if it makes you feel more comfortable . . ." The woman reached up and pulled back her hood, revealing a pale face possessed of high cheekbones and a narrow jawline, where the only concessions to age were the crow's-feet around her eyes. Her silver hair was cut short, lending emphasis to her sharp features.

"What would make me feel more comfortable," Lukan replied, "is for you to untie me." He glanced down, realized his weapons were missing. "I'm not even armed."

"Neither am I." The Scrivener spread her hands.

"You still have me at a disadvantage."

"And that's exactly where I'll keep you for the duration of our conversation."

Not the most promising start. Lukan glanced around, taking in the small room for the first time. The ceiling was low and the walls were lined with wooden racks, the candlelight playing across the dusty glass bottles within. *A wine cellar, though one that's not been used for some time. Wonder if there's any Parvan Red down here.* He turned back to the Scrivener. "Where are we?"

"Somewhere away from prying eyes, you can be assured of that. So let's get down to business. Why have you sought me out?"

"I've already told Juro my story. Did he not tell you?"

"He did, but I would hear it again from you."

"Why? Do you not trust your own man?"

"I trust Juro implicitly," the Scrivener replied, her voice hardening. "His ability to see through falsehoods is just one of his many talents."

"I told him the truth."

"So he tells me, which is why I consented to this meeting—but I warn you now, I *will* abandon it without hesitation if you persist with your aggressive tone."

"Hey, *you're* the one who abducted me and had me tied to a chair."

The Scrivener raised a sharp eyebrow.

"All right, fine," Lukan said wearily. *Have it your way.* "What do you want to know?"

"I understand your late father wrote you a note. I'd very much like to see it."

"Yeah, it's in my left boot—perhaps if you cut my ropes . . ."

But Juro was already beside him, retrieving the folded paper from its hiding place. The man offered the note to the Scrivener; Lukan thought she might express some reluctance to touch the paper—crumpled and bloodstained as it was—but the woman took the note and unfolded it without hesitation. As her eyes scanned the bloody scrawl, Lukan noted how fine her hands were, her fingers long, almost elegant.

"Lukan," she murmured. "Saphrona. Zandrusa." Her eyes met Lukan's.

"And here I am," he replied, giving a rueful smile.

"So I understand," the Scrivener said, folding the paper and setting it down on the table, "that you seek an audience with Lady Jelassi—or Zandrusa, as you call her."

"That's her real name."

"I'm well aware of that." Her expression momentarily softened—or perhaps it was a trick of the light, for her voice retained its edge. "And you want my help getting inside the Ebon Hand."

"That's right. Obassa—he's a blind beggar . . . well, he's not blind, but—"

"I know who he is."

"Right. Well, he said you might be able to help me, that you were the best forger in the city."

"Always playing the charmer, that one," the Scrivener said dryly. "But then that's the nature of his role."

"His role?"

"Yes. Don't tell me you believed that blind beggar nonsense?"

"No, of course not," Lukan replied, a little heatedly. "He's obviously got some sort of game going on, though I'm told he's not with your lot—the Kindred, I mean."

"You were told true, Obassa's not one of us. No, our blind friend is a spy for the Zar-Ghosan crown. How he hasn't yet taken a knife to the back remains a mystery, though you have to admit he has a certain charm."

"He said you could help me. Can you?"

"That depends." She steepled her fingers. "Do you have a plan?"

"Well, originally I was thinking of impersonating a prisoner—"

"A ridiculous notion."

"Yeah, so I've been told," Lukan said, feeling his irritation rising. "Too many risky elements, and so on. I get it. So I was thinking . . . if I could get hold of a constable's uniform—"

"Spare me the talk of amateur dramatics," the Scrivener interjected. "Constable, prisoner, it doesn't matter which of them you impersonate. Neither will get you inside the Hand. Not without the official paperwork."

"But isn't that where you come in? Can't you forge the papers?"

"No."

"No?" Lukan echoed incredulously. "So I played that bloody pyramid for nothing? Endured all that agony for *nothing*?" His rising voice echoed off the cellar walls. "So much for being the best forger in the city. I guess Obassa was wrong about that."

"The Ebon Hand holds some of the worst scum this city has to offer," the Scrivener said, speaking slowly, as if to a child. "Murderers, rapists, child abusers, and many more. Consequently, all paperwork granting access to members of the constabulary bears the signature of a senior inquisitor and is stamped with a seal. A *sorcerous* seal. I can perfectly replicate such a document down to the cigarillo-ash smudges and coffee stains, but I cannot replicate sorcery."

"So there's no way of getting inside?" Lukan asked, his hope fading.

"Oh, there's a way." The Scrivener pursed her lips. "But it won't be easy."

"Just tell me." Lukan could feel exhaustion clawing at the corners of his mind, born of the day's trials—the horrors of the Bone Pit, the various agonies of the pyramid, and now this cat-and-mouse conversation. *Enough.* "Please," he added, as the Scrivener's gaze hardened.

"Members of the constabulary need to show the official paperwork to enter the Hand. Representatives of the Inquisition do not. That means—"

"You're suggesting I impersonate an *inquisitor*?"

"Interrupt me again and I will walk away from this meeting," the Scrivener said coolly. Before Lukan could so much as mumble an apology she continued, "The Inquisition has full access to the Hand, and its inquisitors can come and go as they please. I can procure you the necessary uniform and badge of office that will get you inside."

"As easy as that?"

"Not quite. The higher-ranking inquisitors will be well known at the Hand, so we'll have to present you as an inquisitor of lower rank—an unfamiliar face. A lesser player who, for reasons unknown, has been given the chance to punch above his weight by subjecting Zandrusa to further interrogation."

"Would that not arouse suspicion? Surely the Inquisition would send one of their top dogs to question her."

"It might prompt one or two questions. Which is why I will also provide you with a personal order from the Prime Inquisitor himself."

"Saying what?"

"That you are to be admitted to the Hand in order to interrogate Lady Jelassi, and are to be given every assistance. Such a document wouldn't bear a sorcerous seal, merely the Prime Inquisitor's stamp and signature. And *that,* Master Gardova, is well within my abilities to emulate."

"And that will be enough to get me access to Zandrusa?"

"In theory, yes."

"I often find theory doesn't match reality."

"There is an element of risk, I admit—"

"Is that a polite way of saying there's a good chance I'll end up in chains, hoping not to be eaten by a giant worm . . ." He trailed off as the Scrivener stood, remembering her earlier warning. "My apologies," he said, inclining his head. "It won't happen again."

"If it does," the Scrivener replied, "I *will* abandon this meeting, and I'll leave you tied to the chair when I go. Understand?"

"Perfectly."

"As I was saying, there is an element of risk," the Scrivener replied as she sat back down. "You're an unfamiliar face, not to mention an unlikely candidate for an inquisitor—most of them are native Saphronans. But I can assure you that I will forge a letter so convincing the Prime Inquisitor himself would be fooled into thinking he'd written it. No one will challenge your authority, so as long as you can control that fool tongue of yours, you should be able to walk into Zandrusa's cell without a whisper of challenge. The rest is then up to you."

"And if I'm caught?"

"You'll go to the Bone Pit. Impersonating an inquisitor is a capital offense."

"No pressure then." Lukan stared at the floor, digesting the Scrivener's proposal. If her work was as good as she claimed, no one would have cause to suspect him—and if anyone *did* harbor any doubts, he'd be long gone before they had a chance to verify his identity. Still, the plan was dangerous. Reckless, even. *But worth the risk*, he decided eventually. *Besides, it's my only chance.* Even so, he couldn't shake the feeling the Scrivener was holding out on him. *There's something she's not telling me.* He met the woman's gaze as his suspicion coalesced into a question. "Why are you doing this?"

The Scrivener tilted her head, as if considering. "For the challenge."

"No," Lukan replied, knowing he risked invoking her anger if he pushed too hard. "I think it's more than that. You already knew Lady Jelassi's real name—I didn't mention it to Juro. I think you have some sort of deeper interest in all this."

The Scrivener regarded him silently.

"Perhaps," she said after a long pause, "you're smarter than I initially gave you credit for."

"I have my moments."

The woman sat back in her chair, tapped one finger on the tabletop. "Very well," she continued, as if she had come to a decision. "Zandrusa and I had a business arrangement, many years ago—I trust you know of her original background?"

"Yeah, Obassa said she was a smuggler."

"Not just any smuggler. She was one of the very best. She could get hold of whatever you wanted—for the right price, of course. And she did it all under the noses of the harbormaster and the trade council." She gave a thin smile. "With my help, of course."

"You forged documents for her?"

"Bills of sale, tax certificates, goods orders—the lot. We worked together for nearly ten years, and not once did Zandrusa's little operation fall foul of the law "

"But then she went straight."

"Yes, she did." Her smile faded. "Such a shame; we had quite the lucrative little business going. But she'd always had a philanthropic streak, and I think she grew frustrated with her inability to effect the change she wanted to see. She always cared a great deal about her people. So she set herself up as an investor and moneylender, and within a few years had earned a seat on the Gilded Council. Quite the meteoric rise, but then Zandrusa was . . . *is* in many ways an extraordinary woman."

"Do you still have contact?"

"No, we haven't spoken in many years. She cut all ties with the Kindred when she turned legitimate. I must confess to being surprised—once she started mixing with those corrupt parasites on the Gilded Council, I thought she'd have more need of my skills than ever before. Still, Zandrusa always liked to do things her way."

"That doesn't appear to have worked out too well for her."

"No, which brings us to the reason I decided to meet with you. You're right, I do have a deeper interest in this. You wish to ask Zandrusa about your father's message. I wish to ask her questions of my own. I think we can help each other, Master Gardova."

"What questions?"

"About what really happened that night in Lord Saviola's villa. About how I might be able to help her prove her innocence."

"You think she's innocent?"

"I know it. Zandrusa always cared deeply for others, especially her friends. This murder is not the act of the woman I knew."

"But you just said you've not spoken since Zandrusa went straight. Maybe years of sitting on the Gilded Council with all those corrupt parasites, as you called them, has rubbed off on her. Perhaps she's changed."

"Perhaps," the Scrivener replied, her tone suggesting she thought it unlikely. "Or perhaps she was framed for a murder she didn't commit."

"You think Zandrusa has enemies on the council?"

"Oh, undoubtedly. She's spent years pushing agendas aimed at improving the lives of the city's poorer citizens, often to the detriment of her fellow merchant princes' business interests. It has won her plenty of enemies and few friends, though Lord Saviola was apparently her closest political ally. Strange, then, that Zandrusa decided to open the man's throat with a blade—unless, of course, she didn't."

"So you want me to find out the truth."

"We both seek the truth, Master Gardova. This is our chance to find answers."

"And yet I'm the one putting myself in harm's way."

"Which is why I'm willing to forgo my usual fee. I will provide you with both the letter and uniform free of charge. In return, you will bring me answers."

"And if I don't return with the information you seek?"

"Then you'll wish the Inquisition *had* slapped you in chains."

"I don't take well to idle threats."

"There was nothing idle about it."

Lukan couldn't help but smile at that. "Fine, I accept your terms." *Though it's not like I have much choice.*

"Excellent." The Scrivener's lips quirked in what might have been satisfaction. "I will have the letter and uniform ready in two days. I suggest you spend the time perfecting the scowl and dead-eyed stare that all the agents of our fine Inquisition seem to share. Juro will deliver the letter and uniform to you at the Orange Tree Inn when they're ready."

"How do you know where I'm staying? Wait, have you been *spying* on me—"

"There is one other thing," the Scrivener continued, reaching into her robes. "I want you to give this to Zandrusa." She placed on the table a small clay jar, its stopper sealed with wax.

"What is it?"

"That's none of your concern. Just tell Zandrusa to apply it to her skin before her next appearance in the Bone Pit."

Curious. Lukan waited to see if the Scrivener would elaborate, but the woman remained silent. Clearly her trust in him extended only so far. *Well, the feeling is more than mutual.*

"Fine," he replied. "I'll make sure she gets it."

"Then our business here is concluded." The Scrivener rose and pulled up her hood, casting her face into shadow as she made for the steps in the corner of the room. "Two days, Master Gardova."

Lukan watched her go, his gaze flicking to Juro as the man stepped toward him, sackcloth in one hand and a damp rag in the other. He tensed as he caught the familiar acrid stench.

Oh, Lady's blood—

Darkness took him again.

15

The Inquisition
Never Sleeps

When Juro delivered the forged letter and uniform (exactly two days later, as promised), his advice to Lukan was simple: People are afraid of the Inquisition, so let the uniform do the talking. *And when you have to speak,* the Scrivener's man had said, *deliver each word like a stab between the ribs.*

The advice echoed in Lukan's mind now as he approached the large guardhouse at the western end of the waterfront. Despite the coolness of the evening—a storm had broken earlier that afternoon—he was sweating freely beneath his black and silver uniform, heart fluttering against his ribs. *Keep it together,* he told himself, *this is no different than bluffing at the rummijake table.* Except it was, because this time he was gambling with his own life. *No pressure, then.*

Two sentries leaned against either side of the guardhouse gate, flicking ash from their cigarillos as they talked, their laughter carrying on the breeze. In that moment he envied them—the simplicity of their lives, the quiet humdrum of their responsibilities. *What I'd give for a smoke and some small talk.* Instead he squared his shoulders and affected a scowl that he hoped was worthy of a member of the Saphronan Inquisition. *Now, let's see how intimidating this uniform really is.*

The two guards glanced up as Lukan strode into the lantern light. He caught their fleeting looks of surprise before they snapped to attention, flicking their cigarillos into the shadows in a smooth manner that suggested it wasn't the first time they'd been caught smoking on duty. *Should I reprimand them? Would they expect me to?* Lukan stared at them, struck by indecision. The two men stared at the floor. He took that as a good sign, and allowed the silence to drag a little longer.

"I have business at the Hand," he announced eventually, his authoritative tone sounding laughably forced to his own ears. "Ah . . . so I need a boat." *Smooth, Gardova. Really smooth.*

The guards exchanged looks.

"Now," Lukan snapped. *Before I lose my nerve.*

"Uh, yes. Of course. Sir." The man who had spoken turned and pushed the gate open, its hinges squealing. "Follow me. Please."

Lukan followed the man through the gate and into a small courtyard. "It's just this way," the guard said, perhaps hoping to ease the tension as he led Lukan past the guardhouse. Laughter and light spilled from its windows. *Seems the constables in this city have a good time of things.* "Careful, sir," the man continued as they reached a stone flight of steps that led down to a jetty. "These are a little steep, and can sometimes be slick from the—"

"Enough," Lukan cut in, "I'm not a child."

They descended in silence.

Half a dozen rowing boats were tethered to the jetty, and a similar number of men sat around a glowing brazier by the water's edge, smoke from their cigarillos spiraling above their heads as they conversed in low tones.

"Look alive, you lot," the guard said, more confident now that he was speaking to people who were comfortably below him in the pecking order. "We need a boat."

The men fell silent and exchanged glances. Someone muttered a curse.

"What, *now*?" one of them replied.

"No, next month," the guard snapped, giving the man's stool a kick. "Of course now, you idiot. Hop to it."

"You heard him, lads," the man said, a mocking edge to his tone. He sucked on his cigarillo, exhaled the smoke through his nose. "Whose turn is it?"

"It's Geraldo's," someone said.

"Piss off," the man seemingly called Geraldo replied. "I did the last run . . ."

As the men argued, Lukan noted the guard shooting him a nervous look—clearly he expected a display of Inquisitorial displeasure. *In which case, I best give it to him.*

"Enough," Lukan snapped, stepping forward and drawing the elegant dagger that had arrived along with his uniform. "Will I have to tell the Prime Inquisitor," he asked, firelight playing along the blade as he pointed at each man in turn, "that my report is late because a bunch of layabouts refused to do their job?"

Six pairs of eyes widened and six mouths dropped open.

Silence, save for the crackling of the flames.

Then five of the men shot to their feet, talking over each other in their panic.

"I'll do it, sir—"

"It's my turn—"

"Geraldo, you *idiot*—"

"You," Lukan said, pointing his blade at the one man who remained sitting—the youngest of the group, who still stared at him with wide eyes. "Get a boat ready."

"M-m-me?"

"Don't make me ask again."

Lukan could sense the other men's relief as the boy stood and ran onto the jetty, his hands shaking as he untied the ropes of the closest boat. He felt a twinge of sympathy for the boy, a sense of regret at involving him in this charade, but masked his emotions with another scowl. The young man was clearly terrified of him, and that was all he needed right now—someone who would row him to the Hand and not so much as look at him, let alone ask any questions. As the boy tossed the rope into the boat and hopped on board, Lukan gave the guard and the gathered men a final glare as he made to depart.

None of them met his gaze.

Lukan ignored the boy's outstretched hand as he stepped into the boat, and almost regretted it as the boat pitched beneath him. He sat quickly—a little too quickly, perhaps, but if the boy noticed he gave no sign. As the young man busied himself with the oars, Lukan's eyes moved to the distant lights of the Hand, glimmering in the twilight. *That's the easy part done. Now for the hard part.*

————

The journey to the Ebon Hand should have given Lukan plenty of time to ruminate on the next part of his plan. Instead, he spent most of the time regretting the sea bass and rich white sauce he'd eaten earlier that evening; the sea was restless in the aftermath of the storm, and the choppy waves did their utmost to convince the remnants of the sea bass to attempt a dramatic escape up his throat. He was glad for the brisk wind, and even more so for the gathering darkness, which he hoped masked his discomfort. Not that the boy was watching him anyway. The youth—when he wasn't glancing over his own shoulder to check their direction— had spent the entire trip staring at the floor of the boat, his soft grunts of exertion a counterpoint to the murmur of the sea.

Still, Lukan was relieved when the dark mass of the Ebon Hand loomed above them, blotting out the stars. *Those upper rooms must have quite the view.* Not that any of the prisoners held there ever got to enjoy it—according to Juro, they were all held in cells in the Hand's lower levels below the waterline. *Did you ever see this, Father?* he wondered, staring up at the Phaeron structure. *No doubt you could tell me how they made a tower rise from the sea.*

"We're here," the youth said, easing their boat alongside the wooden jetty.

"I can see that."

The boy flinched at Lukan's rebuke and busied himself with a rope. Once the boat was secured, Lukan stood, gripping a weathered post to stop himself from tumbling into the water. "My business here should take no more than an hour," he said as he stepped onto the jetty. "Regardless, you will be here when I return. Understand?"

The boy nodded.

Lukan gave him a final glare and strode toward the wooden staircase leading up to the tower's entrance. *When this is all over, I'll slip a few coins into his pocket,* he thought, taking the first creaking step. *If I don't end up in chains.*

The tower entrance turned out to be unguarded, a solitary lantern casting a weak glow across the surface of a door that—like the jetty—clearly wasn't original to the building. The Phaeron, as Lukan's father had told him on several occasions, never worked with iron or wood. *Wonder what happened to the original,* he mused, noting the deep gouges that marred the black material around the entranceway. Most likely it had been lost during the same episode of violence that had blown the top of the tower wide open. He stepped up to the iron-banded oak door and glanced about for a bell or some sort of knocker. Seeing neither, he drew his dagger and rapped its pommel against the wood. He paused, listening. The waves whispered below, but all else was silence. He rapped on the door again, with the same result. *Lady's mercy . . .* He was about to try a third time when a panel slid open and a pair of narrowed eyes peered through.

"What's your business?" a muffled voice demanded.

"I'm . . ." *Sorry,* he was going to say. *An inquisitor wouldn't apologize.* "I'm going to give you one more chance to address me correctly," Lukan replied, tapping the tip of his dagger against the badge pinned to his chest: two crossed silver keys.

The eyes widened at the symbol of the Saphronan Inquisition. "Ah—my apologies, sir. One moment."

The panel snapped shut and Lukan heard the rumbling sound of bolts being drawn back. Then the door was creaking open on hinges that hadn't tasted oil in some time, revealing a man in a constable's uniform.

"Terribly sorry, sir, I—"

"I'm here on important business," Lukan snapped as he strode through into the entrance hall beyond. *And that at least is not a lie.* "The Prime Inquisitor has asked me to interrogate Lady Jelassi. You will escort me to her without further delay."

"Ah, of course, sir," the man replied, pushing the door closed. "Only . . ."

"Only *what*?"

"My apologies sir, but I'll need to fetch the lieutenant—"

"Did you not hear me? I said *without further delay*."

The man paled. "I-I . . ." *Seven shadows, people really are terrified of this uniform.* Lukan scowled as the guard took a steadying breath. "My apologies, sir," he repeated, "but Lieutenant Rafaela was clear that she must be notified of all requests to visit Lady Jelassi and—"

"This is not a *request*," Lukan snapped, "and I don't have time for your insolence." *Nor the need for someone of authority to be breathing down my neck.* "You will escort me to Lady Jelassi this *very* instant, or—"

"Is there a problem?"

Lukan turned, his words dying on his lips as he took in the speaker: a tall woman, her dark hair tied back. The entrance hall echoed to the sound of her footsteps, her measured gait and upright posture radiating authority. *And this will be the lieutenant herself, I'll bet. Shit.*

The guard straightened, his relief evident as he snapped a sharp salute. "Ma'am. This is, ah . . . an inquisitor."

"I can see that."

"He wants to see Lady Jelassi."

"Does he now?" The woman regarded Lukan coolly, her eyes flicking to the silver keys pinned to his chest. "Welcome to the Ebon Hand, Inquisitor . . ."

"Ralis," Lukan said brusquely.

"I am Lieutenant Rafaela." A line creased her brow. "I don't believe we've met."

"We haven't."

"I'm not surprised," the lieutenant continued, eyeing the three keys stitched in silver thread on Lukan's shoulder. "We don't often get inquisitors of your rank visiting us."

Is that a gibe at my status? Lukan wondered. *An insinuation about my purpose here?*

"My superiors are all currently indisposed," he replied, "so it falls to me to question Lady Jelassi."

"You're not from Saphrona," Rafaela observed. "Your accent, your appearance—"

"I'm not sure what business that is of yours," Lukan snapped, feigning anger to cover his growing nerves.

"Forgive me, I'm merely curious. The Inquisition doesn't admit many outsiders to its ranks."

"I have friends in high places. Not least in the Prime Inquisitor's office." Lukan slipped the forged letter from a pocket. He'd been hoping the Scrivener's forgery wouldn't be needed, but he didn't like the line of Rafaela's questioning—nor the fact that she seemed unperturbed by his uniform. "I have an order from Prime Inquisitor Fierro himself," he continued, waving the letter impatiently. "It confirms the purpose of my visit."

The lieutenant took the letter and studied the wax seal, which Juro had claimed was stamped with the Prime Inquisitor's personal emblem. Evidently satisfied, she cracked the seal and unfolded the letter.

Now, Lukan thought, his heart quickening as Rafaela scanned the handwriting, *let's see if the Scrivener's as good a forger as she claims to be.*

"How curious," the lieutenant said eventually, "that the Prime Inquisitor feels the need to question a condemned woman whose guilt has already been proven."

"That is no concern of yours," Lukan replied, scowling to hide his relief.

"No, of course," Rafaela acknowledged, handing the letter back. "Though I would have thought a few questions could wait until morning."

"The Inquisition never sleeps," Lukan replied, repeating the same words that Juro had said to him when he had voiced his own doubt about the timing of the mission. He returned the letter to his pocket. "Now, if you could direct me . . ."

"I will escort you myself. This way." The lieutenant spun on her heel and strode toward a doorway at the end of the hall.

Lady's mercy, Lukan thought, almost giddy with elation. *It worked. Seems the Scrivener knows her business.* Some of his relief must have shown on his face, as he realized the guard was frowning at him. "What in the hells are you looking at?" Lukan barked, causing the man to mutter an apology and busy himself with closing the front door. The sound of the bolts rasping into place echoed after Lukan as he followed Rafaela.

The lieutenant waited for him by the far door, which unlike the front entrance was clearly original to the tower, its bronze surface embossed with the sort of geometric Phaeron designs he used to see on papers spilling over his father's desk. It slid sideways at Rafaela's touch, disappearing into the wall without so much as a whisper. Lukan followed her through into a large, circular stairwell illuminated by lanterns. The wide steps spiraled around a central, open space dominated by a single column, grooves visible in its surface. As Rafaela started downward, Lukan leaned over the balustrade and chanced a quick look up, his eyes following the column as it rose into the darkness of the tower's upper levels. *To what purpose?* Far above he could see a jagged sliver of sky, shining with the light of a single star. *And what in the hells happened here to destroy the entire top of the tower? I'll bet Father would have an idea—*

"First time at the Hand?" Rafaela asked, one eyebrow raised.

Idiot, Lukan thought, furious at allowing himself to become distracted. "Actually, yes," he admitted, seeing little point in lying. "I'd heard tell of the Phaeron ingenuity here, but seeing it with one's own eyes is something else."

"Ingenuity? It's said the Phaeron destroyed themselves."

"Well, yes—"

"Then perhaps they weren't as smart as you think." Rafaela

resumed her descent, the sound of her boots echoing around the stairwell. "This way, Inquisitor."

How Father would have liked you, Lukan thought as he followed. *He always did enjoy explaining to people why they were wrong, especially when it came to the Phaeron.* In truth, he was rather starting to like Rafaela himself—particularly for her uniform, which was tight-fitting in all the right places—*Enough,* he thought, forcing himself to look away.

The air grew colder as they descended, the smooth black steps reflecting the light of the lanterns that lit the way. *We must be beneath sea level now,* Lukan thought, as they passed the bronze door to the first lower level. The thought of the dark, impenetrable water pressing against the tower from all sides left him feeling uneasy. He looked for signs of the sea forcing its way through, but saw nothing—not the merest trickle of water on the walls, which left him wondering how the Phaeron had built the tower in the first place—and why. *Circles within circles,* as his father had once said of the long-vanished race. *Mysteries within mysteries.*

A shout cut through his thoughts: a bellow of rage that echoed up the stairwell from the entrance to the second lower level. More shouts followed as another voice joined the first, the words growing clearer as they approached.

". . . off me! Bastard—"

". . . cuffs, get the cuffs . . ."

". . . kill you, I swear!"

". . . hold him still, damn it!"

Rafaela didn't so much as glance at the open doorway as she strode past, but Lukan caught a glimpse of the scene beyond: two figures—one in chains—struggling in the flickering light, while a third raised a club, a snarl of intent on his lips, eyes limned in shadow. He didn't see the moment of impact, but heard the crack of polished wood against skull, the prisoner's furious threats instantly silenced.

"Damned fool . . ."

"I *told* you those cuffs were falling apart—"

"Just bloody get him up . . ."

The guards' voices faded as Lukan followed the lieutenant down the stairwell, though the sound of the club's impact echoed in his mind. No doubt he could look forward to similar treatment if this ruse went wrong—and it *could* still go wrong, he had no doubt about that. *The show's not over 'til the curtain falls,* as they said back in Parva. *Then again, if this all goes to shit, being roughed up by a couple of guards will be the least of my worries.*

As they approached the entrance to the third lower level, the answer to Lukan's question as to the column's purpose slowly came into view: a large bronze disc, seven or eight yards in diameter. Geometric designs covered its surface, radiating out from where the column passed through a hole at its center. *A platform,* Lukan realized, *that must have once traveled up and down. A means of transportation.* He glanced around for a sign of the mechanism that would have propelled the disc, but saw nothing. *Another secret the Phaeron took to their graves.*

"Here we are," Rafaela announced as they reached the entrance to the third lower level. She touched the door, which slid soundlessly open to reveal a sparsely furnished chamber dimly illuminated by a couple of lanterns. Darkened corridors stretched away into shadow on all sides of the room. Two guards sat at a table, rolling dice, cigarillos dangling from their lips. Only one of them bothered to glance up as Rafaela entered.

"Open Lady Jelassi's cell," the lieutenant ordered. "She has a visitor."

"At this time of night?" the man replied, a scowl creasing his rough features. "Bit bloody late, isn't . . ." His complaint shriveled on his tongue when he saw Lukan standing in the doorway. "Ah, of course," he spluttered, rising from his chair and stubbing his cigarillo out. The other guard finally looked up, and her eyes widened at the silver keys on Lukan's chest. She scrambled to her feet and gave a ragged salute. Lukan glared at her until her gaze dropped to the floor.

"Please," the first guard said, snatching up a lantern. "This way."

As they followed him down one of the corridors, Lukan realized it wasn't original to the tower; the walls were made of limestone, and the doors they passed were oak banded with iron. Whatever purpose this part of the tower once had, the Inquisition had refitted it to serve their purpose.

"This is the one," the guard said, fumbling with a set of keys. His hand shook as he unlocked the door and stepped aside. Lukan looked through the grille and saw nothing but darkness beyond.

"Leave the light," he said, without so much as a glance at the guard. The man hung the lantern on a hook by the door, bobbed his head, and retreated back down the corridor. *Now I just need to get rid of Rafaela.* "The questions I need to ask Lady Jelassi," he said in a low voice, "are for my and her ears only."

To his relief, the lieutenant offered no resistance. "Understood," she replied. "I'll wait for you by the stairwell."

"This might be a long conversation."

"All the more time for me to discipline these two idiots." Rafaela nodded in the direction of the two guards, who were sitting at the table in sullen silence.

"Very well," Lukan replied, seeing little point in pushing the issue further. He watched as the lieutenant returned to her subordinates and began giving them a tongue-lashing. As her reprimands echoed off the walls, he turned back to the door before him, his heart racing now that the moment had finally arrived. *Am I about to meet my father's murderer? Or someone else entirely?*

He unhooked the lantern, took a deep breath, and pushed the door open.

16

REVELATIONS IN THE DARK

The tang of old sweat and stale piss stung Lukan's nostrils as he stepped into the cell. Darkness seethed beyond the weak glow of his lantern, pressing against him, as if given weight by the misery and despair of the countless prisoners who had spent their final hours here, locked away in blackness beneath the sea. When he raised his lantern, the light failed to penetrate the far reaches of the cell, and as he gazed into the darkness Lukan couldn't help but feel that it stared back. *Don't be a bloody fool—*

"Are you going to come in, or just stand there and admire the view?"

Lukan flinched at the voice, too loud in the silence. *Clearly this place hasn't broken her. Yet.* Still, that wasn't surprising—he hadn't forgotten the way Zandrusa had stared, unflinching, into the gaping maw of the worm in the Bone Pit. *A woman as brave as that isn't going to be afraid of the dark.*

Whatever the merchant prince's role in his father's murder—if she had any at all—Lukan couldn't help but feel a grudging respect for her. *Let's see if she deserves it.*

He closed the cell door and stepped forward, the light from his lantern forcing the inky blackness into a grudging retreat, revealing the cell's far wall—and the figure sitting against it, legs crossed, manacled wrists resting on her knees. Zandrusa blinked against the light, jaw clenched with the same defiance that she had shown in the Bone Pit. She was an attractive woman, he realized, with high cheekbones and full lips that curled in derision as she watched him set down the lantern.

"Had a feeling I'd be seeing you lot again," she said. Her voice was cracked and hoarse, yet still sharpened by contempt. "What's the matter, can't let an innocent woman die in peace?"

"I would prefer you not to die at all," Lukan replied, squatting before her. "Well, at least not until you've told me what I need to know."

Zandrusa's laugh was little more than a rasp. "How many times," she said, shaking her shaven head, "are you going to make me relive that night? I have nothing to say beyond what I've said already—I didn't kill Lord Saviola, I don't know who did, and I don't care if you think—"

"I'm not interested in who killed Lord Saviola."

That gave the merchant prince pause.

"Then what do you want?"

"Information," Lukan replied, setting down the lantern. "Answers that only you can give me."

Zandrusa's eyes narrowed, a line creasing her brow.

"I saw a lot of faces during my trial, if you can even call that farce by such a name," she said slowly. "But I don't recognize yours."

"That's because we've never met."

"So why are you here now? Who are you?"

"The Scrivener sends her regards." Lukan reached into his coat and pulled out the small clay jar, placing it on the floor. The merchant prince's eyes flicked to the jar and back to Lukan, a gleam of hope in them that hadn't been there moments before.

"The Scrivener," she breathed, smiling faintly. "Now that's a name I never thought I'd hear again. And I believed all my friends had abandoned me." A chuckle escaped her cracked lips. "Are you one of her men?"

"I'm my own man."

"There's a lot to be said for that. What's this?" She gestured at the clay jar, chains clinking.

"I don't know, but I'm told you should apply it to your skin before your next appearance in the Bone Pit."

"Gods within," Zandrusa murmured, leaning forward and

squinting at the jar. "If this is what I think it is . . ." She trailed
off, eyes flicking back to Lukan. "Why is the seal broken?"

"Because I broke it." Lukan shrugged. "Professional curiosity,
I'm afraid. Gets me into all sorts of trouble."

"What's inside—is it a fine white powder?"

Now it was Lukan's turn to frown.

"That's right. How did you—"

"Does it smell like a week-old corpse that's been left to dry in
the sun?"

"Something like that."

Zandrusa sat back, exhaled a slow breath. "I'll be damned. I
heard such a thing existed, but I didn't dare to think . . ."

"You know what it is?"

"An alchemical mixture," the merchant prince replied, her
gaze not leaving the pot, as if she was worried it might disappear
if she looked away. "It's made from several rare ingredients, not
least the powdered bone of a dragon eel. When applied to one's
skin, it's said to be effective at repelling certain large creatures
that might like to eat you."

"Like the worm in the Bone Pit," Lukan said, nodding in
understanding.

"Exactly," Zandrusa murmured, a sudden distance in her gaze,
as if she was recalling Gargantua rearing before her, teeth-lined
maw stretching wide. "So the Scrivener obtained the powder," she
said, eyes snapping back to Lukan, "but she had no way of getting it to me, so she asked you to smuggle it into the Hand—am
I right?"

"Told me, more like."

"And was the inquisitor disguise her idea as well?"

"Of course."

Zandrusa grunted a laugh. "It's a dangerous thing, bluffing
your way into a place like this. I hope the Scrivener's paying you
well."

"She's not paying me a single copper. Smuggling the powder to
you was her price for helping me get inside the Ebon Hand."

"Oh? To what purpose, may I ask?"

"To speak with you."

Zandrusa tilted her head, as if seeing Lukan for the first time. "I was a smuggler once," she said eventually. "Did the Scrivener tell you that?"

Lukan nodded. "She said you were one of the best."

"I was *the* best. You won't get any false modesty from me. You know what my talent was? I could read people like a book—I knew what they wanted before they even opened their mouths. And I knew what they would pay." She leaned forward. "You are going to ask me a question, maybe several questions, and if I don't give you an answer you like, then you're going to leave and take that jar with you. Is that right?"

"It is," Lukan admitted. *But if you murdered my father I won't feel a trace of guilt.*

"Then ask your questions. Though perhaps first you'd do me the favor of telling me who you are."

"You don't know me, but I'm willing to bet you know my father."

"Perhaps. I know lots of people. What's his name?"

"Conrad Gardova."

Zandrusa's lips parted slightly, her only concession to surprise. "Hold the lantern higher."

Lukan did as he was bid.

"Asheru's grace," the woman breathed, eyes widening. "I see it now—the nose, the curve of the jaw . . . you look just like him."

"So people tell me. An irony, really, since that's where the similarity ends."

"Conrad used to mention you," the merchant prince continued, unheeding of the bitterness in Lukan's tone. "Luther, is it? Or Lucas . . ."

"Lukan."

"Ah, yes!" The woman's brow furrowed, confusion replacing her enthusiasm. "But what are you doing here, Lukan? And how is Conrad?"

"He's dead."

Zandrusa bowed her head. "I'm truly sorry to hear that."

"Are you?"

The merchant prince looked up sharply. "Of course I am—your father and I were friends, we went way back. Did he never mention me to you?"

"No, but then he rarely talked to me at all."

"Oh? I'm surprised. He spoke well of you in his letters."

"What letters?" Lukan asked, trying to mask his surprise. "Why was my father writing to you?"

"As I said, we were friends."

"You were close?"

"Yes."

"How close?"

"We were friends," Zandrusa said firmly, sensing the direction of Lukan's thoughts. "Nothing more, nothing less."

"I wasn't aware my father had any."

"Oh, he did, though I understand why you might think that. Conrad was always something of a lone wolf, pursuing his theories about the Phaeron. He was quite obsessed. He'd often speak at length about them—what he thought they were like, what fate he thought may have befallen them . . ."

"I'm sorry you had to listen to all that," Lukan said dryly.

"Oh, I found it fascinating. Some of his theories were remarkable."

"The Academy of Parva didn't see it that way."

"Indeed. I recall Conrad's frustration that they wouldn't acknowledge his work."

"Sometimes I think it was less about his theories and more about him. My father was . . ."

"Not the easiest person to get along with?" Zandrusa offered, one side of her mouth curling in a half smile.

"That's putting it mildly."

"Conrad was driven. People like that can often be hard to reach. To unravel. And he could be difficult at times, I know. Obtuse, stubborn—"

"You *did* know him."

"—but beneath all that he was a good man. And he may not have had many friends, but those he did have would have done anything for him." Her gaze became distant. "I would have."

"Why? How did you know my father?"

Zandrusa blinked, as if jolted from a memory. "That story will have to wait for another time. Please, tell me—how did Conrad die?"

"He was murdered."

"Murdered? By whom?"

"I was hoping you might be able to tell me that."

"Me? I didn't even know he was dead." The merchant prince peered at him curiously. "If you didn't even know of my link to your father, why have you sought me out?"

"Because," Lukan said, withdrawing the creased note from his pocket, "he wrote your name while he was bleeding to death." He unfolded the paper and passed it to Zandrusa, who squinted at the bloody script.

"He wrote this in his own blood?" The merchant prince shook her head, lowered the note. "Gods within. What happened?"

Lukan stared at her, searching for any sign of deception or guilt. He saw nothing. *Still, the woman used to be a smuggler. Deception must come naturally to her.* "I don't know," he replied. "Shafia—my father's steward—found his body in his study, clutching this note. He'd been stabbed. More than once. The place had been turned upside down."

"I am so sorry, Lukan." Zandrusa folded the note and handed it back. "Please believe me when I say that. And I understand why you think I may have been involved in his death, but all I ever had was the greatest affection for your father. I played no part in any of this."

"Why should I believe you?"

"Because why would I deny it if I had?" The merchant prince's chains clinked as she shrugged. "You've come here prepared to kill me, and from where I'm sitting a steel blade in the throat is a more attractive proposition than facing that monstrosity in the Bone Pit again." She leaned forward, her voice softening. "*Think*, Lukan. Your father used to speak of your agile mind. I suggest you use it now."

Lukan blinked, caught off guard. "He told you that? In his letters?"

Zandrusa nodded. "Don't get me wrong; Conrad mostly wrote of his research and whatever was obsessing him at that moment in time. But he mentioned you now and again, and his words were always warm. He was proud of you, Lukan."

"I . . ." Lukan hesitated, unable to find the words—not even sure what he was supposed to feel. "We didn't have the best of relationships," he said eventually. "Especially in the last few years we were together."

"Yes, Conrad mentioned that. It pained him greatly."

"It did? But he never . . ."

"Spoke to you about it?"

"No."

Zandrusa sighed. "Your father was a brilliant man. But I'm not sure fatherhood ever came easily to him."

"That is something we can agree on."

"It's such a shame we couldn't have met under different circumstances," the woman continued, smiling ruefully. "I still have all his letters. I would have been happy to show you." She raised her manacled hands. "Sadly I'm indisposed."

Lukan nodded, a sense of frustration stealing over him. He'd been hoping for closure of some kind, not a dead end. *There's got to be more to this.* "What I don't understand," he said, returning the note to his pocket, "is why my father was thinking of you just before he died. Why did he write *your* name? Why did he want me to find you?"

"Ah, well that I *can* explain. When I last saw Conrad, many years ago now, he gave me a small casket and asked me to look after it. He said that one day you might come looking for me, and that if you did I was to give it to you."

Lukan stared at her, dumbfounded.

"A casket?" he managed eventually. "What sort of casket?"

"A Phaeron casket. Don't ask me what's inside, because I don't know. It will only open for you, or so your father told me. Which is why I've kept it safe, all these years."

"Where is this casket now?"

"In my private vault at the Three Moons Counting House, where it will remain until my death. Once I'm literally in the belly of the beast, who can say? No doubt all my wealth and assets will be seized by my former associates on the Gilded Council." She shook her head. "Bloody vultures."

"Is there any way I could access your vault?"

"None. Only the owner of a vault is permitted entry."

"Then could we forge some sort of document? A letter of authorization or something?"

"Good idea, but it won't work."

"Why not?"

"The bank will only grant access to authorized associates of the vault's owner in the event of the owner's death." Zandrusa forced a grim smile. "As you can see, I'm not dead yet."

"So there's no way I can gain access to the casket?"

"Not with me in chains."

"Is there a chance the Inquisition might repeal your sentence?"

"None. I was interrogated by Prime Inquisitor Fierro himself, and that cold-eyed bastard was clearly convinced of my guilt."

"And are you? Guilty, I mean."

Lukan almost flinched at the fury shining in the woman's eyes as she glared at him.

"Of course not," she snapped. "Emilio—Lord Saviola—was a good friend of mine, and my main ally on the Gilded Council. We shared similar interests and held the same values. He was one of the few decent men in a nest of vipers. Why in Asheru's name would I wish him harm?"

"I was told you were found standing over his body, bloodied blade in hand."

Zandrusa sat back, a great sigh escaping her lips. "Yes, that much is true. We had dinner together at Emilio's villa and then spent the evening discussing policy. I went to the privy and came back to find him on the floor with a blade in his throat. There was nothing I could do—he was already dead. I pulled the blade out and of course that was when Emilio's steward walked in with refreshments. The man always did have a poor sense of timing."

"He called the guards?"

"Of course he did. Can't say I blame him either, I know what it looked like. But I didn't kill Lord Saviola, understand? I wasn't gone long, the privy was just down the hall. Emilio was alive when I left, dead when I returned. And I didn't hear a thing. Not a whisper."

"Do you have any idea who the murderer is?"

"Not a clue—no common thug, that's for sure. This was the work of an expert. But I *do* have an idea who paid them."

"And who's that?"

"Lord Murillo," Zandrusa replied, lips twisting with distaste. "Another merchant prince, one of the most powerful on the Gilded Council. I'll bet that snake is behind all this. He hates me almost as much as he loves coin."

"So you think he framed you? Why?"

"Because I represent everything he despises, everything he's afraid of. I'm a Zar-Ghosan commoner who made a fortune and rose to power, and I want to use my influence to help others do the same."

"And Murillo doesn't like that."

"Damned right he doesn't. Murillo is the head of an old, prestigious family—'old blood, old money,' as the saying goes. He owns several silver mines outside the city and treats his workers like animals, just as his forebears have done for generations. They toil in the darkness for a pittance while he grows rich from their suffering. My legislation will change all that—and Murillo despises me for it."

"Because it'll put a dent in his profit margins?"

"Oh, this is about far more than money," Zandrusa continued, her voice rising with a sudden fervor. "This is about improving the lives of thousands of Saphronans and giving them a voice where they previously had none. It's about changing the very fabric of our society to make it fairer—changing the balance of power in this city so it's no longer solely in the hands of the Gilded Council."

"A noble goal," Lukan acknowledged, "especially given you're part of that same council."

"The Gilded Council's purpose should be to improve the lives of Saphrona's citizens, not to line the pockets of its wealthiest members."

"Is that why you went straight, all those years ago? Why you gave up smuggling for politics?"

"I figured the easiest way, perhaps the *only* way, to realize my vision for Saphrona was to join the Gilded Council and try to effect change from the inside. It took me a long time, but eventually I managed to acquire the necessary wealth and reputation one needs to join that pit of snakes." She smiled ruefully. "I was the first Zar-Ghosan merchant prince. An achievement I wish I'd had more time to savor, but there was too much work to be done."

"How did the other merchant princes react to you joining the council?"

"There was some grumbling from Murillo and the older families. I even caught wind of a campaign to try to have me discredited, but it came to nothing—I'd hidden my smuggling past too well. But most of the other princes accepted me, however grudgingly, because ultimately they respect coin more than anything else—and I had a lot of it."

"Coin is the only true god in Saphrona," Lukan recited, recalling Velleras Gellame's words.

"It is," Zandrusa agreed. "Which is both a blessing and a curse."

"So Murillo has Lord Saviola executed and pins the blame on

you," Lukan mused. "You must have really put his nose out of joint."

"We had him and his allies running scared," Zandrusa replied, clenching a fist in frustration. "What you must understand is that the council is split into two factions: Murillo and his fellow Old Bloods, who inherited their wealth, and the New Bloods—the newer princes like me who made their own fortunes. The Old Bloods might wield more influence, but the New Bloods are more numerous—and many of them supported my plans. We managed to force a vote on a crucial piece of legislation that would pave the way for serious reform. That's why I was with Emilio that night, to talk strategy. And then of course he was . . ." She sighed, shook her head. "We were so close."

"Close enough for Murillo to decide that he needed to take drastic action?"

"The council was going to vote, and Murillo knew it was going to be tight—that the life of immense privilege and power he and his fellow Old Bloods took for granted was under serious threat. So he took matters into his own hands and figured he'd kill two birds with one stone. With Lord Saviola dead and me in chains, the legislation—everything we fought for—is in ruins. The vote will never pass, if it's even held in the first place. And Murillo and his Old Blood allies cling on to their wealth and power."

"There must be a way to prove that Murillo is behind all this," Lukan said. "To prove that you're innocent."

"There isn't. There's not a lick of evidence." Zandrusa held up her hands, rattling her chains. "Which is why I'm wearing these."

"There must be something we can do."

"I appreciate the thought, Lukan. Truly. But you've risked enough already. Please, go with my blessing."

"And leave you here, chained to a wall in the dark for a crime you didn't commit?" Lukan shook his head. "No, I'll not abandon you—not when you were my father's friend. Besides, if you were as close to the old man as you claim, he'll probably come back and haunt me if I left you here to rot. And that's the last damned thing I need."

"Lukan—"

"One good turn deserves another," he continued firmly. "You've dedicated your life to helping others. Now let me help you."

"You don't need to do this."

"Yes, I do. For your sake, and for my father's—and for mine, because I want that Phaeron casket my father left for me, and it seems getting you out of here is the only way I'll get my hands on it. I didn't come all this way to Saphrona to leave empty-handed."

"There's no way out of this for me," Zandrusa said, clasping her hands. "I appreciate your concern for me, Lukan, but there's nothing you can do."

"There's got to be some sort of evidence. Something we can use."

"Well, there is one thing," the woman admitted. "A strange detail that I can't explain. I mentioned it to the Inquisition when they interrogated me, but I doubt they followed it up."

"Go on."

"When I found Lord Saviola's body, there was frost on his clothes. *Frost*, for pity's sake!" Zandrusa shook her head. "It was then that I realized how cold the room was—it felt like an icehouse. Yet the windows were open and outside it was a warm summer's evening. It just doesn't make sense." The merchant prince shrugged. "I know it's not much."

"It's a start," Lukan said firmly, masking his doubt. "Though I don't know where to begin."

"Talk to Doctor Vassilis—he was Lord Saviola's physician and attended to his body. Perhaps he saw the frost too, or felt the cold. He might be able to help."

"Where can I find him?"

"He lectures at the Collegium."

"Then I'll seek him there."

"You'll really do this for me?" Zandrusa asked, a note of doubt in her voice as if she didn't dare to hope. "You'll try to clear my name?"

"My father trusted you," Lukan replied. "And I won't abandon one of his friends in their hour of need." He smiled wryly. "Besides, I want that casket he gave you."

"And you'll have it," Zandrusa promised, "the very moment I'm free of these chains." She smiled, nodding to herself. "You really are Conrad's son. I see now why your father was so proud of you—"

"Quiet," Lukan cut in, raising his hand and turning toward the door. Distant footsteps sounded beyond. "Someone's coming."

"Here," Zandrusa whispered, "take this." She pulled a gold and ruby ring from her left hand and tossed it to him. "Speak to my steward," she continued. "He'll be at my villa. Magellis will do whatever he can to help, you can trust him. Now go."

A sharp rap sounded against the cell door.

"Everything all right in there, Inquisitor?" Rafaela's voice called through the grille.

Lukan was tempted to tell her to leave him alone, to give him more time. The merchant prince had already revealed things about his father that he would never have suspected, and it surprised him now how desperate he was to learn what more the woman could tell him. *Father was proud of me.* That revelation still stunned him. *I had no idea.*

Another sharp rap jolted him from his thoughts.

"Inquisitor? Do you need any—"

"I'm nearly done, Lieutenant," he called back, deciding he'd pushed his luck far enough for one night. "Please await me in the antechamber." Rafaela's footsteps moved back down the corridor. "I wish we could talk more," he said to Zandrusa. "There're so many things I want to ask you."

"We'll speak again," the merchant prince replied. "Of this I'm sure. And when we do, I'll tell you whatever you want to know."

"I'll hold you to that." Lukan picked up the clay jar and handed it to her. "Hopefully you won't need this."

"Hopefully not," she agreed, pulling a face. "I'll never get rid of the damned smell." She concealed the jar beneath her rags. "Now go. And Lukan?"

"What?"

"Be careful."

"I'll do my best." He snatched up the lantern and returned to the door, leaving Zandrusa in darkness. "Lieutenant," he called through the grille. "Attend me." When he heard Rafaela's footsteps approaching, he cleared his throat and said loudly, "You're a traitor and a murderer, Lady Jelassi. I hope Gargantua takes her time with you. It's the least you deserve."

"Begone, Inquisitor," the merchant prince called back, a convincing dose of venom in her voice. "Your very presence offends me."

Lukan grinned and pushed the door open, stepping through without a backward glance. Rafaela was waiting for him in the corridor.

"Did you get what you needed, Inquisitor?" she asked, closing the door and sliding a key into the lock.

"Not exactly," he replied, not needing to lie. "Though Lady Jelassi did reveal some intriguing information. It's given me much to think on." *And a whole load of new problems.*

17

BETWEEN BLADE
AND BOUDOIR

Lukan was ten steps away from freedom when his luck finally ran out.

The guard at the tower's entrance had already seen them coming and was busy drawing back the bolts on the great oaken door. Rafaela was saying something to Lukan but he was barely listening; instead he watched as the door opened to reveal the distant glimmer of the city's lights away across the water. *Almost there.* He could feel the coolness of the night's breeze on his skin, the taste of success on his lips—

"Inquisitor!" a reedy voice called from behind them. "Please—a moment of your time, sir!"

Not a chance, Lukan thought, not even turning round.

"My thanks for your assistance," he said to Rafaela, quickening his pace. "I'll see myself out." Head down, he strode for the door. *Just a few more steps . . .*

"Inquisitor, please!" the voice called again, breathless. "The captain of the Hand . . . would have a word with you."

Shit. Lukan hesitated in the doorway, his gaze traveling down to the wooden jetty, where he could see the shape of the boat and the boy's hunched figure within. *I could make a run for it . . .*

Yet the moment had already passed; he could sense Rafaela just behind him, could hear the echo of approaching footsteps. *So close.* He tightened his fist. *So bloody close.*

Lukan turned and glared at the grey-haired man hobbling toward him. *Not the captain,* he realized, noting the man's lack of uniform. *Must be his servant.* The newcomer wore a frilly shirt and faded waistcoat, both of which seemed out of place in the Hand's austere surroundings, while his face bore the lines of someone who had spent a lifetime faking smiles.

"What is it, Haspar?" Rafaela asked.

"Lieutenant," the man croaked, breath rattling in his throat. "Inquisitor." He bowed as deeply as he was able, straightening with visible effort. Lukan felt a twinge of sympathy but kept his expression firm as stone.

"What can I do for you?" Lukan snapped, making it clear he'd prefer to do nothing at all. The man offered an apologetic smile, though he seemed entirely unfazed by Lukan's tone. *No doubt he's suffered worse.*

"My profound apologies, sir," the servant said, struggling to catch his breath. "I understand you're keen to return to the city, but . . . Captain Varga wishes to speak to you on a matter of . . . some urgency."

Lady's blood. Lukan's instinct was to refuse, to mutter something about pressing duty and leave without a backward glance. Instead he hesitated, his mind racing. What was the etiquette here? Did the captain of the Hand hold more influence than a mid-ranking inquisitor? Refusing a request from a superior would be the quickest way to blow his cover, but no more so than meeting with someone who might easily see through his disguise. *Shit. Damned if I do, screwed sideways if I don't . . .*

The moment stretched. He became aware of Rafaela's gaze, the earlier spark of curiosity rekindling in her narrowed eyes.

"Sir?" the servant prompted. "Are you well? You look troubled."

"I'm fine," Lukan muttered, annoyed at letting his uncertainty show. "I suppose I can spare a moment for the captain," he continued, hoping his show of grudging acquiescence was appropriate. Judging by the flicker of relief on the old man's face, he'd hit just the right note.

"Very good, sir. If you would follow me, please?" The old man turned and shambled off toward the stairwell.

"Decent of you to see the captain," Rafaela said, raising an eyebrow. "None of your colleagues ever seem to have the time. Or inclination."

Shit. Lukan bit his tongue to mask his frustration at misreading the situation. *I could have just walked out—just smirked at the captain's request and strolled out of the Hand, and nobody would have so much as blinked.* The knowledge sat in his stomach like a lead weight. Still, it was too late now. *Just got to run with this and see how it plays out.* To do anything else would merely arouse Rafaela's suspicion.

"Don't presume to question my intent," Lukan replied, attempting to claw back a little authority.

"Oh, I wouldn't dream of it." The lieutenant turned to the guardsman, who was standing nearby, pretending not to hear their conversation. "Close the door. The inquisitor isn't leaving just yet."

If this goes badly I won't be leaving at all, Lukan thought as he set off after the old man.

For the second time that night, the tower's main door boomed closed behind him.

———

Captain Varga's quarters comprised the entire fifth floor of the Ebon Hand, and were adorned in the manner of a man who, having found himself in charge of a tower full of rapists and murderers, had decided to try and make the best of things. *And he clearly has the coin to do so,* Lukan noted as he followed Haspar through the doorway. An elaborate chandelier hung from the low ceiling, light from its two dozen candles illuminating plush rugs, fine tapestries, and bookcases lined with leather-bound volumes. The farther reaches of the room extended away into shadow, though as Lukan glanced around he glimpsed the outline of a four-poster bed and a large bathtub. *Varga's clearly a man who doesn't believe in half measures. When it comes to his own luxury, at least.*

The captain himself sat behind a white desk of polished winter-wood facing the door, the distant lights of Saphrona visible through the large arched windows behind him. He was making a show of reading a letter as they approached, though Lukan was willing to bet he'd snatched it up when he'd heard Haspar's rap on the door. *That glass of red wine would certainly suggest his attention was elsewhere.* For someone holding a position of no little authority, Captain Varga was decidedly unimpressive. His soft, round face gleamed with sweat and his weak chin had a dimple that made it look like an arse. *Hardly the sort of man you'd expect to find in charge of dangerous criminals.* Then again, Saphrona was a city where everything had a price. *I'll bet he comes from money and bought his commission. No way he could afford all this expensive shit on a captain's salary.*

"My lord," the old servant wheezed, using an honorific that the captain was almost certainly not entitled to, "I am most pleased to introduce our guest, Inquisitor . . . ah . . ."

"Ralis," Lukan said evenly, attempting to spare the man's blushes. *Lady knows he's suffered enough already with that flight of stairs.* Haspar's knees had creaked and popped with every step of the climb to the fifth floor.

"Indeed," the servant continued, nodding as if he'd known all along. "Inquisitor Ralis. Ah, here to speak with you, my lord."

"I can see that, Haspar," the captain replied primly, shooting the old man a look of disapproval. "That will be all."

"Yes, my lord."

"Actually, wait," the captain said, tossing down his letter, which Lukan noted he'd been holding upside down. "Bring some tea," the man commanded. "And cakes—those lemon ones with the powdery sugar."

Lady's mercy, Lukan thought, as Haspar bowed and hurried away. *Seems the good captain pays more attention to his food than his work.* He found himself liking the man less with every passing moment, though he was careful to keep his expression impassive. *Just listen to what he has to say, flatter his ego if necessary. Whatever it takes to get the hells out of here.*

"Inquisitor Ralis, welcome!" The captain rose from his chair, revealing a belly that strained against his belt. "I am Captain Varga. You do me a great honor," he continued as he rounded the desk, his demeanor far brighter now that he was talking to someone he considered of similar social standing. "It thrills me to meet an inquisitor of the"—his eyes flicked to the three silver keys on Lukan's right shoulder—"*third* rank . . ." His mouth twitched, as if he was concealing disappointment, but he extended his hand nonetheless. "The pleasure is all mine."

You can say that again. Lukan waited for a few heartbeats—just long enough to make the captain uncomfortable—before shaking his hand, squeezing the man's limp, clammy fingers with a little more force than was necessary. *Just to remind him of who he's dealing with—or thinks he's dealing with.*

The captain's smile seemed pained as he withdrew his arm and gestured at a couple of leather armchairs. "Please, take a seat."

"I'd rather stand."

"Oh . . . of course." The man massaged his hand. "Ah . . ."

Best not to make this any more awkward than it is already. "On second thoughts," Lukan said, "it *has* been a long day." He sat down on one of the armchairs, positioning himself on the edge of the cushion. *Best not get too comfortable.*

"Oh, I can imagine," Varga replied, his relief obvious as he sank into the opposite chair. "I trust you found everything here to your satisfaction? I assure you, Inquisitor, I run a tight ship. Lady Midnight herself couldn't slip past my notice."

Lady Midnight. Flea's hero. And someone I doubt the Inquisition would hold in high regard. "You believe that nonsense?" he asked, eyeing the man coldly. "A thief who can evade any guard and pick any lock? Who can walk through walls?"

"Of course not," the captain said, with a furious shake of his head. "It's mere rumor, of course. She's nothing more than a myth."

"Indeed." *Though I'm sure Flea would argue otherwise.*

"Did you get what you needed from Lady Jelassi?" Varga continued, eager to change the subject.

"I can't talk about Inquisition matters."

"No, of course not." The captain gave a nervous chuckle, waving away his own question. "I must say, though, I don't envy you having to spend time down there with that awful woman. Terrible, terrible business. It was Inquisitor Lucidus who interrogated her last time, though sadly he didn't have time for a chat. Always busy, that man. Are you acquainted?"

"Of course," Lukan replied smoothly. "Though I don't know him well. He's always busy, as you say."

"Indeed. Still, I have a couple of friends in your noble institution—both important figures of high rank. They've already filled me in on the details of Lady Jelassi's awful crimes."

"Is that so?"

"Oh, yes." Varga smirked, evidently pleased with himself. "And the story they told . . ." He tutted as he shook his head. "Dreadful! Simply dreadful."

"And what did they say, exactly?"

"Ah, well . . ." Varga swallowed nervously, as if realizing he might have landed his friends—*if that's what they truly are*—in trouble. "Nothing much, I assure you." He forced another chuckle. "Just that the servants walked in to find Lady Jelassi stabbing Lord Saviola over and over again, screaming at the top of her lungs like a madwoman." He gave an apologetic shrug. "You know the story, of course."

"I do." *And Zandrusa tells a very different version than you.* "Perhaps," Lukan continued, glancing meaningfully at the clock standing on a nearby shelf, "we could move on to the matter at hand?" *Whatever the hells it might be.*

"Oh, of course. Yes, well . . . I, um. I was hoping . . . That is to say—"

"Lady's mercy, out with it man," Lukan snapped, not needing to feign his irritation.

"I was hoping for . . ." Varga winced. "A favor."

"A favor."

"Yes. Not for me, as such." He laughed, as if such a notion had never crossed his mind, let alone his lips. "It's for my nephew, Perras. Wonderful boy, very bright. He's . . . well, he *was* at the Collegium reading natural philosophy. Unfortunately there's been a terrible misunderstanding that has led to the suspension of his studies—not that Perras is in any way to blame, of course—"

"Of course," Lukan interjected dryly. "What sort of misunderstanding?"

"A few books went missing from the library," Varga scoffed, waving a hand. "Several rare first editions, or some such. Apparently they're quite valuable, though why anyone would waste good coin on some dusty old books is beyond me."

I'll bet a lot of things are beyond you, Captain. "And Perras was blamed for this theft?"

"The books were found in a sack under his bed. The poor boy swore he had no idea how they got there, but of course the old fools at the Collegium expelled him anyway." Varga shook his head in disgust. "I'm sure you'll agree, Inquisitor, that the evidence is circumstantial at best, and that it's—well, it's practically a crime in itself to ruin a young man's academic career and reputation in such a fashion."

Sounds like the boy made a mistake and got himself kicked out of the Collegium. And isn't that a story I know only too well. "What do you want from me, Captain?"

"Well, I've had a rather good idea."

I'll bet that doesn't happen often. "Go on."

"Perras has a sharp intellect, and would make an excellent inquisitor." Varga beamed and spread his hands. "The Collegium's loss can be the Inquisition's gain!"

Yes, no doubt a dim-witted book thief will make for a fine, upstanding enforcer of the law. "I'll ask again, Captain, what do you want from me?"

"Well," Varga replied, wringing his hands, "I was hoping you might be able to make a recommendation. You know, put in a good word for him."

"A good word."

"Just to help him get a foot on the ladder, so to speak." The man squirmed in his chair. "Is—is that something you might be able to do?"

"Surely these friends you mentioned earlier are better placed to help you?" Lukan fixed the man with a stare. "Your important, high-ranking friends . . ."

"Sadly they're not able to help," Varga admitted with a wince. "Due to, ah, certain complications."

Complications such as not actually existing. "I see."

"I've already written a letter," the captain continued. "It explains all of my nephew's best qualities. If you could simply hand it to your superior, perhaps with a positive word of your own? I'd be willing to pay you for your efforts, of course." The man tittered, as if what he was requesting was a trivial matter and not blatant nepotism with a side order of bribery. "So, um . . . what do you think?"

I think you're a self-serving, useless bastard. Lukan frowned, as if considering the man's offer, when in fact he was considering something entirely different. *Would a real inquisitor be open to such a bribe?* Accepting the man's offer would certainly be the smoothest way out of this situation. *Still, best not look too eager. Captain Varga might have the wits of a slug, but if I give him any reason whatsoever to doubt my identity . . .* "I'm meant to arrest people for taking bribes," Lukan replied evenly. "Not take them myself."

Panic flashed in Varga's eyes.

"Oh, no—you misunderstand me, Inquisitor," he spluttered. "I'm not offering a *bribe*, I'm just, ah . . ."

"Requesting a favor that comes with a promise of payment?"

"Yes! That's exactly it."

"Well," Lukan said, with mock sincerity, "that's completely different."

The captain sagged in relief. "I'm glad we're in agreement."

"We haven't agreed on anything yet. But I'm sure I could deliver this letter of yours—with a positive word or two of my own, of course—for, let's say . . . ten silvers?"

"Done!" Varga cried, holding out his hand.

Lukan ignored it. "Just give me the letter."

"Of course, of course . . ." Varga jumped up and hurried to his desk, where he pulled some papers from a drawer. "It's already written, as I promised." He snatched up a quill and dabbed it in an ink pot. "All I need to do is address it to the appropriate person." He gave Lukan an expectant look, quill poised over the letter.

Shit. "Yes, of course," Lukan replied slowly. "Best address it to . . ." His mind raced, came up blank. "The . . . Prime Inquisitor." *What did Zandrusa say his name was?* "Fierro," he said, masking his relief.

"The Prime Inquisitor?" Varga said, doubt creasing his round face. "Are you quite sure?" He stared at the paper as if it held an answer. "Forgive me, but surely the Prime Inquisitor has enough demands on his time. There must be someone a little lower down the chain of command who would be more appropriate." He brightened. "What about your direct superior—what's their name?"

"Well . . ." Lukan glanced around the room, desperately searching for some sort of inspiration. His gaze swept across a nearby bookshelf, settling on a copy of *Between Blade and Boudoir*—a Talassian bodice ripper that had scandalized Parvan high society for a season or two. He recalled Jaques laughing as he read out choice passages from the book. More importantly, he could still remember the antagonist's name. "Salvio Costanzo," he said with forced confidence, hoping that—like everything else in the captain's room—the books were just for show. *Surely he won't have actually read the damned thing.*

"Salvio Costanzo," the captain echoed, eyes narrowing. "You mean . . . like the villain from that book, what was it called . . ." His eyes flicked to the bookshelves. "Something *Boudoir*?"

Seven hells . . .

"Indeed," Lukan replied quickly. "Such an incredible coincidence—we used to joke that the author had some sort of vendetta against him and used his name on purpose." *Lady's mercy.* Even to his own ears it sounded laughably unconvincing.

"How curious." Varga looked back at the letter, his quill still poised above the paper. Sweat beaded his brow. "I've met many of your fellow inquisitors," he said, looking up at Lukan. "But never one with that name." He swallowed. "And I can't help but wonder . . . well, it's passing strange that I've never met *you* before, Inquisitor Ralis—"

"My apologies, Captain," Lukan said, rising from his chair, "but I really ought to be going—if you wouldn't mind?" He gestured at the letter. *Go on, sign the bloody thing and be done with it.*

"Yes," the captain replied, his uncertainty clear. "Yes of course." He wet his lips as he stared at the letter. Swallowed. Then he began writing the name, quill scratching on the paper.

Lukan glanced away in relief. *Lady's blood, that was too close—*

The captain's pen scritched to a halt.

Lukan's gaze snapped back to the desk.

Captain Varga met his eyes before glancing to a corner of the room, where a rope of red velvet hung from the ceiling.

A bellpull, Lukan realized, heart sinking. *Oh shit . . .*

Captain Varga moved surprisingly quickly for a man who spent his days behind a desk eating cakes, but Lukan was faster. He drew his dagger and vaulted the desk, scattering papers and paraphernalia, grasping Varga by his collar just as the man lunged for the rope. The captain gave a pathetic squeal as Lukan hauled him back and shoved him against the desk.

"That," Lukan hissed, raising his blade, "was a mistake."

"Please," Varga whined, lower lip quivering. "Please . . ." He began to tremble, staring at the tip of the blade as if he'd never seen a knife before. *I'll certainly bet he's never had one this close to his face.* Lukan felt nothing but contempt for the man, who in that moment had been revealed for exactly what he was: a smug coward who had gained his rank not through merit but by greasing the right palms with gold, who had probably never patrolled the city streets once in his life, nor ever drawn his sword—if he even had one—in anger. *Pathetic. No wonder the constabulary stuffed him away here.*

"Wh-what do you want?" Varga stammered.

"What do *I* want?" Lukan replied, pressing the tip of his blade to the man's cheek, causing him to inhale sharply. "I just wanted to leave this bloody tower, which is exactly what I *was* doing until you insisted on your little act of bribery—and look where that's got you."

"Please! Don't hurt me—I'll do anything you ask . . ."

"I'm sure you will—doubt you have the balls for anything else. Now listen, this is how it's going to go—"

A faint knock at the door, gnarled old knuckles on Phaeron metal. *Shit,* Lukan thought, glancing up. *I forgot about . . .*

The door slid soundlessly open to reveal Haspar, a silver tray balanced in one hand. "Tea, my lord," the servant said, stepping into the room, "and those lemon cakes—" He froze, staring at the scene before him, eyes darting from Lukan to the captain, then to the blade between them. The tray rattled as his hands began to shake.

"Haspar," Lukan called, smiling as he lowered his blade. "The captain and I were just having a friendly chat—"

The tray crashed to the floor.

Lukan winced. "There's no need to be alarmed, Haspar—this is . . ."

The old man turned and fled.

". . . almost exactly what it looks like." *Shit.*

"You fool," Varga wheezed, finally locating his spine now that his salvation appeared to be at hand—and Lukan's dagger wasn't poised at his throat. "Did you really think you could get away with this?" His laugh came out as a strained, high-pitched giggle. "Unhand me at once."

"Sure," Lukan replied, releasing his hold on the captain's collar. "Whatever you say." He slammed the pommel of his blade against Varga's skull and the man pitched sideways, collapsing to the floor. Lukan ran to the doorway and peered through, instantly spying Haspar descending as fast as his old bones would allow—the servant was only a few steps below, but his cries for help were already echoing around the stairwell. *Too late.* The guards' mess hall and dormitories were on the third and fourth levels; the doors to both floors had been ajar as Lukan had ascended, and he'd glimpsed plenty of guards in each, enjoying their downtime. *There's no way I'll get past them—and they'll be up here in moments.* He stepped back into the room and touched the edge of the door, which slid shut. *How in the hells do you lock this thing?*

Sadly, the only person who might have told him was lying unconscious in the corner of the room.

Lukan stepped back and studied the door, his heart racing. *There.* An indented panel bearing a Phaeron sigil. Instinctively he pressed a finger to the panel and was rewarded by the sigil glowing with a golden light—once, twice, three times.

Then it faded.

Hopefully that's it, he thought, backing away. *If it's not, well . . . I'll know soon enough.*

Distant shouts rang out, underscored by the echo of boots on steps.

Lukan turned and surveyed the room, fighting his rising panic. *Now what?* He ran toward the arched windows behind the captain's desk, as if the distant, glittering lights of Saphrona offered some sort of sanctuary. One of the windows was on the latch and he pushed it open, the night breeze ruffling his hair as he looked down at the jetty far below. *Too high to jump.* He squinted at the faint outline of his boat, thought he could see a small shadow sitting in it. *The kid's still there. Not that it's much good to me now.*

Damn it. Lukan slammed a fist on the windowsill and turned back to the room. *Think,* he willed himself, his gaze passing over the chairs, the shelves, the tapestries. *There's got to be a way out of this.*

"Open up," a muffled voice bellowed, followed by something crashing against the door.

Lukan snatched up a candle from Varga's desk and ran into the unlit depths of the room, the candle's weak light revealing the four-poster bed with its silken sheets, the copper bathtub . . . and another window. It was smaller than the window on the adjacent side of the room, but still big enough for Lukan's needs. He flung it open and stared out at the expanse of dark sky and darker ocean. It was almost impossible to tell where one ended and the other began. He glanced down at the inky blackness of the water and almost felt as if it was staring back, waiting to take him in its cold, crushing embrace. *Lady's blood,* he thought, *that's got to be a fifty-foot drop. Maybe more.*

Fear squirmed in his gut. *I can't do it.*

Another crash at the door told him he had no choice.

Lukan scrambled up onto the narrow windowsill, his heart lurching as if only now realizing what his mind had already accepted. He braced himself against the frame, thoughts as dark as the sea below flitting through his mind: his legs breaking on impact, the cold water spilling into his lungs, lion sharks dragging his broken body into the midnight depths . . . *Enough.* Terrifying as the prospect was, it was still better than the alternative: interrogation and torture, then imprisonment followed by visits to the Bone Pit until he eventually found himself between Gargantua's jaws. *Besides, this'll make for a good story. If I survive.*

"Open the damned door, in the name of the Duke!"

Lukan positioned himself so his legs were dangling out of the window, his arse the only thing holding him back. *Never thought I'd see the day.* All it would take to send him hurtling down into the darkness was the slightest push. *Where the hells is Flea when you need her?* The thought of the street girl made him smile. *Bet she wouldn't think twice about giving me a shove.* He took a deep breath. *Guess I'll have to do it myself.*

"Three," he whispered, trying to ignore the frantic rhythm of his heart.

A metallic groan sounded as something heavy struck the door, Phaeron ingenuity giving way beneath blunt force.

"Two." He shifted, inching forward, every fiber of his being pleading with him not to jump.

He sucked in a breath, held it.

Metal squealed behind him.

Voices shouted.

Blood roared in his ears.

"One."

He pushed himself off the ledge.

18

NO STRANGER
TO GRANDEUR

"You jumped?"

"I jumped."

"You jumped into the sea from the *fifth* floor of the Ebon Hand." The Scrivener regarded Lukan over the rim of her steaming teacup. "Did you take leave of your senses?"

Lukan shrugged. "Half the guards in the tower were hammering at the door. What was I supposed to do?"

"You were *supposed* to infiltrate the Hand, make contact with Zandrusa, give her the jar, and obtain the relevant information—"

"Which I did," Lukan interjected. "I just . . . happened to leave in a more dramatic way than I intended."

"I've warned you before about interrupting me." The Scrivener took a sip of her tea without breaking eye contact. "Anyway, yes— *dramatic* is certainly the word. *Idiotic* might be another."

"Oh, come on . . . Don't pretend you're not impressed."

"*Impressed?*" The woman raised an eyebrow as she set down her teacup. "I'm only impressed you didn't manage to kill yourself."

Lady's mercy, this is like going for tea with your least favorite aunt. Perhaps that's what they looked like to the other customers of the little teahouse. *Or maybe they think she's my grandmother, enjoying a little chat with her favored grandchild.* The Scrivener looked just about old enough to play the role, though there was certainly nothing affectionate about her expression. Not that any of the other patrons were paying the slightest bit of attention to them anyway.

"What happened after you jumped into the sea?"

"Well . . ." Lukan paused, remembering the chill of the water, its crushing embrace. His panic in the darkness. "I swam back to the boat and shouted at the kid to row the hells out of there."

"You weren't pursued?"

"By the time they'd realized what had happened, we were well away. We lost them in the darkness."

"They will interrogate the boy."

"The kid was duped by my disguise, just as the guards at the Hand were. They can hardly hold that against him. Anyway, I gave him a few silvers for his trouble. If he's got any sense, he'll lie low for a bit. Either way, he knows nothing."

"But Zandrusa does," the Scrivener replied, pursing her lips. "She knows everything—your identity, and that you had *my* help."

"They'll get nothing from her. You know that as well as I do. Better, even."

"If they find that jar on her, all our efforts will have been for nothing."

"If Zandrusa was half the smuggler you claim she was, they won't."

"That's true enough, I suppose." The woman took another sip of her tea. "I appreciate your wits and courage, Master Gardova, if not your subtlety."

"Coming from you, I'd say that's high praise."

"It is," she replied, with no trace of irony. "So, you met with Zandrusa and heard what she had to say. What will you do now?"

"I'll find a way to prove her innocence, just like I told her."

"That's very honorable of you. Or is it your father's casket you really want?"

"Does it matter?"

"No, I suppose not." The Scrivener's brow creased in thought as she sipped her tea. "How curious that your father gave such an item to Zandrusa for safekeeping. Do you have any notion as to what it might contain?"

"None whatsoever."

"Then you're risking a lot for a reward of uncertain value. Murillo is one of the most powerful men in the city. If he is indeed the villain of the piece, he won't take kindly to you poking around."

"I've little choice," Lukan said with a shrug. "If Zandrusa dies, I'll never get hold of the casket."

"So what's your next move?"

"I'll do as Zandrusa said and speak with her steward, Magellis." Lukan withdrew the merchant prince's gold-and-ruby ring from a pocket and placed it on the table. "Hopefully he'll be able to help somehow. And I'll try and track down this physician, Doctor Vassilis. See what he has to say."

"Yes, I'd be very interested to hear what he might know about this frost on Lord Saviola's body." The Scrivener frowned at her teacup. "Very mysterious."

"I thought so too. What do you think might have caused that?"

"Nothing good, Master Gardova. Nothing good." The woman set her cup down and steepled her slender fingers. "We need to move quickly. Zandrusa will face the Bone Pit again in a week or so—perhaps even sooner if they find that jar on her. I suggest—"

"Hang on, what do you mean *we*?"

"Interrupt me one more time and I will throw the dregs of my tea in your face."

"Given that last time you were threatening to leave me tied to a chair in a darkened cellar, I'd say this marks an improvement in our relationship."

"We have no *relationship*, Master Gardova. I tolerate you and that insolent tongue of yours because so far you have proven useful to me. It is my hope that might continue."

"Is that so." Lukan picked up his own neglected teacup, noted the sediment swirling around the bottom, and set it back down again.

"The tea isn't to your liking?"

"I'd rather have a glass of wine."

"Oh? The bottle you consumed last night at the Orange Tree wasn't enough?"

How in the hells . . . "Are you keeping tabs on me?"

"I pay close attention to all my investments, Master Gardova. Especially the more unpredictable ones."

"Like me."

"Like you."

Lukan sighed, rubbed at his eyes in a vague attempt at banishing the headache he could feel building behind them. A few hours of snatched sleep apparently wasn't enough to offset the exertions of the previous night. "What are you suggesting?"

"I want to see Zandrusa walk free just as much as you do, so I suggest we continue to work together. If you're prepared to share whatever intelligence you uncover with me, I will assist you in any way I can and provide whatever materials you might need going forward. My areas of expertise extend far beyond mere forgeries." The Scrivener snapped her fingers, and a waiter appeared as if from nowhere, refilling her teacup before disappearing just as quickly. "So," she continued, squeezing a slice of lemon over the steaming liquid. "What do you say?"

Lukan had to admit the offer was enticing. The woman clearly knew her business; his little adventure last night had proven she was just as good a forger as he'd been told. Without her assistance, he would never have made it inside the Ebon Hand—not that he would admit that to her. "You're suggesting a partnership?"

"If that's what you want to call it."

"A partnership," Lukan continued, holding the Scrivener's intense gaze, "where the risk isn't evenly shared. If Lord Murillo really is behind all of this, then he's already murdered one merchant prince and imprisoned another—what's to say I won't be next? Even if we're working together, I'm the one putting myself in harm's way while you're . . . doing whatever it is you do in the shadows. It seems the risk is all on me."

"We play the roles that we are best suited for," the woman replied, stirring her tea with a spoon. "My expertise lies in deception and pulling certain strings from the . . . well, *shadows,* as you put it. Yours, Master Gardova"— she raised an eyebrow—"appears to lie in making a nuisance of yourself. Still, I suppose you have a point." The woman took a slow sip from her cup. "Very well," she murmured, as if coming to an agreement with herself. "I own a house in the Seven Arches district, in the shadow of the aqueduct. It's only a modest property, but much nicer than that fleapit you're currently staying in. I'll grant you full use of it and ensure the house is guarded day and night. You can use it as your base of operations for the duration of our association. How does that sound?"

"Does it have a wine cellar?"

"Fortunately not," the Scrivener replied, her expression hardening. "You'll need all your wits about you if we're to uncover the truth and help Zandrusa."

"Shame. There's nothing like a good glass of red to calm the nerves when you're meddling in shit that might just get you killed—"

"If it's that important to you," the Scrivener interrupted, her tone making it clear she was nearing the end of her patience, "I'll ensure there's some wine in the house. And if we're somehow successful in this little endeavor of ours, I'll provide you with enough wine to drown yourself in." Her expression suggested she wouldn't be displeased with that particular outcome.

"Make it Parvan Red, and we have a deal."

"Done. At last." She threw him a withering look as she took another sip of tea. "I will send Juro to the Orange Tree later this evening. He will escort you to my property, which I expect you to treat with the utmost respect."

"I'll look after the place like it was my own."

"I'd rather you didn't, as no doubt it would end up as a burning wreck within days." The woman dismissed him with a flick of her fingers. "Now get out and let me enjoy my tea in peace."

Gladly. "I'll go and speak with Zandrusa's steward," Lukan replied, rising from the table. "I'll keep you informed."

"You do that. Oh, and best you keep this little arrangement of ours a secret. Only reveal what is necessary. You can't trust anyone in this city."

"Can I trust you?"

"Goodbye, Master Gardova."

―――――――

Lukan was no stranger to grandeur. Not that his own family had much to speak of; his grandfather's alcoholism and gambling habit had seen to that. What was left of their fortune had been eroded further by his dueling accident—or, to use his father's words, the day he trampled his family's good name into the dirt and then set fire to it. *The old man always did have a good turn of phrase.* Yet he'd visited most of the old manor houses of Parva, had smoked expensive cigars in their wood-paneled chambers, had danced beneath glittering chandeliers in their ballrooms. In short, he thought he knew what wealth and influence looked like.

How wrong I was.

The mansions of Saphrona's elite made the country seats of Parva's aristocracy look like hovels in comparison. Statements of power in marble and whitewashed stone, they sprawled among the lemon trees and poplars that dotted Arturo's Rise—the exclusive enclave nestled in the foothills above Saphrona. Lukan caught only glimpses as the carriage passed by—flashes of immaculate gardens, columned porticos, and arched balconies—but it was enough for him to reconsider what true wealth looked like.

Yet as impressive as these villas were, they all lay in the shadows of the seven great towers that crowned the highest reaches of the Rise. Stark and imposing, they were home to the seven richest families in Saphrona—the Silken Septet, as Grabulli had called them—and were physical reminders of where the true power in the city really lay. *And the man I'm supposedly going up against lives in one of them. Wonder which one is Murillo's?*

"Look at that house!" Flea gasped. Her freshly scrubbed face was pressed to the carriage window, nose against the glass. "It's got a big fountain—"

"Hey," Lukan cut in, glad for the distraction. "What did I just tell you?"

"Not to stare."

"Exactly."

The girl kept staring. Lukan could hardly blame her. He found the passing mansions impressive, despite having been raised among the trappings of wealth, so he couldn't begin to guess how they must seem to a girl who had grown up on the streets. *Like some sort of dream, perhaps.*

Still, they had an appearance to maintain. "Flea," he said again, more sharply this time.

She gave an exaggerated sigh. "No one's even watching."

"There's always someone watching, kid. Especially when the aristocracy are concerned." *I should bloody know.* "And I'd bet my last copper whoever framed Zandrusa is keeping an eye on her villa, so it's important we blend in—"

"Yeah, you told me already."

"Then stop gawping out the window."

Flea rolled her eyes but did as she was told, sitting back against her cushioned seat. "This thing itches," she complained, tugging at the front of her new dress. "And I look stupid in it."

"You look respectable," Lukan said with a grin. "A proper little lady."

Flea scowled at him. "Yeah, well you look like someone I'd steal from. A frilly."

"Good, because that's entirely the point. Anyway, you think those guards at the gate would have let us pass if you were in your rags?"

"They're not *rags*." She glowered at him. "And they only let us pass because you bribed them."

"I didn't have much choice."

"They would have taken half what you gave them."

"Less than that, I'd imagine."

"Then why did you give them so much?"

"I'm sure you can figure it out."

The girl frowned in thought, and Lukan enjoyed the momentary silence, which didn't last nearly long enough. "Because arguing with them would just attract more attention," she said eventually. "They would be more likely to remember us and what we looked like."

"Exactly, and the less attention we attract, the better—hence why I am dressed like one of your frillies"—Lukan indicated his new shirt with extravagant cuffs—"and you are dressed like a little rich girl who is off to . . . I don't know. Ride a pony or something."

"A *pony*?"

Lukan shrugged.

"I still think this dress looks stupid," Flea muttered, tugging at a button.

"I'm glad you like it."

"And you look stupid."

"Thank you."

"And you *are*—"

"Stupid as well—yes, I get it."

Flea grinned and went back to plucking at the material of her dress. Lukan smiled to himself; the novelty of seeing the girl looking clean and respectable hadn't worn off yet. It had been a battle getting her to take a bath back at the Orange Tree, and even more so getting her to wear the dress and sandals he'd purchased for her. Yet, for all the girl's complaints, he suspected she was secretly pleased with her new acquisitions—not that she would ever show it. *Too much stubborn pride for that. Guess that makes two of us.*

"How old are you, kid?" he asked, realizing he didn't know.

"Thirteen."

"The hells you are."

Flea pulled a face at him. "Eleven. I think."

"And what's your story?"

Flea's eyes narrowed as she met his gaze. "*My* story?"

"Yeah. You already know mine, but it just occurred to me that I don't know much about you." He affected a thoughtful look. "Actually, that's not quite true—I know you're annoying and talk too much—"

"Why do you care?"

Lukan paused, taken back by the sudden intensity of the girl's stare, her mischievous humor for once entirely absent. "I . . ." *Don't,* he was going to say. But that wasn't true, and in any case he figured the girl had heard that too many times before. *Still, I doubt she'll react well to anything too invasive.* "When you're working closely with someone," he replied, choosing his words carefully, "it just helps to know a bit about them." Flea studied him, dark eyes full of mistrust. "Never mind," he said, waving the topic away, "it doesn't matter—"

"We grew up in the Splinters," Flea cut in, her voice lacking its usual impetuous edge. "Matteo and me. Our mother died from the pox. I don't really remember her, but sometimes I think I can hear her voice in my head . . ." The girl blinked, as if surprised at her own words. "We didn't know our father. Matteo always claimed he was a sailor, but I don't know why." Her jaw tightened. "He said a lot of things."

"So you picked pockets to survive?"

"Yeah. We joined a gang called the Blood Rats, but they were just boys a bit older than Matteo. We ran with them for a while. Mostly we dipped in the plaza, but sometimes we worked the Slopes and Seven Arches. At first they'd only let me be the prop, but—"

"Prop?"

"Yeah, like . . ." The girl adopted a mournful expression, her lower lip quivering. "Please, sir," she said, affecting the voice of a frightened young girl, "I'm so hungry . . ." She grinned. "And then, while they were distracted, one of the others would cut their purse."

"The old bait and switch." Flea stared at him blankly. Lukan waved his own words away. "Never mind. You were saying . . ."

"Eventually they let me become the runner, because I proved I was the quickest out of all of them." Seeing his confusion, the girl rolled her eyes. "The cutter *cuts* the purse and then throws it to the runner, who—"

"Runs away, I get it. And you were the fastest?"

"No one ever caught me," the girl said proudly.

"No one?" Lukan asked, indicating her missing finger.

Flea scowled. "That came later."

"What happened?"

"We found out that our leader, Casca, had been skimming from our takings." Her eyes narrowed in remembered anger. "He was reporting lower figures to the Watcher and keeping the difference."

"Ah, sorry—you're going to have to—"

"The Watchers work for the Twice-Crowned King, the ruler of the Kindred. They collect tithes from all the gangs."

"Even ones made up of child thieves?"

"We paid our way, like all the Kindred," Flea said defensively. "That's how it works. The King takes a slice of everything."

"So even Lady Midnight pays a tithe?"

The girl shrugged. "I guess."

"So Casca was tampering with the takings . . ."

"Yeah, and Matteo found out. He was angry, not just because Casca was keeping some of the money for himself, but because if the Watcher found out we'd all be in big trouble." Her expression became pensive. "But it was more than that, I think. Matteo thought if we could impress the Watcher with our takings, we might be able to catch the eye of the King, or someone in his favor. He thought maybe that would be a way out for us."

"So Matteo confronted Casca."

Flea nodded. "Yeah, and they had a fight. Casca was bigger and stronger. Matteo got hurt. We had to spend the coins we'd saved on getting him fixed up, but he was never the same after that. His arm never mended properly. So after we left the gang, I had to become the cutter." She managed a pained smile. "I was good at that too, but . . ." She waggled the stump of her missing finger. "I got caught trying to lift some oranges from a stall. The man didn't even bother calling for the constable, he just held me down and . . ."

Lukan winced. "I'm sorry."

The girl shrugged. "I learned my lesson. Never got caught again."

"Well, that's not strictly true—"

"I didn't get punished when you caught me, so it doesn't count."

"I'm making you wear that dress." Lukan grinned as he indicated her clothes. "Isn't that a punishment?"

"At least I'm getting paid." The girl turned her attention back to the passing mansions.

"If you don't stop staring, I'll deduct a few coins just like Casca did."

Flea's crude gesture made it clear what she thought of that.

"Your brother, Matteo," Lukan said, keeping his tone neutral. "What happened to him?"

Flea remained silent.

"I know how it feels," Lukan continued, feeling suddenly awkward. "I lost my mother when I was about your age. I know how hard it is to lose someone close to you. But I understand if you don't want to—"

"I don't know what happened," Flea interrupted, a hint of sorrow in her voice revealing a vulnerability that she had thus far kept hidden. "Sometimes I think that's the hardest part. Not Matteo being gone, but not knowing what happened to him." She was still staring out of the window, but Lukan could tell she wasn't seeing the mansions and gardens that rolled by outside. "After Casca kicked us out, we mostly worked alone, but sometimes we teamed up with another gang called the Night Hawks. They dropped by one night and said they had a job, something about a warehouse down in the Salts."

"The Salts?"

"Yeah, where all the shipyards are, not far from where we lived in the Splinters. We didn't go there much, but they said they had a big score lined up and wanted Matteo to go with them."

"But not you?"

"They wanted me to, but I wasn't feeling well. I think I drank some bad water or something."

"So Matteo went with them . . ."

"And I never saw any of them again." Flea's jaw tightened. "I . . .

I asked around, but no one knew anything. They just vanished. Someone said it was like they'd been taken by the Faceless."

"Unlikely," Lukan replied, recalling the myth of the Faceless. The children's stories spoke of demons who wore masks and traveled the skies on a flying ship with black sails, landing only to carry off naughty children—or so parents across the Old Empire claimed. Lukan knew better, since the Faceless had been another of his father's obsessions that he had talked about on many occasions. While there was a historical basis for their existence— the Faceless were mentioned in a handful of historical documents across several centuries—the last reference to them was over three hundred years old. They had subsequently vanished from the pages of history, leaving most scholars to conclude that they had probably never existed in the first place. *Not that Father ever stopped believing they were real.* "The Faceless are just a story, kid."

"I know," Flea retorted, rolling her eyes. "I'm not stupid."

"So did you search the warehouse?"

"Yeah, I snuck in the following night, but there was nothing there except lots of rope and planks of wood. Stuff they make ships out of."

"So you found nothing at all? Nothing that suggested what might have happened to them?"

"No. Except . . . there was a strange smell. It was . . . like something had burned—"

"If the warehouse is near the shipyards, it was probably just tar or burning pitch, or something."

"Let me finish!" she retorted, shooting him a glare. "It smelled burned, but also sweet, like, I dunno, flowers or something."

"Flowers?"

"And there was something else. I felt . . . It made me feel uncomfortable. Like something really bad had happened and it was still in the air. It felt wrong. Like it didn't belong. And whatever it was . . ." She hesitated, as if afraid to continue.

"Go on."

"I felt like . . . it knew I was there." Her expression hardened, as if she expected him to ridicule her. When he remained silent, she continued, "That's when I ran. And I didn't go back."

"I don't blame you. Did you tell Obassa about this?"

"Yeah, but he didn't know what the smell was, and he said the weird feeling was probably just me being upset at Matteo being gone. Said I was feeling troo-ma or something . . ."

"Trauma."

"Do you think he's right?"

"I'm not sure, kid. Maybe." *And yet there's something weird about all this.* "Regardless, I'm sorry about Matteo."

"Thanks." Flea went back to staring out of the window, though her expression of wonder had been replaced by harder lines.

"You seem to know a lot about the Kindred," Lukan said, looking to both raise the girl's spirits and change the subject. "Tell me more about the Twice-Crowned King. Why's he called that?"

"*They,*" Flea corrected, looking at him. "There's two of them. They both wear a crown, but there's only one king, twice-crowned."

"I don't follow."

"I've never seen them, so I don't know much. People say they're twins, that they're joined at the hip. I don't really know what that means . . ."

"It means they're close. That they do everything together."

"I guess that makes sense." The girl shrugged again. "One of them is called the Snake, and the other is the Scorpion. The Snake always sits on the left side of the throne and the Scorpion on the right. They have their court down in the catacombs beneath the city. I don't really know anything else."

Two siblings, but only one king. Curious . . .

The carriage juddered to a halt, shaking him from his thoughts before he could think on the matter any further.

"Lady Jelassi's residence," came the driver's muffled shout.

"What did I tell you earlier?" Lukan asked Flea as he reached for the carriage door.

"That we need to blend in?"

"The other thing."

"To keep my eyes open, my mouth shut, and my hands to myself?"

"That's the one." He pushed the door open. "Make sure you do."

Lukan ignored the girl's scowl as he stepped down from the carriage and into the heat of the afternoon. Aside from an elderly man pruning an impressive bougainvillea farther down the lane, the avenue was empty—a far cry from the clamor and chaos of the Northern Boneway, which they'd traversed earlier. He breathed deeply, enjoying the novelty of fresh air laced with the scents of jasmine and honeysuckle, a welcome reprieve from the lower city's aromas of sweat, salt, and shit. He heard Flea disembarking behind him but decided against offering an assisting hand—he'd only get a punch for his trouble. Instead he stepped toward the elaborate wrought-iron gates of Zandrusa's estate. Beyond he could see a well-tended garden of sculpted hedges and paved walkways. The villa itself was partly hidden behind a stand of poplars, but what Lukan could see of it suggested a grandeur easily the equal of anything he'd seen already. *Not bad for a former smuggler.*

"We're going in there?" Flea whispered as she joined him, her wide eyes gazing at the landscaped garden beyond the gate as if it were some sort of fever dream.

"I hope so," Lukan replied in a low voice. "I certainly didn't dress like this just for the fun of it."

"It smells strange here. Different, like . . . I don't know. Like a lady's perfume I once smelled."

"While you were stealing from her?"

Flea smiled coyly. "Maybe."

A polite cough sounded behind them.

"Wait here," Lukan told the girl. He opened his coin purse as he returned to the carriage, where the driver watched him expectantly from his seat. "Four coppers," he said, counting them out into his palm. "That's what we agreed, correct?"

The driver bobbed his head. "Sir."

"I should be no more than an hour," Lukan said, passing the coins to the man. "If you're still here when I return, I'll give you four more. And then another four to take us back to the lower city."

"Very good sir."

"That's twelve coppers. What say I add two more to make it one silver—and you forget that you ever saw me or the girl?"

The driver smiled. "I've been known to suffer the odd memory lapse now and then, sir."

"Good man."

"Enjoy your visit, sir."

"I will." *If it proves worthwhile.*

Lukan returned to the gates, where Flea still stared beyond the bars. He wondered then—not for the first time—whether it was fair to bring her here, to give her a glimpse of a life so far removed from her own. Deep down he knew he should have refused her desire to accompany him, not least because it made him more conspicuous. But the girl wouldn't be denied; she'd cleverly waited until they sat down to lunch, and—when he was on his second glass of wine—made her request, which in truth was more of a demand. Lukan hadn't bothered to argue. He'd quickly learned that letting Flea have her way was the quickest method of shutting her up. *It'll be fine,* he assured himself, although he wasn't entirely convinced. *As long as she keeps her hands to herself.*

Unlike all of the other villas they had passed on their way through Arturo's Rise, Zandrusa's estate had no liveried guards standing before the gates—a sign, no doubt, of her recent fall from grace. Lukan grasped the velvet rope that hung beside the gate and gave it a sharp tug. A bell rang somewhere on the other side.

"Does your house have a garden like this?" Flea asked as they waited, her eyes still locked on the greenery beyond the gates. Lukan thought of his father's crumbling old manse—*his* manse now—and its overgrown garden.

"Not exactly, no."

"But you do have one?"

"Of sorts."

"I'd like a garden."

"I'd like someone to open this bloody gate." Lukan tugged the rope again, and the unseen bell echoed across the neat hedges and potted lemon trees. Silence returned as the sound faded, broken only by the buzzing of cicadas and the distant clacking of the old man's shears. *Lady's mercy, don't tell me I came all the way here for nothing . . .*

He was reaching for the rope again when a figure suddenly appeared round a hedge—a grey-haired woman, dressed in loose clothes covered in grass stains. She approached the gate with a slight limp, her back stooped—presumably from years of tending flower beds. "Help you, sir?" she asked, squinting through the bars.

"I hope so," Lukan replied, relieved. "I need to speak to Lady Jelassi's steward, Magellis. So if you wouldn't mind fetching the butler, or whoever's in charge . . ."

"There's no butler," the woman replied, rubbing her chin with dirt-smudged fingers. "No guards either. They all got given their marching orders after the lady was locked up. Now it's just me and the cook. And Magellis, of course. So you see, I have to be careful who I let in."

"I'm sure Magellis would be very interested in what I have to say."

"That so?" The woman gave him an appraising look. "He didn't say he was expecting visitors."

"He doesn't know I'm coming, though I have no doubt he'll want to see me." Lukan gestured at the gate. "So if you wouldn't mind?"

"Magellis hates to be disturbed," she replied, glancing back at the villa. "Who are you, anyway?"

"My name is irrelevant," Lukan said, his patience slowly fraying. "All that matters is that I have important information and I need to speak to Magellis *now*. Please."

The woman remained unmoved.

"The sooner you let us in," Flea said suddenly, "the sooner you can go back to your plants."

Lady's blood . . . Lukan shot her a warning glare, but the girl ignored him as she continued, "Your garden is very beautiful."

The woman smiled at that. "Not my garden, little one," she replied, "but it pleases me you think so." If she thought anything of a well-dressed girl speaking with the accent of a lower-city gutter rat, she kept it to herself. She glanced at Lukan again, then sighed. "Oh, to the hells with it," she said, pulling a key from a pocket. "I'm a gardener, not a guardswoman. This place is falling apart now anyway, so I don't suppose it matters." She unlocked the gate and pulled it open.

"Thank you," Lukan said as he stepped through, Flea close behind.

"You're welcome," the gardener replied, as she closed and locked the gate. "But if you harm any of my plants, you'll be out on your arses before you can blink."

"Wouldn't dream of it," Lukan replied with a smile.

The gardener gave him a doubtful look, then turned and limped toward the villa. "This way."

They followed her through the grounds, past neatly trimmed hedges and flower beds blooming with color despite the lateness of the season, past a gurgling fountain and a gleaming bronze sundial. Flea hesitated as she saw a butterfly flitting above a lavender bush, and Lukan had to give her a gentle nudge to keep her moving, feeling a stab of guilt as he did so. The villa came fully into view as they rounded the stand of poplars, and was just as impressive as Lukan had suspected—an extravagance of columns and arches, much like the others he'd seen, but with the addition of colored wall tiles that spoke of Zandrusa's Zar-Ghosan heritage.

"Quite the place," Lukan said as they stepped into the shadow of the porticoed entrance.

"Suppose it is," the woman replied, reaching for the bronze door knocker. "If you care for stone and marble. Prefer plants myself." She rapped three times.

"I like the garden more too," Flea said.

"I'm glad you do, little one." The woman muttered under her breath and rapped three more times. Muffled shouting came from beyond the door. "Ah, he's in a good mood as usual," she added, over the sound of bolts being drawn back.

The door flew open.

"Lady's mercy, woman!" the man standing in the doorway snapped. "I told you to use the back bloody door . . ." He paused, blinking at Lukan and Flea. "Unless we have guests," he added, his anger flowing smoothly into a welcoming smile. "My sincere apologies, I wasn't expecting visitors."

"Aye, well, you've got them whether you like it or not," the woman replied, her lip curled. "If you want me to turn people away, you can damn well pay me a guard's wage." She turned and crouched before Flea. "How about I show you more of the garden, little one? Leave the men to their boring business."

"Um . . ." Flea looked askance at Lukan.

What harm can it do? He couldn't see any danger, so long as the girl kept quiet about the purpose of their visit. *And it means I can talk to Magellis without fear of awkward interruptions.* "Very well," he said, giving Flea a pointed look. "Just make sure you behave yourself." The girl nodded, catching his meaning.

"This way then, little one," the gardener said, ushering Flea back toward the garden. "Let's start with the pond."

Lukan turned back to the man, who regarded him with a quizzical expression. "You are Magellis, I take it? Lady Jelassi's steward?"

"I am." The man gave a perfunctory bow. "And who might I have the pleasure of addressing?"

"My name is . . ." Lukan hesitated, the name of his alter ego forming on his tongue. *No, enough with the smoke and mirrors. I need to win this man's trust.* "I'm Lukan Gardova. And I have a story you need to hear."

"I see," Magellis replied, though he clearly didn't, and his wary expression said as much. "And what might that be, may I ask?"

"It concerns Lady Jelassi," Lukan said, dropping his voice even though there was no one else in earshot. "It would be best if we spoke inside."

Something passed across the man's face at the mention of his employer's name—suspicion perhaps, or possibly something else. Either way, he held his ground. "I'm sorry, sir, but I've already told the authorities everything I know about—"

"Lady Jelassi sends her regards," Lukan interrupted, holding out the gold ring she had given him.

Magellis frowned as he took the ring, thumbing the ruby as he turned it over in his hands. "How did you get this?"

"As I said, it's best we talk inside."

"Yes," Magellis replied, stepping aside. "I think maybe it is."

————

"You jumped into the sea—from the fifth floor of the Ebon Hand?"

"Yeah."

"That's . . . well." Magellis forced a laugh and sipped his drink. "That's quite the story."

"I think it lacked a little tension this time round."

"I beg your pardon?"

"Never mind."

They were seated in the atrium of Zandrusa's villa and—much to Lukan's disappointment—were drinking some sort of mint tea that looked revolting and somehow tasted even worse. Whereas the villa's exterior bore hints of Zandrusa's Zar-Ghosan heritage, her atrium displayed them more indulgently—intricate arabesques covered the surrounding columns, while the walls beyond them were covered in bright frescoes. Water tinkled from a fountain, while small, colorful birds flitted amid the variety of plants that offered shade from the sun.

"I must confess," Magellis continued, "to a good deal of curiosity as to this mysterious ally who you say helped you with your disguise . . ."

"As I said," Lukan replied firmly, "the less you know the safer you'll be. If what Lady Jelassi told me is true—if Lord Murillo really is behind all of this—then I'll be not so much poking a hornet's nest as taking an axe to it. I wouldn't want you to get stung, so to speak."

"No, of course. I appreciate that." Magellis set his teacup down, a slight tremble in his wrist. The fingers of his right hand tapped a nervous rhythm on the armrest of his wicker chair.

"You're concerned," Lukan ventured. In truth, the man had seemed on edge the entire time. Distracted. *Which is hardly surprising, to be fair. His employer has been sentenced to death and he's probably wondering what in the hells is going to happen to him. I'd be anxious as well, though I'd be drowning my sorrows with something far stronger than this herbal shit.* He took a sip anyway, hoping the taste might have somehow improved. It hadn't.

"Yes," the man admitted with a pained smile. "My apologies. It's just . . . well, it's been a trying time."

"Of course."

"I've tried to continue as best I can and keep the household running, but with Lady Jelassi's assets frozen by the Inquisition . . ." He shrugged helplessly. "I've had to let many of the staff go. The maids, the guards—"

"But not the gardener."

"No, not Clarena. I should have asked her to leave with the others, but I couldn't quite find it in my heart to do so. Lady Jelassi always had a soft spot for her and she was so fond of her garden. It felt like it would have been, I don't know . . . a stain on her memory."

"She's not dead yet."

"No, of course not—"

"And if I have my way, she won't be any time soon."

"You're serious then?" Magellis picked up the ring from the table, turned it over in his hands. "You're actually going to try and prove the lady's innocence?"

"You sound doubtful."

"No, no—forgive me. It's just . . ." The man sighed, placed the ring back on the table. "I want nothing more than for Lady Jelassi to be exonerated. Of course I do. I know she's not guilty, I know that she never murdered Lord Saviola. But what you're suggesting, what you propose to do . . . Lord Murillo is one of the Silken Septet. He's a very powerful man."

"So I'm told."

"But you're prepared to stand against him? Why? What is in this for you?"

"As I told you, the less you know the safer you'll be when the blades come out." *And they will come out, make no mistake about that.* "Let's just say that I'm determined to see justice served."

"Well, it's a noble cause. I can only offer you my heartfelt thanks."

"Whatever help you can offer would be welcome too. Lady Jelassi said you would give whatever assistance you can."

"And my lady is right, as always." Magellis shifted in his seat. "Though I must admit I'm not sure exactly what I can do for you."

"What can you tell me about this physician, Doctor Vassilis? The one who attended to Lord Saviola's body?"

"Well, there's not much to tell. He's said to be the best doctor in the city and certainly counts many of the merchant princes among his patients." Magellis frowned. "I did hear that he's been out of the city for a while. I asked if he would come and see me about my, ah . . . Well, it doesn't matter. But I was told by his secretary that he'd taken leave. He seemed unsure when the doctor would be returning, or even where he was."

"That's interesting." *Not to mention frustrating, since he's my only lead in all this. A strange coincidence.*

"However," Magellis continued, forehead creased in thought, "perhaps . . . Hmm. I wonder. Yes, it's worth a try, I think . . ."

"You have an idea?"

"Only a vague one, but . . ."

"Let's hear it."

"Well, it just occurred to me that Lady Valdezar is holding a ball tonight to mark the upcoming celebrations."

"Lady Valdezar? She's another merchant prince?"

"Yes, one of the Silken Septet." Magellis sounded bemused. "Forgive me, you're obviously new to the city if her name is unfamiliar to you."

"Never mind that. What's the importance of this ball?"

"Well, it's likely that Doctor Vassilis will be there. If he's returned to the city, of course."

"How can you be sure?"

"Lady Valdezar is a patron of the Collegium and makes regular donations. The patronage of a merchant prince is a fickle thing, and once lost it's very hard to get back." The man gave a faint smile. "Failure to attend the ball will be regarded as a snub and could have damaging social and financial consequences. My guess is that Doctor Vassilis will be there—as will many of the other merchant princes, Lord Murillo among them. It could be a good chance for you to speak to the doctor, and also get a look at the man you're setting yourself against." Magellis shrugged. "You'd need some sort of cover story, of course."

"That won't be a problem."

"Given your exploits so far, I don't imagine it would be. If you'll excuse me a moment . . ." Magellis rose and left the courtyard, disappearing through one of the arched doorways. Lukan took the opportunity to pour his tea into a plant pot. The steward returned a moment later. "Here you are," he said, offering Lukan a cream-colored envelope, the red seal already broken. "Lady Jelassi's invitation arrived shortly before, ah . . . the tragedy with Lord Saviola. The circumstances being what they are, I'm sure my lady would be only too pleased for you to attend in her stead."

Lukan slid the invitation from the envelope. The textured card smelled faintly of violets. *No expense spared,* he thought, as his eyes took in the swirling script, embossed in gold leaf. *And it's not personalized. Perfect.* If the invite was anything to go by, Lady Valdezar's soirée promised to be quite the occasion. *A shame I need to put business before pleasure yet again.*

"I can't thank you enough," he said, rising to his feet and offering his hand. "You've been a great help."

"Anything to help Lady Jelassi," Magellis replied, smiling as he clasped Lukan's hand. "Anything at all."

19

JUST LIKE OLD TIMES

The distant bells of the Lady's House were tolling to mark the ninth hour of the evening as Lukan's carriage approached Lady Valdezar's tower. *Two hours later than I'd intended.* Still, at least he wasn't to blame. He couldn't help that his nocturnal adventure had taken its toll, exhaustion turning his afternoon siesta into a deep, four-hour slumber. Nor could he be held accountable for the antics of the Scrivener's chef, who—to Lukan's bleary surprise— had arrived at the house just before the sixth bell and informed him that she was to be his personal cook. The woman—who hailed from one of the ports of the Mourning Sea, as far as Lukan could judge—might have had a limited grasp of the Old Empire's common tongue, but she didn't need words to express her disgust at Lukan's request for some cold meat and cheese. The tight line of her lips was more than enough.

An hour later Lukan and Flea found themselves sitting down to an impressive three-course dinner, each dish more delicious than the last. While Flea gorged herself, Lukan ate more reservedly, distracted by the evening's task. Aware that time was marching on, he'd told the chef not to bother with dessert, causing Flea to howl in protest. The chef merely pursed her lips and disappeared into the kitchen, returning with a huge lemon pie. "You eat," she said firmly. Having seen the way the woman wielded her chopping knife, Lukan had thought it best not to argue.

Hence why he was now arriving fashionably late for Lady Valdezar's soirée, with a large slab of the lemon pie sitting uneasily in his stomach, alongside a churning knot of trepidation. *Relax,* he told himself, as the carriage lurched to a halt. *You've attended dozens of these galas. You know the ropes.* Which was true, but also overlooked a minor detail: He'd never attended such a social event while pretending to be someone else. *Still,* he thought, as he disembarked and flicked a coin to the driver, *there's a first time for everything.*

A sudden movement overhead drew his attention. He glanced up at the dark sky and froze as a huge shadow blotted out the stars. *What in the hells . . .*

"Just one of the bats, my lord," a well-dressed footman called from the gates.

Of course, Lukan thought, recalling mention of the giant creatures in Velleras Gellame's booklet. *Seven shadows, that thing is massive.* He watched as the creature circled the top of Lady Valdezar's tower and headed back toward the mountains, wings beating with indolent grace. "Quite the sight," he said as he approached the footman. "No wonder they're the symbol of your city." *Better than a giant worm, at least.*

"Quite right, my lord," the man replied, inclining his head. "May I see your invitation?"

"Of course." Lukan showed him the embossed card.

"Very good, my lord," the man replied, though his brow creased as his eyes flicked back to Lukan. "Ah—you must forgive me, but I don't think I've had the pleasure . . ."

"Lord Bastien Dubois of Parva," Lukan replied, puffing out his chest a little, as if the name was something special and not one he'd made up a couple of days ago.

"Of course," the footman said, feigning recognition with well-practiced ease. "A pleasure, my lord." He coughed into a white-gloved fist. "Lord Dubois of Parva," he announced in a clear voice.

Few of the guests within earshot paid any attention as Lukan strolled through the gates. Those who did gave him a dismissive glance before returning to their drinks and gossip. *Perfect.* Being unmemorable was exactly what he aspired to tonight, and he'd chosen his outfit accordingly: black hose, a silk shirt, and a gold-embroidered velvet doublet that was expensive enough to pass muster, but not so fashionable—so the tailor had assured him—as to attract attention. The clothes had been expensive, but Juro had covered the cost without complaint, and the initial reaction to his arrival suggested he'd pitched his appearance just right.

Lukan felt his trepidation melt away as he started down the paved walkway, weaving between groups of guests. After the events at the Ebon Hand, he wasn't thrilled to once again be going undercover armed with only a false identity and his wits, but at least the dangers tonight were less immediate, and the price of failure not quite so severe. Besides, he *knew* these people—not personally, of course, but he knew their type, he knew how they acted and how he should act in turn. *After all, I used to be one of them.* He shouldn't have any trouble blending in. After that, it was just a case of finding the doctor and learning what he could about Lord Saviola's death before slipping away into the night. *And this time I won't even have to jump fifty feet into the bloody sea.*

Still, he couldn't afford to be complacent—he'd been to enough balls and galas to know that an ill-judged word could attract all sorts of unwanted attention. Yet as he looked around, he realized that—for all his familiarity with such social events—he'd never attended anything quite as extravagant as this before.

Lady Valdezar's gardens were comfortably three times the size of Zandrusa's. Alchemical globes lined the central walkway, bathing the flower beds and hedgerows in soft hues of rose and gold. *An effective way to set the mood,* Lukan mused as he continued along the winding path, *but an even more effective display of wealth.* Such globes were expensive, manufactured exclusively by the famed alchemists of Korslakov, and using them to light one's home was considered the height of luxury in the circles he had once moved in. To use two dozen of them simply to create a bit of atmosphere at a party was something else entirely. *Lady Valdezar clearly has money to burn.* Not that the merchant prince needed alchemical globes to prove that—the tower that rose from the center of the estate was proof enough of the woman's standing. *Not to mention a reminder of the sort of power I'm up against.* Lukan felt a twinge of unease as he stared up at the structure, which was not nearly as tall or broad as the Ebon Hand, yet still radiated a sense of power and authority. *Lady's mercy, I need a drink.*

"Drink, sir?" a servant asked, appearing as if from nowhere with a tray of glasses.

"How did you guess?"

"Sir?"

"Never mind." Lukan selected a tall, fluted glass filled with a bright green liquid. *Even the bloody drinks look expensive.* He took a sip as the man bowed and retreated. *Tastes like shit, though.* He worked his tongue around his mouth, trying to scrub out the lingering taste of anise, as he pondered his next move. His priority was to speak with Doctor Vassilis, but he wouldn't pass up the opportunity to catch a glimpse of Lord Murillo and get a sense of the man who was his nemesis in all of this. *Where to start looking, though?* He glanced around the grounds, and his gaze settled on the lawn away to his left, where some twenty or so guests mingled and chatted over the sounds of a string quartet. *Guess there is as good as anywhere—*

"By Brandur's frozen cock!"

Lukan looked to his right to see a large figure shambling along a side path toward him.

"Take some . . . fresh air," the figure continued, words slurred by alcohol and thickened by a heavy Korslakovan accent. "Who the hells do . . . they think they are?"

The man staggered into the light and Lukan realized he was wearing a fur-trimmed cloak despite the warmth of the evening. *No wonder his face is as red as a smacked arse.* The man belched as he almost collided with a potted plant. *Or perhaps it's from the drink. Bloody fool has clearly had enough to sink a battleship.* Lukan turned away. *Best escape before he—*

"You!"

Oh, here we go.

Lukan turned back, forced a smile. "Sir."

"That's . . . *General* to you," the man replied, thumping his chest. His deep-set eyes rolled around in their sockets, above a bulging nose and an unruly white beard that might have been impressive had it not been soaked with booze. The man belched again, treating Lukan to a blast of alcoholic fumes. "Get some air, that's . . . what they said." He scowled and rubbed at the white fuzz of hair that hovered above his head like an ironic halo. "Damned fools, the lot of them. More interested in gossip than a good war story. And I was just getting to the good bit."

"Well, it's their loss."

"Damned right! I was about to tell them how the northern clans came streaming out of the forest and hit our baggage train. By the Builder, you should have seen them! Painted faces howling just like the damned bears that ran beside them." He shook his head and hiccoughed. "It was a bloody massacre."

"I'm sure it was," Lukan said quickly, before the man could get too deep into his tale. "Here," he added, offering his glass of foul green luminescence. "You look like you could use another drink."

"Oh . . . very kind." The stranger accepted the glass and sniffed its contents. "Smells like horseshit."

"Tastes like it too. Enjoy."

Lukan tried to move away, only for the man's other hand to clamp round his arm. "And who might you be?" he asked, squinting at Lukan as if seeing him properly for the first time. "Another of these perfumed princes, eh?"

Lukan forced a smile and gently eased the man's fingers from his elbow. "No one so grand, I'm afraid. Lord Bastien Dubois of Parva, at your service."

"General Leopold Razin at yours," the man replied grandly, accepting Lukan's offer of a handshake—he might have been drunk as a newt, but his grip was like iron. "You know my story, of course," the man continued, puffing out his chest. "Liberator of the Frostfort, victor of the Battle of the Black Ice—that worm Colonel Orlova might claim the credit, but the strategy was *all* mine, I assure you."

"Yes, of course," Lukan replied, not having the faintest idea what the man was on about. "Anyway, I really ought to—"

"And it was *me* that the so-called King of the Crags surrendered to! The greatest of the northern clansmen bowing at *my* feet, not Orlova's! It was *my* triumph, not hers! Damn her eyes . . ." Razin took a mouthful of his drink, grimaced, and sprayed the liquid across the paving stones.

"A fascinating tale," Lukan said, stepping back, "but I *really* must be—"

"The debacle at Cauldron Pass, on the other hand, was *all* Orlova's fault. A foul-up of the highest order, yet I took the blame, me—the hero of Korslakov! They took my title, my reputation . . . but not my pride." Razin waved an admonishing finger. "This city," he continued, glancing around in a conspiratorial fashion, "is too damned hot, and you can't find a good bottle of vodka anywhere, *but* . . . there's money here. Serious money. And that's what I need—money to raise an army. Then I'll march it to the gates of Korslakov and smash them down. Orlova and those cowards on the Frostfire Circle won't be laughing then. I just need the coin." His flushed face seemed to droop. "A lot of coin."

"Well, you've come to the right place."

"You'd think so, eh?" The man snorted and shook his head. "These coin-kissers cling to their wealth like . . . like . . ."

"A drunk to his bottle?"

"Yes! Exactly. But one day I'll get the money I need. And with it, sweet vengeance!" He raised his glass, frowned at the green dregs inside and hurled it into a nearby bush.

"Well, I wish you every success," Lukan replied, with as much false sincerity as he could muster. "Before I leave you to your noble quest, perhaps you might help me with mine? I'm looking for a doctor by the name of Vassilis. You wouldn't happen to know him?"

"Of course." Razin frowned, as if annoyed the conversation was no longer about himself. "The good doctor treated me for a case of . . ." He scratched at his white whiskers. "Yes, well . . . Best keep that to myself."

"Indeed." *I'm sure that's the first sensible decision you've made all night.* "Would you happen to know if he's here?"

"Hmm?" Razin was staring at the gathering on the lawn, no doubt seeking another target for his fundraising efforts. *Or his overblown war stories.*

"Doctor Vassilis," Lukan pressed. "Is he here tonight?"

"I think I saw him in the tower." The general didn't sound convinced, nor did he seem to care. "My apologies," he continued, stepping away, "but there are many people I need to speak to. You understand, of course."

"Of course," Lukan replied, relieved to see the man go. "Good evening, General."

"And to you, Lord . . ." Razin feigned a cough. "Um . . . Yes. Well. Good luck."

"Thank you," he replied, watching the drunken general totter away. *Chances are I'll need it before this night is through.*

———

"Drink, sir?" the footman in the tower's entrance hall asked as Lukan stepped through the doorway. *Well, that depends.* He glanced at the silver tray and was relieved to see that the crystal glasses appeared to hold nothing more threatening than red wine. "The other guests are up on the second floor," the man continued, gesturing at the spiral staircase at the end of the opulent hallway. Lukan nodded his thanks and made his way toward it, reaching the bottom just as two well-dressed women were making their way down.

". . . absolute nonsense! I *told* him the market was unstable—"

"Not as unstable as his state of mind. The man was always a fool."

"Well, quite. I mean, *really*. As if the guild would *ever* have agreed . . ."

Lukan paused, one hand on the elaborate balustrade and a forced smile on his face, but neither of the two guests so much as glanced at him as they swept off down the hallway. *Here's to*

*hoping the rest of the guests find Lord Bastien Dubois equally un-
remarkable*. He made his way up the staircase, only to pause when
he reached the top, his breath catching at the sight before him.

It was as if the last seven years of his life had melted away.

Servers in yellow tunics bobbed and weaved with practiced elegance between groups of lavishly dressed men and women, like
minnows darting around sharks. The guests barely seemed to notice them, busy as they were sipping from their wineglasses and
puffing on fashionably fat cigars, whispering to each other behind
raised hands that glinted with jewelry. They stood in separate
groups, regarding partygoers outside their own circles with looks
that were dismissive at best, disdainful at worst. Another string
quartet played on the far side of the room, gently teasing out the
last few bars of an Alfrezo signature piece and lending the pro-
ceedings an air of civility that they probably didn't deserve.

Just like old times, Lukan thought, finally remembering to
breathe. The scene before him, even after many years, felt ach-
ingly familiar. After all, such events had once been his natural
habitat. Even after his family had lost most of their fortune (but
before his own spectacular fall from grace) the Gardovas had still
been invited to Parva's most exclusive balls, the prestige of their
family name weathering the years better than their finances had.
His father had dispensed with most social engagements after Lukan's mother had died, but for Lukan they became an escape from
the rift that was growing between the pair of them. He'd become
adept at navigating the treacherous waters of such events, where
lineage and reputation were a currency, and a scandalous rumor
concerning a rival was something to be treasured.

But that had been many years ago.

Now he was a stranger, watching a glimmer of his old life as it
danced before his eyes.

He looked around the lavishly decorated room, only this time
he wasn't searching for some willing female company to while
away the night with, but a man he had never even met—a man
who might know something about Lord Saviola's murder. *How*

about that for a mood killer. Yet as he eyed the male guests in the room, recalling the description of Vassilis that Juro had provided earlier that afternoon, he didn't see anyone who resembled the doctor. *Seems General Razin was wrong. What a surprise . . .*

A male guest suddenly dropped to one knee, spilling half his wine across a plush rug as he made a jest to his tittering companions, revealing another man sitting in an armchair on the far side of the room. A man with thinning hair, a waxed mustache, and, most significantly, a monocle.

Vassilis. It has to be. Looks like the general was right after all. Lukan took a sip of his wine, not even registering the taste. *Well, let's see what the good doctor has to say.*

He made his way across the room, weaving between the gossiping circles, the chatter of the guests filling his ears.

". . . prices to double by the end of the next quarter . . ."

". . . the latest fashion, though as to why I couldn't *possibly* say . . ."

". . . oh, you *didn't* . . ."

"I most certainly did!"

Laughter.

He noted one or two glances in his direction as he passed by, but was careful to keep his eyes lowered, and thankfully none of the other guests deemed him intriguing enough to strike up a conversation. *Amazing what an unfashionable jacket will do for you.*

The seated man didn't so much as glance up as Lukan reached his side; instead he stared into space, apparently deep in thought, a cigarillo slowly turning to ash between his fingers.

"Doctor Vassilis?"

No response.

Lukan cleared his throat. "Doctor Vassilis," he repeated, a little louder this time.

The man jolted, cigarillo tumbling from his fingers. He swore under his breath and snatched it up, glaring at Lukan through his monocle.

"Do I know you?" he asked stiffly.

"We haven't met," Lukan replied, keeping his voice low. "My name doesn't matter. I was hoping to ask you a few questions—"

"I don't offer free consultations, particularly not at social events. I suggest you speak to my secretary about an appointment."

"I'm not looking for medical advice."

"Oh. I see." The man took a drag on his cigarillo, exhaled purple-tinged smoke. "Then what can I do for you?"

"Perhaps we could conduct this conversation somewhere more private."

The doctor tensed. "I'm quite comfortable here," he replied, eyes darting round the room before settling back on Lukan. "So please, say your piece or leave me to my thoughts."

And what thoughts are those? Whatever they were, they were rattling him—that much was obvious. *The man's on edge, but why?*

"As you wish," Lukan said, checking to make sure none of the other guests were within earshot. Satisfied, he continued, "I would like to ask you about the death of Lord Saviola."

"You can ask, but I have nothing to say on the matter."

"I understand you were there."

"I was."

"And that you attended to Lord Saviola's body."

"He was already dead when I arrived, so there wasn't much to attend to."

"How did he die?"

The doctor gave him a withering look. "I mean no disrespect," he said, his tone suggesting that on the contrary he meant a good deal of it, "but that has literally been the talk of the city for the last few weeks. I can't imagine there's so much as a ratcatcher who doesn't know how Lord Saviola died."

"Oh, I know his throat was slashed open. It's the frost on his clothes that's of interest to me."

The doctor swallowed and tapped some ash into a silver tray.

"I have no idea what you're talking about," he said quickly. *Too quickly.* "There was no frost—the idea is completely absurd."

"That's why it interests me."

"Lady Jelassi slashed Lord Saviola's throat open with a blade," the doctor replied sharply. "She was caught standing over the body, still holding the knife. That's all there is to it."

"That's not what I heard."

"I don't care what you *heard*. I was *there* and I can tell you that's all there is to know."

"Then why did Lady Jelassi claim there was frost on Lord Saviola's body?"

The doctor shrugged. "Desperate people will say desperate things. You'd have to ask her yourself."

"I did."

"I-I see . . ." The man tried to mask his unease by taking another drag on his cigarillo. "You're with the Inquisition, then?" He asked the question casually, but there was nothing casual about the way his left hand gripped the chair's armrest, knuckles whitening.

"I might be." *Let's just see where this goes.*

The doctor briefly met Lukan's gaze—a glance that seemed equal parts fear and desperation—and opened his mouth, only for his words to catch in his throat. He winced and looked away. *He's got more to say,* Lukan mused. *And I'd even guess he wants to say it. He just can't find the courage.*

"I'm sorry," the doctor said, stabbing his cigarillo into the silver tray with a little more force than was necessary. "This matter is *confidential*." He seemed to regain a measure of composure, as if the word were a shield he could hide behind. "I have nothing more to say to you, sir." He rose from the chair, forcing Lukan to step back. "Good evening."

"Doctor, wait . . ."

But the man was already moving, slipping between the groups of guests as he made for the stairs. Lukan made to follow, only to pause as he noted several guests breaking off their conversations and giving him curious looks over the rims of their glasses. *Damn it.* He watched helplessly as Vassilis disappeared down the stairwell. *What are you hiding, Doctor? What are you so scared of?* It seemed unlikely now he'd ever find out. The doctor had vanished, and with him the one possible lead that Lukan had. *What now?* He remembered the glass of wine in his hand and took a sip. The notes of it blossomed across his tongue like a kiss from an old lover. *Lady's mercy,* he thought, glancing down at his glass and the wine within. *Parvan Red, a '31 or '32 . . .*

"You look perfectly well to me, I must say."

Lukan started, almost spilling his wine. He hadn't even heard the old man approach, though as he regarded him now he realized that *old* wasn't quite the right term: the man's hair and ducktail beard might have been entirely white, his face bearing all the lines of a life well lived, yet there was a youthful glint in his dark eyes.

"I'm sorry?" Lukan said.

"I saw Doctor Vassilis beating a hasty retreat, almost as if he was fleeing for his life." The man's lips quirked in amusement. "But you don't look like you're carrying any deadly diseases to me."

"Only a dangerous love for Parvan Red," Lukan replied, raising his glass.

"Ha! I'll drink to that." The man touched his own glass to Lukan's. "My name is Marquetta—*Lord* Marquetta, I should add, though my title counts for little at a party where half the guests are fellow merchant princes."

Oh, I don't know about that. Lord Marquetta, according to Juro, wasn't just one of the so-called Silken Septet, but was the leader of the Gilded Council, a largely honorary title, as far as Lukan understood; but, given that the council was the true political power in Saphrona, that made Marquetta a man of great importance. He was certainly dressed in a manner befitting his status; even in a room full of well-dressed guests, Lord Marquetta stood out in a green velvet doublet slashed with cloth of gold, the emerald set in the top of his walking cane flashing every time it caught the light.

"Lord Bastien Dubois of Parva," Lukan replied, inclining his head. "Though I must say, my title also counts for little in a room full of such esteemed guests."

"Then that makes two of us." Marquetta chuckled. "Parva, hmm? I thought you had the look of the Heartlands about you. Beautiful part of the world. Good wine. What brings you to our fair city?"

"Business, actually."

"Ah, a man after my own heart!" The merchant prince swept a hand at the room. "Not to mention those of many others here tonight. What are your interests?"

"Gems, fine jewelry, that sort of thing." Lukan shrugged in the manner of a young nobleman with plenty of coin and not much idea what to do with it. "I've heard wonderful things about the silver mines here, so I thought I'd come and make a few inquiries, press a few palms—"

"And kiss a few arses," Marquetta cut in, giving Lukan a conspiratorial wink. "Oh, I know the tune. I've danced to it many times over the years." His face creased into a mock frown. "Though these days it seems to be *my* arse that's being kissed."

They both laughed. Lukan found himself warming to the older man; he'd met plenty of men with much smaller fortunes and far bigger egos, and he found Marquetta's apparent lack of arrogance refreshing.

"Well," the merchant prince continued, "you've certainly picked an interesting time for your visit, what with the Grand Restoration in a few days, and all the associated festivities." He took a swallow of his wine and grimaced, as if it tasted sour. "And then, of course, there's the recent business with Lord Saviola's murder."

"Indeed," Lukan said, careful to keep his tone measured. "I've heard plenty of talk about that. Terrible business. Did you know him well?"

"Not particularly, no. He was a fellow prince, of course, but our paths rarely crossed outside the council chambers. Our business interests were quite different."

"And Lady Jelassi?"

"A fine woman," Marquetta said, shaking his head. "Quick-witted, generous, principled . . . Or so it seemed. I guess I was wrong. We all were." He brightened. "Still, life goes on, eh? Especially when there's money to be made. Oh, speaking of which—have you met Lord Murillo?"

Lukan's heart lurched. "No, I've not had that pleasure."

"Then it would be *my* pleasure to introduce you. Lord Murillo owns several silver mines, so his is an arse well worth the kissing, I'd say. Follow me."

Marquetta turned and strode away, his jeweled cane clacking on the polished floor. Lukan ignored the curious stares of his fellow guests as he followed the merchant prince across the room. He was aware that he was attracting a little more attention than he felt comfortable with. Still, there was no time to worry about that—not when he was about to come face-to-face with the man who was behind Lord Saviola's murder and the framing of Zandrusa for the crime. *The villain of the whole piece.* His heartbeat quickened as Marquetta led him toward three men standing before a large marble fireplace, two of whom were listening with rapt attention as the third man regaled them with some sort of anecdote. *That'll be Murillo,* Lukan thought, studying the speaker. If the man's extravagant attire didn't give his status away (and with its red velvet, lacy cuffs, and absurdly large frill, it most certainly did), then the way the two other men guffawed with forced laughter was proof enough of his superior social standing. Lukan had spent enough time among aristocrats to know a couple of sycophants when he saw them. He'd always regarded such fawners with disdain, and now—as he watched the pair of them chortling over their wineglasses—he felt the old contempt stirring inside him. It was strangely comforting. *Even if now I have to pretend to be one of them myself.*

"A wonderful jape, Lord Murillo," one of them said, raising his glass. "Perhaps I might share one of my own—"

"Good evening, gentlemen," Marquetta said grandly, tapping his cane twice on the floor as if to announce himself.

The man who was speaking threw him a dark look, only for his wine-flushed face to pale when he realized who had interrupted him. He stammered an apology and quickly excused himself, his fellow sycophant following suit. Marquetta ignored them.

"Lady's blood," Murillo swore, piglike eyes narrowing as he scowled at Marquetta. "I had those two fools eating out of my hand. Why'd you have to ruin it?"

"If those young men had spent another moment in your company," Marquetta retorted, a wry smile dancing on his lips, "their tongues would have been so deep in your backside you'd have never pried them loose."

Murillo waved a hand in dismissal, bejeweled fingers glinting in the light. "The hells do you want, Marquetta?"

"Well as it happens, I have someone here to meet you." He beckoned Lukan forward. "May I introduce Lord Bastien Dubois of Parva."

"An honor, my lord," Lukan said, offering the man a deep bow.

"Likewise," Murillo replied, his tone one of cool disinterest.

"Lord Dubois is new to the city," Marquetta continued, "and is keen to discuss business." He turned to Lukan and offered his hand. "I will leave you to it, my lord. Good fortune to you."

"Thank you," Lukan replied, shaking the merchant prince's hand. "You've been too kind." *And more helpful than you can possibly know.* "I hope we meet again."

"Oh, I'm sure we will." Marquetta smiled. "I look forward to it."

With those words he swept away, leaving Lukan alone with a man who, he suspected, would think nothing of ordering his murder, should he discover Lukan's true identity and purpose at the party. *No pressure then.*

"So," Murillo said, slurping from his wineglass. "You wish to discuss business."

"If it pleases you, my lord," Lukan replied, resisting the urge to wrinkle his nose as the man's scent—an overpowering citrus perfume undercut by a whiff of stale sweat—tickled his nostrils.

"And what sort of business might that be?" Murillo didn't even look at Lukan as he asked the question; instead his eyes swept the room as if in search of more stimulating conversation. *Or someone else to bore with his anecdotes.* The merchant prince's sense of self-importance had been clear to Lukan even from a distance—it was reflected in every curl of his lip, every flick of his ringed fingers—but now he could see that the man's vanity also extended to his appearance, as evidenced by the fake beauty mark on his left cheek and the fact that the impressive dark curls atop his head were clearly a wig.

"One of my interests is fine jewelry," Lukan said, spinning out the ploy he had developed with Juro's help. "I was hoping to discuss acquiring a shipment of silver—"

"You're from *Parva*." Murillo said the word as if it tasted like ashes in his mouth.

"I am, my lord."

"Which trading company?"

"Ah, well . . . we're a new venture, just starting out, so you won't have heard of us—"

"I'll be the judge of that."

"Of course. We're called the Silver Owl Trading Coaster."

"Ah yes, the name is vaguely familiar." Lord Murillo smirked and swilled the wine in his glass. "I pride myself on knowing the names of all mercantile ventures that deal in silver in the Old Empire, no matter how newly established."

Including ones that don't even exist. "We are humbled by your recognition, my lord—"

"Yes, yes." The merchant prince silenced Lukan with a sweep of his hand. "I don't discuss business affairs in such surroundings, but if you care to make an appointment with my secretary at the council chambers I may be able to spare you a few moments of my time."

"You are most kind."

Lord Murillo grunted in apparent agreement, his gaze wandering once more. "Anyway, if that'll be all—"

"Actually, there was something else."

"Make it quick."

"Of course. Forgive me, my lord, but . . ." Lukan affected an apologetic expression. "I've heard one or two rumors concerning an upcoming motion to be debated in the council, concerning the rights and privileges of laborers in the city—"

"*Privileges,*" the merchant prince sneered, taking a swallow of wine as if to wash the taste of the word from his mouth. "My peers and I offer them stable jobs and fair—no, *generous*—pay, and they have the nerve to demand more. Ungrateful swine, the lot of them. The whole thing is a disgrace."

"Indeed," Lukan said, nodding in feigned agreement, "but I must confess to being curious as to what impact such a motion might have on the price of silver—"

"It won't happen. The motion won't pass."

"You're sure? Forgive me, but I had been led to believe that the motion had found favor with some of your fellow council members—"

"Fools and charlatans, the lot of them. They allowed that upstart Jelassi to get inside their heads and poison their minds with this . . . this *nonsense* about civil rights." Murillo practically spat the last two words. "She convinced them to look down on the very things that made this city great. But they forget. They forget that it was blood and sweat and backbreaking toil that built Saphrona."

"Quite." *Just not yours.*

"And they forget too that it was *my* silver mines that originally brought prosperity to this city." He relaxed then, lips curling into a smirk. "Still, it hardly matters now. Not with Jelassi in chains."

"Yes, I heard about that unfortunate event—"

"There's nothing unfortunate about it," Murillo snapped, giving Lukan a sharp look. "Jelassi got exactly what she deserved, the damned murderer. The very motion she fought so hard for is going to go up in flames, and it's entirely her own fault." He snorted a laugh. "I've never heard an irony so sweet."

"Indeed . . . Though I must say, it strikes me as most strange that she should murder her closest ally." Lukan took a sip of wine, watching the man carefully over the rim of his glass. *There—was that a flicker of unease?*

"Yes, well . . ." Murillo tugged at his oversized ruff, as if feeling suddenly flushed. "Lord Saviola was a decent man," he continued, wincing as if the admission somehow caused him pain. "And a good businessman, though I didn't agree with his politics." He gestured dismissively, rings glinting. "In any case, the business with Jelassi makes little difference in the grand scheme of things. Her motion would have failed anyway. I had more than enough support to ensure that."

So why did you murder her ally and frame Zandrusa for the crime? The question danced on the tip of Lukan's tongue, where it would have to remain. Still, the short time he'd spent in Murillo's company had confirmed what he'd suspected: that the man was an utter bastard, and that he was likely behind Zandrusa's predicament. "I'm most reassured by your words, my lord," he said, offering the man another bow. "My sincere thanks for your time. It has been most enlightening."

"My pleasure," Murillo muttered, his eyes already sweeping the room once more. "Now, you really must excuse me . . ."

"Yes, of course." Lukan bowed again and turned away. *Time to get the hells out of here.* He'd learned as much as he could and didn't dare push his luck any further—all he wanted now was to get out of his expensive clothes and think over what he'd seen and heard. *Preferably with a glass of wine.* Keeping his eyes lowered, he made for the staircase and descended as quickly as he dared, the chatter and laughter of Saphrona's elite citizens gradually fading behind him.

———

Lukan was making his way along a gravel path, the faint strain of music and voices carrying across from the nearby lawn, when a figure stepped out from behind a hedgerow to block his way.

"Sir," the figure said in a hushed voice, features concealed by shadow. "A moment, please."

Lukan froze, hand instinctively reaching for a sword hilt that wasn't there. He glanced over his shoulder, half expecting to see another figure blocking his retreat, but the path behind him was empty. "Who goes there?" he demanded.

"It's me," the figure replied, rather unhelpfully.

Lukan frowned. "Doctor Vassilis?"

"Shh! Not so loud." The doctor stepped forward, the light of an alchemical globe illuminating his face in a rosy glow that seemed at odds with his fearful expression. Another cigarillo had turned to ash between his fingers.

Lady's mercy, Lukan thought, drawing a breath, *the man's terrified. But of what?* "Doctor? Is everything all ri—"

"Quiet!" the man hissed, glancing around as if expecting the very shadows to come alive and strangle him. When they didn't, he swallowed and edged closer. "You want to know what really happened to Lord Saviola?" he asked, his voice barely above a whisper. "Because . . ." He hesitated, as if trying to find the will to continue. "Because I will tell you."

Well, this is interesting. "Go on."

"Not here." The man wet his lips with a nervous tongue. "Meet me in my office at the Collegium at midnight. It's in the western wing on the second floor. The main entrance will be locked but there's a door at the rear of the building that I'll leave open." He raised the cigarillo to his lips, saw it was mostly ash and dropped it to the ground. "Midnight," he repeated, grinding his heel against the embers. Then he turned and strode away in the direction of the lawn.

Lukan watched him go, then continued toward the gates. *Looks like that glass of wine is going to have to wait.*

20

CABINET OF CURIOSITIES

It was fair to say, when it came to secret midnight trysts, that Lukan was something of an expert. He'd certainly enjoyed more than his fair share during his years at the Academy, mostly with Amicia. However, he'd never found himself hiding in a shrubbery in the middle of the night, hoping to speak to a man with a dubious eyepiece about the mysterious death of a merchant prince.

"So are we going in, then?" Flea asked, leaves rustling as she shifted beside him.

"In a moment."

"You said that several moments ago."

"I just need some time."

"What for?"

"To try and think," he replied, shooting her a glare that would be lost in the darkness, "without being constantly interrupted."

The girl muttered under her breath; Lukan thought he caught the word *stupid* but couldn't be sure, and wondered again whether he should have left Flea behind at the Scrivener's house. Yet after missing out on Lady Valdezar's soirée, Flea had made it clear she had no intention of being sidelined a second time, and Lukan had been too distracted to argue. *In any case, it won't hurt to have another pair of eyes.* He moved a branch out of the way and peered through the foliage. *Especially if this goes wrong.*

The Collegium of Saphrona stood some twenty yards distant, the columns and arches of its facade limned in moonlight. The impressive building crowned a hill in the upmarket commercial district of the city known as the Silks, and was surrounded by a crumbling wall that had proven no difficulty to climb; the vines that covered its surface had offered plenty of handholds. The grounds within were dark, the neat lawns and paths shrouded in a silence broken only by the chirp of cicadas—and by Flea, who as usual was having trouble keeping her mouth shut.

"You know this could be a trap?" the girl whispered.

"It had crossed my mind," Lukan replied irritably. In truth, the thought had gnawed at him ever since he'd left Lady Valdezar's estate, his optimism at a fresh lead soon tempered by a sense of foreboding. He'd spent the subsequent couple of hours mulling over his last encounter with the doctor, searching for any sign of deceit but finding none. The man, as far as he could tell, had been scared out of his mind, and his promise to spill his secrets about Lord Saviola's death was entirely genuine. *And yet . . .* Lukan couldn't shake the fear that it had all been an act, that Vassilis might somehow be in league with Lord Murillo, his invitation to a clandestine meeting in fact an invitation to something far more sinister. He'd managed to push the thought aside, but now—with the Collegium looming before him—the fear was much harder to ignore.

"Well, there's no point sitting here," Flea insisted, plucking a leaf from the bush beside her. "We won't know if it's a trap until we get inside—"

"Hush, little mouse," a voice said from Lukan's left, the soft words at odds with the cigarillo-coarsened growl that delivered them. "Let the man think in peace." He couldn't see Hector in the darkness, but he could imagine the lopsided grin on the man's face; the guard's expression rarely seemed to change, and Lukan imagined that he wore that smile all the time, whether he was smoking a cigarillo or cracking someone's skull. Hector was one of the guards the Scrivener had assigned to them, and Flea—to Lukan's surprise—had taken an instant liking to the gruff man. Even more surprising was the guard's ability to keep the girl quiet, a skill he demonstrated again now as Flea fell silent without complaint. It was one reason why Lukan had asked Hector to come along on this little midnight jaunt, the other being that the man was built like an ox and had hands that could crush grapefruit. *Or skulls. Let's hope it doesn't come to that.*

"Let's move," Lukan whispered. "We'll learn nothing by sitting here."

"That's what I just said," Flea hissed.

"You sure about this?" Hector rumbled.

"No," Lukan admitted. "But we don't have much choice."

"The mistress won't like it."

"No, I don't suppose she will."

There had been no time to discuss his plans with the Scrivener and obtain her approval—the best he could do, after arriving back at the safe house, was to scribble a quick message about what had happened at Lady Valdezar's gala and his intention to meet with Vassilis. He'd asked Hector's counterpart, a guard called Vetch, to deliver the message to Juro. Then he'd changed into more suitable clothes and hit the streets again, Hector and Flea in tow. The Scrivener, as Hector had noted, was not going to be happy, and the fact that he'd taken her guard along for the ride would only anger her further. Still, there was precious little he could do about that now. In any case, if Vassilis proved true to his word, what he learned tonight could prove vital in their fight to prove Zandrusa's innocence. And if instead it turned out to be a trap . . . *Well, she can shout at my dead body.*

"All right," he said, with a conviction that was as much for his own benefit as anyone else's. "Let's go and see what Doctor Vassilis has got to say for himself."

"Finally," Flea muttered.

"And if this doesn't end with blades pressed against our throats, perhaps I'll ask the good doctor if he can prescribe a cure."

"A cure?" the girl echoed. "For what?"

"Your big mouth."

Lukan moved away before Flea could punch him, the soft rasp of Hector's laughter in his ears.

————

They stole through the moonlit grounds, passing the locked front gates and keeping to the shadow of the vine-choked wall as they circled around the western wing of the Collegium.

"Lukan," Flea whispered as they reached the rear of the building.

"I see it."

A light glowed in a room on the second floor, bright against the darkness.

"Hector, you're with me," Lukan murmured as they crouched behind a towering poplar. "Flea, I need you to stay here and—"

"Nope," the girl cut in, shaking her head. "I ain't staying out here."

Lady's mercy, here we go. "Someone needs to stay here and keep watch."

"So make Hector do it."

"Hector is coming with me. I need him in case . . . um . . ."

"Someone tries to stick a knife in your back," the guard said.

"Right." Lukan squeezed Flea's shoulder. "You're smaller"—he felt the girl tense under his hand—"and *quicker* than either of us," he added quickly, before she could voice the protest that was clearly forming on her lips. "I need you out here to watch for anyone following us, in case this is a trap."

"If this is a trap," the girl replied, shrugging off his hand, "then they'll be inside already, waiting for us."

"Then you'll be safer out here."

"I can look after myself."

Lukan looked askance at Hector, hoping the guard might back him up, but the man merely shrugged.

"Fine," Lukan said grudgingly, "but stay close to us. And don't—"

"Touch anything," Flea said, rolling her eyes. "Yeah, I got it."

Lukan turned his gaze back to the darkened building, the light still shining on the second floor. A candle, judging by the softness of the glow. It flickered as he watched, as if beckoning to him—an invitation. *But to what, exactly?* "Vassilis said there was a door . . ."

"There," Flea said, pointing.

It took Lukan a moment to spy the entrance. Once again he was impressed by how sharp Flea's eyes were. "Hector," he said, glancing at the big man. "You ready?"

"All set," the guard replied, hefting the unlit wooden torch he carried in one hand.

"Flea?"

"I'm ready."

"Then let's go."

Lukan broke from the cover of the tree and ran across the lawn to the entrance, Flea and Hector following close behind. They regrouped in the shadows of the arched doorway, Hector keeping an eye out while Lukan gripped the door handle and gave it a gentle push. *Come on . . .* To his relief the door opened, the squeal of old hinges too loud in the silence of the night. *Vassilis is proving true to his word. So far at least.* He peered through the doorway. The darkness seemed to stare back.

"Hector?" he prompted, but the big man was already pulling a flint from his pocket.

"Hold this, little mouse," the guard said, handing the torch to Flea. The girl obliged, holding it steady as Hector struck sparks from the flint with a knife. A flame quickly blossomed from the oil-soaked cloth wrapped around the torch's head.

"All right," Lukan said, taking the torch from Flea, "let's go."

He stepped through the door, the torchlight revealing white walls hung with oil paintings in ornate frames, and the bronze bust of a man that stared indignantly at them from a nearby pedestal. The polished floor stretched away before them into blackness. Flea and Hector followed, the latter pulling the door closed.

Silence, save for the hissing of the torch.

"Stay alert," Lukan whispered, drawing his dirk. It felt reassuring in his hand. Hector slid a large cudgel from a loop on his belt; its surface was scored and pitted, suggesting it had already cracked a hundred skulls and was good for a hundred more. "The light we saw is coming from the second floor," Lukan continued, "so we need to find a staircase. Wait—what the hells is that?"

"What?" Hector grunted, tensing as he squinted at the darkness.

"*That*," Lukan repeated, gesturing at the knife Flea had just drawn.

"It's my weapon," the girl replied nonchalantly.

"I can bloody see that. Where the hells did you get it from?"

"Stole it from your room."

"Of course you did. Silly question."

"You want me to come in here unarmed?"

I'd rather you didn't come in at all. He kept the thought to himself; this was not the time to start an argument, nor did he fancy being on the receiving end of a jab from the girl's dagger. *The punches are bad enough.* But most of all, he knew that Flea wouldn't understand—she would think he was trying to exclude her because of her age, her inexperience. The truth was entirely different; he was trying to protect her. He didn't want the girl to get hurt because of him. *But that's not the entire truth, is it? Admit it, you're growing fond of her.*

"The hells you looking at?"

Lukan realized he'd been staring at Flea, who was glaring back, eyes full of defiance.

"Nothing." He looked away. "Let's just get this over with."

———

Lukan led the way down the corridor, Flea silent as a cat at his side, Hector a reassuring presence at his back. The light from his torch spilled through doorways on either side, revealing glimpses of wood-paneled classrooms—blackboards covered in chalk diagrams and formulae, rows of empty desks and stalls. It reminded Lukan of his time at the Academy, not that he'd spent much of that time in lessons. The taverns of Parva had proven a far more enticing prospect.

At the end of the corridor they found a staircase and climbed the timeworn steps in single file. The upper floor was just as dark as the lower, save for a slash of light away to their left—the glow of a candle spilling through an open door.

"Lukan," Flea whispered.

"I see it." He exchanged a meaningful look with Hector, then crept toward the light, knife raised, heart racing.

The door stood ajar. A bronze plaque adorned its wooden surface. DOCTOR BENITO VASSILIS—FACULTY OF MEDICINE. No sound came from beyond, and, when Lukan peered through the narrow gap between the door and its frame, he saw nothing more than the edge of a desk and a bookcase behind it. He took a deep breath.

"Doctor Vassilis?" he called softly.

There was no response.

Lukan rapped lightly on the door and tried again. "Doctor Vassilis?"

Silence.

"Not sure I like this," Hector murmured.

"Nor do I," Lukan admitted. "Stay sharp."

He eased the door open and slipped into the room.

Doctor Vassilis was sitting behind his desk. He was still wearing the same clothes he'd worn to Lady Valdezar's gala, though he'd lost his bow tie and waistcoat, and had somehow contrived to spill red wine all over his fine shirt.

Lukan's heart lurched. *Not wine.*

Vassilis stared intently at him, but offered no greeting. No doubt the deep slash across his throat made speaking difficult.

"Shit," Lukan murmured, his mouth suddenly dry. "Shit, shit, *shit* . . ."

"Lady's blood," Hector swore. "We need to get out of here."

Lukan barely heard him as he glanced around the room. The

place was a mess, with books piled on the floor and papers scattered over every surface, but it was the untidiness of a distracted mind, rather than the result of someone turning the place over. There were little signs—a mug of cold coffee here, a plate of abandoned food there—that suggested Vassilis was just another absent-minded academic. *Or had been before someone opened his throat.* He approached the desk and leaned over it, pressing his fingers to the side of the man's neck. No pulse—the doctor was too far gone for that, of course—but warmth still lingered beneath his skin. *He's not been dead long.* The wound looked no better up close: a vivid slash of red, neat as you like. *The mark of a professional killer. One who might still be close by.*

The thought should have worried him, but it barely registered in the face of a greater concern: that his one lead in this entire mystery had been snuffed out, quite literally. *Who were you so afraid of, Doctor?* he wondered, searching the man's vacant, glassy eyes. *What did you know?* That the man had known *something* was beyond doubt. Lukan was now sure this hadn't been a trap; the doctor had been prepared to reveal some sort of truth to him, even though he feared it might cost him his life. *Well, he was right about that.*

"What a bloody mess," Hector muttered, joining him at the desk. "We need to go, Lukan. It's not safe."

"Just give me a moment."

"For what?" The guard jabbed his cudgel at the corpse. "Hate to break it to you, but *he* ain't going to be talking any time soon. Face it, lad—whatever secrets the man had, they died with him."

"Perhaps," Lukan replied, his gaze drifting to the surface of the desk and lingering on the stacks of papers and ledgers. "Or maybe he wrote them down."

"Why would he do that?" Flea asked, squeezing between them. The sight of the corpse didn't appear to bother her. No doubt she'd seen worse.

"Because he was a scholar. And I'd wager that like most scholars he kept a record of his thoughts and discoveries—"

"Forget it," Hector cut in. "Look at the state of this place; you could spend hours searching it and still not find what you're looking for."

"Then we'd best get started."

"Listen to me, lad—whoever killed the doctor could return at any moment."

"All the more reason for you to get back outside and keep watch."

"We should go. *Now*. Get back to the safe house and consider our options—"

"He *is* the option," Lukan snapped, pointing at Vassilis. "Or was, at least. And I'm not leaving until I've found out what he had to say. One way or another."

Hector's jaw tightened, a vein throbbing in his forehead. Lukan held the man's gaze, refusing to so much as blink. They remained that way for several moments, until Flea sighed.

"You're both idiots."

Hector grunted and nodded at Lukan. "He's the idiot. Get to it then, Gardova." He turned toward the door. "I'm going to count to a hundred and then I'm leaving, with or without you."

"So what are we looking for?" Flea asked as Hector left the room.

"I don't know," Lukan admitted, riffling through the nearest stack of papers. "A diary perhaps, or some sort of journal . . ." He trailed off at the girl's blank expression. "A book," he clarified, "full of the doctor's handwriting."

The girl glanced around the room. "But there must be hundreds of books in here."

"Right, but it won't look like the others. It'll be full of handwriting, not printed text."

"But I can't even read."

"Doesn't matter, you'll know it when you see it. Try not to break anything."

Flea gave him a glare as she wandered over to some shelves on the far side of the room. Lukan turned his attention back

to the desk, trying to ignore the corpse's glassy-eyed stare as
he rummaged through the piles of papers. Finding nothing of
interest, he moved around to where the doctor sat and tried the
two drawers. Both were stuffed with more papers and assorted
curiosities, but nothing that looked like a diary. *Damn it, there's
got to be something—*

He jolted as a crash interrupted his thoughts, something smashing on the floor. He whirled round to see Flea standing on a stool,
one arm extended into a bookcase. What might have once been a
glass sculpture lay in jagged shards at her feet.

"Damn it," he snapped, "I told you to be careful."

"The bloody hells was that?" Hector hissed, sticking his head
through the doorway.

"Just Flea being careless."

The man muttered under his breath and disappeared again.

Click.

Lukan frowned. "What was that sound?"

"Oh, nothing," Flea said nonchalantly. "Just this fake book
that seems to be a lever." She grinned as the whole row of leather-
bound volumes swung out of the bookcase in an arc, revealing a
darkened compartment behind.

"Let me see," Lukan said, moving to join her.

"Uh-uh," the girl replied, reaching into the space. "It's my find,
so I get first call on any valuables."

"Fine. Just tell me what you can feel. Is there a—"

"Give me a chance." Flea's brows knitted as she groped around
inside. "Ah, got something." She withdrew her arm, a piece of
dog-eared card clutched in her hand. It bore the likeness of a
woman, sketched in charcoal.

"Let me have a look."

Flea was more than happy to relinquish the item and immediately reached back into the recess. Lukan turned the card over,
revealing a message on the back. *To my darling Benito. Yours
always, Mathilde.* He glanced at the dead doctor. *Well, it seems at
least one person will mourn his passing.*

A sharp intake of breath told him that Flea had found something else. The girl's face lit up as she pulled out a small leather pouch, which clinked as she shook it. Her smile grew wider as she pulled the drawstrings back, revealing the gleam of silver coins within.

"That's more like it," she murmured.

"Is there anything else?"

Flea thrust her arm back into the hidden space. "Nothing . . . no, wait. I think there's something . . . Got it." She withdrew a notebook, the leather cover scuffed and worn, and opened it to reveal pages of neat handwriting comprising paragraphs beneath underlined dates.

"That's it," Lukan said excitedly. "That's got to be the doctor's journal."

"Then let's get the hells out of here," Hector said, poking his head round the door.

"Agreed," Lukan replied, slipping the book into a pocket. There would be plenty of time to read it later. "Come on," he said, tapping Flea's shoulder. "Let's go."

"But there might be more stuff here," the girl protested.

"Doesn't matter. We've got what we came for."

Lukan started toward the door, only to hesitate as he realized he was still holding the charcoal portrait. On a whim, he returned to the corpse and tucked the card under the doctor's hand where it rested in his lap. Ignoring Flea's questioning look, he gestured to the door. "Let's get out of here."

"About bloody time," Hector muttered.

21

A Good Turn of Phrase

Yet another day where I found myself questioning why I ever chose to pursue a career in medicine. I spent the morning up at the Rise, tending to the afflictions of the wealthy. That is to say, supplying Lord Firenze with another pot of cream for his piles and providing Pontifex Barbosa with some lotion to cure the side effects of his various indiscretions. You'd think the holiest man in the city would know better, but apparently celibacy is yet another virtue that he preaches but deigns not to practice himself. Then I had to explain to Lord Valderamos—for the umpteenth time—that there's nothing more I can do about his thrice-damned gout. Oh, but the highlight of the morning was pulling a rotten tooth from Lady Taranzia's lower jaw. The old hag made her usual pass at me, fluttering what was left of her eyelashes, as if I might be persuaded to overlook the fact that she's an eighty-three-year-old widow whose breath smells like a cesspit.

Lukan laughed, almost spilling his wine over the journal. He glanced over at where Flea lay sprawled across a divan, but the girl didn't stir from her sleep. She'd crashed out not long after they'd returned to the safe house, the night's adventures clearly having caught up with her. Sleep, however, was the last thing on Lukan's mind. His thoughts were racing after the evening's events, and at the prospect of what he might find in the doctor's journal—proof, if he was lucky, that Lord Murillo was behind the murder of Lord Saviola. Such evidence would also, he hoped, serve to temper the Scrivener's wrath. He'd spoken to Vetch soon after they'd returned from the Collegium, and the guard confirmed he'd delivered Lukan's message to Juro. He said no reply had yet been forthcoming, but the man was in little doubt as to what his employer's response would be. *She's going to have your balls for breakfast, lad,* he'd said cheerily.

All the more reason to find something of worth in the journal.

So, leaving Hector and Vetch to a game of cards downstairs in the kitchen, Lukan had retired to the first-floor living room and—with a bottle of Parvan Red for company—had delved into the private life of Doctor Benito Vassilis. He resisted the urge to skip straight to the entry for the night of Lord Saviola's murder, instead starting with an entry dated some two months before; he wanted to try to get the measure of the doctor. After all, he'd met the man only twice before he died, and his behavior had been erratic to say the least. It seemed important to try to establish the doctor's state of mind in the weeks before Lord Saviola's murder, to provide some context for whatever had happened on that fateful night.

Or at least that's what he told himself.

The fact of the matter was that the journal made for absorbing reading. Vassilis possessed a dry humor and a talent for a good turn of phrase, and while many of the entries detailed mundane concerns—lack of funding, perceived slights from students, the difficulty of obtaining fresh human organs for his studies—others were far more revealing. The doctor's meticulous handwriting took on a furious edge as he railed against his peers' criticisms of one of his recent academic papers—an episode that triggered a slide into depression, which in turn fueled an addiction to alcohol and a variety of illegal substances that he regularly took in the company of courtesans. Vassilis wrote with particular bitterness about a failed romance he'd had with a student, which ended in blackmail and acrimony, though the doctor's anger seemed mostly reserved for his own conduct in the sordid affair. *He clearly despised most of his patients,* Lukan thought, as he turned a page, *and held his students and fellow scholars in equal disdain. Yet the person he seems to have hated most of all was himself.*

The more Lukan read, the more he sensed an unseen—and unmentioned—force behind the doctor's writings. A presence, or perhaps an absence, that seemed to shape his bitterness and resentment, that acted as a focus for his self-loathing. *The woman in the charcoal sketch, perhaps?* Yet for all the doctor's failings—and Vassilis himself acknowledged there were many—Lukan found nothing to suggest that the doctor was involved in any conspiracies, or that his life was in any danger.

Until he finally reached the entry for the night that Lord Saviola was murdered.

Lady's mercy, what a strange night. Even now, thinking about the events of the last few hours, I can scarcely comprehend them. Where to even begin . . . well, at the start I suppose.

I was awoken in the early hours of the morning by someone pounding on my front door. I'm not sure of the exact time, though I was still a little drunk, so perhaps between the first and second bells. I ignored the hammering for a while, hoping whoever it was would go away, but then they started calling my name and the banging intensified. Eventually I went to see who it was and what they wanted at such an hour. I opened the door, to be confronted by a man stricken with panic. He spoke so quickly I could scarcely understand a word he said, and if it wasn't for the sight of Lord Saviola's motif on his tunic I would have slammed the door in his face. Instead I managed to calm him down and he told me that his master had been attacked and was in desperate need of medical attention.

The man's distress was clearly genuine, so I dressed as quickly as I could. Besides, Saviola was one of the few merchant princes I can say I quite liked. Anyway, I climbed into the waiting carriage and we raced to Saviola's villa halfway up the Rise. During the short journey I questioned the man as best I could. He knew very little, only that Saviola had been entertaining Lady Jelassi (another merchant prince I will admit to a liking for) and the two of them had dined together and then retired to Saviola's study. At some point one of the other servants apparently arrived with refreshments, to find Lady Jelassi—and this is the part I can scarcely believe—standing over the body of Saviola, with a bloody blade in hand. Jelassi apparently called for a doctor, which was why I had been summoned. The man knew nothing more, and, when I asked him whether he believed Lady Jelassi had attacked his master, he could only stare at me with wide eyes as if he couldn't even grasp the question.

When we arrived at Saviola's villa, we found the constabulary had got there before us, and were leading Lady Jelassi through the garden—in chains, no less, though she appeared calm and didn't resist. I dashed inside, following the servant to the study.

Upon entering the room, I was immediately struck by how cold it was, despite it being a balmy night. But that wasn't all—there was a strange weight to the air, a lingering sense of something I instinctively knew was unnatural.

I cast these thoughts aside, assuming them nothing more than the product of my tired mind, and attended to Lord Saviola's body. He was lying near the center of the room, limbs askew, eyes glassy. He was dead, I could tell that before I even knelt beside him. The cause of death appeared obvious: a stab wound to the throat. The man should have been lying in a pool of his own blood, yet there was surprisingly little, save for a few drops on his shirt. I examined the wound further and found, to my surprise, that the blood had congealed—something known to happen when a wound is inflicted after death has already occurred.

As I examined the corpse further, I discovered the skin was very cold to the touch, too cold for a body that had been dead for barely half an hour. The limbs were also stiff, as if rigor mortis had already set in, even though that usually doesn't happen for hours after death.

But that was not all.

As I leaned closer, I saw flakes of frost on the man's eyelashes. Frost. In late summer.

In that moment I knew the truth. It wasn't a blade that killed Lord Saviola. It was sorcery.

I rose shakily to my feet, my heart pounding. My only instinct was to leave as quickly as possible—I wanted no part of whatever had happened here.

Gathering my wits, I informed the steward that his master was dead
and beyond my help. Then I took my leave—I couldn't bear to spend another moment in that room. As I left the villa I saw Prime Inquisitor
Fierro disembarking from a carriage. Fearing he would want to talk to me
about what I'd found or, worse, ask me to accompany him, I hid behind
a hedgerow and waited until he'd gone inside. Fortunately the carriage I'd
arrived in was still in the driveway, and the driver didn't object when I told
him to take me home.

My hands were trembling by the time I got back. Unlocking my front
door was tricky, filling my pipe with shimmer was even harder. Still, the
drug calmed my nerves somewhat, if not the thoughts that whirled in my
mind. Eventually exhaustion overcame me and I retired to bed. A particular side effect of shimmer, as I've noted before, is that it will often make me
hard. That was the case again tonight, and, as any honest man will tell you,
trying to concentrate on anything—even falling asleep—is difficult when you
have a raging erection. I resolved to do something about it, figuring such an
action might serve to dissolve any lingering tension. Summoning what little
energy I could, I set to work.

It was then that I heard the footsteps on the stairs.

I can honestly say I've never lost an erection so fast in my life.

They were in my room before I'd even got out of bed: three of them,
little more than shadows in the moonlight. I felt an absurd rush of embarrassment at my nakedness and pulled the bedclothes over me. My
heart pounded as I sat there staring at them. They stood still, apparently staring back, though I couldn't see their faces. This bizarre stand-
off seemed to last an age, though it couldn't have been more than a
few moments. Then the central figure stepped forward and I heard the
unmistakable whisper of steel being drawn. I remember the moonlight
playing along the blade's length, and its coldness as the tip touched my
throat a moment later. I somehow found the strength to ask them what
they wanted.

The figure replied in a woman's voice (and I quote verbatim): "Lord
Saviola died from a stab wound to the throat. There was nothing otherwise remarkable about his death, nor the corpse he left behind. You
will make this clear in any reports you write, and to anyone who asks. If

*you don't . . ." I gasped as the tip of the blade bit into my skin—a clear
warning.*

Then the three figures left my bedroom, silent as shadows.

*That was over two hours ago. The sun is now rising, I've smoked all
the shimmer I have left, and yet I'm still shaking like a leaf. What to
make of all this? That there's some sort of conspiracy here, I have no
doubt. But who is behind it? Who really killed Lord Saviola? Because it
wasn't Lady Jelassi, I'm sure of it—in fact, it seems likely the murderer
intended for her to take the blame for the crime. She may have been
found holding the blade, but Saviola was murdered by sorcery, and
Jelassi is no gleamer. Besides, they always work in pairs and Jelassi
was found alone in the room. Someone must have hired the gleamers,
but who? Only someone with plenty of coin could afford their services.
Could it be another merchant prince?*

*If I was a better man than I am, I would go to the Inquisition and tell
them what I know, but every time the thought crosses my mind I feel the
bite of the blade's tip at my throat. Damn them. Damn them to the hells.
I'll do what they ask. I'll report that Saviola was killed by a stab wound
to the throat, even though it's likely that wound was inflicted after he was
already dead. I know such an action will likely condemn Lady Jelassi,
but what am I supposed to do? It's my life or hers.*

Lukan lowered the journal and drained the last of his wine,
swilling it around his mouth as he considered the doctor's words.
*No wonder he almost choked on his cigarillo when I mentioned
Lord Saviola's murder. Poor bastard was scared out of his wits.*
Any lingering doubt he might have had about Zandrusa's innocence was gone now. The doctor's account verified the merchant
prince's claim about the frost on the corpse, but more importantly
it lent serious weight to her belief that she had been deliberately
framed for the murder—the threat against Vassilis's life was proof
enough of that. Yet there was nothing in the doctor's journal to
suggest Lord Murillo was involved, no way of knowing if the three
mysterious figures in the doctor's bedroom had been sent by him.
Smoke and mirrors. This damned city is full of them.

Lukan refilled his wineglass and turned to the next entry.

Two inquisitors visited me at the Collegium today, as I knew they would.
They were grim-faced and steely-eyed as they asked me about Lord Sav-
iola's death. I told them he died from a stab wound to the throat, though
my heart was hammering and I could feel sweat on my brow. They asked
if I had noticed anything else, anything unusual. I said that I had not. I
was sure they could tell I was lying, but they merely nodded and asked
me to write a statement. As I took up my quill I felt an overwhelming
urge to tell them everything, to reveal the truth. Yet my nerve failed me.
And so, feeling sickened to my very bones, I wrote my false statement
and knowingly condemned an innocent woman to death. As soon as the
inquisitors left I vomited into a desk drawer, my entire body shaking. The
fact that I am nothing more than a pawn—that someone else is pulling
the strings of this little conspiracy—does nothing to alleviate the guilt that
gnaws at me. I had a chance to save Lady Jelassi's life, to help her prove
her innocence. Instead I lied to save my own worthless hide. Perhaps
that's why I've recorded the truth in this journal. It makes me feel a little
better knowing that there's a true account of Lord Saviola's death in the
world, even though its very existence might well lead to my own. Perhaps
that would be fitting.

Lukan turned the page to find that there was only one further
entry, dated that very day and scrawled in a hasty hand.

Someone knows. I don't know who this man is, but he claimed to have spoken
to Lady Jelassi. He knows about the frost on Saviola's corpse. And worse, he
knows that I know. I can't even begin to—Lady's mercy, my mind is racing
away from me again. All I know is that my life is in danger, and it's entirely
because of my own actions.

  Since my last entry, I'd been lying low. I hid my journal and I
told the Collegium I needed time off to attend to a private matter,
which was ironically close to the truth—I badly needed to get my head
straight, to somehow come to terms with my guilt. I didn't want to stay

at home in case my midnight visitors returned, so I rented a room at an inn just outside the city. I had hoped for some peace and quiet in which to think, but the damned place was full of travelers, all here for the celebrations. Still, I wasn't troubled any further by the Inquisition, or anyone else.

With so much on my mind, I scarcely had a thought to spare for the upcoming celebrations, and it was with some anguish I remembered my invite to Lady Valdezar's gala this evening. Given her generous donations to the medical faculty over the past few years, it would have been remiss of me not to attend. I figured that if I was going to pick up the threads of my life and carry on with my career, I would need Valdezar's continued goodwill. Besides, I knew I couldn't hide from society forever.

The evening initially proceeded perfectly well—there were plenty of inquiries about both my health and my absence, which I had expected, and I deflected them with a story about a death in the family. Much of the conversation, inevitably, was about Lord Saviola's murder and Lady Jelassi's conviction (and her first appearance in the Bone Pit, which I'd already heard she survived). I managed to maintain my composure, even as the guilt struck me with renewed force. Yet my mask finally slipped when a stranger approached me as I was smoking alone. He began asking about Lord Saviola's death, but I managed to fend off his questions. Then he mentioned the bloody frost.

I panicked. I can't recall what I said, but I managed to escape him. Yet as I made my way outside, my heart hammering, I realized that any belief I had that I could merely continue my life as before was a lie. I couldn't go on like this, the guilt was—is—just too much. I took a hit of shimmer behind a hedgerow and knew in that moment I couldn't keep my secret any longer. I had to share it, relieve myself of its burden and to the hells with the consequences.

When the stranger appeared a short while later, I accosted him and told him to meet me at my quarters in the Collegium at midnight. That was over two hours ago, and the midnight hour now draws near. When this man arrives—whoever he is—I'm going to tell him everything. And then

I'm going to leave Saphrona. My home. I'm going to leave and never come back. Perhaps I can start afresh—a new city, a new life.

Hopefully soon this nightmare will be over.

"Oh, it's over all right," Lukan murmured, closing the journal and picturing the doctor's bloody throat. *Though I'm not sure it's quite the ending you had in mind.* He set the journal on the table beside him and sat back in his chair, taking a sip of wine. *Something doesn't add up here.* Vassilis had surely been murdered by the mysterious figures who had previously visited him in the night—somehow they'd learned of his plan to reveal his secrets, and had fulfilled their deadly promise. Yet why had they stopped there? They'd had the perfect opportunity to spring a trap and remove Lukan from the equation as well. Instead they'd murdered the doctor and left. *Unless . . .* His stomach lurched. *Unless they didn't leave. Maybe they were still there, hiding in the shadows as they waited to see who turned up . . . and where they went afterward.*

The wine suddenly tasted like ashes in his mouth.

Lukan sprang up from his chair just as a loud *crack* sounded through the floorboards, followed by the sound of splintering wood.

"What was that?" Flea asked, awake now and sitting bolt upright on her divan.

"Get upstairs," Lukan replied, snatching up his sword.

"But—"

"Now!"

Lukan shoved the girl in the direction of the door and followed her through onto the landing, both of them hesitating at the shouts and sounds of clashing steel rising from below.

"Lukan—"

"Get upstairs," he whispered, gesturing frantically at the staircase to their right. "Go."

For once the girl didn't argue, instead darting across the landing and taking the steps two at a time. Lukan made to follow, only to pause as the sounds of violence continued below. It was impossible to say how many attackers there were, but it was more than likely that Vetch and Hector were badly outnumbered. *Lady's blood . . .* He couldn't just leave them to their fate. Heart racing, he started down the stairs. A sudden bellow—of pain or rage, perhaps both— caused him to freeze. *Hector.* The cry cut off and was followed by the thump of a body hitting the floor.

"Find them," a woman's voice said, her tone clipped and cold.

Shit. Lukan spun and darted back up the stairs. The thick carpet muffled his footsteps as he ran for the other staircase at the far end of the landing. He heard booted feet on the lower stairs as he took the steps two at a time, the wood creaking beneath his weight. The upper floor was shrouded in darkness; his foot struck the edge of a corner table and he all but fell through the doorway to the master bedroom. "Flea," he hissed, glancing around as he tried to regain his balance. "Where are—"

"Here," the girl called softly as her shadow emerged from beneath the four-poster bed. "What's going on?"

"No time to explain." *Even if I could.* He shut the door as quietly as possible, turned the key in the lock. *That should buy us a moment or two.*

"What are we going to do?" the girl whispered, her voice unafraid.

"We get the hells out of here." Lukan strode toward the large windows.

"Wait . . ."

"If we stand still, we die." He reached for the heavy drapes.

"No, *don't.*" Flea grabbed his arm just as his fingers brushed cloth.

"Flea, what the hells are you—"

"There's someone out there. Down in the alleyway." The girl tugged his arm again, insistent. "We can't go out that way. They'll kill us."

"They'll kill us if we stay." Yet he made no effort to reach for the drapes again. He swore and glanced around the darkened room, his mind racing, desperately seeking a solution.

"The bolt-hole," Flea said breathlessly. "We can hide there."

Lady's mercy, of course. In his panic, he'd somehow forgotten about the hidden room that Juro had shown to them just the day before. He followed Flea as she scampered over to the empty fireplace. Voices sounded on the stairs. "Quickly," he urged, as the girl's hands probed the mantelpiece.

"I'm trying, I just can't find the—Wait, that's it!"

He heard, rather than saw, the back of the fireplace sliding upward with a soft murmur of grinding stone.

"Get in," he said, giving her a push. The girl replied with a sharp elbow to his ribs as she dropped to all fours and crawled into the large fireplace, and then the bolt-hole hidden behind it. Footsteps—hesitant, as if their owners expected a trap—sounded from the stairs beyond the bedroom door as Lukan dropped to a crouch. He could barely see a thing.

"I'm in," Flea whispered from the darkness before him. Lukan began to crawl forward, one hand raised before him, only to pause as a thought struck him. "Stay here," he ordered Flea.

"Where are you going?"

Lukan rose and returned to the drapes, reaching between them and unclasping the latch on the window. Then—as slowly as he dared, so as not to attract the attention of the guard in the alley below—he pushed the window open.

The door handle rattled from the other side of the room.

Lukan crept back to the fireplace, grateful for the plush carpets the Scrivener had furnished the bedroom with—and for the solid door, which held firm against a powerful blow. He dropped to his knees and crawled through the fireplace, into the impenetrable blackness beyond. Another blow struck the door.

"Lukan, quick!" Flea whispered, her voice close in the darkness.

"Almost there." Lukan scrabbled to reposition himself, praying the door would hold a few moments longer. He winced as his shoulder scraped the rough stone wall—the bolt-hole was tiny. He could see back through the fireplace now, could see the glow of torchlight below the bedroom door, which shuddered again beneath another blow. Wood splintered.

"The lever," he whispered, half remembering Juro's instructions. "Where—"

"On the right side of the entrance," Flea hissed.

Lukan groped around blindly, felt the lever beneath his fingers, and pulled down hard. He was rewarded with the murmur of grinding stone as the wall of the fireplace started to slide back down. He could only hope the noise was lost beneath the sound of splintering wood as the bedroom door gradually gave beneath the attackers' blows. *Just need it to hold for a little longer.* The wall seemed to take an age to descend, but eventually a soft click sounded as it slotted back into place, plunging the bolt-hole into total darkness. Suddenly all he could hear was his own ragged breathing.

He jumped as Flea gripped his shoulder.

"Just as well one of us was paying attention," the girl whispered.

The bedroom door crashed open before he could answer.

22

Rats in a Cage

Lukan didn't dare to breathe as booted footsteps entered the bedroom. *Two people,* he thought, listening as they suddenly stopped, the newcomers no doubt lowering their weapons and glancing around in confusion. He grinned in the darkness. *Surprise, arseholes.* As the intruders began searching the room, Lukan fancied he could hear their frustration in every chair they kicked aside, every wardrobe door they threw open.

"They're not here." A man's voice.

"You don't say," another man replied.

"Diamond's going to be pissed."

"Oh, you think?"

"Shit, look at this . . . the window's open. They must have climbed through—"

"Not a chance. Emerald's out there with a crossbow. If they'd so much as stuck their heads through she'd have stuck bolts in their eyes."

Flea was right, Lukan thought. *If she hadn't stopped me . . .*

"Then where'd they go?"

"The hells should I know?"

"Maybe they were never in here."

"The door was locked from the *inside,* genius . . ."

Both men fell silent as someone else entered the room.

"Report," the newcomer said—the same woman Lukan had heard earlier.

"Mistress," the first man acknowledged, his tone deferential. "They're not here—"

"I can see that."

"Uh . . . we think they must have gone through the window—"

"Nonsense. Emerald would have dealt with them."

"That's what I said," the second man put in. "I think that—"

"I don't care what you think, Topaz," the woman snapped. "They're still hiding in this house somewhere. Find them. *Now.*"

"Mistress," another voice—female this time—called from the doorway. "I found this downstairs. Looks like the doctor's personal diary."

Shit. In his haste Lukan had forgotten about the journal. *My only proof that Zandrusa was framed . . .*

"Ah, so the doctor *was* holding out on us after all. The man had more steel than I thought. Good work, Sapphire."

"Thank you, Mistress. Your orders?"

"Well, it seems that Garnet here has little faith in your sister's ability with her crossbow, and thinks that our quarry may have escaped through the window."

"Mistress," the first man protested, "I was just saying—"

"Silence, Garnet. Sapphire—go and check with Emerald that this was not the case."

"Yes, Mistress."

"Topaz, Garnet," the woman continued, her voice moving toward the doorway, "I'll be downstairs. Fetch me the instant you find anything. Do not disappoint me again." Her footsteps faded away, leaving a silence broken only by the occasional creak of a floorboard as the men moved around. *Searching for a secret room,* Lukan thought, fear tightening his chest. He'd hoped the open window might throw them off the scent, but it had always been a long shot. *They'll find us eventually.* Flea had clearly reached the same conclusion, for the girl's fingers found his in the darkness. He gave them a reassuring squeeze and turned his face toward her.

"We'll be okay," he whispered.

An empty promise. The truth was that there was nothing they could do but wait in the darkness, clinging to each other as their hunters prowled the room. *Tap tap.* One of the men was tapping the wall with what Lukan guessed was a blade. *Tap tap tap.* He listened as the sound drew closer to the fireplace. If he recalled correctly (and he hadn't exactly been paying much attention when Juro had shown it to them), the secret button was the center of one of the symbols carved into the mantelpiece—small and subtle, but if the man was vigilant enough he'd find it. *And what then?* They would be helpless as the fireplace wall slowly rose, light spilling in to reveal them. Lukan didn't even have room to raise his sword; the blade lay in the dust at his side. *We're trapped like a couple of rats in a cage.*

The footsteps moved in front of the fireplace, the tapping now coming from directly above the mantelpiece. *Any moment now.* Flea squeezed his hand; he could hear her breaths in the darkness, short and sharp. Scared. He stared at the darkness before him, waiting for the crack of light to appear, for the grinding of stone as the fake wall began to rise . . .

Instead he heard a series of rapid footsteps enter the room.

"The Watch is coming," a brusque male voice said. "We're pulling out."

"Lady's tits," Topaz swore, but neither he nor Garnet made any argument as they followed the newcomer out of the room. Lukan listened as their footsteps faded away, scarcely able to believe his luck.

"Lukan," Flea whispered, breaking the silence. "Are we safe?"

"Yeah, I think so," he whispered back. "You all right?"

"Yeah. What do we do now?"

"We stay here."

"Why? If the Watch is coming then maybe they could help us."

"With two dead bodies downstairs, they're more likely to throw manacles round our wrists."

"You . . . you think Hector is dead?"

"Probably." Lukan grimaced, feeling a stab of guilt. *Another man dead because of me.* He squeezed Flea's hand. "I'm sorry, I know you liked him."

"He was nice to me." The girl sighed. "Lukan?"

"Yeah?"

"Who are they? These people?"

"You're meant to be answering *my* questions," he replied, trying to strike a light tone. "It's what I'm paying you for."

"I—I don't know," Flea replied, for once uncertain.

"Hey, I'm kidding." He gave her hand another squeeze. "They're assassins or something, right? So surely they're Kindred?"

"Maybe. I didn't recognize their names."

"Diamond, Garnet, Emerald, Topaz . . . damn, what was the other one . . ."

"Sapphire."

"Right. All the names of gemstones, so clearly they're aliases."

"Alia-what?"

"Fake names. You sure you've never heard them?"

"I'm sure."

"Well don't worry. We'll find the bastards, whoever they are."

Voices sounded below, faint and edged with alarm—no doubt the Watch had found the bodies of Hector and Vetch and were trying to piece together what the hells had happened. *They're not the only ones.* The identity of the attackers was also the foremost question in Lukan's mind. *They must have followed us from the Collegium, then waited for the moment to strike.* Their plan had failed, but he found no solace in that—not with two men lying dead downstairs, and the journal in the hands of his enemy. *Whoever the hells they are.* He ground his teeth, guilt fueling his anger at the loss of the journal. *The only proof I had that pointed to Zandrusa's innocence, and it slipped through my fingers.*

Footsteps sounded on the stairs. Someone entered the bedroom, paused as they presumably glanced around at the overturned furniture. They did a quick circuit of the room before heading back through the door, stairs creaking as they descended.

"Lukan," Flea whispered. "We could still—"

"We wait."

The girl sighed but didn't argue. Lukan kept his ear to the false wall, listening to the vague sounds of movement below. Occasionally he caught a raised voice but couldn't decipher any words.

Eventually a door slammed, leaving silence in its wake. The Watch had apparently seen enough.

"What now?" Flea asked.

"We wait."

"Still?"

"Still." Lukan imagined the girl rolling her eyes in the dark.

"For how long?"

"Until I think it's safe."

"But the Watch has gone—"

"They might have left a guard. Or perhaps whoever killed Hector and Vetch will come back to finish the job."

"You think they will? Come back, I mean?"

"Count on it. We've not seen the last of those bastards. They killed Vassilis and now they're after us. Seems they don't want the truth about Saviola's death getting out."

"But if they wanted to kill us, why didn't they do it at the Collegium?"

"I asked myself the same question. I guess they wanted to see where we went, who we spoke to. Whether we might be—"

"Working for someone else."

"You're too smart for your own good, kid."

"Yeah, well, you're too stupid for yours."

"That's something we both agree on." *I've certainly not covered myself in glory tonight. Hector and Vetch dead, the journal lost. The Scrivener's not going to be pleased.* "We'll give it an hour or two and then I'll take a look around. Try and get some sleep."

"Sleep? In *here?*"

"Fine, just . . . try and keep quiet. I know that's hard for you." Cloth rustled as the girl shifted position; he twisted away as she tried to hit him. "But not as hard as trying to land a punch in the dark."

"I'll wait until I can see you. Then I'll punch you extra hard."

"I won't stop you." *It's the least I deserve.*

———

Time passed slowly in the darkness.

Lukan's thoughts circled around the events that had transpired since he'd arrived in Saphrona, but kept returning to the same concern: how he was going to explain all this to the Scrivener. He'd broken the terms of their agreement by going to meet Vassilis without her approval, but the discovery of the doctor's journal had vindicated his decision. Now it was lost and two of the Scrivener's men were dead. The woman had previously threatened to leave him tied to a chair simply for interrupting her—what fate could he look forward to now? *Perhaps it's best just to stay in this hole and never crawl out.*

"Lukan."

"Hmm?"

"Can we go now?"

"Best just to give it a little longer."

"But we've been in here for *hours*. And I need to pee."

Lukan suddenly became aware of the pressure of his own bladder. *We can't stay in here forever.* He pressed his ear to the false wall and listened. *Nothing.* "All right," he said, grasping around until his fingers found the lever. "Ready?"

"Yeah."

Lukan pulled the lever before he could change his mind, the soft grinding of stone filling his ears as the fireplace wall began to rise. It seemed louder than before, *too* loud in the deathly quiet. *Surely if anyone's still here they'd have heard that.* He braced himself, half expecting to hear footsteps in the room beyond, to see masked figures entering with blades drawn . . .

The darkened room was empty.

Lukan crawled out of the fireplace, Flea close behind him. He caught the girl's arm as she tried to slip past.

"Wait here," he whispered. "I'm going downstairs."

"I'll come with you. I just need to—"

"No, stay here. If anything happens to me, get back behind the fireplace."

"Fine," the girl said grudgingly. "Can I pee now?"

"Chamber pot's under the bed." He released Flea's arm. "Stay away from the window."

The girl muttered under her breath as she padded away, though for once Lukan was glad of her insolence; it suggested she remained unfazed by the evening's events. *Then again, she's probably endured worse experiences than this.*

As Flea hunted for the chamber pot, Lukan moved to the door, which stood wide open. He peered through. The outline of the staircase was barely visible in the darkness. He moved slowly along the landing and took the stairs one at a time, wincing at every creak. No one challenged him as he descended to the first floor. He glanced through the door to the living room, but nothing moved within. It was only as he reached the staircase leading down to the kitchen that he saw the faint glow of light from below. He paused at the top of the stairs, his heartbeat quickening as he listened.

Silence.

Either someone was waiting down there, or the Watch had carelessly left an oil lamp burning. *Only one way to find out.* He took the stairs quickly—if anyone was in the kitchen, they'd see him coming, making speed a better option than stealth. Heart racing, he leaped off the final step, his sword raised as he glanced around . . .

Empty.

His relief faded as he saw the shattered crockery, the broken furniture—and the blood on the floor. *No bodies, though. The Watch must've taken them away.* He was glad for that; Lady knew he felt guilty enough about the deaths of Hector and Vetch already. The last thing he needed was their dead eyes judging him. He moved slowly through the kitchen, surveying the mess. An oil lamp stood on the central table, though its weak light failed to penetrate the shadows in the corners of the room. *The Watch must have left it behind, the useless bastards—*

"I knew you were still here."

Lukan started at the voice, his heart lurching. *Shit.* He took a deep breath and turned slowly, watching as a figure emerged from the shadows beneath the staircase. A hood concealed the stranger's features, but their outfit of supple leathers and dark cloth (not to mention the belt of throwing daggers strapped across their chest) made it clear their professional interests concerned breaking the law rather than enforcing it.

"Diamond said you'd be long gone," the stranger continued, the voice familiar. "She thought I'd be wasting my time coming back here. But I knew better."

"Topaz," Lukan replied, recalling the man's voice from the earlier conversation he'd heard from behind the fireplace.

The figure gave a mocking bow. "And you're Lukan Gardova."

Lukan fought to mask his surprise. "How do you know my name?"

The man's only reply was to pull back his hood, revealing dark curls, olive skin, and a face that—save for a light scar below his left eye—was unremarkable. The small crossbow he was pointing at Lukan, by contrast, was a thing of beauty—sleek, black as sin and no doubt twice as deadly. The tips of the two loaded bolts gleamed in the flickering light.

"Who is Diamond?" Lukan asked, resisting the urge to back away. "Who are you working for?"

"I could ask you the same thing. And since I'm the one holding this"—Topaz tilted the crossbow—"I'll be the one asking the questions."

"Fair enough. Want me to put the kettle on?"

"I'd rather you put your sword on the table."

Lukan hesitated, eyes flicking to the crossbow.

"Don't be a fool," the man said, shaking his head. "We both know the outcome." There was no malice in his voice, no arrogance, just the calm assurance of a professional who knew he had the upper hand.

Lukan forced a smile. "I was merely admiring your weapon. Lovely piece."

An amateur might have taken their eyes off Lukan in that

moment, cast a prideful glance at their weapon that would have given him the chance he needed.

Topaz was no amateur.

"Put your sword on the table," he repeated. "Slowly."

"I could do it quickly, if you like. Save us a bit of time—"

The crossbow thrummed and Lukan felt a rush of air as a bolt flashed past his face.

"Any more lip from you," Topaz said coolly, "and the next bolt goes in your balls. Drop the sword." Lukan obliged and the man kicked the blade away across the tiles. "Where's the girl?" he demanded.

"What girl?"

"Don't play games. Where is she?"

"Lady's mercy, she's just a kid—"

The man's finger tightened on the trigger. "Where is she?"

"I don't know—"

"I will ask one more time. Where is the girl?"

"Right here," Flea replied.

Topaz glanced round—and gasped, his wide eyes moving to the girl's face and down to the length of steel she'd just stuck in his thigh. His breath hissed between gritted teeth as Flea pulled the dagger free. Topaz raised his crossbow, but before he could squeeze the trigger Lukan slammed into him, sending him sprawling across the kitchen table. The crossbow flew from his hands and struck the oil lamp, which fell to the floor and shattered on the tiles.

As the man tried to rise, Lukan snatched up a heavy frying pan and slammed it across the back of his head. Topaz slumped to the floor.

"Thought I told you to stay upstairs?" he said to Flea, tossing the pan aside.

"Lukan . . ."

He looked where the girl was pointing, saw flames devouring a pair of curtains that hung across a nearby window. "Oh *shit* . . ."

"We need to get some water," Flea said, glancing around. "Otherwise—"

With a *whoosh* that sounded almost triumphant, the flames spread to a pile of flour sacks and engulfed a wooden workbench.

"Seven shadows," Lukan murmured, shielding his face from the rising heat, "half the bloody kitchen's on fire."

"We need to go!" Flea snatched up the man's crossbow and unclasped the quiver of bolts from his belt, then made for the back door, which was hanging askew on a single hinge. "This way."

Lukan remained where he stood, his expression grim. *The Scrivener's going to kill me for this.* For a moment he wondered whether burning alive was preferable to facing the piercing cold of the Scrivener's furious gaze. *There's not much between them, to be fair—*

"Lukan!" Flea called from the doorway.

Coughing as he caught a mouthful of smoke, Lukan glanced at his sword—too close to the flames to be rescued. Instead he grabbed Topaz's tunic. Gritting his teeth, he dragged the unconscious man toward the door.

"What are you doing?" Flea asked. "We need to *go*."

"We still need answers," Lukan replied, coughing again, "and this arsehole is going to give them to us."

23

TEA AND RECRIMINATIONS

"You burned down my house." The Scrivener spoke softly, but her words were sharp as any blade.

"I can explain." Lukan sank into the chair opposite her.

"You burned down my house," she continued, her voice rising, "*and* you got two of my men killed." A man sitting at a nearby table glanced over, brows knitted in curiosity. The Scrivener gave him a glare and he quickly looked away, busying himself with some papers.

"You think I don't care?" Lukan replied, tone hardened by quickening anger. "Believe me, I deeply regret their loss—"

"Not half as much as their families do. Juro tells me Hector's daughter was particularly distraught when she learned the news."

Lady's mercy, I didn't even know he had a family. Lukan stared at a faded coffee stain on the table as a fresh wave of guilt struck him. "I didn't mean for this to happen," he said wearily. "Vetch, Hector . . . I never meant for them to die."

"But they did." The woman took a sip from her cup, letting the accusation hang in the air between them. "I can only hope," she continued, setting the cup down with a clink, "that they did not die in vain."

The question might have been rhetorical, but it was loaded all the same. Lukan had no doubt the Scrivener already knew the broad thrust of the night's events—he'd given Juro a detailed account. *And yet she insists on this little dance all the same.*

"Sir?" a waiter said, appearing at his side. "Can I fetch you anything?"

"Coffee, as strong as you make it."

The man bowed and slipped away.

The prospect of coffee steeled Lukan's resolve just enough for him to meet the Scrivener's piercing gaze. "Look, I'm sorry about your house. It was an accident—"

"I don't give a fig for the house, Master Gardova. What bothers me is that you broke the terms of our agreement and betrayed my trust. You were supposed to share all of your intelligence with me." Her eyes narrowed. "*All* of it."

"I know, I know, but . . . Look, there was no time—the doctor told me to meet him at midnight. I had to move fast. That's why I sent Vetch to you with a note—"

"Yes, how thoughtful. Had you bothered to visit me yourself I would have had the chance to point out the obvious trap you were about to walk into. Instead you went gallivanting halfway across the city on a fool's errand that resulted in my house burning to the ground and two of my men dying for nothing."

"Not for nothing."

They regarded each other in silence as the waiter returned and placed Lukan's coffee on the table.

"Explain," the Scrivener said, once the man was gone.

"Zandrusa was right about the frost on Lord Saviola's body. Doctor Vassilis saw it as well, but left it out of his report after his life was threatened. Instead he lied to the Inquisition and said that Saviola died from a stab wound, even though he suspected that wound had been inflicted after the merchant prince was already dead."

The Scrivener was silent for a moment. "You told Juro," she said, a note of accusation in her voice, "that the doctor refused to discuss Saviola with you at the gala, and that he was already dead when you reached the Collegium."

"That's true." Lukan blew on his coffee.

"Don't play games with me, Master Gardova—I am *not* in the mood. If you never spoke to Vassilis about Saviola's death, how do you know what he saw?"

"Because I found his journal in a secret compartment in his study."

The Scrivener's only concession to surprise was a slight tensing of her jaw, but Lukan took pleasure in the sight all the same. It was, he hoped, a reminder to the master forger that she shouldn't doubt his abilities. As for the fact that it had been Flea who actually found the journal . . . well, she didn't need to know that detail.

"How interesting." The Scrivener took a sip of her tea. "Tell me more about this journal."

"Well, Vassilis talks at length about the night of Lord Saviola's death. He reached the same conclusion as Zandrusa—that the timing of the murder was to ensure Zandrusa took the blame. He claims that later the same night he was visited by some masked strangers who warned him his life would be forfeit if he disputed the notion that Saviola died from a stab wound."

Interest gleamed in the Scrivener's blue eyes. "Did he guess at their identity?"

"He had no idea, but assumed they were working for whoever murdered Saviola. He feared for his life, so he did as they asked. He wrote his last journal entry just before his death; said he couldn't live with the guilt, which is why he decided to tell me the truth."

"And he was killed before he could do so." The Scrivener pursed her lips, tapping a finger against the rim of her cup. "But how did his killers find out about his meeting with you?"

"I've been wondering that myself."

"Do you have the journal with you? I'd very much like to read it."

"I, um . . ." It was an effort not to wince. "I sort of lost it . . ."

"You lost it."

"Look, everything happened at once. The attack came without warning, I had to get Flea to safety—"

"Spare me your excuses, Master Gardova. What happened to the journal?"

"Whoever attacked your house—they took it. I heard them talking while we were hiding behind the fireplace. One of them found it."

"So you lied."

Lukan frowned. "About what?"

"You told me," the Scrivener said, dropping a sugar cube into her tea with the aid of some silver tongs, "that Vetch and Hector did not die for nothing. But it seems that's *exactly* what they died for."

"That's not true."

"Isn't it?"

"We know so much more now," Lukan insisted, loud enough to draw another glance from the man sitting nearby. Lowering his voice, he continued, "We know that Saviola was killed by unnatural means dressed up to look like a simple stab wound. We know that the blame was intended to fall on Zandrusa, and that whoever is responsible killed Vassilis to keep the truth a secret. We *know* there's a conspiracy here."

"We guessed at that already; this merely confirms our suspicions," the Scrivener said, her expression as sour as the lemon slice she was squeezing over her tea. "If you had the wits to keep hold of the journal then it might have been enough to prompt the Inquisition into reopening their investigation, but without it there's no chance of persuading them. It seems, Master Gardova, your misadventure gained us very little but cost us a great deal."

"There's still the man I subdued. I didn't drag him halfway across the city in the middle of the night for nothing. If Juro can get him to talk . . ."

"Oh, Juro will get him to talk. I just hope for your sake that he has something interesting to say."

"And if he doesn't?"

The Scrivener didn't reply, merely sipped her tea. Lukan swallowed a curse and turned his attention to his coffee. He took a swallow. On another day he would have appreciated the deep, rich taste upon his tongue, but as it was he barely noticed it. Still, after a few more mouthfuls he thought he could feel his fatigue lifting—though the coffee did nothing to alleviate the guilt and anger that sat in his stomach like a burning coal. *Should have bloody listened to Hector.* In the heat of the moment, when he was caught up in his own enthusiasm, the prospect of meeting Vassilis had seemed an opportunity too valuable to pass up. But now, sitting in the sunlight that shone through the teahouse's windows, he could see it for what it truly was: an obvious trap, just as the Scrivener had said. *You bloody fool, Gardova.*

The arrival of Juro drew him from his thoughts.

"Mistress," the man said, offering the Scrivener a respectful bow. "My apologies for keeping you waiting." He nodded at Lukan, his familiar half smile in place. If the night's events had taken a toll on him, Juro gave no sign. His eyes were bright and clear, his clothes immaculate, without so much as a speck of blood on them. He looked for all the world like a clerk preparing to deliver a financial report to his superior, rather than a man who had spent the last few hours teasing truths from a captive with the edge of a blade. *Or perhaps he's more of a hot irons sort of man.* Whatever variety of interrogation Topaz had endured, Lukan had little sympathy for him.

"Do sit, Juro," the Scrivener said, motioning to an empty chair. "Tea?"

"Very kind, Mistress."

The Scrivener requested a fresh pot of tea from a passing waiter, not bothering to ask Lukan if he desired anything. "And another coffee," Lukan called as the man hurried away. He could already feel his fatigue creeping back, dulling the edges of his mind.

"So," the Scrivener said, fixing Juro with a meaningful look. "How is our guest?"

"Still alive, or he was when I left him."

"Good. I don't want him dying without my permission."

"Of course, Mistress."

"Who is he, anyway?"

"He claims his name is Enzo Varassi—"

"A Talassian? I should've known." She pursed her lips. "Where there's trouble, there's—"

"A Talassian denying involvement," Lukan muttered, completing the well-known refrain that painted all citizens of the Talassian Isles as rogues and scoundrels. It was a popular saying throughout the Old Empire and, like most regional stereotypes, it was a significant exaggeration (even if it carried more than a hint of truth). Still, Lukan had found most of the Talassians he'd met to be good—if slightly boisterous—company, save for the one individual who had tried to stick a knife in him during an ill-tempered card game. On another occasion he might have made this point to the Scrivener, but given the way she was currently glaring at him he thought it better to keep quiet.

"What else?" she asked, turning her gaze back to Juro.

"The crew he runs with are a mercenary company called the Seven Jewels. Their leader is one Delphina Delastro, who is also known as—"

"Diamond," Lukan said, realization dawning as he recalled Topaz's words. *Diamond said you'd be long gone.* "There were others too—Emerald, Garnet, and Sapphire. The man we caught is called Topaz. I don't know who the other two are."

"Ruby and Amethyst," Juro confirmed.

"The Seven Jewels," the Scrivener said slowly, as if testing the words. "Can't say I've heard of them, or this Delastro figure."

"Neither had I, Mistress, so I took the liberty of making a few discreet inquiries. It seems the Seven Jewels mostly operate in the northern cities, where they've developed a reputation for being ruthless and efficient. Delastro herself fought for Vispana in the Seventh Talassian War, during which she acquired the nickname 'Diamond,' though it's not clear why. What *is* agreed is that she was highly decorated. It's also rumored she was one of the few survivors of Serpent Rock."

"Lady's blood," Lukan murmured as memories of long-ago lectures flitted through his mind. "I studied that siege at the Academy. A few Vispanians held that fort against a force of Virenzians nearly twenty times their number. When their supplies ran out they ate rats, then boiled leather . . . It's said they eventually resorted to eating their own dead—"

"Yes, thank you for the history lesson, Master Gardova." The Scrivener gave him a withering look. "We're all familiar with the story. The point is that we're dealing with a formidable mercenary whose skills—and those of her company—no doubt command a high price. A price that *someone* in this city was willing to pay." She fell silent as the waiter returned with a fresh pot of tea and—much to Lukan's relief—a mug of coffee. As the man departed, the Scrivener continued, "I don't suppose that our guest revealed the identity of this mystery employer?"

"I'm afraid not, Mistress."

"Pity."

"Topaz has only seen them a few times," Juro elaborated as he poured the tea. "On each occasion the person was masked and hooded, though he believes it's a man—a view apparently shared by his colleagues. He claimed that only Delastro knows the employer's identity and that she's not revealed that information to her crew."

"Smart woman."

"Lord Murillo has both the money and the motive," Lukan said. "Zandrusa is convinced he's behind all this, and, having met the arrogant bastard myself, I think she's right."

"There are many rich, arrogant men in Saphrona," the Scrivener replied. "Women too. And more than a few of them would stand to gain from Saviola's death and Zandrusa's downfall. Still, I agree that it's hard to look beyond Lord Murillo." She took a sip of tea, her gaze flicking back to Juro. "Did this Topaz reveal what kind of duties his crew have been performing for this masked man? Besides murdering Lord Saviola and Doctor Vassilis, of course."

"This is where it gets interesting," Juro said. "Topaz denied that his crew murdered Lord Saviola."

"Of course he bloody did," Lukan put in. "He's hardly going to admit to the murder of a merchant prince, is he?"

"I know when a man is lying to me," Juro replied calmly. "He denied the Seven Jewels were responsible for Lord Saviola's murder, but had no idea who was. However, he did admit they had threatened Doctor Vassilis and later killed him."

"So the Seven Jewels—or three of them, at least—were the masked intruders who appeared in the doctor's bedroom," Lukan mused. "And then they murdered him last night when he broke his promise, before coming after us."

"But if they didn't kill Lord Saviola," the Scrivener said, "then someone else did. Murillo must have more hired blades working for him besides the Seven Jewels."

"There's more," Juro said. "Topaz told me the Seven Jewels arrived in Saphrona a month ago." He paused, one eyebrow raised meaningfully. "Which was around the time that the Sandino Blade was stolen."

"You're not serious," the Scrivener murmured, her teacup half raised to her lips.

"I am."

"Lady's blood." The Scrivener set her cup down. "It was *them*? They stole the blade?"

Juro nodded. "Topaz claimed it was the first task given to them."

"I'm sorry," Lukan said, raising a hand, "but you've totally lost me. What's this blade you're talking about?"

The Scrivener ignored him, leaving Juro to explain.

"About a month ago," he said, "someone broke into Lord Sandino's villa and stole a ceremonial dagger, said to have been in his family for generations—the so-called Sandino Blade. No one among the Kindred claimed responsibility. Given that the theft broke the Midnight Charter, we thought—"

"Midnight Charter?"

"My apologies." Juro smiled and spread his hands. "The Midnight Charter is a list of rules that all members of the Kindred must abide by. One rule states that no one may steal from a merchant prince or a person of significant authority without first obtaining the Twice-Crowned King's permission. The Twice-Crowned King is—"

"The ruler of the Kindred, I know. One king, twice crowned—is that right?"

"Indeed. And only they can approve any crime to be committed against the city's elite citizens—and they rarely do. Lord Sandino's blade was stolen without their permission, and there's only one thief in the city who would dare to defy them in such a way."

"Let me guess: Lady Midnight, the mythical thief who can walk through walls."

"She's no myth, Lukan, though the rumors about her are certainly exaggerated. But yes, the popular opinion among the Kindred was that she stole the blade, for reasons unknown. Lady Midnight denied the charge, but the King has been hunting her all the same. So far she's proven elusive. Now we know she's telling the truth. It wasn't her."

"But why would Lord Murillo hire the Seven Jewels to steal Sandino's family heirloom?" the Scrivener asked, surfacing from her reverie. "I can't think of why he would want such a trinket, nor how it possibly connects to the murder of Lord Saviola or a desire to frame Zandrusa." She tapped a finger against her teacup. "None of this makes any sense at all."

"There's one other thing, Mistress. Topaz said that several times—always at night—his crew have escorted this masked man to the cemetery, specifically to a mausoleum on the western side. Within this tomb are several sarcophagi, one of which apparently hides an entrance to the catacombs. On each occasion they have accompanied him down into the tunnels beneath the cemetery, whereupon they've been instructed to guard certain passages."

"Where does this masked man go and to what purpose?"

"Topaz doesn't know. He claims the man only takes Delastro with him, and she's never spoken about where they go or what they do."

"Stranger and stranger," the Scrivener murmured, pursing her lips. "If Murillo is the man behind the mask, then what in the Lady's name is he doing down in the catacombs?"

"We might have a chance to find out."

"Oh?"

"Topaz said that his crew are due to escort the man to the cemetery tonight. It's possible that plan may change—Delastro might decide that Topaz's disappearance compromises their security. But if it does go ahead, Topaz believes they'll arrive at the mausoleum sometime after midnight."

"Did he provide a description of this mausoleum?"

"He said there's a stone swan above the entrance."

"Excellent work, Juro. As always." The Scrivener met Lukan's gaze. "Best get some rest, Master Gardova," she added, the ghost of a smile on her lips. "Looks like you've got the graveyard shift."

24

An Undeserved
Reputation for Elegance

Death is the great equalizer, the philosopher Volendt declared in his treatise *An Unseen Philosophy,* a text that Lukan had been forced to read during his first year at the Academy. *A dark mistress who holds no regard for wealth, nor power, nor birthright. All souls are equal before her gaze.*

It seemed Saphrona's wealthy citizens hadn't received the memo.

The mausoleums of the city's elite families lined the cemetery's winding paths, impressive affairs replete with elegant sculptures, marble pillars, and lintels chased with gold. Many bore depictions of the Lady of Seven Shadows, usually with Her leashed hounds but occasionally standing alone, Her features always concealed beneath a veil. Other tombs bore statues of gods from the pantheon of the Southern Queendoms, and even the divine symbols of Linesh, far to the east, where idolatry was forbidden. Religion, it seemed, was no barrier to those who wished to be interred on the prestigious western side of Saphrona's cemetery. That, as with everything else in the city, came down to coin. *And the folks resting here clearly had money to burn.*

The same couldn't be said for the inhabitants of the cemetery's eastern side, where the city's poorer citizens were buried. No grand tombs for them—just countless gravestones, their descriptions long faded and covered by vines and lichen. They tilted at drunken angles, packed so closely together they seemed to be fighting among themselves. *Death the great equalizer, indeed.*

The sound of crying drew Lukan from his thoughts. A young

woman, draped in black, knelt before a nearby tomb sobbing into a handkerchief, while a man of similar age stood behind her, one hand on her shoulder. He looked bored. They were the first living souls Lukan had seen in nearly half an hour—not counting the numerous cats that appeared to have made the graveyard their home. He could see one now, sprawling across the steps of a nearby mausoleum, enjoying the late-afternoon sun. The animal sat up as they passed, watching them through narrowed eyes, tail flicking. *Volendt can keep his dark mistress. No one has less regard for wealth, power, or birthright than a cat.*

"I think I see it!" Flea exclaimed, pointing with her half-eaten peach. "Over there."

Lukan shielded his eyes from the sun and squinted at the tomb in question. "That's a bird."

"Swans *are* birds."

"A *small* bird, then."

"Swans aren't small—"

"No, *that* bird," Lukan cut in, jabbing a finger, "is small. Swans are . . ." He trailed off as Flea dissolved into giggles. "You're winding me up."

"Yep."

"Perhaps you could stop."

"Nope." The girl took a bite of her peach, pulling a face as she swallowed. "Why would someone have a swan on their tomb anyway?"

"Maybe it was their family crest or something. Swans have an undeserved reputation for elegance, but really they're just moody bastards."

"Bit like you, then."

Flea dodged his half-hearted swipe at her head. "The only thing that's elegant about me," Lukan replied, "is my swordplay, and in that respect my reputation is well deserved."

"Didn't do you much good last night, did it?" the girl asked, grinning at him.

Oh, here we go . . . "Topaz had a crossbow pointed at me,"

Lukan said, with the weariness of a man who already knew he'd lost the argument. "I'd have taken him in a fair fight—"

"But it wasn't a fair fight, was it? Just as well I was there to save you."

"That's the third—no, *fourth* time today you've dined out on that little fact. At this rate you'll never go hungry again."

"I never go hungry anyway. I'm too good at stealing." The girl hurled the remains of her peach at a nearby mausoleum, the fruit exploding across the stone doors.

"For the love of . . ." Lukan glanced around to make sure they were unobserved, then glared at her. "What the hells did you do that for?"

Flea shrugged. "Guess I'm full now."

Lukan swallowed a sharp retort. *It'll only provoke her.* Besides, he couldn't deny that the girl's good humor—as annoying as it was—at least suggested she'd already swallowed the pain of Hector's death. "You want to play a game?" he asked instead.

"What sort of game?"

Lukan fished two copper coins from his pouch. "If you find the swan first, you get to keep these."

"And if you find it?"

"If *I* find it," Lukan replied, smiling, "you have to keep quiet for half an hour." *If such a thing is even possible.* "Deal?"

Flea grinned. "Deal."

———

The shadows were lengthening, the late afternoon lapsing into evening, by the time Flea gave a cry of triumph and pointed to a stone swan looming above them. Time and the elements had conspired to rob the statue of its finer details, but there was no mistaking the elegant sweep of its neck or the curve of its wings. Any annoyance Lukan might have felt at having to flick the girl his copper coins was offset by his relief that they'd found the damned thing at all.

The swan perched above the columned entrance of a mausoleum

similar to the many others they'd passed—a little smaller perhaps, but no less extravagant. A family crest was carved into the lintel above the doorway, but the symbols were weathered beyond recognition. Lukan climbed the stone steps to the wrought-iron door and peered through the bars. In the gloom beyond, he could see the vague outline of two sarcophagi, but of greater interest were the footprints in the dust that led toward them. *Several people passed this way recently.* He tried the handle, but the door was locked. *Still, this is the place.*

"So what now?" Flea asked.

"We find somewhere to keep watch." Lukan returned to the path and glanced around. "There," he said, pointing to a flat-roofed mausoleum some twenty yards away. "That should give us a decent view." *If we can get up there.*

In that regard, luck proved to be with them; vines sprawled up and across the mausoleum's far side, clinging so tightly that they might as well have been carved from the same stone. Flea scurried up with the ease of a street rat, while Lukan followed with rather less finesse.

"Too much wine," Flea remarked as he pulled himself over the lip of the roof, flushed and puffing. "And too many of those little pastries back at the taverna."

"I only had a couple. Too sweet for me."

"You had four," Flea replied, and ticked them off on her fingers. "Two while I was there, and two when I went to pee."

"Seven shadows, do you ever miss *anything*?"

"I miss Hector." The girl looked away.

"Yeah, well . . ." *What to say?* "It gets easier," he offered, reaching out to her.

"I know," Flea replied, slapping his hand away. "It hurts for a while and then goes away. It was the same when my brother left and didn't come back."

Old beyond her years. "Topaz is just the first. We'll catch the others and whoever is paying them. We'll see justice is done for Hector and Vetch." Lukan crawled on his elbows and knees to the front edge of the roof, where a statue of the Lady stood. He scanned the surrounding pathways. *Perfect. We'll see them coming from any direction. But they won't see us.* Satisfied, he moved back into the center of the roof and unslung his new sword from his back, taking a moment to admire the blade. It was a nice piece, sleek and well-balanced. On Juro's advice he'd avoided the arms merchants in the Plaza of Silver and Spice and instead sought out a particular blacksmith in the Smokes. The weapon had cost him nearly all his remaining coin, but that was preferable to saving a few coppers and having to rely on a second-rate blade. Still, he wondered whether he might be able to persuade Juro to cover the purchase. *Probably not, with his mistress's house a smoking ruin.*

"I don't suppose," he said, as he laid his sword down, "you feel like being generous in victory and giving me those two coppers back?"

"Nope."

"Didn't think so." He lay down next to his sword and put his hands behind his head.

"What are you doing?"

"Catching up on some sleep."

"You slept earlier."

"Not nearly enough. Keep watch, will you? Your eyes are sharper than mine."

"But it's not even dark yet."

"Then go and get us something to eat. There was a fruit cart near the entrance." Lukan dug in his pouch and winced at how few coins nestled inside. Reluctantly he pulled out a copper and flicked it to the girl. "See if they have any grapes. And pay for them, all right? I don't want to eat stolen fruit."

"Why? It tastes the same."

"And don't pickpocket any mourners in the cemetery. Got it?"

"You are such a bore."

"And you're a brat."

The girl grinned as she flicked an obscene gesture and disappeared over the edge of the roof.

———

"Lukan."

His eyes flicked open. High above, the stars burned silver. He felt the stone beneath his back, the caress of the night's gentle breeze upon his skin, and for a blissful moment he couldn't remember where he was or what he was doing.

"Lukan," the voice said again, more insistently this time. *Flea's voice.* He groaned as his memory returned. *Shit, it's already night* . . . He rolled onto his side and squinted at the girl, who crouched near him in the darkness, her body tense as she peered around the statue.

"What is it?" he whispered.

"Someone's coming."

He crawled toward her. "Why didn't you wake me earlier?"

"I like you better when you're asleep. Even if you snore like a pig."

"I do not."

"Yeah, try telling that to all the dead people that you just woke up. Hey—"

Lukan's gentle shove sent the girl tumbling onto her backside. Ignoring her hissed insult, he looked over the statue's right shoulder. *There.* Distant flames, bright against the darkness. A succession of burning torches that floated like fireflies as they moved down the pathway, drawing steadily closer.

"Is that them?" Flea whispered as she crouched beside him. "Is it the Seven Jewels?"

"Six Jewels now," Lukan replied wryly, watching as the torchbearers approached. "But yeah, I reckon that's them." He could see the figures more clearly now—six in total, all clad in the same outfit of dark cloth and leather that Topaz had worn. He squinted at each in turn, wondering which one of them was Delastro, but the hoods that concealed their features made it impossible to tell them apart. "And that'll be our friend Lord Murillo," he added, his gaze shifting to the grey-robed figure that walked in their midst, the only one not carrying a torch. He was disguised, just as

Topaz said he would be, but Lukan had little difficulty imagining the merchant prince's piglike eyes beneath the ornate silver mask, which glinted whenever it caught the torchlight.

A moment later the group reached the mausoleum bearing the swan statue, and the torchbearers formed a semicircle round the entrance as Murillo climbed the steps. He withdrew a key from his robes and inserted it into the lock, while his armed escort surveyed the silent tombs around them. "Down," Lukan hissed, flattening himself against the roof as one of the hooded figures glanced in their direction. Flea obeyed and for several moments they lay together, until the night's silence was broken by the sound of old hinges squealing in protest. Lukan looked up again in time to see Murillo entering the mausoleum. The torchbearers followed him inside—all save the last one, who instead set their torch in a bracket by the doorway and remained outside on the steps.

"What now?" Flea whispered.

Lukan barely heard her; he was too busy staring at the door, which stood ajar. *Murillo hasn't locked it.* The torchlight within the mausoleum dimmed, then faded altogether.

The door remained open.

Overconfidence or forgetfulness? Or maybe he just wants to ensure a quick escape if he needs one. Whatever the reason, Murillo had presented him with an opportunity that Lukan knew he couldn't afford to pass up.

"I'm going in," he said.

"You're *what*?"

"Stay here, keep out of sight. If I'm not back in an hour, go and find Juro and tell him what happened."

"But the Scrivener said—"

"I know what the Scrivener said. But if all we ever do is watch from the shadows, we're never going to get anywhere. I can't just walk away when there's a chance to find out what the hells Murillo is up to down there."

"But what about the guard?"

"I'll charm them with my wit."

The girl punched his arm.

"Just kidding." He gave her a humorless smile and patted his sword. "I'm going to show you just how elegant my swordplay really is."

You might think you fight a duel with your blade, Shafia had told Lukan, the first time she'd placed a wooden practice sword in his hand. *But you'd be wrong. You fight a duel with your mind, before the swords have even been drawn. A show of confidence—whether a smile, a stare, or a strut—can sow doubt in your opponent, even fear. And that can be just as deadly as a perfect thrust or a well-timed riposte.*

Lukan had always remembered Shafia's words, and had found the advice to hold true on numerous occasions. *Hopefully this will be one of them,* he thought as he approached the guard standing before the mausoleum's doorway. While he had no desire for violence, despite what he'd told Flea, if what Juro had learned about these mercenaries was true he doubted the guard would be swayed by words or the promise of silver.

Which left only one possibility.

"Evening," Lukan said brightly. "Lovely night for it—"

"That's close enough," the guard said, her clipped Talassian accent sharpening her words. He half expected a small crossbow to appear, to hear the *snap* of a bowstring—to fall to the ground with a bolt between his eyes. Instead the guard pulled back her hood, the torchlight revealing tanned, angular features, dark hair tied back. She gave him an appraising look. "What brings you here?"

"Just coming to pay my respects," Lukan replied, holding up the dried flowers he'd just snatched from a nearby tomb.

"Strange time of night for it."

"It's been a strange couple of days." That was true, at least.

"You always pay your respects with a sword strapped to your back?"

"Says the woman with a sword sheathed at her side."

A hint of a smile. "Who are you? Or are you going to lie about that as well?"

"You already know my name."

"True enough . . . Lukan Gardova."

"You're Talassian. Let me guess . . . you're from Vispana?"

"Virenze," she replied, jaw tightening. "You do me an insult."

"You Talassians are a funny lot, with your notions of honor." Lukan tossed his flowers aside. "You know, I'd heard that your people were all liars and thieves—"

The woman's hand moved to her sword.

"—but," Lukan quickly continued, "that you're also excellent lovers. A hypothesis I've sadly not had the chance to test."

"Don't worry," the woman replied, smirking. "I'll be sure to kiss your corpse."

"You're too kind. Which one are you, anyway? Emerald, perhaps?"

"Amethyst. If I *was* Emerald, you'd now look like a pincushion. She has a tendency to shoot first and ask questions later."

"Then perhaps Delastro made a mistake not putting her on guard duty."

"Diamond doesn't make mistakes."

"Yeah? Then how come Topaz is currently tied to a chair in a darkened room?"

"Because he's a fool who can't follow orders." Amethyst didn't betray so much as a flicker of concern for her comrade. "If he ever comes crawling back, I'm sure Diamond will string him up by his balls—unless you've already removed them, of course."

"There was no need to go that far. Topaz started talking at the first sign of a blade." Lukan had no idea if that was true, but it sounded good. "He had a lot to say for himself."

"He always does. Usually bullshit."

"So you deny that your crew stole the Sandino Blade? That you murdered Doctor Vassilis—"

"Why do you care?" Amethyst tilted her head in apparent curiosity. "What's it to you?"

"That's my business."

"Have it your way." She drew her sword and held it loosely at her side. "Shall we dance, then?"

"Yes," he replied, drawing his own blade. "Let's."

Amethyst leaped from the steps, firelight rippling along her sword as she unleashed a flurry of strikes that surprised Lukan with their ferocity; he managed to parry the first three and twist away from the fourth—but not quickly enough to avoid the tip of her blade slicing across his right shoulder. *Shit*. Ignoring the flash of pain, he retaliated with a wild slash that Amethyst deflected with ease, almost catching him with a smooth riposte. *Lady's blood*, he thought as he backed away. *She's good*. The woman's smile as they circled each other suggested she knew it.

They closed again, blades a blur of silver, their steel song echoing among the darkened tombs. Lukan forced Amethyst back with a series of feints and thrusts, almost catching her out with his final attack. As she fought to retain her balance, he lunged—only to realize it had been a ruse. He leaped aside, narrowly avoiding getting some sharp steel in his gut. Suddenly he was retreating before a fresh flurry of attacks, his heart pounding, blood roaring in his ears. As he desperately deflected Amethyst's strikes, Lukan became aware of a doubt growing in his mind. *I can't win this*. Amethyst easily matched him for skill; even on his best day he would have needed some luck to beat her, and this was *not* his best day—he'd barely slept since the previous night, and exhaustion clung to him like a cloak that only became heavier with each stroke of his blade. *Concentrate*, he willed himself, ignoring the blood trickling down his right arm. *Don't panic*—

Amethyst came at him again, her sword describing a deadly arc aimed at removing his head from his shoulders. He knocked her blade aside, managing to deliver a punch to her face as he twisted away—not nearly as powerful as he would have liked, but enough to send her reeling. He tried to press his advantage but she recovered quickly, deflecting his thrust and stepping in close to deliver a vicious elbow to his jaw. This time it was Lukan's turn to stumble backward, but Amethyst didn't press her advantage—instead she grinned, licking her bloody lips. *She knows,* Lukan realized, panic flaring. *She knows she's got the better of me.*

"You should have walked away," Amethyst said, smiling as she traced lazy circles in the air with her sword. "Such a shame I'm going to have to cut your pretty face."

Lukan made to reply, only to fall silent as a small figure emerged from the shadows behind the mercenary. *Flea.* He felt a flicker of hope. *What in the hells is she doing?*

"You can't best me," Amethyst continued, oblivious to the girl creeping toward her.

Lukan grinned. "I don't need to."

A flicker of realization passed across the mercenary's face. She spun, carving the empty air with her blade.

"Nice try," Flea said, raising the crossbow cradled in her hands. Amethyst moved quickly, but not as fast as the bolt that hissed from the weapon, which skewered her thigh. The woman gasped and staggered but recovered swiftly and lunged at Flea. The girl skipped away. *Slippery as an eel,* Lukan thought, as he leaped forward, slashing at the mercenary's back. Amethyst whirled and deflected his attack, but at the cost of her balance. Lukan slammed her with a shoulder and sent her tumbling to the ground. Again she recovered swiftly, rolling and rising to one knee, only to freeze as Lukan pressed the tip of his sword against her throat.

"Drop your weapon," he ordered, his arm trembling.

Amethyst glared at him but tossed her blade aside. "You dishonor yourself, Lukan Gardova."

"It's been known to happen."

"Relying on this little street rat to save your skin—"

"My name's *Flea*." The girl strode to Lukan's side, her face dark with anger. "My friend's name was Hector—"

Amethyst spat at her feet. "Tell someone who cares."

Flea's jaw tightened and she raised her crossbow; Lukan thought she was going to skewer the woman between the eyes with the second bolt, but instead the girl showed surprising restraint. "His name was Hector," she repeated, holding the mercenary's gaze. "You killed him, just like you killed Vetch. And the doctor—"

"It was just business, you little bitch."

"So is this." Lukan slammed the pommel of his sword against Amethyst's skull. The woman slumped to the ground, her body limp.

"Is she dead?" Flea asked.

"I hope not."

Flea stared at him, confusion replacing her anger. "But . . . but she deserves to die."

"Probably."

"Then why don't you kill her?"

Lukan sheathed his sword. "Why don't you?"

Flea frowned, glanced down at her crossbow. Set her mouth in a tight line. "Fine, I will." Her finger tightened round the trigger. A moment passed. Another.

"It's easy to wish death on someone," Lukan said softly, "but much harder to actually deliver it to them."

"She killed Hector."

"I know. She deserves to die, for that and her other crimes. But if you take her life, you'll wear it round your neck for the rest of your own." He placed a hand on the girl's shoulder. "Is that a burden you're prepared to bear?"

Flea shrugged his hand away, lips thinned in determination. *Lady's mercy,* he thought, *she's going to do it.* But instead the girl lowered her crossbow and drew a dagger from her belt. Crouching over the unconscious woman, she ran the tip of her blade down the mercenary's cheek; a deep cut that drew blood. "There," the girl said. She wiped her blade clean on Amethyst's tunic and sheathed it. "She said she would cut your face, so I've cut hers. She deserves more, but . . . this will do." Flea tried to pull her bolt free, but it remained lodged in Amethyst's thigh. "I can't . . ."

"Here," Lukan said, tugging it loose and handing it to her. "Good shot, by the way." He'd initially been concerned about Flea claiming ownership over Topaz's crossbow. While it was small and sleek, it was certainly no toy, and in the girl's hands he worried it might do more harm than good. Yet his suggestion that she give it up had been met with a scowl and a crude gesture. In any case, the hour he'd spent watching her shoot bolts into a fence post behind the Orange Tree Inn had left him surprised at how quickly she'd mastered the weapon.

Flea grinned as she loaded the bolt back into the crossbow. "Did you see me? I moved as quietly as Lady Midnight."

"I saw you. You did great, kid."

"That's twice now."

"Twice what?"

"Twice that I've saved your life."

"Really? I've not been counting." Lukan grinned as Flea punched him. "Anyway, I was in full control of the situation—" He leaned away from her second punch and started searching Amethyst's body, finding a dagger; a couple of silver coins; a vial of unknown liquid, which he discarded; and a length of fine rope, which he sliced in two and used to bind her hands and feet. Satisfied that the knots would hold, he cut a strip from her undershirt and tied the rag round the wound in her thigh.

"What should we do with her?" Flea asked.

"Leave her somewhere she won't be easily found. Give me a hand."

The girl rolled her eyes and half-heartedly picked up a leg. Together they dragged the unconscious mercenary away from the path, leaving her in the darkness beside a nearby tomb. With any luck she'd be out for a good half hour, and groggy for a lot longer than that. *Enough time to get down into the catacombs and see what the hells Murillo is up to.* As they returned to the mausoleum, Flea made a beeline for Amethyst's sword, which lay beside the path where she'd tossed it.

"Put that down," Lukan said as he removed the burning torch from its bracket beside the door.

"Why? It's mine now."

"Do you know how to use it?"

The girl took an experimental swing and almost lost her balance.

"I'll learn," she said tightly, grimacing at the effort of keeping the blade raised.

"A sword in unskilled hands," Lukan said, "is just as much a danger to the wielder as anyone else." He drew the mercenary's dagger from his belt. "This is more your size. I'll trade you this dagger for the sword. You'll have two, one for each boot."

The girl pulled a face but handed over the sword, accepting the dagger in return.

Well-balanced, Lukan thought, as he hefted the sword. *Talassian craftsmanship, quality steel.* With a touch of regret, he hurled the blade as hard as he could, sending it spinning away into darkness until it clattered against the side of an unseen tomb. *Even if Amethyst wakes up soon and somehow frees herself, she won't be much of a danger without a blade.*

"So what now?" Flea asked, still studying her new weapon.

"I'm going in."

Flea finally looked up, raising a single eyebrow.

"Fine. *We* are going in."

Lukan eased the door open and stepped into the mausoleum. The torchlight played across the plain stone walls, revealing the fresh footprints in the dust that led toward the two sarcophagi that lay side by side in the center of the tomb. As he moved forward he half expected another guard to emerge from the alcoves, but nothing stirred in the shadows. He followed the prints toward the sarcophagus on the left, realizing as he drew closer that its lid had been removed and placed on the floor. *This'll be the entrance to the catacombs.* Sure enough, when he looked inside there were no dusty bones or scraps of clothing—merely a set of steps that descended into darkness. "If I told you," he said to Flea, as the girl stood on her tiptoes and peered over the rim of the sarcophagus, "that it might be best if you waited here . . ."

"I'd shove my new dagger up your arse."

"Thought so." He sighed. "Come on then. Follow me."

25

DUST AND DISQUIET

Lukan led the way down the steps, Flea following silently. His own footsteps sounded loud in comparison, echoing off the rough walls. *Not that it matters.* Even the most inattentive guard couldn't fail to notice the approaching glow of their torchlight. *And the Seven Jewels are nothing if not attentive.* All he could do was hold his sword ready and hope for the best.

It took them only a few moments to descend, the steps leveling out into a passage. An arched doorway loomed ahead.

"Stay behind me," Lukan whispered. Not waiting for Flea's reply, he surged through the doorway, his sword raised. His pulse raced as he scanned the room, expecting to see the flash of silver as a hooded assassin came at him with blade drawn.

Instead all he saw were bones.

There were thousands of them, stacked in moldering piles that reached halfway up the walls. Cobwebs clung to some, scraps of cloth to others. The air was cold but strangely close, as if weighed down by the memory of so many lives. A heavy silence lay in the room, broken only by the skittering of tiny feet on stone. *Rats. Must be thousands of them down here.*

"Look," Flea whispered, pointing to a set of footprints on the dusty floor that disappeared into the shadows.

"Let's go," Lukan replied. "Stay close."

They followed the prints as they wound between the mounds of bones. The chamber proved larger than Lukan had thought, but soon they reached another arched doorway that was lined with skulls, all of which seemed to stare at him with sightless eyes.

"Look at that," Flea said, pointing to a line of script carved into the lintel above. "What does it say?"

Lukan held his torch higher, squinting at the graven words. "'Take heed, you who drew . . . no, *draw* breath, for you now enter . . . the realm of the dead.'"

"Is that meant to be scary?" Flea asked dismissively.

"I don't know," Lukan replied, lowering his torch. "Do you feel scared?"

"No," the girl said, a little too quickly.

"Me neither," he lied, trying to ignore the inky stares of the skulls as he strode through the arch, Flea following closely behind.

———

The footprints led deeper into the catacombs, through passages lined with hundreds of skulls and vaulted chambers choked with bones. The torchlight flickered across the silent mounds, the dancing shadows lending them the impression of movement—as if at any moment they might suddenly shift and collapse, spilling over the pair of them in a skeletal tide and burying them in darkness. A harrowing fate, yet still preferable to what this Delastro character might have in store for them, should they fall into her hands. *Best not think about that.*

Every so often a set of prints would break away from the main group and disappear through a different chamber exit, or down another branch of a passage, and Lukan remembered what Topaz had told Juro: that the Seven Jewels patrolled different corridors while Murillo ventured deeper into the catacombs with Delastro. *Hopefully we can slip through the net.* With every new chamber and passage they entered, he braced for an attack, his blade raised as he scanned the shadows.

None came. It seemed Delastro—whether she thought the mission compromised or not—had believed Amethyst to be a sufficient deterrent. *Or perhaps,* Lukan mused, recalling what he'd been told about the Twice-Crowned King's subterranean kingdom, *she's more concerned with threats from below, not above.*

Either way, he was relieved by their smooth progress—he had no desire to tangle with another of Delastro's mercenaries. *Can't have Flea saving my life a third time,* he thought, glancing at the girl as she padded along silently beside him. If she was unnerved by the darkness or their macabre surroundings, she gave no sign. She was, he reasoned, like a little protective shadow that was both irritating and reassuring at the same time. *Not that I'd ever admit the latter to her.* He couldn't deny that it felt good to have someone watching his back, someone he could trust. And he *did* trust her, that was the surprising part; this willful street girl he'd known for only a few days, though it felt much longer. He certainly trusted her more than anyone else in Saphrona. *Not that I'll be telling her that either.*

"Hold up," Flea whispered as they walked a winding corridor, shadows pooling in the eye sockets of the skulls that lined the walls. "I think I heard something."

Lukan listened carefully, hearing only the sound of his own breathing. "I don't hear anything—"

The girl motioned for silence. "There," she said, "can you hear them?"

Voices. So faint they were little more than a murmur.

"I hear them." *We're getting closer.* His heartbeat quickened at the thought. "Stay sharp."

The passage opened into another chamber full of bones. Only two sets of footprints were visible in the dust. *Delastro and Murillo.* They led toward the left side of the room, where light spilled through an archway some twenty yards distant.

"Lukan . . ."

"I see it." He wedged the torch in a pile of bones. "Now listen—"

"Stay behind you," Flea muttered, rolling her eyes. "I get it."

"And do exactly as I say. If something happens to me, you grab this torch and get the hells out of here. Get back to the Scrivener and tell her what happened."

"What about you?"

"I'll be fine. I can look after myself."

The girl snorted.

"I mean it, Flea," he said, his tone hardening. "No heroics this time. Got that?"

"Okay."

"All right. Let's see what sort of party we've invited ourselves to."

Lukan followed the prints across the chamber, Flea following behind. The voices grew louder as they approached.

". . . don't tolerate failure, you understand? I want him dead."

"I will see to it."

"You do that. Lady knows I'm paying you enough."

Lukan pressed himself to the left side of the archway and peered through. A flight of steps led down into the chamber beyond, which was the largest he'd seen so far. Hundreds of skulls lined the walls, illuminated by flames that leaped from a dozen braziers. Tattered banners, their colors long faded, adorned the columns that stood in each corner of the room, their upper reaches disappearing into the shadows of the vaulted ceiling. The sunken floor was clear of bones and dominated by a large marble sarcophagus, its surfaces covered in intricate carvings. Lukan's eyes moved to the two figures standing beside it.

". . . come too far now to have my plans ruined," the silver-masked figure was saying as they paced back and forth, cloak stirring up dust from the floor. *Murillo,* Lukan thought, *though his voice sounds different. Must be the mask.*

"As I said," the other figure replied, "I will see to it." *And that'll be Delastro.* The mercenary leader looked just as intimidating as Juro had made her sound. Time and hardship had left their mark on the woman's sharp features; her olive skin was lined and bore several nicks and scars, while her dark hair was streaked with grey. Yet Lukan sensed they had also sharpened her spirit, like a whetstone honing a blade. Her conviction was clear in the way she spoke—coldly, sharply—and in the way she remained perfectly still, arms folded. *A dangerous woman.*

"We should have killed the bastard after Valdezar's gala,"

Murillo said, ceasing his pacing. "But instead we let him dig too deep and he found that damned journal."

Lukan tensed. *They're talking about me.*

"The journal told him nothing," Delastro replied, unmoved. "And it's in our hands now."

"Yet Gardova is not."

"A mistake that will be rectified."

"You don't even know where he is." Murillo shook his head. "We should have just killed him when we had the chance."

"We needed to discover who Gardova is working for so we can remove them *all* from the equation," Delastro replied. "Trust me on this, my lord. I understand the stakes involved—"

"You know nothing of the stakes," Murillo snapped, making a sharp gesture. "Nothing, do you understand? You can't even *begin* to comprehend them."

Lukan frowned, doubt growing in his mind. *That voice . . .* He listened as the man continued speaking, not following the words but trying to imagine the shape of them passing between Murillo's lips. His heart lurched as the realization struck him. *Lady's blood . . . that's not Murillo.*

As if sensing Lukan's thoughts, the man pulled back his hood and removed his silver mask, placing it on the sarcophagus. Lukan's jaw dropped as he stared at the man's white hair and neatly trimmed beard. *I don't believe it . . .*

Lord Marquetta stepped toward Delastro. "You will find Gardova, and this time you will kill him," he said, with no trace of the good humor that he had shown to Lukan after approaching him at Valdezar's party. On that occasion his eyes had gleamed with mirth; now they shone with a cold fury. "No excuses. Have I made myself clear?"

A shadow of anger passed across Delastro's face, but was gone in an instant. "Perfectly."

We were wrong, Lukan thought, his mind reeling. *We were completely wrong.*

"Excellent." Marquetta turned away and began pacing again.

"Now, where have these guests of mine got to . . ." He paused, glancing toward an archway on the far side of the chamber; previously dark, it was now illuminated by a faint glow. "Ah, here they come."

A tall, broad-shouldered man entered the room. He held a lantern before him, while his military bearing suggested he knew how to use the blade he held loosely in his other hand. His grey hair was cropped short, his strong jaw clean-shaven. Smoke rose from the cigarillo clamped between his lips as he surveyed the chamber like a general studying a battlefield, his face devoid of expression.

"Prime Inquisitor Fierro," Marquetta exclaimed, raising a hand. "Welcome."

The man offered Marquetta a brusque nod and set the lantern down. He took the steps to the floor with a slow, measured pace, sheathing his blade as he descended. *Seven shadows,* Lukan thought, *what in the hells is the head of the Inquisition doing here?*

His attention was drawn back to the archway as a second stranger appeared. Whereas Fierro was all hard edges, this man was smooth curves, his round face gleaming with sweat despite the chill. He paused at the top of the steps, pursing his lips as he brushed cobwebs from his ermine-trimmed robes. *Hardly the sort of thing you'd wear to a midnight meeting in the catacombs.*

"And Pontifex Barbosa," Marquetta said, a note of reproach in his voice. "You got my message about nondescript clothing, I see."

Pontifex? Lady's blood. Lukan stared at Barbosa, who looked more like a preening peacock than the holiest man in Saphrona. Then again, experience had taught Lukan the two were not mutually exclusive. *The highest religious authority in the city,* he thought, as the Pontifex tottered down the steps, *the head of the Inquisition, and the most powerful merchant prince. Quite the little cabal.*

"The Lady's Chosen must always look his best," the Pontifex replied, reaching the floor with a swish of cloth. "I am Her representative at *all* times, of course, so it's important that I look suitably dignified—"

"Dignified?" Fierro cut in, his voice a gravelly rasp. "You look like a whore in silks."

"Better that than a boy in cuffs, which I hear is your personal preference."

Fierro removed the cigarillo from his mouth and blew a cloud of smoke at the other man. "I'd think very carefully about your next words, *priest*."

"Or you'll what? Slip bitterbloom into my tea, like you did to your illustrious predecessor?"

Steel rasped as Fierro drew his blade and stepped toward the Pontifex, whose face paled as he backed away.

"Gentlemen, please," Marquetta said, hands sketching a placating gesture. "We're all friends here."

"I'll never be friends with this sniveling sack of shit," Fierro replied, but he sheathed his sword and returned his cigarillo to his lips.

"The feeling is mutual, I assure you." Barbosa glared at the Prime Inquisitor and made a show of smoothing his robes before turning to Delastro and offering her a beatific smile. "Madame Delastro, a pleasure as always."

The woman ignored him.

"So, Lord Marquetta," the Pontifex continued, "might I ask why we couldn't have met in more comfortable surroundings?" He feigned a cough and patted his chest, his many rings glittering in the light. "The chill down here is terrible for my lungs."

Fierro snorted but said nothing.

"My apologies for the cold and cobwebs, and for the lateness of the hour," Marquetta replied, "but I have something to show you and I can only do so here, away from prying eyes."

"And where exactly is *here*?" Fierro asked, glancing around. "What is this place?"

The merchant prince smiled wolfishly and approached the sarcophagus. "This, gentlemen," he said, running his hand over the marble lid as he walked down its length, "is the tomb of Baltasar del Vasca, who ruled our great city nearly a century ago."

"The Jackal of Saphrona," the Pontifex offered, glancing at the sarcophagus. "Isn't that what they called him? A tyrant who killed thousands—"

"He was no tyrant," Marquetta snapped, shooting the man a glare. "Though it is true history has not been kind to his name. But then history is written by the winners, and when this is all over I intend to write a few words of my own."

When what is over? Lukan wondered.

"Baltasar was a great man," Marquetta continued. "Under his rule Saphrona flourished like never before—was *feared* like never before. He understood that some men are meant to rule and others are meant to serve. That strength lies in an iron will and refusal to back down, not in compromise. And he knew a dead enemy to be a thing of beauty."

"Until he was murdered," Fierro said.

"Indeed. By a damned *coward*." Marquetta spat the final word. "How Baltasar would turn in his grave if he could see what Saphrona has become. He would sneer at how we have traded conviction for compassion. He would rage at how, in our weakness, we have let the Zar-Ghosans settle and prosper in our own city, where once we crushed them beneath our heel. But then he would smile when he sees us, my friends. Because in us his vision lives on. Together, we will restore Saphrona's glory and drive these Zar-Ghosan leeches back across the Scepter Sea. Soon a glorious new chapter in our city's history will begin—and we shall be the ones to write it."

"Well said, my lord," the Pontifex replied, clapping enthusiastically. "Well said indeed—"

"And your plans?" Fierro asked, silencing Barbosa with a glare. "Do they proceed as intended?"

"They do," Marquetta said with a nod. "Everything is in place."

"And what of Gardova? Is he still a threat?"

Lukan's heart skipped a beat.

"He's not a threat," the merchant prince replied dismissively. "Merely a nuisance. He attended Lady Valdezar's gala last night, posing as a merchant from Parva. I spoke with him briefly to

get a measure of the man and can't say I was overly impressed."
Marquetta began pacing again, hands clasped behind his back.
"Gardova spoke with Doctor Vassilis, as I had anticipated. What
I hadn't foreseen was that the doctor would agree to reveal his
suspicions about Lord Saviola's death."

"I thought you'd warned him about that," Fierro said, glancing
askance at Delastro. "You said he wouldn't talk. Seems he wasn't
as scared of you as you thought."

"He seemed scared enough when I put my blade in his throat,"
Delastro replied, deadpan.

"So he's dead?"

"That's normally what happens when you cut someone's jugular."

"If you'd both allow me to continue," Marquetta said, a hint
of annoyance in his voice, "Vassilis invited Gardova to meet
with him at the Collegium at midnight. Madame Delastro paid
the doctor a visit of her own and bought his silence. Perma-
nently. So there's no need to worry—Vassilis's little secret died
with him."

"He's not the only one who knew," Fierro said, flicking ash
from his cigarillo. "Some of the servants mentioned the frost on
Saviola's corpse, and the unnatural coldness in the room. The constables who arrested Zandrusa noticed it too."

"Vassilis was the only one who mattered," Marquetta replied
firmly, "the only witness whose claims might have carried weight.
With him gone, there's nothing to fear. No one cares about the
words of a few witless servants."

"Be that as it may, you still haven't told us what all that strange-
ness was about. The frost, the coldness—there are far more subtle
ways of killing a man." The Prime Inquisitor looked at Delastro.
"I thought you were meant to be the best."

The mercenary's eyes narrowed, lip curling as she prepared a
sharp retort, only for Marquetta to intervene.

"Please, Prime Inquisitor, all will be revealed in time." The
merchant prince smiled and spread his hands. "I know you have
questions. Tonight you will receive answers."

"So Vassilis is dead," Fierro growled around his cigarillo, which glowed red. "What about Gardova?"

"We tracked him to a town house in Seven Arches," Marquetta replied. "Delastro and her crew raided the place in the early hours of the morning. They killed a couple of guards, but Gardova and that little brat sidekick of his managed to give them the slip."

"They got away?" the Pontifex exclaimed, nervously clutching at the amulet round his neck. "My lord, if the Seven Jewels can't catch Gardova then perhaps we should find someone who can . . ." The man trailed off as Delastro stepped toward him, a dagger gleaming in her hand. He took a step back as she raised her arm, his eyes wide, then flinched as—with a deft flick of her wrist—the mercenary sent the knife flashing toward him . . . and past him, skewering a rat that had been scrabbling across the floor a few yards away. The rodent twitched as it died.

"Never liked rats," the woman said, staring coldly at Barbosa.

The man swallowed and forced a weak laugh. "I meant no offense, of course . . ."

"You must forgive the Pontifex, Madame Delastro," Marquetta said. "This sort of business makes him a little jittery. But I'm sure he has absolute faith in your ability to locate and eliminate Gardova. As do I."

Delastro made no reply as she went to retrieve her knife. Barbosa stiffened as she strode past him, a fresh sheen of sweat on his brow.

"In any case," Marquetta continued, "Gardova is an irrelevance. He knows nothing of our plans, nor does he know of our involvement in Lord Saviola's death and Lady Jelassi's imprisonment."

I do now, you bastard, Lukan thought.

"But my lord," the Pontifex said, "surely Gardova suspects . . ." He fell silent as the merchant prince made a sharp gesture.

"Suspicions are all he has," Marquetta replied firmly, "and he's directing them in entirely the wrong direction. Lady Jelassi thinks that Lord Murillo is the culprit, that it was he who murdered Lord Saviola and framed her for the crime, just as I knew she would. Fear not, my dear Pontifex, Gardova is no threat to us, merely a nuisance. I have no idea who he is or why he has thrown his lot in with Jelassi, nor what he hopes to gain from her release, but it will prove to be the last mistake he ever makes. Madame Delastro will find him and we'll get his story from him one way or another. Once we're finished with him, he'll meet the same end as Doctor Vassilis."

Delastro's not told him about Topaz, Lukan realized. He couldn't be sure, of course—and Delastro's stony expression gave nothing away—but something about Marquetta's relaxed confidence suggested that the mercenary had left out some of the finer details of the raid on the safe house. *But why?* Whatever the reason, Lukan knew it was to his advantage; he didn't doubt that Marquetta would have called off this meeting if he had an inkling that his secrecy might have been compromised. *Thank the Lady for small favors.* Still, it would count for nothing unless he learned more about Marquetta's plans.

"That's most reassuring, my lord," Fierro said, dropping the stub of his cigarillo and grinding it beneath a heel. "But I must admit to being curious as to where you got all this information— Gardova's infiltration of the Ebon Hand, his conversation with Jelassi, his decision to seek the doctor out at Lady Valdezar's gala . . ." He slipped another cigarillo from a silver case and knelt by a nearby brazier to light it. "How did you learn all of this?"

How indeed, Lukan thought. *I was wondering that myself.*

Marquetta's smile returned. "A fair question, my friend, and one I would expect from the head of the Inquisition. As it happens, that was one of my motives for summoning you both here tonight." The merchant prince walked toward one corner of the chamber and gestured at the shadows. "You can come out now, my friend," he called.

A figure materialized from the gloom. Lukan's jaw dropped again as the newcomer stepped into the light of the braziers. *Lady's blood, it can't be,* he thought numbly. He blinked several times, as if this were a mirage he could simply dispel. It wasn't.

"My friends," Marquetta said, turning back to the Pontifex and Prime Inquisitor, "allow me to introduce you to Magellis."

The man bowed to Marquetta and nodded politely to the two other conspirators as he joined them by the sarcophagus.

"I know you," Barbosa said, eyes narrowed. "You're Lady Jelassi's steward."

"What's going on here, Marquetta?" Fierro asked, dispensing with formality, his rough voice taking on an even harder edge.

"Not Jelassi's man," Marquetta said, grinning as he placed his hands on Magellis's shoulders. "He's *mine*. I plucked Magellis from the debtors' prison, about . . . eight years ago? Nine? I forget. Anyway, I had heard that Lady Jelassi was looking for a new steward, and I told her I knew *just* the man." Marquetta clapped Magellis on the shoulder. "Magellis did a wonderful job for Jelassi, just as I promised he would. He also kept me apprised of my dear colleague's business affairs and passed on any information he thought I might find useful . . . such as Jelassi's intention to visit Lord Saviola's villa for a secret meeting about the impending council vote."

"So that's how you were able to implicate her in Saviola's murder," Fierro observed, puffing on his new cigarillo. "I admire your ingenuity, my lord. And Gardova?"

"He visited Magellis and sought his help in proving Jelassi's innocence. Magellis sent word to me immediately. His timely actions have saved us a lot of trouble."

You bastard, Lukan thought, staring at the steward, who was smiling at his master's praise. *Just as well I didn't tell him everything.*

"But can we trust in his silence?" Fierro asked, staring at Magellis. "The more people who know of our plans, the more we risk discovery."

"Have no fear, Prime Inquisitor," Marquetta replied. "It's all in hand." He nodded at Delastro, and the mercenary strode forward, approaching Magellis from behind. Realization dawned in the steward's eyes; he turned and raised his hands—

Too late.

Delastro's blade flickered silver and opened his throat. Magellis staggered, grasping numbly at the wound as blood gushed between his fingers, turning them crimson. He looked to Marquetta as he fell to his knees, eyes wide with shock, lips quivering. The merchant prince stared back, his expression betraying not a hint of remorse. Magellis toppled sideways, convulsed once, and then lay still as his blood pooled around him.

"No one keeps secrets better than the dead," Marquetta said.

"Lady protect us," the Pontifex murmured, his face pale. "Was—was that truly necessary, my lord? Killing him just . . . well, it seems rather extreme, and—"

"We killed Lord Saviola too," Fierro interjected, eyeing the Pontifex over the glow of his cigarillo. "I don't recall you having an issue then."

"I voiced my objections at the time," Barbosa replied hotly, anger bringing some color back to his pale face. "I've always argued against bloodshed in this . . . endeavor of ours."

"Indeed. How noble of you."

"My conscience is clear," the Pontifex said tartly, raising his chin. "After all, I didn't wield the blade that killed Lord Saviola—"

"Of course you didn't," Fierro sneered. "The most dangerous weapon you've ever held is your limp cock."

"You dare insult the Lady's Chosen? I'll have you—"

"*Enough.*" Lord Marquetta's voice echoed around the chamber. The two men fell silent.

"As I was saying," the merchant prince continued, his anger disappearing as quickly as it had come, "we have nothing to fear from Gardova. It is our upcoming plans that we should be focusing our energies on, and I am pleased to say that everything is in place. The time, gentlemen, is nearly upon us. We shall proceed as planned and strike during the Grand Restoration, just as the Silver Spear is being exchanged." He smiled. "A moment meant to symbolize our peace and friendship with Zar-Ghosa will instead be the harbinger of a glorious new age for Saphrona. A delicious irony, I'm sure you agree."

"And the Zar-Ghosan ambassador?" Fierro tapped ash from his cigarillo. "You still intend to . . ."

"I do. The ambassador is the key to my entire plan."

"Forgive me, my lord." The Pontifex was toying with his amulet again. "You still haven't revealed how you intend to commit a murder in front of the Grand Duke's entire court, not to mention half the city."

"Now *that*," Marquetta replied, with a wolfish grin, "is a good question."

Seven shadows, Lukan thought, his stomach lurching. *They're planning to murder the Zar-Ghosan ambassador.* His mind raced through the implications. Murdering the ambassador would in itself carry severe political consequences, but to murder them at a ceremony intended as a celebration of peace between the two nations . . . well, that was something else entirely. *It's nothing short of a declaration of war.*

"I'm grateful to you both for indulging me this far," the merchant prince continued, pacing once more. "I appreciate that I have demanded both your trust and loyalty with one hand, while concealing the truth of my plans with the other. It is only natural that you should wonder how I intend to pull off such an ambitious endeavor. That you might question my ability to deliver on my promises. But I assure you, such concerns are unnecessary." Marquetta spun on his heel and spread his arms. "As I will now show you."

A glowing scarlet orb appeared in the air behind the merchant prince. *Sorcery,* Lukan realized, as the orb began to move in a circle. *Marquetta must have hired gleamers.* Two more orbs appeared, green and purple in color, and joined the first in its circular movement, all three moving in tandem. Suddenly the orbs began to move faster, until they were indistinguishable, their movement forming a ring of white light. Lukan frowned as the ring began to expand. *What in the hells . . .* The air within the expanding ring was moving. The movement was subtle at first, like the ripples of a lake, before growing more intense, like a storm-tossed sea. *What manner of sorcery is this?*

The Pontifex and Prime Inquisitor were clearly wondering the same thing, as both backed away, placing the sarcophagus between them and the disturbance. Delastro held her ground, though she gave Marquetta a sharp look. The merchant prince merely stood and smiled, stroking his beard.

A flash drew Lukan's attention back to the sorcery. Light was flickering across the churning air, staccato bursts of pure white. *Almost like lightning.* Lukan's mouth fell open as the realization hit him, his father's words—stories he'd long dismissed—rising from the depths of his memory. *Lady's blood, it's a damned portal.*

But surely it couldn't be. Such powerful sorcery—the ability to alter the very fabric of reality—was far beyond the ability of any gleamers, though many had tried. Lukan had heard rumors of their failures; those who hadn't lost their lives had instead lost their minds. Some scholars argued that the Phaeron had been capable of using powerful sorcery to travel great distances in the blink of an eye, but the Phaeron had disappeared long ago, and there was no one else who was capable of such a feat. *Except . . . no, that's impossible. They're a myth, a children's story. They don't exist—*

"Gentlemen," Marquetta said grandly, gesturing toward the portal. "Behold the Faceless!"

Lukan stared in horror as a figure emerged from the writhing surface of the portal, the lightning flickering across its form as it stepped into the chamber. Icy vapor steamed from crimson armor of unfamiliar design, its sharp edges chased in silver. A dark cloak swirled behind the figure like liquid shadow, flowing down from pauldrons shaped like snarling wolves, their garnet eyes gleaming in the firelight. *The Wolf,* Lukan thought, remembering the stories. The Wolf wore a featureless helm that lacked even eye slits. Nonetheless, the figure's head turned slowly, as if examining the room and the people within. Lukan felt ice on his spine as the unseen gaze seemed to linger on the archway where he stood. *Did I imagine that?*

Movement drew his gaze back to the portal as two more figures stepped through. They looked much like their companion, with the same cloaks of shifting shadow, ornate armor, and featureless helms. Yet as Lukan stared at the newcomers, he noticed certain differences. The second figure's armor was dark green chased in gold, with pauldrons shaped like coiled snakes, their emerald eyes flashing, fangs bared as if they were preparing to strike. *The Viper,* he thought. The third figure wore armor of deep purple embossed with bronze, the pauldrons forged in the shape of a tentacled squid with eyes of amethyst. *The Kraken.*

A deep, aching fear uncoiled in Lukan's gut as he watched the two newcomers join their comrade, forming a silent line. Behind them, the lightning flared as the portal began to shrink, its glowing edges growing smaller in diameter until the ring became a single ball of pure white light, which pulsed once before winking from sight.

Silence fell across the chamber.

"Lukan." Flea's whisper was fear mixed with awe. "I thought you said they were just a story."

"I . . . I thought—" His breath caught in his throat as the three figures stepped forward as one, their movements slow and measured.

"We should go," Flea urged.

We should. Yet as he watched the Faceless approach the conspirators, moving in unnerving synchronicity, Lukan found he couldn't look away, his gaze transfixed by a children's story come to life—a myth of mask-wearing demons revealed as terrible truth. *You were right, Father,* he thought, as the armored figures stopped before Marquetta. *You were right all along. They truly are real.* He swallowed, his throat dry, and steadied himself against the arch. His knees felt weak.

"Lukan," Flea hissed again. "We need to *go.*"

He managed only a croak in response.

"My lords," Marquetta said grandly, offering the three armored figures—the *Faceless*—a deep bow. "Welcome. You do us great honor with your presence."

No shit, Lukan thought, his wits returning. There were only a few recorded sightings of the Faceless across nearly a millennium of history, the last of them over three hundred years before, so for the three men on the chamber floor this was a rare blessing indeed.

Or more likely a curse. While the historical accounts were few and far between, all imparted the same fact: that whenever the Faceless appeared, trouble followed.

The disbelief Lukan felt was reflected on the faces of the Pontifex and the Prime Inquisitor. The former's face was white, lips moving rapidly as he murmured an entreaty to his goddess, while the latter's jaw was clenched, hand on his sword as he stared at the armored figures. No doubt they had always assumed—like Lukan—that the Faceless were nothing more than a myth. *How wrong we were,* he thought, feeling a sudden, absurd need to laugh. *How terribly, terribly wrong.*

The Faceless remained silent, unmoving.

"Don't be shy, gentlemen," Marquetta called, giving his co conspirators a glare that was at odds with the warmth in his voice. "My new friends here mean you no harm—"

The Faceless stepped forward in perfect unison.

Marquetta, to his credit, didn't so much as flinch. The same couldn't be said of his two allies; the Pontifex squealed and hid behind the sarcophagus, while the Prime Inquisitor drew his blade and held it before him—as if a few feet of steel were any defense against beings that could bend reality's fabric to their will.

"Put that away," Marquetta snapped at him before turning his glare on the Pontifex, who was peeping over the top of the sarcophagus. "On your feet, Barbosa. Show some damned dignity, the pair of you. You're embarrassing yourselves." Lukan could hardly blame the two men for their reaction, not when his own heart was threatening to burst from his chest. Delastro, to her credit, was doing a better job than the men of keeping her composure, but the uncertainty in her gaze was unmistakable. *Interesting,* Lukan mused, as the mercenary's hand hovered over the sword at her hip. *This seems to be as much a surprise to her as everyone else. Clearly Marquetta's been holding back, even from her.*

The Faceless halted a couple of yards from Marquetta and

Delastro. Fierro—at a brusque nod from the merchant prince—finally lowered his blade. Barbosa rose shakily, but remained behind the sarcophagus.

"When I first came to you both," Marquetta said, a smile tugging at his lips as he glanced at his co-conspirators, "you asked me how we could possibly commit a murder in front of the Grand Duke's court—not to mention the entire *city*—and cast the blame precisely where we wanted. Well, my friends . . ." He swept an arm toward the Faceless. "This is how."

"You would ask . . . *them* to work for us?" Fierro asked hoarsely.

"They already are." Marquetta's voice contained a note of triumph. "They murdered Lord Saviola at my request."

"Saviola? But I thought the Seven Jewels . . ." The Prime Inquisitor looked at Delastro.

"We are mercenaries," the woman replied, meeting his gaze. "Not gleamers. We trade in steel, not *sorcery*." She spat the last word as if it was acid on her tongue.

"So they killed him?" Fierro said, glancing at the Faceless. "Better it *had* been the Seven Jewels. The damned frost on Saviola's corpse set too many tongues wagging."

"The frost was an . . . unfortunate side effect," Marquetta admitted. "One I don't fully understand, and the cause of which our esteemed friends here prefer to keep to themselves." He smiled and spread his hands. "No matter. Only Doctor Vassilis could have made trouble for us, and—thanks to Madame Delastro—he's dead. History will record that Lord Saviola died from a stab wound to the throat, delivered by Lady Jelassi. No one knows the truth, save for us."

"Gardova knows."

"I already told you," Marquetta said, a hint of annoyance in his tone, "that Gardova is nothing more than a nuisance. He believes in Jelassi's innocence but has no way of proving it; nor does he know of our involvement. Besides, Delastro will find him and kill him, and that will be the end of it. In the meantime, we have more important things to concern ourselves with. Our moment of triumph approaches, and the Faceless stand ready to help us make our dream a reality."

"Why?" the Prime Inquisitor said, asking the same question that was tugging at Lukan's own mind. "Why would they do this for us? What have you offered them?"

"That is between me and the Faceless." Marquetta turned back to the three armored figures and offered them a bow. "My lords, please excuse my friends' poor manners—this is a little much for them. Allow me to introduce the Prime Inquisitor and—" The merchant prince jolted, pain spasming across his face as he touched a hand to his right temple. "Yes . . . I—I have it," he stuttered, gritting his teeth against whatever invisible force assailed him. "Please . . . allow me to . . . show you."

Another myth revealed as truth, Lukan thought grimly. The accounts of the Faceless all held that they never spoke, instead communicating by projecting images into the mind of the subject, and that such an action took both a physical and psychological toll on the recipient. *But what the hells is Marquetta talking about?*

"Here," the merchant prince said, reaching beneath his robe. He withdrew a dagger and held it before the Faceless, his arm trembling. "The Sandino Blade," he added, his voice strained. "I told you . . . I always keep my promises. Now . . . will you keep yours?"

The Sandino Blade, Lukan thought, as the pieces of that little mystery fell into place. *The old family heirloom the Seven Jewels stole from Lord Sandino. Marquetta's using it as payment for the Faceless . . . but why? What could they possibly want with it?* He squinted at the dagger, but could see nothing remarkable about the dull blade.

The Faceless remained unmoved.

"It's yours," Marquetta continued, slipping the dagger back beneath his robes. "All you need to do is carry out the final act as we agreed." He gasped, face contorting in pain as he raised a shaking hand to his head. "No . . . of course not . . . No one outside this room knows of our plans . . ."

Lukan's heart leaped into his mouth as the three eyeless helms all turned toward him. *Seven shadows . . . they know we're here.*

"No . . . that's impossible," the merchant prince gasped, squinting in Lukan's direction. "No one knows of this meeting . . . I set guards—"

"What's going on, Marquetta?" Fierro demanded.

"The Faceless . . ." Marquetta grimaced, pointing a shaking finger toward Lukan's hiding place. "They . . . they say there's someone there . . . an intruder."

"Lukan." Flea's voice was a startled whisper. "We need to—"

"Go," he finished. *We should have gone already.*

Steel rasped as Delastro drew her blade and started forward, only to freeze as the Wolf raised its right hand. Scarlet light glowed between its gauntleted fingers as they weaved an intricate pattern. With a lazy flick of its wrist—as if to suggest that the manipulation of such power was little more than child's play—the Wolf sent a bolt of light streaking toward the chamber floor. The energy struck stone with a sharp crack, scattering dust as it coalesced into a glowing scarlet form of powerful limbs, sharp claws, and bared fangs. *Lady's blood,* Lukan thought, as the sorcerous wolf threw back its head and howled.

"Run!" he gasped, but Flea was already moving, racing back toward the burning torch. He took off after her, his chest tight with rising panic.

Behind them, the wolf began its pursuit.

26

A HEROIC ACT OF DEFIANCE

Bones skittered to the floor as Flea pulled the burning torch free.

"Follow me," she called, darting back into the passage they'd traversed earlier. Lukan raced after her, the echo of their footfalls and his own heavy breathing almost combining to drown out the howls that rose behind them.

Almost.

Just keep running. He gritted his teeth, breath hissing between them. *Don't look back, don't look back—*

He looked back, saw only darkness.

They entered another chamber and followed the prints into a skull-lined passage, countless empty eye sockets bearing witness to their panicked flight. Lukan realized that Flea was slowly pulling away from him, the distance between them growing. "Flea," he gasped, forcing his limbs to renewed effort, "slow down . . . I can't see my bloody feet!"

"This way," the girl called as the passage forked, her light disappearing into the left-hand tunnel. Lukan swore as he barreled after her. *If I trip on a bone . . .* He rounded the corner, breath exploding from his lungs as he collided with the girl, sending them both staggering. The torch spun from Flea's hand, flickering as it struck the stone floor. *What in the hells . . .*

A man stood before them, clad in dark cloth and supple leather. He held a burning torch in one hand and a dagger in another. *One of the Jewels,* Lukan realized. *Shit.* "Get back," he said, grabbing Flea and shoving her behind him.

"Shouldn't have come here," the mercenary said in a Talassian accent.

"Not going to argue with that," Lukan replied. He reached for his sword, only to hesitate as his fingers brushed the hilt. In the narrow confines of the passage, he would be at a disadvantage. *Knives it is then,* he thought grimly. His gaze flicked to a skull lying at the base of the wall. *Unless . . .*

The mercenary charged, lips bared in a snarl. Lukan scooped the skull up by its eye sockets and hurled it, striking the man full in the mouth. The mercenary stumbled against the wall, his torch falling to the floor as he spat blood and a single tooth. Lukan leaped at him and felt the man's blade scrape his forearm as they collided, his momentum bearing them both down. The mercenary lost his hold on the blade as they hit the ground, but recovered quickly, scrambling on top of Lukan and wrapping both his hands round Lukan's throat. Darkness crowded the edges of his vision as Lukan tried to break the man's vise-like grip. Together they thrashed in the flickering light of the torches.

A howl sounded from the darkness behind them.

The man glanced up in surprise, his grip slackening. "What in the hells was—"

Lukan surged upward and headbutted him in the face before shoving him away. *Not going to die here,* he thought, terror lending strength to his limbs as he grabbed a fistful of the mercenary's hair and slammed his head against the stone floor. *Not going to*—he slammed the man's head again—*bloody die here.* He released his grip, the mercenary slackening beneath him.

Lukan rose shakily to his feet, chest heaving. "Flea?" he called, his words sounding like they came from a great distance, barely audible over the pounding of blood in his ears.

"Here." The girl picked up her torch and stepped toward him. "Are you okay?" She glanced over her shoulder. "Because the wolf is—"

"I know." He snatched up the mercenary's own torch. "Quickly, let's go. You lead."

The girl didn't need to be told twice and raced off down the passage without another word. The mercenary groaned but Lukan didn't spare him another glance as he ran after her.

They were halfway across the next chamber when they heard a snarl from behind them, followed by a scream—a rising note of pure terror that was quickly silenced. *Not a pleasant end,* Lukan thought as Flea led the way into another passage, *but one he more than deserved.* They emerged into a new chamber, the flames from their torches casting fleeting shadows across the mounds of bones that surrounded them; to Lukan it seemed like the piles were shifting, as if the bones were conspiring to block their escape. If Flea shared his thought, she gave no sign as she tracked the footprints into another skull-lined passage. *We can't be far now.* Lukan glanced over his shoulder, saw nothing but darkness. He felt a flicker of hope. *Perhaps we lost it. Perhaps it's given up the chase—*

Another howl echoed through the catacombs in mocking response.

Dread tightened his chest. *We're not going to make it.* "Flea," he called, stopping in the middle of the chamber.

The girl turned and shot him a questioning look.

"We can't outrun this thing." Her mouth formed an objection but he pressed on. "Get out of here—get back to the Scrivener and tell her everything. *Everything, you understand? Don't look* back." He tried to shove her away, but the girl resisted.

"What about you?" she asked, eyes wide.

"I'll lead the bloody thing away," he replied, glancing at one of the other passages. "Try and buy you some time."

"No." She shook her head. "I'm not leaving you—"

"Listen to me! This is far bigger than we thought. If you don't get word to the Scrivener, the Zar-Ghosan ambassador will die. This isn't just about Zandrusa anymore, understand? Marquetta's looking to start a *war.*" He gripped her shoulder and gave what he hoped was a reassuring squeeze. "Besides, you've saved my life twice now. Time for me to repay the favor."

Flea swallowed, caught in indecision.

Another howl echoed behind them.

"Flea . . ."

The girl surprised him by grabbing him in a hug. "Stay safe," she whispered before darting away.

"I'll try," he murmured after her, watching as the light from her torch faded. *But I don't rate my chances.*

Lukan started toward another passage on the far side of the chamber. Where it led was anyone's guess. *They stretch in the darkness for miles,* Juro had said of the catacombs. Evading the beast at his heels would serve little purpose if he ended up lost in the tunnels. He'd merely be trading a quick death for a slow one, shivering and starving in the darkness, long after his torch had burned out—

A growl sounded behind him.

Lukan swore under his breath and turned round.

The beast emerged from the passage on the far side of the chamber. It was at least twice the size of a real wolf, its powerful body—which possessed a ghostlike quality—casting a red glow across the piles of bones. Yet for all that it was a creation of sorcery, the creature prowled like a living wolf—head slung low, fangs bared. Its movements were slow, purposeful—those of a master predator content to bide its time, knowing its prey couldn't escape. Every instinct Lukan possessed screamed at him to run, but he couldn't. Not yet—not until he was sure Flea was safe.

The wolf—or whatever it truly was—paused as it drew level with the tunnel Flea had taken, its great head turning, as if sensing her recent passage.

"Hey," he yelled. "Over here, you big bastard."

The creature's head swiveled, its eyes glowing crimson as they regarded him.

"Come on," Lukan shouted, fear thickening his voice. "It's me you want."

A low growl escaped the wolf's throat as it looked back to Flea's passage.

Seven shadows . . . Lukan picked up a skull and hurled it at the wolf. "Come on, you stupid—"

The beast snarled as the skull struck its right flank. *It's not ethereal*, Lukan realized, as the wolf finally started toward him. *And if it can be hit, then maybe it can be harmed.*

Lukan turned and fled down the corridor, terror lending his limbs a frenzied energy. His heart pounded as he raced through a network of tunnels and chambers, trying not to think of the beast at his heels, or what would happen if his torch guttered and died. *Just keep moving.* He ducked into another passage, skulls leering at him in the torchlight. Maybe, just maybe, he could lose the wolf in the depths of the catacombs.

It was a faint hope.

Far more likely he'd hear its claws skittering on the stone behind him, feel the chill of its sorcerous breath on his neck as it lunged . . .

Panicked by the thought, Lukan whirled and slashed with his sword.

The blade sliced empty air.

He stood alone in the passage, lungs heaving, limbs trembling. A cold sweat stinging his eyes.

No, he realized with growing dread. *Not alone.*

Lukan could feel the weight of the wolf's gaze, watching him from beyond the torchlight. He took a deep breath and lowered the torch.

Darkness . . . and a faint crimson glow at the far end of the tunnel. A low growl rumbled from the wolf's throat as it stalked toward him.

Shit.

He turned and ran, forcing his aching body to one last effort even though he knew it was hopeless. The torchlight revealed an archway ahead—the entrance to yet another chamber piled high with bones.

No doubt his own would soon join them.

Lukan burst into the room and spun round, bellowing as he

raised his sword—a final act of heroic defiance. The effect was spoiled somewhat by the flagstone beneath his right boot sinking into the floor, causing him to almost lose his balance. *What in the hells . . .* A rasp of metal drew his attention back to the archway, where several thick iron bands were descending to block the entrance. Lukan watched, stunned, as the ends of the bars disappeared into a series of holes in the floor.

He flinched as the wolf crashed against the bars barely a moment later. Scarlet sparks flew.

The bars held.

The wolf snarled and threw itself against the bars again, then a third time. Metal screeched as they bent inward. The creature howled in apparent triumph and hurled its huge bulk against the bars again and again. Each time they seemed to give a little more. Lukan stood still, not daring to remove his foot from the sunken flagstone. *It's too strong,* he thought, despair rising. *They're not going to hold . . .*

But they did. The bars bent further beneath the wolf's furious assault, yet somehow refused to give entirely. The wolf stilled, growling low in its throat as its scarlet eyes glowered at Lukan.

Each passing moment felt like an eternity.

Then the beast snarled and turned away, its crimson glow disappearing back down the passage. *Searching for another way in.* Perhaps it would find one. *Best get out of here before it does.* Slowly he removed his foot from the sunken flagstone. The bars remained in place. He closed his eyes, feeling almost dizzy with relief, scarcely able to comprehend what had just happened. *That was too close. Far, far too close—*

His eyes snapped open as he heard a noise behind him.

He whirled round, expecting to find the wolf stalking through another entrance. Instead his gaze fell upon another iron-barred archway on the chamber's far side—the only other exit from the room. The bars were rising, revealing steps beyond. *A way out.*

Lukan's hope died as three figures descended the steps and swept into the chamber. His first thought was that they were part of Delastro's crew, but these newcomers—two rough-looking men flanking a hard-eyed woman—were dressed in mismatched leather armor rather than the sleek black outfits favored by the Seven Jewels. The men bore crossbows, while the woman held nothing more dangerous than a lantern, though hatchets were tucked in her belt.

"So, what do we have here?" she asked in a throaty voice, making a show of looking Lukan up and down, lip curling as if she was unimpressed with what she saw. "Drop it," she added, thrusting out her chin.

"With pleasure," Lukan replied, letting his torch fall to the floor.

The woman's jaw tightened. "I meant the sword."

"I know."

The woman grunted in what might have been amusement. "Who are you?"

"I might ask you the same question."

"I'll be asking the questions."

"Lady's blood," the man to her right muttered, staring past Lukan. "Look at the other gate."

The woman's gaze flicked to the bent iron bars; her eyes narrowed as they turned back to Lukan. "What happened here?" she demanded.

He managed a laugh at that. "You wouldn't believe me if I told you."

"That's for me to decide." She glanced at the two men. "Bind him."

"Drop your blade," one of them growled as they approached.

Lukan eyed the two men and the crossbows they had aimed at him. Even at his best there was little chance that he could have taken them both on and lived, and he was a long way from his best—as it was, he barely had the strength left to stand up. He smiled weakly at the irony of escaping a terrifying creature of powerful sorcery, only to be captured by . . . whoever these thugs were. His smile faded as he let his sword fall to the floor. He suspected he already knew.

One of the men kept his crossbow trained on Lukan while the other snapped some manacles round his wrists.

"Where are we going?" Lukan asked, as the woman started toward the steps. She frowned at that, while the men exchanged amused snorts.

"You're not from around here, are you?" she replied, one eyebrow raised. "We're off to see the King, of course."

Fear flared anew in Lukan's chest. "The Twice-Crowned King."

"Ah, so you're not as clueless as you look." She stepped up to him and patted his cheek. "What's the matter, you not excited to meet royalty?"

"I've met royalty before. It's overrated."

"Trust me," the woman replied with a smirk, "this will be very different."

Lukan sighed. "I don't doubt it."

27

THE COURT OF MIDNIGHT

Lukan stared at the monster.

The monster stared back through its single, lidless eye, set above a gaping maw lined with sharp teeth. He raised a hand and pressed it to one of the creature's tentacles. *Blood,* he thought, staring at the rusty residue on the end of his finger. *It's painted in blood.* A myriad of graffiti surrounded the painting, words and phrases scratched into the stone by way of pottery shards that still lay at the base of the wall. *Why is it so dark?* asked one. *I can't get out,* said another. *I didn't do it. I love Selisse. Heiron is a liar.* On and on, a litany of pleas and fears, their authors long since departed to fates unknown. *Why me?* the last one to catch Lukan's eye said.

Why me, indeed.

"Curious, isn't it?"

Lukan turned to find a man standing beyond the bars of his cell. The light of a nearby torch softened the harsh angles of his face, yet he still retained a cadaverous aspect that wasn't helped by his shaven pate or pale skin. A golden chain ran from his nose to the top of his left ear, glinting as he tilted his head, his kohl-rimmed eyes staring past Lukan to the nightmare daubed on the wall.

"I often wonder," the man continued, his soft voice almost a purr, "how accurately it depicts the creature of the Black Maze. A shame that none of those who know the answer are around to tell us." He smiled, black-stained lips parting to reveal teeth studded with tiny jewels. "Perhaps you'll soon learn the truth yourself.

After all, the punishment for trespassing in the Twice-Crowned King's domain is death."

"Who are you?"

"I am called Scipio."

"And you're what, the royal arse-licker?"

"A humble servant of the King, nothing more." The man's eyes flicked to Lukan. "And you are . . ."

"Someone who is regretting their recent life choices."

"As did all the previous inhabitants of your cell. Precious good it did them."

"Listen, I wasn't—I didn't *mean* to intrude on your king's domain. I was—"

"Hush, little fly. You flew in here without so much as a by-your-leave, and now you're trapped in the Twice-Crowned King's web. Only by their word shall you flutter free."

"Then take me to them. Let me explain."

"All in good time. You'll get the chance to prostrate yourself before the King. Though when you do, I suggest you show a little more humility, otherwise it won't end well for you."

"The Black Maze you mentioned."

"Just so. Do you know of what I speak? Of what we call the Long Swim?"

"Never heard of it. If I knew I would be getting wet I'd have brought a towel."

"A comedian!" Scipio exclaimed, clapping his hands together. "How wonderful. Perhaps I should petition the King to keep you alive to cheer this dreary place up a bit. Goodness knows we could use a little laughter around here, isn't that right, Reinhardt?" The question was directed at another cell, beyond Lukan's vision; he thought he heard a faint whimper in response. "Just so," Scipio continued, smile slipping from his face as he turned back to Lukan. "If you knew of what I speak, little fly, you would not be so quick to jest."

"Then tell me."

"The Black Maze is an older part of the catacombs that has been reclaimed by the sea—a flooded network of tunnels and chambers, all dark as night. At the center of this maze is a staircase that leads to the surface and freedom . . . if you can find it. *That* is the Long Swim, the bone that the Twice-Crowned King throws to the condemned. No one can say they are without mercy."

"And that?" Lukan asked, gesturing to the nightmare painted on the wall.

"Ah, yes." The man's smile slithered back. "There is a . . . creature said to live in the Maze. Some insist it's a pale shark with glowing eyes, others claim it's some sort of giant octopus." He shrugged. "The only thing anyone agrees on is that the monster has a taste for human flesh."

"Drown or be devoured in the dark. Not much of a choice."

"Or swim to your freedom. Whatever the outcome, you won't suffer it in the dark, nor will you be unarmed. We give all swimmers a lantern and a dagger."

"How thoughtful."

"As I said, the King is not without mercy." Scipio turned away. "I shall return soon. Think on what I've said, little fly."

"I'd rather not."

"Your choice. Soon the Twice-Crowned King will make theirs. Best hope they're in a forgiving mood."

"Is there much chance of that?"

Scipio looked back at him, his smile widening. "No."

———

Lukan spent the hour that followed pacing his cell, trying to recall everything Flea had told him about the Twice-Crowned King. Instead his thoughts kept returning to the catacombs. To Marquetta's conspiracy, the murder of Magellis, and the appearance of the Faceless. But most of all he thought about the spectral wolf, a chill creeping down his spine as he recalled the beast hurling itself against the metal gate, eyes glowing crimson. *Should have let the damn thing take me,* he thought, his gaze moving back to the monster on the wall. *Better than the alternative.*

Footsteps echoed on stone, drawing him from his thoughts.

Scipio reappeared beyond the bars, several guards at his back. "I come to bear you to your judgment, little fly," he purred, voice oily with ill promise. "Best not to struggle."

Lukan watched as they unlocked his door. One or two guards might have presented an opportunity, but four offered only the chance for a severe beating. It took some effort to remain still as they flooded into his cell and slapped manacles round his wrists. Even more not to react to the sly punch one of the guards drove into his side.

"That's enough," Scipio snapped as they dragged Lukan into the corridor. "Now fetch Reinhardt."

The occupant of the cell next to Lukan's did not come nearly so quietly. Reinhardt—for all that he was an emaciated fellow covered in filth and threadbare rags—fought like a wildcat, and in the end it took three of the guards to subdue him. "Bastard smells like a bloody corpse," one of them muttered, wrinkling her nose.

"That's what you'll be if he dies without the King's permission," Scipio replied, giving her a hard stare. "Now let's be away."

Two guards flanked Lukan as they followed the cadaverous man through a series of passages. Between the echo of their footfalls and Reinhardt's endless sobbing, Lukan first sensed it—whatever *it* was—as a vibration, so subtle he thought he'd imagined it. It quickly became stronger, accompanied by a sound that grew from a murmur to a distinctive rhythm—a frenetic beat that echoed through the tunnels, drowning out all other sound. The stone thrummed beneath Lukan's feet. He swallowed the fear rising in his throat as a large doorway loomed ahead, two guards standing on either side. One of them pushed the door open as they approached.

"Behold," Scipio said, raising his voice above the sudden roar of sound, "the Court of Midnight."

A heady aroma of smoke, sweat, and sex assailed Lukan's nostrils as he was dragged through the doorway and into the chamber beyond, the sudden rush of heat stealing the breath from his lungs. He blinked, his eyes watering against the brightness of flames leaping from braziers, illuminating the cages that hung from the chamber's vaulted ceiling. Naked, oiled bodies writhed behind the bars, moving to the frenetic beat provided by three drummers who sat on one side of the chamber, muscles rippling as they pounded their huge drums. Below them, on the sunken floor, courtiers lounged on divans, drinking, smoking, and grasping at the flesh of courtesans. Servants, wearing nothing more than loincloths, circled the floor bearing trays of narcotics and wine, doing their best to keep the hedonism going.

On the far side of the chamber, seated on a raised throne, the Twice-Crowned King looked down on their court with all four of their eyes, smiling with both of their mouths. *People say they're twins, that they're joined at the hip,* Flea had said—words Lukan had not taken literally at the time. Now the truth stood—or rather *sat*—before him. *Conjoined twins,* he thought, the phrase rising from the depths of his memory. Such a phenomenon wasn't unknown—the celebrated artists Porcelina and Polindra were said to have been sisters joined by flesh. *But there's a difference between being an artist and the king of . . . whatever the hells this is.* He couldn't even begin to guess at how such twins had risen to lead the Kindred of Saphrona. *Perhaps the Scrivener can enlighten me.* That, of course, would depend on whether he ever had the chance to enjoy the master forger's waspish company again, a possibility that was looking more remote with every passing moment.

Lukan felt the collective gaze of the court on him as he was marched toward the throne, curiosity sparking in drug-glazed eyes. He sensed a wider movement as the court roused itself, dispensing with languid revelry at the prospect of something far more entertaining. *Like sharks drawn to blood.*

He could only hope they'd be disappointed.

As they neared the throne, Lukan saw the King clearly for

the first time. *The Snake and the Scorpion,* he thought, recalling
Flea's words as he eyed the twins. They were identical as far as he
could tell, both round-faced and clean-shaven, their scalps shorn
save for a long central plait of dark hair. Their bronze skin spoke
of eastern ancestry, and their smooth features made it hard to
put an age to them, though he guessed they were well into their
fourth decade. The left-hand twin—the Snake, if he remembered
correctly—sipped from a glass of water, his cold gaze locked on
the struggling Reinhardt. Lukan didn't like the cruel twist of his
lips. His brother, the Scorpion, didn't pay the new arrivals any
attention at all—instead he was busy sucking at the nipple of a
courtesan perched on one knee. *Two men, but one king . . . and
one body.* Even so, with all the silks and velvets the twins wore it
was unclear where one of them ended and the other began.

Reinhardt, upon seeing the King, began thrashing again, eyes
wide with terror. Drool dangled from his lips as he mouthed a litany of pleas lost beneath the pounding drums. A blow from one of
his captors silenced him and a shove sent him sprawling beneath
the throne.

The drums shuddered to a halt. A hush fell across the chamber,
charged with anticipation.

"Look, brother," the Snake said, speaking from one corner of
his mouth, his voice a guttural rasp. "Our dear friend Reinhardt
graces us with his presence again."

The Scorpion glanced up from the courtesan's glistening nipple,
his lips quirking in a half smile. "Reinhardt," he purred, his own
voice silk to his brother's steel. "What a delight!" He eased the
courtesan from his knee and sent him on his way with a slap to his
bare buttocks. "To what do we owe the pleasure?"

"No doubt the fool's finally come to tell us where he hid those
diamonds," the Snake said.

"Now, brother," the Scorpion replied, raising a finger in mock
admonishment. "Don't be so harsh on the dear boy. After all, he
did promise us he had nothing to do with our gems . . . didn't you,
Reinhardt?"

"Please," Reinhardt wheezed, clasping his hands in supplication. "I-I am a loyal subject—"

"Look at your king when you address them, you wretch," the Snake barked, his stare as predatory as his namesake's. One of the guards grasped the prisoner's hair and yanked his head back. *Lady's mercy,* Lukan thought, seeing the man's face properly for the first time, *he's barely out of his teens.*

"P-please," Reinhardt stammered, blinking furiously, "Your Majesties—"

"Majes*ty*," the Scorpion corrected. "There are two of us, dear Reinhardt, but only one king—twice crowned."

The young man swallowed, licked cracked lips. "Your Majesty. Please . . . I-I've made a mistake—"

"And *there* it is." The Scorpion raised a hand and tilted his head, as if hearing a melodious note. "Tell me, Reinhardt, what delivered this moment of revelation to you, hmm? Was it the sound of the rats, gnawing bones in the dark? Or perhaps it was the red glow of the poker?" He waved the question away. "No matter. I take it you have miraculously remembered something about those diamonds? *Our* diamonds."

"Y-yes, Your Majesties—*Majesty.*"

"Splendid! In that case, I'll ask you the same question as before. Hopefully the answer won't prove so elusive this time round." The Scorpion leaned forward, a smile playing at his lips. "What happened to the diamonds?"

"I . . . sold them, Majesty."

"You traitorous bastard," the Snake began.

"Language, dear brother," the Scorpion said jovially, though his smile had tightened. "You were saying, Reinhardt?"

The prisoner seemed to shrink before the twins' gaze. "I sold them, Majesty."

"And to whom did you sell our diamonds?"

Reinhardt took a long, shuddery breath, as if he knew his next words might be his last. "I—please, Your Majesty, I swear I didn't know the diamonds were yours. I *swear* it—"

"If that tongue of yours wriggles around the question again," the Snake interjected, "I'll slice it out." He drained his water and hurled the glass at Reinhardt, who cringed as it shattered beside him.

"There's no need for threats, brother," the Scorpion said. "The dear boy just needs a little encouragement, that's all. Something to help jog his memory." He tapped his cheek in mock thoughtfulness. "The promise of freedom, perhaps."

The young man looked up, hope gleaming in his eyes. "Please," he blurted, "I'd do anything . . ."

"Give us a name and you'll go free."

Liar, Lukan thought. The murmurs and titters that sounded from the watching courtiers suggested the wider court shared his opinion. But Reinhardt was a drowning man flailing for a branch.

"You're too kind, Majesty," he blurted, punch-drunk at his apparent salvation. "I-I won't let you down again—"

"The diamonds, boy!" the Snake rasped. "Who did you sell them to?"

"I, um, sold them to Tarantio Hess."

The Scorpion's smile slid from his face. "Tarantio Hess," he echoed, a sharp point swathed in the silk of his voice. "You sold them to Tarantio Hess, the corsair lord?"

"Ah . . . yes, Your Majesty—like I said, I didn't realize they were—"

"Tarantio Hess, the corsair lord who recently raided no fewer than *three* of our ships and stole cargo to the sum of . . . what was it, dear brother?"

"Two thousand ducats."

"Two *thousand* ducats," the Scorpion echoed, raising an eyebrow. "Quite the sum."

Reinhardt winced, as if hearing the sound of a metaphorical door booming shut. "I . . . I . . . *please*—"

"Silence!" the Scorpion snapped, his temper striking as fast as the arachnid he was named for. "One more word from you and I'll flay your hide so finely it'll make the softest bedsheets this side

of the Scepter Sea." He looked at Scipio. "Take this traitor back
to his cell."

"And slather his balls in honey," the Snake added, lips hooked
in a grim parody of a smile. "A little treat for our rodent friends."

"No, please . . ." Reinhardt struggled as the guards hauled him
to his feet. "You promised me my freedom," he screamed as he
was dragged away. "You *promised*!"

"Wait," the Scorpion called, raising a hand. A murmur passed
through the court as he chewed his lip, his anger of a moment before all but disappeared. "Our dear friend Reinhardt is right," he
said finally. "I *did* promise him his freedom, and I am nothing if
not a man of my word."

Reinhardt sagged in his chains, relief written across his filthy
face. "Thank you, Majesty . . ."

"Oh, don't thank me just yet, dear boy." The Scorpion's smile
returned, a savage glee shining in his eyes. "If you want your freedom, you'll have to swim for it . . . and hope our little pet isn't
hungry." He thrust out an arm. "Take him to the Black Maze."

The roar that greeted his words seemed to shake the chamber to
its vaulted ceiling, quickly coalescing into a chant: "Swim! Swim!
Swim!"

Reinhardt's face was a study in terror, his bulging eyes bright
white against the filth of his face. "No," he mouthed, his voice
lost beneath the din. He said something else that might have been
mercy before his pleas turned into an anguished wail as he was
dragged away, the chant breaking into a chorus of jeers. Lukan recalled Scipio's words from earlier, about all swimmers being given
a lantern and a dagger. He doubted either would do Reinhardt
much good.

"Your Majesty," Scipio said, raising his voice over the lingering
shouts. "I have another guest waiting on your pleasure."

Lukan's heart lurched. *Here we go.*

The Scorpion was already beckoning to the courtesan, as if
sentencing a man to death was nothing more than a distraction.

"Really, Scipio," he replied, as the man slid back onto his knee. "Can't you see we're busy?"

"*You're* busy," the Snake grated, snapping his fingers. A servant quickly placed another glass of water in his hand. He swirled it, his eyes flicking to Lukan and back to Scipio. "Who is this fool?"

"An intruder in your domain, Majesty. He was taken at the eastern gate. He declined to tell me his name, only that he sincerely regrets his recent life choices."

The Snake barked a laugh, echoed by much of the court. "Oh, I'll bet he does." He drank from the corner of his mouth, water spilling over his chin. "But you'll tell *us* your name, won't you, boy? Step forward and kneel before your king."

The guards released Lukan's arms, one of them giving him a shove. He staggered forward, the court's murmur of anticipation a mocking echo in his ears. He could feel their eyes on him like a hundred knives against his back, a counterweight to the Snake's cold glare that speared him where he stood. For a moment he stood helpless, breathless, as if paralyzed by the two forces.

"Kneel," the Snake barked.

Stay calm, Lukan told himself as he knelt. *If they sense weakness, they'll seize on it.*

"There, that wasn't so hard, was it?" the Snake rasped. "What is your name, boy?"

Lukan considered lying, but the Snake's piercing gaze caused his false name to die on his tongue. "Lukan Gardova . . . Your Majesty."

"Scipio claims you intruded on our domain."

"Not intentionally."

"Do you know the price for such a transgression?"

"I . . . Yes, Your Majesty."

"Swim," someone called, a shout echoed by several others. "Swim, swim, sw—"

"Silence," the Snake barked, dark eyes never leaving Lukan. The Scorpion's had never even left the courtesan; he was busy tracing a finger around the man's nipple, apparently oblivious to the exchange.

"You know the punishment," the Snake continued, taking a sip of water, "yet still you trespassed in our domain. Why?"

"I was being chased, Your Majesty."

"By whom?"

"A wolf born of sorcery, Majesty."

A murmur swept the court. Even the Scorpion looked up, his object of affection momentarily forgotten. The corner of the Snake's mouth twitched. "A wolf," he bit out, grimacing as if the words tasted foul. "A *sorcerous* wolf."

"Yes, Your Majesty."

"Are you so desperate to swim the Black Maze that you lie to your king?"

"No lie, Majesty." Lukan swallowed. *Tread carefully.* "The wolf pursued me through the catacombs. I stumbled into your realm by accident, which saved my life. I tripped the gate and it blocked the wolf's path, though even then the beast almost broke through—"

"Nonsense. That gate is made of wrought iron."

"Ask Scipio, Majesty." A risk, perhaps, to demand something of the King, but Lukan needed the confirmation.

The Snake's eyes narrowed but flicked to the cadaverous man. "Does this fool tell the truth?"

"I'm told the gate did sustain some . . . minor damage," Scipio replied, inclining his head. "I haven't yet verified the claim—"

"Minor damage?" Lukan cut in, throwing the man a glare. "The wolf nearly bent the bars backward—"

"Silence," the Snake barked again.

Lukan bowed his head in contrition. *Idiot,* he scolded himself. *Watch your tongue.*

"How do you know this wolf was born of sorcery?" the Scorpion asked, pursing his lips as if the thought amused him. "Did it sparkle?"

Laughter rippled across the court.

"It glowed, Majesty," Lukan replied, "with a crimson light. In truth it was no wolf, but merely a sorcerous construct that took the aspect of one. I saw it take shape with my own eyes."

"And this creature chased you how far?"

"I couldn't say, Majesty . . ." Lukan trailed off as he recalled his desperate flight. The fear. The panic. The dying scream of the man the wolf had set upon. "But it was some distance through the catacombs."

"So the wolf traveled far from its creator?" the Scorpion asked. His tone was mild, but there was a sharp point buried beneath his words. A point seeking its mark.

"Yes, Majesty."

"How curious." The Scorpion smiled, preparing to drive his metaphorical dagger home. "You see, there are six known pairs of gleamers in this city, and only one of them might have the power to fashion such a creature. But I doubt even they could control it over such a distance."

"The wolf wasn't created by gleamers, Majesty."

Under different circumstances, Lukan might have enjoyed the surprise that flickered across the Scorpion's features. As it was, he knew that the next part of this conversation could well see him condemned to the same fate as Reinhardt.

"Whatever do you mean?" the Scorpion asked, his mask of amused indifference firmly back in place. "If gleamers didn't create your sorcerous wolf, then who did?"

There it was. The question that could seal his fate more surely than any other.

Lukan took a breath. "The Faceless, Your Majesty."

Silence fell.

The Scorpion let loose a high-pitched giggle. "The Faceless?" he repeated, to hesitant laughter from the court. "The bogeymen from myth?" He chuckled again and looked to his twin. "We should keep this one, brother. I've always wanted a jester."

The Snake shared none of his twin's amusement and scowled as he glared at Lukan. "You ridicule your king," he rasped.

"Your Majesty, I speak the truth," Lukan replied, fighting to keep his voice even. "I swear, I saw them with my own eyes—"

"Still your tongue, lest I rip it out." Fury smoldered in the Snake's gaze. "You lie to your king."

"No, I—"

"Guards," the Snake barked, "seize him. The Black Maze awaits."

A cheer erupted as guards swarmed toward him, coalescing into the now-familiar refrain. "Swim, swim, swim . . ."

"Your Majesty," Lukan cried, panic nearly stealing the words from his throat. "I have to tell you something—" He felt a hand on his shoulder and reacted by flinging an elbow in the direction of its owner. The hand fell away. "Your Majesty—" He leaned away from a cudgel swing and dispatched his attacker with a punch. The man stumbled back, fumbling at a newly broken nose, but another guard took his place. There were too many. Lukan managed to dodge another blow, only for something to crack against his skull from behind. He staggered, the world reeling as black stars danced across his vision. He felt the stone of the floor beneath him, then a boot driving into his side, forcing the breath from his lungs. *No,* he thought, desperation rising as other blows landed, *I've got to speak.* He knew his next words might be the most important ever to pass his lips. "Your Majesty," he shouted, summoning what little strength remained to him, "I know who really stole the Sandino Blade." He barely heard his own voice over the roaring in his ears. *They didn't hear me,* he thought, fear knifing him along with the blows that continued to rain down.

"Hold." The Snake's voice was the grating of drawn steel, but to Lukan it was the sweetest sound he'd ever heard. "Get him up."

Rough hands hauled Lukan to his feet, the world pitching around him again. He coughed, felt blood on his tongue, his lips. Darkness and light swam before his eyes. He blinked, his vision slowly clearing to reveal the Snake and the Scorpion both watching him intently.

"Did you say," the latter said, "that you know who really stole the Sandino Blade?"

"Yes," Lukan gasped. "I do—"

"We already know who stole it," the Snake cut in. "Only Lady Midnight would dare insult her king by breaking the Midnight Charter."

"It wasn't Lady Midnight," Lukan replied, "I swear . . ."

A murmur swept the court as he struggled for breath, for the strength to voice the words. "But I know who did steal it," he continued. "And I know why. It's all connected. The wolf, the Faceless, the Sandino Blade . . . there's a conspiracy here that will . . . start a war . . ."

"Enough," the Snake barked, looking at his twin. "This fool's a liar. A coward so desperate to avoid his fate that he's invented a ridiculous fantasy."

"Perhaps, brother," the Scorpion replied, his brow creased in thought as he regarded Lukan. "Or perhaps he's a man with a very peculiar story to tell." He returned his brother's gaze. "I say we hear what he has to say. After all, if it's not to our liking, we can always send him to the Maze afterward."

The Snake's scowl deepened. The moment stretched, Lukan's hope stretching with it. "Fine," the Snake grunted. "Let's hear what the fool has to say."

"Scipio, have him taken to the outer sanctum," the Scorpion added. "We will have a little chat in private."

Lukan sagged with relief as the guards dragged him away. *A literal stay of execution,* he thought, a breathless laugh escaping his lips. *For now.*

28

BOLD CLAIMS

The noise of the court faded as Lukan's captors dragged him through a series of torchlit passages, but he could hear the drums as they started up again, the frenetic beat signaling a return to the court's pursuit of pleasure. *As if a man hadn't just been condemned to death before their very eyes.* Under different circumstances he might have felt disgust, or even anger, but in that moment all he could feel was relief that it wasn't him facing the Long Swim—and fear that it soon might be.

"You're lucky that your impertinence hasn't cost you your life," Scipio said, as if sensing Lukan's thoughts. The tiny gems on his teeth glinted as he glanced back at Lukan and smiled coldly. "Yet, anyway."

"I don't feel lucky," Lukan muttered, wincing at the pain in his ribs. Other aches and pains were blossoming over his body, but as far as he could tell nothing was broken.

"Such insolence," the cadaverous man replied, nose chain jingling as he shook his head. "If you wish to see daylight again, I advise you to speak the truth when next the King asks."

"I already did."

"The Faceless? Sorcerous wolves?" Scipio gave a reedy laugh. "You must take me for a fool."

"I took you for a fool anyway."

That drew a snigger from one of the guards at Lukan's side, only for the man to fall silent as Scipio threw a dark look over his shoulder. "I'd watch your tongue, Lukan Gardova. The King will have it out otherwise." He stopped before a set of double doors and produced a key, which he slipped into the lock and turned until it clicked. "Wait in here," he said, easing the door open. "Don't touch anything."

Lukan raised his manacled hands. "Not much chance of that. Unless—"

"Inside," the man hissed, clearly still irked by Lukan's insult. *Small victories,* Lukan thought as he stepped through the door, which closed behind him. *Though I'll need a bigger one to get out of this mess in one piece.* He took a few steps into the chamber— the so-called outer sanctum—and glanced around, finding it to be richly appointed with plush rugs and exquisite tapestries. A dozen silver candelabras bathed the room in a warm, inviting light. *Almost feels like I'm here for a dinner party, rather than an interrogation.* The candlelight played across the edges of several glass-topped display cases set against one of the walls. Lukan wandered over and peered inside them, finding a series of objects set upon velvet cushions. None of them looked valuable—he could only guess why an empty glass vial and a withered fig-like fruit were worthy of such presentation—with one obvious exception: a golden ring set with a sparkling sapphire. Any sense of grandeur was ruined by the severed finger that still wore the ring, which appeared to have been embalmed somehow to prevent decay. A woman's finger, if Lukan had to guess, but what the significance of it was he couldn't say.

It was then that he noticed the large glass aquarium in one corner of the room, filled with red-tinted water. Two shapes floated within. He thought the fish might disappear into the weeds that rose from the tank's sand-covered bottom, but they remained still as he approached, apparently more interested in each other than the newcomer outside their domain. One was crimson in color, the other indigo, but otherwise they were identical, watching each other with black, bulbous eyes, their long frills flowing out behind them like bridal dresses.

"Gladiator fish," a voice said, causing Lukan to jolt in surprise.

He turned to find the Twice-Crowned King sitting in the doorway in a large, wheeled chair. "Imported all the way from the Mourning Sea," the Scorpion continued. "At great expense, I might add."

"At *too* great an expense," the Snake rasped beside him. They rolled slowly into the room, their chair pushed by a powerfully built man who must have stood over seven feet tall, his naked upper body gleaming with oil. A bronze helm covered his face, the eye slit revealing nothing but shadow.

"Their venom can kill a man in a matter of heartbeats," the Scorpion continued, ignoring his twin. "Marvelous, don't you think?"

Lukan wasn't sure whether the man meant the fish themselves, or their lethality, but decided that the best response either way was a murmur of agreement. "So, uh, do they fight or something?"

"Oh, yes," the Scorpion said, lips quirking. "When the mood takes them. Like some men, they only get their blood up when a pretty lady swings by." He affected a mock gasp. "Oh! Here she comes now! Such impeccable timing."

A yellow fish with bloodred fins emerged from the fronds of a plant at the back of the tank, gliding toward the two males with deft flicks of her tail. As the female gladiator fish drew closer, the males became agitated, their trailing frills whipping forward to form intimidating halos round their heads.

"Taunting each other," the Scorpion murmured. "Here it comes . . ."

Lukan blinked in surprise as both fish attacked, coming together in a blur of color, twisting and thrashing as they snapped at each other—a brutal dance, yet somehow elegant at the same time. The fight didn't last long. The female, apparently uninterested in the spectacle, disappeared back into the fronds of the plant with a flick of her red tail. The males immediately ceased their struggle and returned to their aimless drifting as if the violence of a moment ago had never happened, their manes deflating until they once more trailed listlessly in their wakes.

"Such ferocity in desire," the Scorpion said with a sigh.

"Enough frippery," the Snake grated. "Let's get to business."

"As you wish, brother dear."

At a snap of the Scorpion's fingers, the bronze-helmed giant pushed the King toward a pair of nearby divans. Lukan hesitated and glanced at the door, which stood wide open. *Best not.* Even if he somehow managed to evade the guards and escape from the King's domain—an unlikely scenario—he would only find himself back in the catacombs, with no sense of the way out. *Besides, that damned wolf could still be out there.* No, better to try to talk his way out of this mess—after all, he'd managed to squirm out of dangerous situations before with a few well-chosen words. Yet those instances had often involved selling a plausible lie, not telling a truth that was so far-fetched he barely believed it himself. *Even though I saw it with my own eyes.* He felt a stab of panic but forced it down. If the King sensed his fear, they'd seize on it, believing it was indicative of his guilt. Whatever happened next, he needed to keep calm.

He followed the King and waited as they rose from their wheeled chair, moving in a crab-like fashion across to one of the divans.

"Ah, that's better," the Scorpion said as they settled themselves against the cushions. "Far more comfortable."

"No king should ever sit comfortably," the Snake replied.

"Ah, yes . . . which of your tiresome philosophers said that? Diagoras?"

"Actually," Lukan put in, the name stealing into his mind, "I believe it was Dagorian. Uh, Your Majesty."

For a moment he thought he'd overstepped, but the gleam of amusement in the Scorpion's eyes suggested otherwise.

"Well," the Scorpion asked, glancing at his brother. "Is he right?"

The Snake's cheek twitched as he glared at Lukan. "Sit down," he grunted.

The Scorpion giggled. "Pretty *and* smart," he purred, raising an eyebrow at Lukan. "What a novelty. But yes, do sit." He wiggled his fingers at the divan opposite.

Lukan sat as the giant in the bronze helm wheeled the empty

chair away, passing Scipio as the gaunt man approached in a rustle
of silk, a silver tray in his arms.

"Refreshment, Your Majesty?" he asked, presenting the tray to
the Scorpion.

"Always," the Scorpion replied, eyeing the collection of glasses.
"Ah, but what to choose . . . sherry, I think," he said, lifting a
glass. "That dry vintage the harbormaster gifted us is *delectable*."

"And for you, Majesty—"

"Nothing," the Snake rasped.

Scipio bowed and made to turn away.

"Don't be a bore, Scipio," the Scorpion said lightly. "Offer our
guest a drink."

The gaunt man gave Lukan a cold look but did as ordered.

"Pick wisely," the Snake grated, as Lukan looked over the assortment of glasses. "If I have my way, this'll be the last drink you
ever take."

"If," Lukan replied mildly, keeping his face impassive as his
heart quickened. He knew insulting the Snake was a dangerous
gamble, but he had the sense that he needed to convince only one
of the brothers that he was telling the truth, and the Snake had
already made his position more than clear. The Scorpion, on the
other hand, seemed willing to listen, and Lukan fancied he could
win him over by standing up to his brother. All it would take was
the right combination of wit, flattery, and sincerity. *And a lot of
luck.*

The Scorpion's smile told him he'd played it just right.

"Insolent wretch," the Snake grated, "I should have your tongue
out."

"Manners, dear brother," the Scorpion chided gently. "We
don't cut out tongues over drinks." He met Lukan's gaze. "We do
that afterward."

Suddenly his smile didn't seem so reassuring.

"You're from the Heartlands, yes?" the Scorpion continued,
watching Lukan intently.

"Yes, Your Majesty. Parva."

"Ah, the City of Song and Spectacle! In that case, you'll appreciate this Parvan Red." He indicated a glass. "Go on. Try it and tell me you don't feel the fruits of summer bursting upon your tongue."

Lukan would have preferred to keep his wits about him, but decided some wine might help settle his nerves. "Thank you, Scipio," he said, smiling at the gaunt man as he picked up the glass. Scipio glared back at him and departed without a word. Lukan sniffed the wine and took a mouthful, rolling it around with his tongue before swallowing. "Oh, that's good," he said truthfully. "Very good. If I had to guess, I'd say that's the '23 vintage."

"Ah, a connoisseur! This is in fact a '26, though I'll admit the taste notes are very similar." The Scorpion trailed off as his twin gave a growl of impatience. "You must forgive my brother," he continued, waving his glass airily. "The poor boy was poisoned many years ago and it ravaged his throat, which is why he speaks like he's got a mouth full of gravel. But worse, it's why he can't drink anything other than water." The Scorpion shook his head in mock pity. "A fate worse than death, I'd say. Which is precisely what we gave to the poisoner once we caught him. Perhaps you saw the glass vial that contained the poison? We keep it over there." He fluttered his fingers in the direction of the glass cabinets. "Along with our other trophies."

"Trophies?" Lukan asked, sensing an opportunity for a little flattery. "So these objects are all . . . mementos from your rise to power?"

"Quite so. My dear brother is often telling me that one's own ego is the true enemy, but I like to look back at these trinkets and remind myself just how far we've come. Akabane's vial, the ring of Shivari Twice-Shy . . . oh, and her finger." The Scorpion giggled.

"Who was she?"

"The former queen of the Kindred of Saphrona, deposed by our own fair hands. She wasn't so shy in the end, when the blades came out."

"And the fruit? I saw some sort of fig, or . . ."

"No mere fig," the Scorpion replied, eyes gleaming. "But a fruit from the Tree of Last Laments, one of the wonders of the Mourning Sea! A prize that told us we were truly destined for greatness—"

"Enough, brother," the Snake cut in. "This peacockery is unbecoming."

"Very well," the Scorpion said, affecting a sigh. "To business then."

"Best drink up, boy," the Snake rasped.

"If I didn't know better, Majesty," Lukan said, keeping his tone light, "I'd say you were trying to loosen my tongue."

"No need," the Snake replied, gesturing at the bronze-helmed giant who stood silently across the room. "We have Borlos for that."

At the sound of his name, Borlos approached the divans. Lukan couldn't help but tense as the huge man moved behind him, an unseen but powerful presence at his back.

"Borlos the Bull," the Scorpion said, taking a sip of his sherry. "That's what they called him in the fighting pits we found him in. Isn't that right, Borlos?"

The giant remained silent.

"Not much of a conversationalist," the Scorpion continued. "Not having a tongue or any teeth will do that to a man. But he's good at crushing skulls with his bare hands."

The Snake shuddered and made a dry, rasping sound. For a moment Lukan thought he was choking, before he realized the truth—the man was laughing. "Best choose your words carefully, boy," the Snake said, lip curling as he met Lukan's gaze. "*Very* carefully."

———

". . . and the gate came down just as the wolf threw itself at me," Lukan said, shaking his head as he remembered the bars bending beneath the wolf's assault, the creature's eyes burning with crimson fury. "It was just, I don't know . . . pure chance that I stepped on the floor plate." He shrugged. "And that's how I ended up in your domain. By pure accident."

"Wondrous!" the Scorpion exclaimed, clapping enthusiastically. "Truly a tale for the ages! What say you, brother?"

"I say it's all a fantasy," the Snake replied, lip curling. "An illusion. A *lie*." He glanced at his twin. "A lie you seem to have fallen for, *brother*."

"I said it was a wondrous tale," the Scorpion replied mildly, tilting his head as he regarded Lukan. "I never said I believed it."

Lukan swallowed, fear squirming in his stomach. "Your Majesty, I swear I'm telling—"

"The truth, yes," the Scorpion interjected smoothly. "Reinhardt told us the same thing, repeatedly. Until he admitted it was all lies."

"Borlos," the Snake rasped.

Lukan sensed the giant moving behind him and tried to rise, only to be hauled back down as the man's huge hands clamped round his neck.

"Admit you lied to your king," the Snake barked.

"I'm telling the truth," Lukan replied, gritting his teeth as Borlos's grip tightened.

"Admit it!"

"I'm not . . . lying."

Borlos's grip tightened further round his throat.

"Admit your lie and your king will be merciful," the Snake said, with a leer that made it clear how much he was enjoying Lukan's suffering. "The Twice-Crowned King is not without mercy."

"No . . . lie . . ." Lukan gasped, the words little more than a strangled whisper. "And . . . you're no . . . king of mine."

The Snake shouted something, spittle flying from his mouth as his features contorted in rage, but all Lukan could hear was his own blood roaring in his ears. His vision was blurring, turning black at the edges. He felt as if he were floating, detached from his body—and for a horrible moment wondered if he actually was, if Borlos had wrenched his head from his neck. A memory sparked in his mind as the darkness closed in: an old oak tree, butterflies flitting over colourful wildflowers, Amicia's smile as she reached for him, hair glinting gold as she weaved her fingers through his—

"Enough."

Somehow the word cut through the memory, ringing in his head like a distant bell. Instantly the pressure eased and the darkness receded, leaving him gasping on the divan as he sucked in great lungfuls of air.

"Pretty and smart *and* brave," the voice said again—the Scorpion, Lukan realized, as his vision slowly cleared. The man was watching him with an amused quirk to his lips. His twin, by contrast, wore a murderous expression. "My brother thinks you're a liar and that you should face the Long Swim," he continued blithely, "but I couldn't possibly sentence a man with such excellent taste in wine to so grim a fate."

"So . . . you'll let me go?" Lukan croaked.

"Oh, I'm afraid not," the Scorpion replied, his amusement fading. "You've given us much to think on. I care nothing for Lord Marquetta's plot, but your claim that these mercenaries—these so-called Seven Jewels—stole the Sandino Blade, well . . ." He shook his head, mouth twisting as if tasting something sour. "Lady Midnight breaking our sacred Midnight Charter is one thing. But to have outsiders challenging our authority in such a manner? No, that will not do. We cannot allow it. There are questions that need answers. And you, my dear boy, may be of help to us in obtaining them. If you're telling the truth, of course." The Scorpion snapped his fingers. "Take him back to his cell."

Despair washed over Lukan as Borlos hauled him up.

"Hold," the Snake grated, a cold fury in his eyes. "This wretch insulted me. He insulted *us*. That cannot go unpunished."

"No," the Scorpion said, affecting a sigh. "I suppose not. Borlos?"

Lukan grunted as the giant pushed him back down and moved to stand in front of him. Lukan looked up and felt, rather than saw, the man's eyes staring back at him from the shadowed eye slit of his bronze helm. Slowly the giant raised his huge hands and cracked his knuckles.

Lukan took a deep breath and nodded. "Let's get this over with."

———

The manacles being eased from his wrists came as a relief. The shove that sent him stumbling to the floor of the cell, not so much. Nor the kick one of the guards delivered to his side as they left, the sound of the key turning in the lock cutting through their coarse laughter. *Alone again.* Lukan groaned as he sat up, his eyes flicking to the blood-daubed monster on the wall. *Well, not quite alone.* "You've got no prettier," he said, gingerly raising a hand to his face. *Not that I can talk.* Borlos had left him with a swelling eye, a bruised cheek and a pair of split lips. *And without a tooth,* he realized, pushing his tongue into the empty space in his lower gum. *Perhaps the Scorpion will put it in one of his display cases.* Still, all things considered, he'd got away lightly compared to Reinhardt, who was most likely a bloated corpse by now. Yet Lukan knew he'd won only a temporary reprieve. He didn't fancy his chances of winning the Scorpion over a second time. Sooner or later the Snake would get his wish.

"Got to get out of here," he muttered, wincing as he rose to his feet.

The next half hour proved that was far easier said than done. The iron bars at the front of the cell stood strong and firm, while the walls felt solid. He even blundered around in the darkness at the very back of the cell, running his hands blindly over the stone, but couldn't find so much as a hairline crack.

"Guess I'll just have to fight my way out," he murmured as he returned to the iron bars, knowing that in his current state he would probably struggle to best Flea in an arm-wrestle. *Flea.* Thinking of the girl brought fresh concern, underscored with guilt. He wondered again whether she'd made it out of the catacombs, or whether she'd got lost, her torch eventually guttering out and leaving her alone in the dark with the bones and rats . . . *No, she made it out. Kid's too smart for her own good. She made it back to the Scrivener, told her everything.* Not that it helped him. Flea knew nothing of his fate and the Scrivener would presume him dead. Perhaps she would scratch his name out in a ledger, an investment that didn't pay off. He ground his teeth in frustration. Right now he should have been with the Scrivener, Juro, and Flea in that teahouse, figuring out how they were going to stop Marquetta.

Lukan thought back to what he'd witnessed in the catacombs, and shook his head at the absurdity of it all. All he'd wanted was to prove Zandrusa's innocence and get his hands on his father's casket—and whatever was inside. Instead he found himself caught up in a conspiracy involving the Faceless that could plunge two cities into war. Yet strange as it was, the two threads were tied together—and there was a single needle that could untangle them. *Marquetta is the key,* he thought. Revealing the merchant prince's conspiracy would avert a war and save thousands of lives—Zandrusa's included.

"Defeat the villain, save the city, free the prince," he said aloud, his bitter laugh echoing off the walls. "Easy."

There was just the matter of his own imprisonment to overcome first. And the fact that he had no evidence of Marquetta's plot, nor the first idea of how to stop it. *Not to mention that going up against Marquetta means taking on the Faceless.* The very thought caused his heartbeat to quicken. *Still, better that than facing the alternative.* He glanced at the painting on the wall. "No offense," he murmured.

The monster stared back, blood almost black in the torchlight.

———

Lukan soon lost track of time, or perhaps it lost track of him. On two occasions a guard brought him a crust of bread and a cup of water—a morning and evening meal, he assumed—so he guessed he'd passed an entire day in the cell, possibly longer. In the permanent gloom it felt as if he had become lost to the world, disconnected from its turnings. He thought of all the life happening somewhere above him, the mundane acts of living and all the joy and rage and despair bound up in them. Simple things he took for granted, like the burst of peach juice on his tongue. Perhaps this was how the dead felt, shrouded in darkness, cut off from the world and yet condemned to remember it. *Was that Giorgio's fate? A twilight existence where his every thought turns back to our duel and the moment my blade punctured his throat?* The Lady's priests claimed that worthy souls—those who had lived without sin or vice—would join Her in some sort of blissful afterlife, but Giorgio Castori had been far from worthy. Not that Lukan believed the priests anyway. People would say any old shit if it brought financial reward, and the Lady's faithful had perfected the art of parting people from their coin. *And now the Pontifex himself is involved in plots of murder. But why? What does he stand to gain from a war? Or the Prime Inquisitor, for that matter? Do they share Marquetta's hatred of the Zar-Ghosans and his desire to put the torch to decades of peace, or is there something else that drives them?* Doubt lingered at the edges of his mind, a gnawing suspicion that he was missing something—an elusive detail that would cast the conspiracy in a new light.

He was still searching for it when sleep finally took him.

———

Lukan jolted awake, eyes bleary, limbs aching. His mind reeled, then reasserted itself. The cell, the monster on the wall, the flickering torch beyond the bars. All the same as before. *So what woke me?*

Footsteps echoed on stone, as if in answer.

They're coming for me. He rose unsteadily, fear lending him strength as he snatched up a shard of pottery and backed into the darkest reaches of the cell. In his current state he wasn't capable of putting up much of a fight, but the only other option was to go meekly to his doom, which was no choice at all. *Death or glory.* Or, more likely, a minor scuffle and then death. *If I could just disarm one of them, use their blade on myself . . . Bleeding out on* the cell floor was hardly an attractive proposition, but still preferable to the alternatives. He steeled himself as voices rose above the footsteps.

He expected to see Scipio appear beyond the bars, a detachment of guards at his back, but the cadaverous man was nowhere to be seen. Instead, two guards held a prisoner between them—head bowed, body slack—while another fumbled with the lock to Lukan's cell. Three more stood close by, eyes alert. *Five guards for one prisoner. Someone's taking no chances.* The door to his cell squealed open and the guards shoved the prisoner inside. Lukan tensed, expecting them to come for him, but instead they beat a hasty retreat, their eyes never leaving the figure lying on the floor. *Almost as if they're afraid.* There was little to fear, as far as he could see: the woman made no move to rise; in fact she hadn't stirred at all. Even so, it was only once the key turned again in the lock that the guards regained their composure, trading grins and leering at the prisoner.

"Enjoy your new quarters, Lady Midnight," one of them sneered.

Lady Midnight, Lukan thought. *Flea's hero. The thief who can walk through walls.* The woman didn't look like doing any of that right now as she slowly climbed to her feet. Still, that movement alone was enough to cause the nearest guard to back away from the bars. As if embarrassed at his own nervousness, the man forced a grin. "Looks like the Long Swim for you," he taunted, while his fellows muttered agreement. "You'll be seeing the monster soon enough, and—"

"Enough," Scipio snapped as he finally made his entrance. "I will talk to Ashra alone, without your pathetic bleating. Begone."

The guards seemed just as scared of the Twice-Crowned King's steward as they were of the woman in the cell, and departed without a word. As the echoes of their footsteps faded, Scipio turned to Lady Midnight—or Ashra, as he had called her. His black lips parted in a smile, tiny jewels gleaming. "Hello, little bird," he purred. "Caged at last, I see." He tutted. "Pity."

"Save me your false sympathy," Ashra replied, her voice carrying no trace of fear.

"But you *do* have my sympathy, little bird." Scipio made a sweeping gesture. "I picked out the largest cell for you. I even had the previous occupant moved to give you some privacy."

"How kind of you."

"I appreciate it's a little . . . rough and ready, but—"

"You forget, Scipio," Ashra cut in coolly, "I grew up in a tenement in the Splinters. This is luxurious in comparison."

"Lost none of your fire, I see, even now. No doubt the Long Swim will dampen your spirits."

"Such wit. No wonder the Scorpion chose you for his lapdog."

"Better a lapdog than a sacrificial lamb."

"Are you saying I'm innocent?"

"Innocent? You?" The man giggled. "You broke the Midnight Charter, little bird. You stole the Sandino Blade and then denied your guilt in front of the entire court."

"I didn't steal the blade."

"So you keep saying." Scipio smiled, enjoying himself. "But who else would have the impudence, the *arrogance,* to insult their king with such an action?" He tutted. "Such flagrant disloyalty cannot go unpunished."

"I've always been loyal," Ashra snapped back, voice like a whip. "Always paid my tithes in full."

"And yet you've always been elusive, always refused the King's generosity. And by stealing the Sandino Blade, you've sent a clear message that you consider yourself beyond the King's authority."

"It. Wasn't. Me." The thief delivered each word like a dagger thrust. "Not that it matters. We both know what this is really about."

"I don't know what—"

"You know exactly what I'm talking about." Ashra strode toward the iron bars. "This isn't about the blade," she continued, her words taut. "This isn't even about me. It's about Lady Midnight. How it's her name on everyone's lips and not the King's. How the

Kindred regard her with the kind of awe and respect they'd never show the King. It's about how the King is afraid of her."

"Afraid?" Scipio tittered. "You think the King fears you?"

"Not me." Ashra thrust her arms out and grasped an iron bar in each fist. Scipio flinched and took a step backward. "But they fear the myth of Lady Midnight. They fear what she represents."

"And what's that?" the man asked with a sneer.

"A threat. A challenge to their authority. A shadow that looms over them. And with every coin Lady Midnight steals, it grows larger." Ashra lowered her hands. "The King doesn't care about the Sandino Blade. It's just a smoke screen. A convenient accusation to blame on Lady Midnight. To reveal her apparent betrayal and justify her execution. To destroy her myth before it devours the King. *That* is why I'm here."

"You're here because you refused the King's offer," Scipio retorted. "How generous of Their Majesty to overlook your transgressions and once again offer you a place at their side. Anyone else would have shown wisdom and thrown themselves on the King's mercy." His black lips twisted. "But not you. Not the fabled Lady Midnight."

"I don't need their mercy. I'm my own woman. I always have been."

"And where's that got you?" The man made a sweeping gesture. "A cell. A terrifying death in the dark."

"I'm not afraid."

"Oh, little bird." The man shook his head in mock sadness. "Stubborn to the very end. You could have been great, you know. You were always the King's favorite, despite your disobedience. Just think of the power and influence you could have had as their right hand. Your legend would not have been that of a rogue thief, but as a loyal servant of the crown. In time, the King might have even named you heir—you could have been the Queen of Midnight!" He affected a sigh. "But no. Instead your insolence has proven your downfall. Where once your name was spoken with awe, now the Kindred will speak it as a curse. You won't be remembered as a master thief, but as an upstart who defied her king and died a traitor's death. Such a tragedy. We all had the highest hopes for you." Scipio turned away. "Farewell, little bird. I don't expect we'll speak again."

"You've heard the rumors about me."

The man paused and looked back. "Of course." He raised a hand and fluttered his fingers. "Fly free, little bird. If you truly can." His laughter echoed as he swept away in a rustle of silk. Ashra muttered something under her breath and ran a hand through her short, dark hair.

"Slippery bastard, isn't he?" Lukan asked.

Ashra turned—not with the quickness of surprise, but with the slow motion of someone always in control of their actions. No concern was reflected in her sharp features as her eyes immediately found Lukan in the shadows, flicking to the shard of pottery he held in his hand. "Who are you?" she asked, meeting his gaze. There was no challenge in her tone, merely curiosity.

"You can see me?" Lukan asked, unable to mask his surprise.

"Of course."

"How? I can barely see my own hands—"

"Who are you?" the thief repeated.

"My name is Lukan Gardova."

"The interloper," she said, with a slight tilt of her head. "I heard about you and your sorcerous wolf."

"And you're the famous Lady Midnight."

"So others call me."

"I know a girl who idolizes you. Lady Midnight this, Lady Midnight that . . . Seems you've made quite the impression."

"Best tell her to find a new hero."

"I won't be telling her anything if I'm stuck in here." He stepped toward her, into the torchlight. "She told me you can walk through walls. I don't suppose that's true? Because it would be pretty helpful right now."

"Looks like the King gave you a hard time," she replied, ignoring the question as her eyes tracked over the bruises on his face.

"Can't say I'm surprised, with all your talk of sorcerous wolves and the Faceless."

"You don't know the half of it."

"I don't want to. Sounds like bullshit to me."

"I could say the same thing of these rumors about you."

"You can say what you want."

"It's not me saying it. This girl who idolizes you told me that nowhere is safe from you, that you can break into the most secure places. And if you can break *in,* then you must be able to get *out* just as easily. Can you?"

"That's none of your business."

"On the contrary," Lukan replied, gesturing at the cell, "I'm stuck in here and you're my only hope of getting out. So whether these stories about you are true is very much my business."

"Your fate is not my concern."

"You might feel differently if you knew what I can offer you."

"You have nothing I want."

"Even the name of who really stole the Sandino Blade?"

Ashra regarded him silently. "You know who stole it?" she asked eventually. Her expression was impassive, her voice measured, but there was an intensity to her gaze.

"It's been a thorn in your side, hasn't it?" Lukan replied. "Someone stole the blade and you took the fall for it. I'll bet you'd love to know who to blame—"

"Tell me."

"You answer my question first. Can you walk through walls?" He almost winced; the question was ludicrous. *Of course she bloody can't. Flea's just got swept up in her myth like everyone else—*

"This girl," Ashra replied. "What's her name?"

"Flea. She's a pickpocket and probably your biggest admirer. I'd hate to have to tell her she's wrong—"

"She's not."

Lukan blinked at her. "You mean . . . you're saying you can actually walk through walls?"

"In a manner of speaking." Ashra tilted her head. "Tell me who stole the Sandino Blade."

"No."

Anger flashed in the thief's dark eyes. "I answered your question," she said, an edge beneath her even tone. "Now answer mine."

"I will. But not here." Lukan raised a hand to forestall the objection forming on the thief's lips. "Get me out of this cell and I'll tell you who stole the Sandino Blade."

"How do I know I can trust you?"

"You don't."

"Then perhaps I should just leave you here."

"Do that and you'll never get your answer."

Ashra stared at him in silence, her jaw working. "Fine. But if you're lying . . ."

"I'm not," Lukan replied, feeling a rush of relief. "I'll tell you everything once we've escaped."

"If we escape."

"If?" Lukan's relief faded. "What do you mean, *if*? You said you can walk through walls."

"It's not as simple as that."

"Of course not," he replied wearily, feeling like a fool for believing there'd actually been a chance. "I don't suppose you'd care to explain . . ."

The thief sighed in response, her cool mask slipping for just a moment, allowing Lukan a glimpse of the person beneath it—an exhausted woman, hollowed out and overtaken by recent events. A kindred spirit, perhaps. "It's hard to explain," Ashra said eventually, her guard raised once more. "I doubt you'd believe me."

"Try me. After what I've seen in the past few days, I'm willing to believe anything."

"Fine," the thief replied. "But it's easier if I show you. Turn round and close your eyes."

"I love it when a woman says that."

"So do I."

Lukan grinned and turned his back on her. *Locked in a cell with Lady Midnight,* he mused, closing his eyes. *Who'd have thought. Can't wait to see the look on Flea's face when I tell her this*— The sound of retching drew him from his thoughts.

"Everything all right?" he inquired.

"Fine."

Lukan frowned as more retching followed.

"You quite sure about that? If I can help . . ."

"Just keep quiet." Heavy breathing followed, accompanied by the sound of spitting. "Actually," the thief continued, "perhaps you can. Come here." Lukan turned round to find Ashra on her haunches. She rose as he approached, and tapped her stomach. "Hit me."

"Ah . . . that's not quite what I had in mind."

"You want to get out of here? Then hit me. Hard."

"Well, if you're sure . . ." Lukan clenched his fist. "Ready?"

The thief nodded.

Lukan drove his fist into Ashra's stomach. The thief—who hadn't so much as blinked—doubled over, then fell to one knee and vomited. "I must admit to"—he paused as she vomited again—"feeling rather conflicted." Ashra ignored him, taking several breaths before vomiting a third time. Lukan frowned as a small object appeared, clinking as it struck the floor of the cell. "What's that?"

"Our way out of here," Ashra replied hoarsely, snatching up the object as if afraid Lukan would steal it from her. *Not bloody likely.* He watched as the thief cleaned the object on her sleeve and held it up.

"A ring?" Lukan said, his hope fading as he leaned in for a closer look. The signet ring was made from a translucent material that Lukan had never seen before, its flat surface shaped like a teardrop. *Or like a pear, which more accurately represents how this escape plan is turning out.* "Is your plan to try and bribe our way out of here?"

Ashra slipped the ring onto a finger and rubbed a thumb against its surface.

"Because if I was one of those guards," Lukan continued, "there's nothing in the world that would tempt me to cross the Twice-Crowned King. And this ring—look, no offense, but it doesn't look all that valuable . . ."

A symbol appeared on the surface of the ring, glowing with a turquoise light. It flared three times, illuminating Ashra's face, before fading away as if it had never been.

"Then again," Lukan murmured, catching a glimpse of what might have been amusement in the thief's eyes, "that symbol . . . it looked like a Phaeron glyph."

"It was."

"A Phaeron ring . . ." Lukan trailed off as understanding dawned. "All of those rumors about you," he continued, "this is the source of them, isn't it? This is how you do whatever it is you do . . . walk through walls and whatnot. The secret to your success—"

"The secret to my success," the thief cut in, "is years of practice." She held up the ring. "This is a fail-safe. Nothing more."

"What does it do?"

"It opens a gateway."

"A gateway?" Lukan frowned. "What sort of gateway?"

"One born of sorcery."

"You mean a *portal*? As in a . . ." He traced a circular motion in the air.

Ashra's eyes narrowed. "You've seen one before? When?"

"When I saw the Faceless." As the woman's lips thinned, Lukan added, "I know what you're thinking. But I swear to you that I saw them. A portal appeared in the air—"

"Describe it."

Lukan sucked in a breath, thinking back to what he saw in the catacombs. "Three colored orbs appeared and traced a circle in the air, which began rippling. There were little streaks of lightning . . . and then they stepped through. Three of them, their armor steaming with icy vapor as if they'd come from somewhere cold—"

"Cold?" Ashra repeated, looking at him intently.

"That's right. Why?"

"It doesn't matter," she replied, though her expression was thoughtful. "Let's just say I feel more inclined to believe you than I did a moment ago."

Encouraged by the thief's words, Lukan said, "So this ring of yours can open a portal?"

"It can."

"And we just walk through it?"

"We do."

"Where will it take us?"

"Somewhere safe."

"As simple as that?"

The thief remained silent.

Lukan laughed. "I knew it. There's more. There always is with the Phaeron. Will it set us on fire, or something?" He waved his own question away. "You know what, forget it. I'd rather not know. Let's just get on with it."

Ashra shook her head. "We can't. Not yet."

"Why not?"

Anger gleamed in the thief's eyes—not at the question, Lukan felt, but at the memory it evoked.

"The King has been hunting me since the theft of the Sandino Blade," she replied, her gaze distant as if recalling past events. "I managed to evade his enforcers but they finally cornered me last night. I used the ring to escape, but . . . they later caught me again." Her jaw tightened, as if the admission stung.

"I don't follow," Lukan replied.

"The ring always takes time to recover its power after being used. It's not yet ready to be used again."

"So until it is," he ventured, "we're stuck here."

"Yes."

"How long will it take?"

"It's hard to know. An hour. Maybe two."

"They might come for us before then."

"They might."

Lukan forced a wry smile. "If they do, we'll just have to fight our way out."

"With *that*?" The thief raised a questioning eyebrow.

Lukan realized he was still holding the shard of pottery. He tossed it away. "Perhaps I'll attack them with my wit."

Ashra sat back against the wall and closed her eyes. "Let's hope it doesn't come to that."

The spectral wolf loomed over Lukan, jaws wide, eyes flaring crimson.

He felt paralyzed by that lupine gaze, his limbs unresponsive, his throat constricting so that he couldn't even scream as the jaws flashed toward his throat—

He jolted awake, breath rasping in his chest as he looked wildly around, eyes taking in the iron bars, the bloody monster— and Ashra, watching him from where she sat against the opposite wall.

"Whatever you were dreaming about," the thief said dryly, "it can't have been worse than this." She gestured at the cell. "I'd go back to sleep if I were you."

"Trust me," Lukan replied, the snarling visage of the wolf lingering in his mind, "I'd rather take my chances with you and your Phaeron ring. Speaking of which . . ."

In response to his meaningful look, Ashra rubbed the ring with her thumb. The glyph glowed with turquoise light, flared three times and vanished again. "Still not ready," the thief said, frowning as if that was a minor disappointment as opposed to a life-threatening problem.

"You don't seem too bothered."

"Calmness is the key to success. The first rule of thievery."

"You have rules? I thought the whole point of being a thief was to break rules, not make them—"

"The point of being a thief is to survive," Ashra cut in, a sudden edge to her voice. "No one goes into thievery by choice. Instead it's thrust on them."

Lukan recalled the moment he had caught Flea dipping her hand into his pocket. The fear in her eyes as he threatened to call the constables. "It was a joke. Forget it. I didn't mean to—"

"Quiet," Ashra said, raising a hand, her eyes flicking toward the bars. "I thought I heard—"

"Footsteps," Lukan finished, fear knifing him as he listened to the echo of boots on stone. "Looks like we're out of time. Guess we'll have to do this the old-fashioned way."

"You mean fight our way out? Forget it. There'll be too many of them."

"But we have one advantage."

"And what's that, this sharp wit of yours?"

"Surprise."

"Surprise?" She glanced at the bars again as the footsteps grew louder. "What are you talking about?"

"Remember what Scipio told you? That little gibe about wanting to give you some privacy?"

Realization dawned in the thief's eyes. "He said he'd had the cell's previous occupant moved . . ."

"But I'm still here," Lukan said, "so someone's screwed up. And Scipio never saw me when he was talking to you because I hid in the shadows at the back of the cell."

"They won't be expecting you to be in here," Ashra said, brow furrowed as she followed the logic. "Which means—"

"I can take them unawares while they're focused on you."

"You don't look in the condition for a fight."

"If I can move quickly enough, there won't *be* a fight."

"Fine," Ashra said, with another glance beyond the bars. "It's worth a try."

"Put up a struggle when they try to put the cuffs on you. Distract them as much as possible."

"I'll do what I can."

Lukan picked up the shard of pottery he'd previously discarded. *Not much of a weapon, but it'll have to do.* "Any other words of thieving wisdom you'd care to share?" he asked, his lightness of tone belying the fear tightening his chest.

"When backed into a corner, always go for the eyes. The eighteenth rule of thievery."

"I'll try to remember." With those words, Lukan gave the thief a nod and backed away into the darkness that enveloped the farthest reaches of the cell. Ashra moved toward the bars just as several figures strode into the torchlight beyond, Scipio at their head. *But only three guards,* Lukan realized, feeling a surge of hope. *If I can take two out before the third realizes what's happening . . .*

"Still here, little bird?" the cadaverous man said, smirking as he regarded Ashra. "I'm disappointed in you. All those bold claims . . ."

"I meant every word."

"And yet here you are, still waiting on the King's pleasure. And they have demanded that pleasure now." The gaunt man nodded at a guard, who unlocked the cell door. "The Long Swim awaits, Lady Midnight. Best come quietly."

Ashra remained still as the door squealed open and two of the guards entered.

"Turn round," one of them grunted, raising a pair of manacles.

Ashra leaped at the guard instead.

Even though Lukan had been expecting it, he was still surprised by the speed at which she moved. The guard managed to block the chop the thief aimed at his neck, but not the knee she slammed into his groin. The manacles fell from the man's hand as he gasped and fell to one knee. Ashra tried to twist away as the second guard swung a club at her, but the weapon caught her on the shoulder and knocked her off-balance. *Not yet,* Lukan thought, his heart racing as the guard forced the thief back against the wall, her club pressed across Ashra's throat.

"Oh, little bird," Scipio tutted, with mock disappointment. "Struggling *really* doesn't become you."

The third guard entered the cell, picked up the manacles from the floor, and went to snap them round Ashra's wrists.

Now. Lukan charged out of the darkness. The kneeling guard glanced up just before Lukan slammed into him, sending him sprawling to the floor.

"You—you *fools,*" Scipio squealed. "I told you to move Gardova to a different cell!"

The two other guards turned and gawped at Lukan, their grip on Ashra easing enough to allow the thief to kick herself away from the wall, bearing the club-wielding guard to the floor. The other guard swore, torn between helping his comrade and facing down the new threat. Lukan took advantage of his indecision by hurling his shard of pottery. It caught the man on the side of the head, causing him to fall back against the wall. With a groan he slid to the floor. Lukan moved toward Ashra, who was still struggling with her opponent, only to hesitate as he glimpsed Scipio backing away from the cell.

The two men's eyes met, each reading the other's intent.

Scipio turned and fled. Lukan followed, racing out of the cell and into the corridor beyond, closing the distance to the man in just a few strides. Scipio squealed as Lukan grabbed a fistful of his silk robe.

"Unhand me!" he demanded, flailing uselessly as Lukan dragged him back into the cell, where Ashra stood over the limp form of her opponent. "Let me go!" Scipio tried to twist free. "Get your filthy vermin hands off me!"

"Gladly," Lukan replied, releasing his grip.

Scipio tottered, then whirled round, eyes flashing. "When the King hears of this they'll—"

Lukan punched the man in the face, sending him crashing to the floor in a whirl of silk. "Tired of your bullshit," he said, before looking to Ashra. "You all right?"

"Fine."

Lukan glanced at the guards. The woman at Ashra's feet was out cold, while the man he'd struck with the pottery shard was still slumped by the wall, one hand pressed to his head. The other man—the unfortunate recipient of Ashra's knee in his groin—was on all fours, taking deep breaths. He glanced up as Lukan approached, eyes widening with fear. "No, please—"

Lukan kicked the man in the face, silencing him.

"Effective," Ashra said, raising an eyebrow, "if lacking in subtlety."

"Subtlety is overrated." Lukan drew a dagger from the guard's belt and held it up to the light. *Poor-quality steel,* he thought, *but better than a pottery shard.*

"We should go," Ashra said.

"What about this one?" Lukan asked, pointing his blade at Scipio, who had pressed himself against the wall, both hands held to his jaw.

"Leave him."

"You sure? Might be best to knock him out—"

"I want him conscious."

Lukan frowned. "For what?"

The thief remained silent.

"Fine, have it your way," Lukan replied, striding toward the cell door. "But let's get out of here before—"

"Not that way."

"What? This is the only way out."

"Is it?" Ashra raised her hand, revealing her ring. The Phaeron glyph was glowing again, but this time it was shining gold.

Lukan's hope surged. "You mean . . . it's working?"

The thief pointed. "See for yourself."

Lukan turned and saw another symbol—a twin to the glyph on Ashra's ring—suspended in the air, bathing the back wall of the cell in golden light. As he watched, the glyph flared brightly and dissolved into a thousand sparks, which smoothly rearranged themselves to form a glowing golden ring. The air within began to contort, reminding him of the Faceless's portal in the catacombs.

Yet this is different. The distortion of the air was less violent, and no lightning flickered across its gently rippling surface. *Different sorcery, perhaps . . .*

"Time to leave," Ashra said. She approached Scipio, who sat with his hands clasped before him, mouth hanging open as he stared at the portal.

"I told you I could walk through walls," Ashra said.

The man glanced up, disbelief in his eyes, his mouth trying to form words that never came.

"Give the King my regards," Ashra added. Leaving Scipio gaping after her, she walked toward the portal.

Lukan followed her, trepidation sitting like a dead weight in his stomach as he watched the shimmering air.

The thief eyed him, the hint of a smile on her lips. "Hope you don't mind the cold."

"The cold?"

Her flicker of humor faded. "Follow me."

29

THE RINGS OF LAST RESORT

A pressure against his cheek, then his entire body—that was the first thing. A dull roar echoing in his ears was the second. Then something else, something . . . *cold*. Lukan gasped, convulsing as shivers racked his body and talons of ice raked his flesh. His teeth rattled in his jaw as he trembled, a groan—equal parts fear and panic—escaping his throat as he forced his eyes open. Light blinded him, sudden tears blurring his vision. He closed them again as he shook uncontrollably, desperately trying to remember what had happened.

Ashra.

The thought seemed to reach him from a great distance, as if ice had formed around his mind. He held to it as best he could, forcing his lips to form the word even as its meaning eluded him. *Ashra, Ashra, Ashra . . .*

Then it all came flooding back, a tide of memories that ended with the fight in the cell . . . and the portal. He recalled the glyph flaring and dissolving, the golden ring, the rippling air. *She went through, and I followed.* He laughed, though it was no more than a hiss through gritted teeth. *Bad idea, that.* Yet as he lay there—wherever *there* was—he sensed that the numbing cold was receding. He wasn't shaking quite as badly as before. The roar in his ears—*my own blood*—was fading as well, and in its wake he could hear something else.

Voices.

". . . you sure . . . bolt in him . . . safe than sorry . . ."

With what felt like a great effort, Lukan pushed himself to his knees. He took a deep breath, opened his eyes again. The light was more forgiving this time; he blinked as his vision settled, the dark blur above him solidifying until there was no mistaking what it was. *Oh shit . . .*

He was staring at a loaded crossbow.

Lukan's gaze moved upward, across the shaft of the weapon, along the burly arms that held it, and up to the crossbowman's face. Deep-set eyes glowered at him from above a grey walrus mustache, which framed lips set in a grimace.

"Don't move," the man warned.

Lukan managed only a croak in response.

"How do you feel?" Ashra asked. The thief was sitting nearby, wrapped in a blanket, her expression lending the impression that her question was born of curiosity rather than concern. "It's difficult the first time."

"You don't . . . say," Lukan managed. He coughed, felt his throat clear. "I'd feel better if . . . I didn't have a crossbow pointed at me."

"Alphonse," Ashra murmured.

"You sure, Ash?" the man asked, eyes not leaving Lukan.

"I'm sure."

As Alphonse grudgingly lowered his crossbow, Lukan realized the man's right leg was made of wood. *Former soldier,* he thought. There was something about the man's bearing, about the way he held his weapon, the ease with which he took orders. *Best not provoke him.* Satisfied that—for the moment, at least—he wasn't going to take a bolt in the throat, he glanced around at the room. Lanterns hung from a low ceiling, illuminating the bare stone walls. "Where are we?"

"An abandoned cellar," Ashra replied. "No one knows we're here."

"So we're safe?"

"Ashra's safe," Alphonse grunted. "Can't say the same for you. Not yet."

"And what are you, peg leg?" Lukan replied, forgetting his own advice of a moment before. "Her butler?"

"I'm whatever Ash wants me to be. Adviser, guardian . . ." He grinned, hefted his crossbow. "Executioner . . ."

"Lady's mercy, I helped her escape—"

"So Ash tells me. It's the only reason I've not pulled the trigger on Old Berta here." He hefted the crossbow. "Best you tell me who the hells you are before I change my mind."

"Ashra already knows my name. Ask her."

"I'm asking you."

"This is Lukan Gardova," the thief put in, the edge in her voice suggesting she was growing tired of the exchange. "Who claims to have been chased into the King's domain by a sorcerous wolf created by the Faceless."

"The Faceless," Alphonse echoed, glancing at her. "You mean those demons from the children's stories?"

"So he says."

"It's true," Lukan replied, looking at each of them in turn. "I swear. I saw them with my own eyes—"

"Lady's mercy," the big man muttered, raising his crossbow again. "A shimmer addict. I should've bloody known. Let's put a bolt in him and be done with it."

"This how you treat people who help you?" Lukan snapped at Ashra. "I would have thought better of Lady Midnight."

"Shut your fool mouth," Alphonse replied, finger tightening round the trigger. "Just say the word, Ash."

The thief stared at Lukan, her face unreadable. The moment stretched.

"It's okay, 'Phonse," she said eventually. "Lower the crossbow."

"You sure?" the man asked, not taking his eyes off Lukan. "This one's bad news, I can tell."

"He helped me escape, 'Phonse. I wouldn't have made it without him."

"And *he* wouldn't have made it without your portal—"

"You heard Lady Midnight," Lukan said, grinning at Alphonse. "Lower the weapon, old man."

"Oh, I'm old all right," Alphonse replied, jaw tightening. "So old that I sometimes get tremors in my hands. Might be that I accidentally squeeze this trigger and—"

"*'Phonse*," Ashra said pointedly.

The man glared at Lukan but lowered the crossbow.

"I'm glad we're even," Lukan said to Ashra. "For a moment there I thought—"

"Call me Lady Midnight one more time," the thief cut in, "and I *will* tell him to shoot."

Lukan raised both hands. "Understood."

"And we're not even," Ashra continued. "Not until you tell me who stole the Sandino Blade."

Alphonse gave her a sharp look, but the thief kept her intense stare on Lukan. "So start talking."

Such was Lukan's disorientation after his experience of the portal—not to mention having a crossbow shoved in his face—that he'd forgotten the deal they'd struck in the cell. "Look . . . it's a long story," he replied, "and I actually have somewhere I really need to be—"

"'Phonse."

The man raised his crossbow again.

"Do you know who stole the Sandino Blade?" the thief demanded.

"Yes."

"Let me guess," Alphonse said, his tone one of derision. "It was the Faceless." He looked at the thief. "We're wasting our time, Ash."

"It wasn't the Faceless," Lukan retorted, glaring at the man. "But they're involved. So is Lord Marquetta."

"Lord Marquetta? The merchant prince?" Alphonse barked a laugh. "What the hells does he have to do with the Sandino Blade?"

"If you shut *your* fool mouth, maybe you'll find out."

"I'd much rather stick this bolt in your gut and live in blissful ignorance—"

"*Enough,* the pair of you," Ashra snapped, glaring at them in turn. "Barking at each other like dogs . . . Lower the crossbow, 'Phonse." The man glowered but did as he was told. "And you," Ashra said, the smirk slipping from Lukan's face as he saw the intensity of her stare. "You start talking. Leave nothing out. And if I *do* think you're bullshitting us, I *will* let 'Phonse put a hole in you. Understand?"

"Perfectly."

"Good." Ashra settled back in her chair, pulling her blanket around her. "Now talk."

"Well," Lukan began, "it all started when I learned my father had been murdered . . ."

———

Neither Alphonse nor Ashra interrupted Lukan as he told his story. The man's expression slid from surprise to disbelief and back again, while Ashra remained impassive for the duration—even Lukan's description of the Faceless and the wolf yielded only a raised eyebrow. But there was an intensity to her gaze as she listened to the revelations about the Sandino Blade, while the details of Marquetta's plan caused her features to harden.

"That's quite a story," she said when Lukan had finished.

"You can say that again," Alphonse muttered as he rose from his chair. The big man hobbled across to a shelf and returned with a bottle and a glass. "The Faceless," he continued, pouring a measure of liquor. "A sorcerous wolf. A conspiracy involving the three most powerful men in the city—"

"It's the truth," Lukan replied, more brusquely than he'd intended. The grasping cold of the portal had long since retreated, leaving a numbing headache in its wake. That, along with his growing exhaustion, left his patience running thin. "Every word of it."

"I believe you," Ashra said.

He blinked in surprise. "You do?"

"Yes."

"And you?" Lukan asked, looking to Alphonse.

The burly man scowled but placed his crossbow on the table. "If Ash believes you, that's good enough for me," he replied grudgingly. "Besides," he continued, his brow furrowed, "the tale you've just spun . . . It's madness. Only a fool would make up a story as far-fetched as that to save their own skin. And whatever you might be"—his eyes narrowed as if to say *and I'm still wondering about that*—"you're no fool."

"Thanks. I guess." Lukan's gaze moved to the table and he gestured at the bottle. "Now that you've decided not to shoot me, I don't suppose . . ."

Alphonse regarded him for a moment longer. "Fine," he said eventually, shrugging his broad shoulders as if to cast off any lingering doubts. He handed Lukan the glass. "Reckon you've earned it after that little scuffle in the cell."

"To be fair," Lukan said, accepting the glass with a nod of thanks, "you were right. We'd still be there if it wasn't for Ashra's ring." *Or somewhere far worse . . .*

"Mmm." The man's grizzled expression became guarded, as if the mention of the ring had made him wary. *Best not push too much on that.* Lukan had a dozen questions about the ring and how it worked, but decided they'd keep for the moment. Particularly when he had a glass of liquor in his hand. He took a sniff—brandy—and then a swallow, rolling the amber liquid around on his tongue. It was rough . . . and also one of the finest things he'd ever tasted.

"So," he said, enjoying the warmth spreading through his chest, "what now?"

"I need to think," Ashra replied, throwing off her blanket as she stood. "Stay here."

"Hey," Lukan called after her, as the thief moved toward a flight of stone steps. "Where are you going?" But the thief had already gone, silent as a shadow. Lukan rose to follow her.

"Sit down, lad," Alphonse said.

"But I need to—"

"Sit. Down."

Lukan locked eyes with the older man, who stared back, un-blinking. *A soldier's gaze,* Lukan thought, as he sank back down to the floor. *No doubt he's stared down worse things than a sleep-deprived lunatic babbling about sorcerous wolves and stolen swords.* "I can't stay here," he said, staring at the brandy in his glass before knocking it back. "I need to find Flea. I need to speak to the Scrivener. Marquetta's plan, we need to . . ." He trailed off, mouth hanging open. *I don't even know what day it is. It might already be too late—*

"It's just past the third bell of the morning," Alphonse said, as if reading Lukan's mind. "Today's the big day."

"You mean . . ."

"The Grand Restoration."

Lukan sagged with relief. "Then I've not missed it."

"You that keen to see the ambassador get murdered?"

"What? No, of course not—I don't want to see the murder, I want to *stop* it."

"If you're right about Marquetta, lad, and I pray to the Lady you're not, then you'll stay the hells away." The older man's mouth twitched into a grimace. "Because things are going to get messy."

"That's why we need to do something—"

"What you need to *do,* lad, is thank your lucky stars that Ashra and her rings got you out of that cell. You've been given a second chance. Not many who find themselves at the mercy of the Twice-Crowned King get to say that. So don't throw it away."

"Rings."

"Huh?"

"Rings," Lukan repeated, emphasizing the last letter. "So there's more than one?"

Alphonse winced and tugged at his mustache. "Ash didn't tell you then?"

"About how her ring works? No."

"Right. Well, it's not for me to say—"

"I've already given you my story."

"That's because I'm holding the crossbow."

"You've put it down."

"Figure o' speech, lad. And I can easily pick it up again."

"Have you ever tried it?" Lukan asked. "Stepped through a portal? Because I tell you, it's not pleasant."

"But still better than taking the Long Swim, eh?"

"A fate Ashra only avoided because I was there to help her."

"Lady's mercy, we've been over this—"

"We helped each other and now we're even. I know. But I still think I'm owed an explanation as to how one moment I'm in a cell and the next I'm"—Lukan gestured with his empty glass at the room—"wherever *here* is."

"Stubborn, aren't you," Alphonse muttered, drumming his fingers on the tabletop. "Well, I suppose it can't hurt. But don't you go getting any ideas about the rings, understand?"

"Got it."

"Fine." The older man let out a heavy breath and reached into a pocket, pulling out a signet ring that was a twin to Ashra's own. "There are two rings," he confirmed, placing the ring down on the table. "Ash calls them the Rings of Last Resort, because she only uses them when she has no other choice."

"I can see why."

"Both must be activated to summon the portal," Alphonse continued. "Did you see what Ash did with hers?"

"She rubbed it with her thumb and a Phaeron glyph appeared. It glowed turquoise and then faded."

"Because it wasn't ready to use. See, the rings take time to recover their . . . powers, or what have you, after they've been used. Normally it takes a full day and night—so if you used them at, say, the eighth bell of the morning, they'd need until about the same time the next day to recover. Sometimes it takes less time, sometimes a little more. We never figured out why."

"The final time she used the ring," Lukan replied, "the glyph shone gold, not turquoise—presumably because it had regained its power?"

The man nodded. "And when one ring glows gold, so does the other."

"So you knew to activate your ring to summon the portal."

"Exactly."

"And the portal took us here," Lukan continued, brow furrowed as he followed the logic, "because the destination is determined by the second ring's location. So if *you* had been the one to initiate the connection, and Ashra had activated *her* ring in response, you could have joined us in the cell."

The man grunted in admiration. "You've got some smarts, lad. Just don't go getting any ideas."

"These rings must be priceless. The amount of coin people would pay to be able to summon *portals*—"

"What did I just say?" Alphonse growled.

"I have no designs on the rings," Lukan replied, raising a placating hand. "I just . . . Where did Ashra get them, anyway—they're both hers, I take it?"

"They are," the man replied gruffly, "and that *definitely* isn't my story to tell."

"Ashra's ring wasn't ready to use when she was thrown in the cell," Lukan mused, thinking back to the turquoise glyph pulsing and fading. "She said she'd used it to escape the King's enforcers."

"Aye, she did. Came tumbling through the portal about this time last night, come to think of it." Alphonse took a swig from the bottle. "We were in one of the other safe houses—Ash has got several across the city. I tried to convince her to stay there for a while, but she was worried it was compromised, so she kept moving. We were supposed to meet up later that day. When she failed to show I assumed the worst." He winced. "Seems I was right to worry."

"We got out just in time," Lukan replied. "If her ring had taken any longer to regain its power . . ."

"The Long Swim," Alphonse said, his expression grave. "Aye. Be glad it did." He sat back with a deep sigh, his chair creaking beneath his weight. "At least now we know who stole the Sandino

Blade. These Seven Jewels have a lot to answer for. Marquetta too."

"On that we can agree."

"A month," Alphonse continued, thumping the bottle down on the table. "A whole month Ash was having to skulk around, hiding from the King's enforcers—all for a crime she didn't commit. I told her to leave the city, told her she couldn't hide forever, but . . ."

"She didn't listen?"

"Oh, she listened all right. Ash always listens. It's just that . . ."

"She's her own woman," Lukan offered, recalling the thief's own words.

"I see you've got the measure of Ash already."

"I got the measure of her when she chose the Long Swim over throwing herself on the King's mercy."

Alphonse leaned forward, his gaze intent. "You were there?"

"No. But I heard her talking to Scipio after she was thrown in the cell. Sounds like the King made her an offer of some sort."

"Aye, I'll bet it was the offer they always make her," the man replied, lip curling in derision. "Power and prestige in return for becoming their puppet. She's always refused them."

"Seems she refused them again."

"And so they condemned her to the Long Swim." Alphonse sat back and took a swig from the bottle, grimacing as if it tasted sour. "It was always going to end this way. The myth of Lady Midnight grew too big. Ash had become too much of a threat. I knew the day would come when the King forced her to choose between death or servitude."

"Lucky that her ring gave her a third option."

"Aye, but we're just back to where we started," the man replied, tugging at his beard. "The King will be scouring the city for Ash—you as well. They'll want to make an example of both of you."

"Are you sure we're safe here?"

"Safe enough. No one knows about this place. We can stay here 'til dawn, then try to blend in with the festival crowds. You'll both need to leave the city as quickly as possible. The western gate's your best bet—"

"I'm not going anywhere."

"Listen to me, lad," Alphonse said firmly. "Between Marquetta and the Twice-Crowned King, you've managed to make two very dangerous enemies. Best get out while you still can."

"No. I have to stop Marquetta."

"And how do you propose to do that?"

"I don't know," Lukan replied, a touch of heat in his tone, "but I'll find a way. I can't let him murder the ambassador and start a war. Besides, unmasking his conspiracy is the only way to free Zandrusa and get my father's casket. I'm not leaving Saphrona without it."

"Better to cut your losses and walk away," Alphonse advised. "There's nothing you can do. You'll just end up in more trouble. Dead, even."

"Thanks for the vote of confidence."

"What's this city to you, anyway? You only arrived here a few days ago. Why do you care?"

"Why don't you?" Lukan asked pointedly.

"I *do,*" Alphonse insisted, his voice hardening. For a moment Lukan thought the man might reach for his crossbow; instead he sat there, jaw tensing. "I do care," he continued, his tension easing. "It's just that . . . Look, I was a boy during the last war with Zar-Ghosa. I remember the joy when the fighting finally stopped—it was thick as honey, you could almost taste it in the air. The whole city was dizzy with the thought of peace after decades of war, with the belief that our enemies across the sea could become our friends. But the world turns and younger generations forget the lessons learned by the old . . . and the wolves of greed and prejudice come slinking back from the shadows." The man took a swallow of brandy. "You can't stop human nature, lad. Even if you somehow manage to stop Marquetta, someone else will take up his cause. We'll war again with the Zar-Ghosans sooner or later, because ultimately there's not enough profit in peace. Conflict is the only thing we truly understand."

"I had you pegged for a soldier, not a philosopher."

"I'm just an old man who knows there's some battles you can't hope to win. I've seen the world turn enough times to see what a mess we've made of it. Sometimes all you can do is keep your head down and wait for things to blow over. This is one of those times. You can't stop what's coming."

"That doesn't mean I shouldn't try."

"Heroism is overrated, lad. Forget all this. I know you want your father's casket, I know you want to do right by your old man, but what Marquetta is planning is bigger than you. It's bigger than all of us. And I've seen too many young men who thought they were invincible throw their lives away for nothing. Don't make the same mistake as them, lad. Go and live your life."

Lukan stared at the brandy in his glass, wishing he could do as Alphonse urged. The old soldier was right, he'd got himself into a tangled mess that would probably get him killed. *And yet . . .*

"I can't," he said, voicing the realization that had settled within him, that he'd accepted without a flicker of resistance. "What sort of man would I be if I walked away now, knowing what I do? Knowing that I could have saved thousands of lives, but instead chose to just save my own? I have enough on my conscience already. Besides, I swore an oath. I made a silverblood promise that I'd find justice for my father. And I keep my promises."

"Admirable words, lad."

"I mean them."

"I know. But they'll get you killed. If you want to honor your father's memory, then walk away."

"I've tried that before," Lukan replied, recalling the sight of Giorgio Castori lying on the ground. *Blood on cherry blossoms.* "It didn't work out so well."

"At least you're alive to acknowledge that. Time heals all wounds, lad. Well . . ." He grinned and raised his wooden leg. "Most of them, anyway."

"I'm staying," Lukan replied firmly. "I'm going to stop Marquetta."

"And go up against the Faceless?" Alphonse gave a low whistle. "You're a braver man than me. You know, I didn't even think—"

"They were real?" Lukan finished, a bitter laugh escaping his lips. "Neither did I. But they are. Trust me."

"In that case, you'll need all the help you can get, but I doubt the Scrivener will aid you this time," the older man mused. "That woman's too smart to get caught up in this madness. Face it, lad, if you go up against Marquetta, you'll be doing it on your own."

"No he won't." Lukan and Alphonse both looked up in surprise as Ashra emerged from the shadows of the steps.

"Damn it, Ash," Alphonse muttered, "how long've you been there?"

"Long enough." The thief met Lukan's gaze. "You swear that you're telling the truth? That Marquetta wants to start a war with Zar-Ghosa?"

"That's what he said."

"Then I'll help you. However I can."

"Lady's blood," Alphonse swore, "this is madness, Ash. This isn't your fight."

"Of course it is. What's that saying of yours, 'Phonse? 'In times of war . . .'"

"'. . . the rich prosper and the poor perish,'" the man finished, his face creasing in annoyance. "And that's true, but—"

"I grew up in the Splinters," Ashra continued, eyes glazed as if she was seeing a different place, another time. "My mother and I rarely had a copper to our name. In those early years we survived on the charity of others, paupers like us who had very little but tried to share what they could. I'm not going to let Marquetta throw them to the wolves. Nor am I going to stand idle while he drives my mother's people out of the city and makes war on their country."

"What I'm trying to say, Ash, is that—"

"This is my city, 'Phonse," the thief continued, a dangerous gleam in her eyes, "and the people in the Splinters and the Zar-Ghosan quarter are *my* people. I'll be damned before I let Marquetta take a

torch to forty years of peace." Her jaw tightened. "Besides, I have
my own score to settle with him. The Sandino Blade was stolen
on his orders. He's the reason I almost ended up facing the Long
Swim. So I'll do whatever I can to bring him down." Her eyes
flicked to Lukan. "Will you accept my help?"

"Uh . . ." Lukan didn't even know why he was hesitating. Having the best thief in the city could only improve his chances of
foiling Marquetta's plan. *The fact that she can summon portals
can't hurt either.* "Yes," he replied. "Of course."

"You sure about this, Ash?" Alphonse asked, raising a hand
to forestall her rebuke. "No, hear me out. It's just . . . well, you
hardly know this lad."

"I know enough," Ashra replied, her expression thoughtful as
she regarded Lukan. "He can think on his feet and seems to know
his way around a fight—"

"Those are two of my better qualities," Lukan said with a grin.

"—although he could certainly learn when to keep his mouth
shut." Her lips twitched in what might have been amusement. "We
should get some sleep," she continued, turning away, the glimpse
of humor gone as quickly as it had appeared. "Dawn's only a few
hours away. We'll leave at first light. Try and blend in with the
festival crowds." She looked at Lukan. "You know how to contact
the Scrivener?"

"I do," he replied. "But we should go now. Leaving it until tomorrow doesn't give us enough time—"

"Too risky. The King's enforcers will be looking for us. Better
to stay here and get some rest. We'll need it if we're to have chance
at stopping Marquetta."

Can't argue with that. Lukan couldn't even remember the last
time he'd properly slept. "Fine," he said, stifling a yawn. "I guess
I'll bed down in the corner."

"Luckily for you," Alphonse said, rising from his chair, "I
brought a few extra pillows and blankets."

"I don't suppose you brought another bottle of that brandy as
well?"

The man raised an eyebrow. "Might be that I did."

"Perhaps we should open it." Lukan ignored Ashra's hard stare. "You know . . . have a little nightcap."

"Now *that*," the man said with a grin, "is the first bit of sense you've spoken all night."

30

TWO WEAKNESSES

They left just as the bells of the Lady's House were tolling to mark the eighth hour of the morning—later than Lukan would have liked, but then he'd still been dead to the world when Alphonse's hand had shaken him awake from what had been a mercifully dreamless sleep. He'd been twitchy as they'd left the cellar, his tired eyes flicking from alley to doorway to open window, but the attack he expected never came. Even so, he remained on edge as they passed through streets that were already bustling with people, the air alive with their laughter and chatter. *Five hours,* he thought. *Five hours until Marquetta murders the ambassador in front of the entire city.* Yet at that moment Lukan had a more pressing problem.

He was hungover as shit.

Shouldn't have finished that bloody brandy. Alphonse had opened the second bottle and a solitary nightcap had become several, much to Ashra's disdain. Lukan's mind was swimming by the time he surrendered to his exhaustion, his vision blurring as he collapsed into his makeshift bed in one corner of the cellar. He didn't recall closing his eyes, but he sure as hells remembered waking up, a vicious headache squeezing his skull like a vise. A skewer of spiced chicken from a street cart, washed down with coffee blacker than sin, had momentarily helped to drive the hangover back. But now, as he followed Ashra through the busy streets, he could feel the headache clawing its way back inside his skull. Worse, his stomach was churning and making gurgling noises, as if it was assessing its contents and deciding whether to . . .

Oh, shit.

Lukan dashed toward the nearest alley, reaching it just as his stomach decided (after what seemed an unfairly brief deliberation) that it didn't like the combination of chicken, coffee, and liquor swirling in its depths. He fell to his knees just as his stomach gave a final gurgle, and vomited against the side of someone's house. Several heaves got the job done. *Lady's mercy, that brandy was strong.* He wiped away a strand of drool and stared at the puddle before him, slightly surprised it hadn't dissolved the stone on contact and then burst into flame.

"You should have left that bottle alone."

Lukan looked up to see Ashra leaning against the alley wall, face impassive.

"If you knew me better," he replied, rising to his feet, "you'll know I have two weaknesses."

"Only two?"

"Dark-eyed women and unopened bottles."

"In that case I'm glad I have green eyes."

"I mean, green is a close second . . ."

"Are you done?"

"I think so," Lukan replied, only for his stomach to gurgle in apparent disagreement. Ashra raised an eyebrow.

"Actually," he said with a wince, "maybe not."

———

The sun rose above the red-tiled rooftops as they crossed the city, and the late-summer heat rose with it. Lukan wiped sweat from his forehead, his damp shirt clinging uncomfortably to his skin. *Sweating like a priest in a brothel,* he thought as he followed Ashra down a series of bustling avenues, which the thief preferred over the quieter side streets. It meant a slower journey, but Lukan didn't bother to argue—partly because his hangover was still giving him grief, but mostly because it made sense to use the cover of the crowd. *Safety in numbers and all that.* Besides, he doubted anything he could say would change Ashra's mind or elicit anything more from her than a cool glance.

He quickened his pace and stole a look at her. In the bright sunlight he could see her clearly for the first time: a much younger woman than he'd thought, at a guess barely into her twenties, average of height, lithe of build and sharp of feature. She'd referred to the Zar-Ghosans as her mother's people, and he could see her Southern Queendoms ancestry in her dark hair, which was cut short and choppy, and her light brown skin. Save for her pale green eyes, which were constantly moving, drinking in every detail, nothing about her appearance hinted at her status as the best thief in the city. *Yet surely the very point of a thief is to blend in and appear nondescript.* That the Twice-Crowned King felt threatened by her was proof enough of her ability, while her rejection of whatever ultimatum they'd given her revealed a strong will. *She's got steel, no doubt about that.* Otherwise, there was precious little Lukan knew about his new companion—save for one thing. *She's deadly serious about stopping Marquetta.* Her words in the cellar had left him in no doubt as to her determination, and he could see it now in the tight line of her mouth, in the set of her jaw. *Marquetta might have the Faceless, but I've got Lady Midnight.*

He could only hope that evened the odds.

They made slow progress through the streets, pausing only once so Lukan could douse his head in a fountain. By the time they reached the Western Boneway, his head felt clearer and his stomach had settled. The ceremony was still several hours away, but already thousands of people lined the wide thoroughfare, all eager to catch a glimpse of the Grand Duke's procession as it passed by on its way to the Lady's House, where, in the shadow of the huge temple, the Silver Spear would be exchanged to renew the peace between Saphrona and Zar-Ghosa. *That's if Marquetta doesn't kill the ambassador first.* Lukan eyed the gathered citizens—men, women, and children all wearing their colorful, festival-best clothes, faces alight with anticipation. Their laughter and conversation—undercut by the occasional strain of music—filled the air between the tall buildings on either side of the street, echoed off the bleached bones that towered above the crowds. *If only they knew this celebration might end in blood.* But they didn't, and Lukan envied them that. Right then he would have gladly traded his knowledge of what was to come for ignorance, for the chance to drink and dance like so many of the people around him. Half the citizens weaving past him seemed to be drunk already, on pomp and circumstance as much as alcohol. *Perhaps I'll join them if we manage to stop Marquetta.* Wishful thinking, given that he didn't have the faintest notion of how they would achieve that. *The Scrivener will know what to do. She always does.*

"We're being followed."

Those three words were enough to snap Lukan to attention. "By who?" he asked, glancing sidelong at Ashra, resisting the urge to look over his shoulder.

"A girl."

"A girl?"

"She doesn't look dangerous," the thief said, with the flicker of a smile, "but she *does* have a small crossbow hanging from her belt. Very fancy piece for a street rat."

"Flea," Lukan breathed, hope soaring as he turned round and scanned the crowds. "I don't see . . ." He trailed off as a gaggle of revelers parted and the girl slipped through the gap. *I'll be damned.* He couldn't help but grin as Flea saw him and hesitated, uncertainty stealing across her features as she eyed Ashra.

"Give me a moment," he said, stepping toward Flea and raising a hand in greeting. The girl's uncertainty melted into delight and she raced forward, covering the few yards between them in a flash. Lukan grunted in surprise as she flung her arms round his waist and hugged him tightly.

"I thought you were dead," she said after a moment, glancing up at him, eyes shining.

"Not yet." Still taken back by her uncharacteristic show of affection, he settled for awkwardly patting her head. "How in the hells did you find us?"

"I was up on the rooftops and I saw you in the crowd. I climbed down as quickly as I could, but this stupid thing"—she tugged at her dress—"got stuck. I thought I'd lost you." She pulled away, her gaze turning to Ashra. "And I wasn't sure . . ."

"It's okay, she's a friend."

"What happened in the catacombs?" Flea asked, her gaze finding his again. "Why didn't you come back?"

"Long story. The short version is that I ended up as the Twice-Crowned King's prisoner."

"Oh . . ." Flea grimaced. "That's bad."

"You don't say."

"But you escaped?"

"I did, thanks to Lady Midnight here."

Flea's eyed flicked to the thief and widened, her mouth dropping open.

"Hello, Flea," Ashra said, her tone edged with amusement as she joined them. "Lukan's told me a lot about you."

"Lady Midnight," Flea breathed, as if the words stole the air from her lungs.

"I never much liked that name," the thief replied, giving the girl a wink. "So call me Ashra." She held out her hand, palm facing downward.

"Ashra . . ." Flea grinned, her face lighting up as she slid her hand beneath the woman's so their palms met. "I've heard all the stories," she said, giddy with excitement. "Is it true you can walk through walls?"

Lukan snorted. "You don't know the half of it, kid."

Flea turned. "I told you," she said, balling her fist, "I'm not a *child*." She punctuated the last word with a solid punch to Lukan's thigh.

"Ahhh." He grinned at her. "How I've missed our little talks."

"Really?"

"No."

She drove her fist at him again, but this time Lukan caught it. "We can fool about later. Right now we need to speak to the Scrivener. Did you tell her everything we saw in the cata-combs?"

"Yeah, I did. She said she found it hard to believe."

"That so?" Lukan managed a wry smile. "Well, trust me—she's heard nothing yet."

31

PASSION BEFORE REASON

"We need to talk."

The Scrivener glanced up, frozen in the act of adding a sugar cube to her tea. "Master Gardova," she replied, a raised eyebrow her one concession to surprise. "I must confess, I hadn't expected to see you again." She dropped the sugar into the steaming liquid. "You smell like a week-old corpse."

"My apologies, Mistress," Juro said as he joined them at the table. "I suggested to our friend that he might prefer to bathe before making his report—"

"And I already told *you,*" Lukan cut in, "that there's no bloody time."

"You're attracting attention, Master Gardova," the Scrivener said, raising her cup and blowing gently on her tea. "Please lower your voice."

"Lady's blood, this is *important*—"

"And yet Lady Midnight appears perfectly calm." The Scrivener's sharp gaze flicked to Ashra. "Greetings, Ashra. We've met once before, a few years ago. Do you recall?"

"I do." Ashra stepped forward and offered her hand, palm upward. "It's a pleasure to see you again."

"Likewise," the Scrivener replied, placing her palm against Ashra's. "Though I can't say the same for the danger you bring to my door."

"So the word is out?"

"If you mean the rumor that you were condemned to the Long Swim and then somehow escaped from the King's custody, then yes, I'm afraid it is." The Scrivener cocked her head. "Is it true?"

"It is."

"Then your presence here leaves me in a bind."

"The King has denounced you as a traitor," Juro said. "Anyone among the Kindred found to be offering you sanctuary or assistance faces the Long Swim."

"Then I apologize for placing you at risk," Ashra replied, showing no emotion at the news. "I wouldn't be here if it wasn't urgent, but if you'd prefer me to leave . . ."

"Leave?" the Scrivener scoffed, arching an eyebrow. "Goodness, no. Not when we have a chance to hear the story straight from the horse's mouth, so to speak."

"I will go and watch the street, Mistress," Juro said, turning away.

"Stay, Juro. I would have your counsel." The woman took a sip of tea and placed her cup down. "Flea, my dear?"

Flea stepped closer. "I'll only do it if I can have another one of those cinnamon buns."

The corners of the Scrivener's mouth creased in faint amusement. "You can have two, if you like."

"Done." Flea shrugged away Lukan's questioning look and headed for the door. She'd already heard his tale on the way to the teahouse, but only after promising Ashra she would keep the secret of the rings. As enthralled as she'd been, her sweet tooth was always going to win out over hearing the story a second time. He smiled as the girl almost collided with a waiter and responded to his bluster with a crude gesture before ducking out of the door.

"So," the Scrivener said, steepling her fingers as she regarded Ashra, "the city's most famous thief is blamed for the theft of the Sandino Blade, declines the King's offer of mercy, and is thrown into a cell from which she disappears into thin air. The entire underworld is in uproar." Her gaze flicked to Lukan. "And as usual, Master Gardova, you appear to be right in the middle of it all."

"Not by choice," Lukan replied.

"But you blundered into it all the same. Still, I must confess to being curious as to how you both escaped from the King's

custody. The rumor is that you both simply . . . vanished." The
master forger's eyes flicked to Ashra. "I suspect there's a little
more to it than that."

The thief glanced at Lukan. He caught the flash of warning in
her eyes and remembered her words to him shortly before they
arrived at the teahouse. *Don't mention my rings or what they can
do,* she'd said, her tone brooking no argument. *No one else can
know.*

"That tale can wait," Lukan said. "We have more important
things we need to discuss."

"Ah, you mean Lord Marquetta's conspiracy. Flea told me
about his little party in the catacombs, with its . . . special guests."

"She said you didn't believe her."

"If someone told you, Master Gardova, that they'd seen some
mythical figures from childhood tales appear and conjure up some
sort of glowing beast, would you believe them?"

"I know it sounds outlandish—"

"Outlandish?" The Scrivener raised an eyebrow. "It sounds
utterly ludicrous."

"I know what I saw."

"You know what you *think* you saw. But firelight and shadows can play tricks on a tired mind, particularly when wine is
involved."

"Lady's blood, I wasn't *drunk*—"

"Language."

Lukan took a deep breath, forcing down his anger. "Just hear
me out," he said through gritted teeth. "Please."

"I wouldn't be here if I didn't believe his story," Ashra offered.
"Please listen to what Lukan has to say."

The Scrivener's eyes flicked between them, her expression unreadable. "Very well," she replied, lips thinning as she gestured
to the seats before her. "I must confess Flea was rather vague on
some of the details, so let's hear this little tale again. Perhaps it
will prove more believable this time round."

Unlike Alphonse and Ashra, the Scrivener did not listen quietly as Lukan told his tale—instead she interrupted him again and again, questioning nearly every detail. Lukan almost lost his temper on several occasions, only to rein his anger in as the Scrivener's eyebrow rose in warning. When he was finally done, the master forger sat back, finger tapping absently against her teacup.

"A highly fanciful tale, Master Gardova," she said, brow creased in thought. "Even more so the second time round."

"It's the truth," Lukan said wearily. "Take it or leave it."

"A conspiracy reaching to the very top of society, involving mythical figures who haven't been seen in centuries, if they even exist outside of fairy tales. Sorcerous portals, a glowing wolf . . ." The Scrivener looked to her subordinate. "What do you make of all this, Juro?"

The man was silent for a moment. "If we take the story at face value," he said eventually, raising a hand to forestall the objection that was already spilling from Lukan's lips, "then it leaves us with one obvious question. *Why?* What is the purpose of Marquetta's plot?"

"As astute as ever," the Scrivener replied, snapping her fingers for more tea.

"Surely it's obvious," Lukan said, waiting impatiently as a server placed a fresh teapot on the table. "He's obsessed with restoring Saphrona's former glory, whatever the hells that means. He wants to drive Zar-Ghosans out of the city. By murdering the ambassador he hopes to start a war—"

"Did you hear him say those exact words?"

"You mean—"

"Did you hear him say he wanted to start a war?"

"Yes . . ." Lukan frowned, casting his mind back. "Well, no. Not exactly . . ."

"Then how can you be sure of what he intends?" The Scrivener picked up the teapot and refilled her cup. "Marquetta's main interests are in shipping. A war would severely disrupt his business. It's hard to see what he gains from engineering such a conflict."

"The same goes for his allies," Juro said. "A war would lead to heightened tensions and tightened purse strings, meaning more work for the Inquisition and less coin in the temple's collection plate. It's difficult to see what the Prime Inquisitor and the Pontifex gain from a war with Zar-Ghosa."

"You're looking for logic where none exists," Lukan said, struggling to contain his exasperation. "These men are pursuing a vision, a shared fantasy. Their reasons are emotional, not rational—"

"Then there's the question of Zandrusa," the Scrivener continued, ignoring him. "Where does she fit into all of this? Why would Marquetta have the Faceless murder Lord Saviola and then frame Zandrusa for the crime?"

"They must have known about his plans," Ashra put in.

Juro nodded. "That's the only explanation."

"If that's the case," the Scrivener said, "Zandrusa would have told Master Gardova about Marquetta's conspiracy when he spoke to her in the Ebon Hand. But she was convinced that Lord Murillo was behind her imprisonment."

"There's a piece of the puzzle missing," Juro mused. "We're not seeing the full picture."

"Agreed," the Scrivener replied. "Still, it doesn't matter now."

"Doesn't matter?" Lukan echoed, eyes narrowing. "What do you mean?"

"You've proven most resourceful, Master Gardova," the Scrivener continued, fixing Lukan with her piercing stare as she set her cup down. "More than I could have imagined. You have my gratitude for relating this information to me, which I'm satisfied fulfills the terms of our agreement."

Lukan gaped at her. "But—"

"As a sign of goodwill," the Scrivener continued, "which is entirely unwarranted, since you did burn my house to the ground, I will provide you with an additional sum of money for services rendered. And should I have any need of your talent for getting into trouble and emerging unscathed, I'll be sure to let you know." She turned her gaze to the thief beside him. "I wish you good fortune,

Ashra. I do hope you work out your current difficulties. Now, Juro—if you would kindly see our guests out—"

Lukan thumped his fist on the table, rattling the crockery. "What in the *hells* are you playing at? You can't just—*we* can't just let Marquetta get away with this. We can't just leave Zandrusa to rot in the Ebon Hand. We have to do something."

The Scrivener's lips thinned. "Passion before reason," she said, with a shake of her head. "That's your weakness, Master Gardova."

"He's going to murder the ambassador. He's going to start a *war*—"

"That will be all. Juro—"

"If you don't care about saving the city then at least think about saving your friend," Lukan continued, his raised voice drawing a few curious stares. "Revealing Marquetta's treachery is the only way to prove Zandrusa's innocence. Surely you see this—"

"Don't presume to question my intelligence," the Scrivener snapped. "Of course I recognize that."

"Then why are we still sitting here?" Lukan demanded, rising. "There's no time to waste—"

"*Sit. Down.*" Whether it was because the master forger's expression could have curdled milk at fifty paces, or because her words were delivered as sharply as dagger thrusts, Lukan couldn't say, but he sat regardless.

"You promised to help me free Zandrusa," he said, trying to seize back the initiative. "You promised—"

"I promised nothing."

"Oh, here we go. We had a *deal*—"

"We had a mutually beneficial agreement," the Scrivener cut in, voice smooth and cold as ice, "whereby I offered you financial support and a base of operations, which you burned to the ground—"

"Lady's mercy, it was an *accident*—"

"—and in return you were to investigate whether Zandrusa truly *had* murdered Lord Saviola, and, if she hadn't, to find out who had framed her for the crime and why."

"But the point of all this was to prove her innocence, to free her from prison—"

"The *point,*" the Scrivener said, raising a finger, "was to determine if Zandrusa was innocent, and if so whether there was anything we could do to help her."

"She *is* innocent. And we *can* help her."

"How?"

The question caught Lukan off guard. "I . . . Well, we need to stop Marquetta—"

"So you keep saying, Master Gardova. To the point where I'm starting to suspect you haven't thought beyond that."

"We'll get word to Obassa," Lukan said, thinking quickly. "You said yourself that he's a Zar-Ghosan spy. He'll be able to warn the ambassador."

"Who will dismiss the threat without a second thought," Juro said patiently. "The ambassador's role in the upcoming ceremony is a huge honor for her and her family, one that she will have expended a great deal of financial and political capital to achieve. She's not going to throw it away on the word of a stranger."

"Particularly when the warning involves mythical creatures from children's stories," the Scrivener added tartly.

"Then we'll go to the Grand Duke," Lukan replied. "We'll warn him of what Marquetta intends to do."

"And how will you prove it?" Juro asked. "What evidence do you have?"

If only I'd hung on to that damned diary. Not that the drug-fueled scribblings of Doctor Vassilis really prove anything. "None," he conceded. "But perhaps we can convince him."

"No one will believe you without proof," Juro said mildly. "You won't even make it past the palace gates."

"We have to at least *try*—"

"No," the Scrivener interjected. "We don't."

"So that's it, then?" Lukan asked, gesturing as he slumped back in his chair. "We're just going to watch Marquetta murder the ambassador and throw the whole city into chaos? We're going to leave Zandrusa to rot in a cell for a crime she didn't commit? I thought she was your friend."

"Don't play games with me, Master Gardova," the Scrivener warned. "Zandrusa was—*is*—someone I retain a great deal of fondness and respect for, which is why I tasked you with investigating the circumstances of her arrest. I expected some sort of foul play, but *this* . . ." She pursed her lips and shook her head. "This is far worse than anything I could have imagined. Believe me, Master Gardova, if there was anything I could do, I would do it gladly. But we have no evidence of Marquetta's treachery, and challenging him directly would mean going up against three of the most powerful men in the city. That's beyond me. It's beyond all of us. And if you're right about the Faceless being involved . . ." She shook her head again. "It's a hopeless task. There's nothing we can do."

"There's always something you can do," Lukan replied hotly, standing once more. "I'll stop Marquetta and get Zandrusa out of that cell even if I have to do it on my own."

"You won't be on your own," Ashra said, rising with him. "A pleasure, Mistress," she added, inclining her head at the Scrivener.

"Likewise." The master forger's eyes flicked to Lukan. "As for you, Master Gardova, contrary to what you might think, I wish you good fortune. Though if you continue with your current course, I don't expect our paths shall cross again."

"I wouldn't be so sure. You said yourself I have a talent for getting out of trouble." With that he left the table, Ashra at his back. He was almost at the teahouse door when a voice called his name.

"Lukan."

He turned to find Juro walking after him, a hand raised imploringly. "Lukan, please . . . think carefully about this." The man kept his voice low so the nearby patrons wouldn't overhear. "I've read the historical accounts of the Faceless. Every time someone has challenged them—"

"They've died a violent death. I know. And I don't care."

"Lukan," the man said again, gripping his arm as he reached for the door. "I know you and my mistress don't see eye to eye, but she's right about this. Don't throw your life away."

"I already have." *I threw it away years ago, the moment I agreed to that damned duel.* With a grim smile, he clapped Juro on the shoulder and turned for the door, Ashra following behind.

32

THE BIGGER PICTURE

"So let me get this straight," the constable said, giving his companion a knowing look, as if this were a joke they'd shared many times before. "You're telling us that Lord Marquetta is planning to assassinate the Zar-Ghosan ambassador in front of half the city."

"That's right," Lukan said tiredly. He already knew where this was going.

"And he's doing it with the help of the Faceless." The man chuckled, shook his head. "The *Faceless*."

"I know you think I'm mad . . ."

"No, I think you're *drunk*. And whatever you've been drinking, I can only hope I might get a taste sometime." The two constables shared a laugh and continued on their way down the crowded street.

"I'm not drunk," Lukan said, grabbing the man's arm and pulling him back. "You have to believe me—"

"Hands off," the constable barked, humor evaporating. "And piss off before I clap you in irons."

"That's all you're good for, isn't it?" Lukan snapped back, the heat and frustration of the morning boiling over.

"Lukan," Ashra said, "let's just go—"

"Taking bribes and bullying people," Lukan continued, his rising anger drowning out the thief's words. "Slapping people in chains regardless of their innocence or guilt, content in your own little sphere of ignorance—"

The second constable moved quickly, raising his halberd and

ramming the base of its shaft into Lukan's stomach. Lukan doubled over, stumbling backward. A second thrust of the shaft struck his shoulder and sent him sprawling to the ground. The man stepped forward to deliver another blow, only for Flea to dart in front of him. "Leave him alone," she shouted.

The constable's lip curled in derision. "Gladly," he muttered, turning away. "Drunken prick's not worth the trouble." He glanced at his companion. "Let's go." The two men ambled away without so much as a backward glance.

"You know," Lukan said, wincing as he gingerly rubbed his belly, "there was a moment there where I thought I'd almost convinced him."

"Are you okay?" Flea asked him, offering her hand.

"Fine," he replied, reaching up.

The girl snapped her hand back and punched his shoulder.

"What in the hells—"

"That's for being an idiot," the girl told him. "You should have learned by now you can't talk to them like that."

"She's right," Ashra put in. "How many more times do you need to end up in the dust before you realize that no one is going to listen?"

"As many as it takes."

"Lukan—"

"Let's try one of the other guardhouses," he said, climbing to his feet. "See if we can actually speak to someone with real authority."

"Yes, because our last attempt at that went *so* well."

Lukan winced again, and not at the pain in his belly. "Don't remind me," he muttered.

The memory of that incident was still raw. They'd visited one of the larger guardhouses in the Silks district, where the duty sergeant and her constables had listened to Lukan's claims with a mixture of amusement and indifference, which quickly changed to hostility—not to mention the raising of a crossbow—when he refused to leave and demanded to see their commanding officer.

Ashra had to drag him away before he got a bolt in the throat for his trouble.

Undeterred, and with his desperation rising with every passing moment, Lukan had approached every single constable they could find, only for all of them to react with similar disdain. Perhaps on another day they might have felt more inclined to listen, but instead they were hot, bothered, and had a dozen more pressing things to attend to. Lukan could hardly blame them; if someone had rushed up to him, stinking of sweat and last night's liquor, and had rambled about how mythical figures from a children's story were going to murder the ambassador, he would have given them short shrift as well. Yet every glare, every insult was a blow that he felt all too keenly, and with each successive brush-off he felt Juro's words echo in his mind all the clearer: *No one will believe you without proof.* As much as he hated to admit it, it was starting to look like the Scrivener's man was right.

"So what now?" Flea asked.

"We should try to reach the ambassador," Lukan said. "If we could just talk to her, perhaps—"

"She'd believe us when no one else does?" Ashra offered, shaking her head. "She won't. You heard what Juro said. Would you give up the opportunity of a lifetime on the basis of a stranger's warning? Besides, we don't even know where she is. If I wasn't being hunted by the entire underworld, I could find out easily. As it is . . ." She shrugged.

Lukan eyed the thief, wondering how afraid she was of her predicament. Her even tone and impassive expression suggested she wasn't fearful at all, but he'd seen her surveying the crowds, her gaze flicking from one person to the next, never resting. Whatever unease she felt, though, the thief kept it to herself.

"I'll bet Obassa knows where she is," Lukan said, glancing around as if the Zar-Ghosan spy might suddenly appear. *We should be so lucky.* They'd already looked for him at the Blue Oyster taverna and in the Zar-Ghosan quarter, but the blind man was nowhere to be found. "Maybe we could try the Inquisition," he ventured. "I know the Prime Inquisitor is involved in all this, but I'll bet none of the other inquisitors know anything about the conspiracy, nor their leader's part in it. Perhaps they'll listen to us."

"We'll just come up against the same problem," Ashra replied. "They won't believe us without proof. Besides, if they realize it was you who broke into the Ebon Hand, they'll clap you in chains. You'd be putting yourself at risk."

"Speak for yourself, Lady Midnight."

"That name means nothing to the Inquisition. Even if it does, they have no idea what I look like." The thief's brow knitted. "But I wouldn't be surprised if one or more inquisitors are in the Twice-Crowned King's pocket. Best we steer clear for both our sakes."

"Are we going to give up then?" Flea asked, her tone suggesting she wasn't against the idea.

"The Scrivener's right," Ashra replied, shrugging. "Without evidence of Marquetta's plan, there's nothing we can do."

"So we're just going to let him get away with it?" Lukan asked heatedly.

"No," the thief replied, without a flicker of emotion. "We need to look at the bigger picture. The ambassador's murder is just the start. The spark that lights the flame. We can't stop that, but we can fight what comes after. We can still prevent this war from happening. This is just the beginning, not the end."

The distant bells of the Lady's House pealed across the city, barely audible over the noise of the crowds.

"An hour until the ceremony," Flea said, chewing a nail.

"Then we'd best find somewhere to watch it," Ashra replied.

"Forget it," Lukan said, glancing around at the crowds with a sense of hopelessness. "It's too late for that. We won't get anywhere close."

"On the contrary," Ashra said, beckoning them to follow her, "I know where we'll find a perfect view."

"Look at all the people," Flea said, awe in her voice as she leaned out of the bell tower's window. "There must be five thousand of them."

"More like ten," Lukan replied.

The crowd filled the large plaza, pressing up against the two lines of constables, who struggled to maintain a central path from the triumphal arch at the plaza's entrance to the steps of the Lady's House on the far side. Those citizens unable to squeeze into the plaza watched from windows and rooftops. Some had even clambered up onto the bronze statues that lined the square, desperate for a glimpse of the grand procession.

Lukan doubted that many of them had a better view than the one he and Flea enjoyed. He'd been skeptical when Ashra had led them to the tilting bell tower rising above the roofs just south of the plaza, and the warning nailed to its door—DANGER, STRUCTURE UNSAFE—hadn't inspired confidence. Ashra claimed it was nothing more than a ruse, that the crumbling tower was structurally sound and until recently had been used as a hideout by a gang of pickpockets. The sign, she claimed, was nothing more than a deterrent to keep prying eyes away. The thieves had recently fallen foul of the law and their hideout still stood empty. Ashra had led the way up to where the old bell hung in a cramped room that nonetheless offered superb views across the plaza. *The perfect place to watch this mess unfold,* Lukan mused as he leaned on the windowsill.

A murmur from the crowd drew his attention to the great oaken doors of the Lady's House, away to his right, which were slowly opening. A lone figure stepped through, draped in a cloth-of-gold cloak trimmed with ermine. *The Pontifex,* Lukan realized, eyeing the man's symbols of office—a golden staff capped with crystal and a ridiculous hat that looked like a wilting cock. A cheer rolled across the crowd as the man ambled forward and took up position just before the stone steps that descended to the plaza.

"He's nervous," Ashra said. "Look at the way he's fingering his amulet."

"I'm not surprised," Lukan replied. "If there's two things I learned from my trip to the catacombs, it's that our friend down there is about as devout as the dregs at the bottom of a wineglass—"

"I could have told you that."

"—and that he's missing a spine."

"That too."

"Look," Flea exclaimed, pointing at the triumphal arch on the left side of the square, "here they come!"

The excitement in the girl's voice, despite what she knew was to unfold, reminded Lukan just how young Flea really was. He could hardly begrudge her such emotion, not when he also felt a touch of awe as the head of the procession passed beneath the arch and the crowd roared in response, the front rows hurling fistfuls of rose petals into the air.

Two standard-bearers rode at the head of the column, their gilded armor gleaming in the sun, the hooves of their white destriers crushing the petals that already covered the ground. Their polished lances bore two banners: the bat of Saphrona, black against gold, and the three rings of Zar-Ghosa, silver on blue. The emblems of two cities, once bitter enemies that had warred for centuries, now fluttering side by side in the breeze. *It's almost enough to stir the blood,* Lukan thought, *if it wasn't all about to go to shit.* Five white horses sporting black plumes followed behind, drawing a golden carriage that was heavy on the gilding and light on good taste.

"The Grand Duke of Saphrona," Ashra commented, as Lukan squinted at the old man who sat hunched against the cushioned seat. His impressive mustache twirled upward even as the rest of his face slumped in the opposite direction, and he waved to the crowd with all the enthusiasm of a man who feared his hand might snap off at any moment. Nonetheless, a great cheer rolled across the plaza as the carriage progressed down the central avenue, both lines of constables struggling to hold back the excitable crowds.

"Seems the Duke's a popular man," Lukan observed.

"The Duke's a pampered old fool," Ashra replied. "The cheers are for his wife, Duchess Catalina."

"That's his *wife*?" Lukan stared at the young woman sitting beside the Duke, smiling as she waved to the crowds. "She looks young enough to be his granddaughter."

"Great-granddaughter, you mean. She just turned nineteen. The sun apparently shines out of her perfect arse, but you probably can't see that from here."

"Seems the crowd can."

"They adore her for her charitable donations. The fact it's not her own money apparently doesn't matter."

"Who are the men riding behind?" Lukan asked, eyeing the two figures who rode in a second, less impressive, carriage.

Both wore high-collared black tunics of fine cut, the sleeves slashed with gold. With the same dark hair, jutting chins, and aquiline noses, they looked identical, yet their expressions couldn't have been more different. The man on the left side of the carriage smiled and nodded at the crowd, while his twin wore a look halfway between a grimace and a scowl.

"The Duke's sons, Gaspar and Lorenzo. Gaspar is the heir, on account of being born a few moments before his brother. Lorenzo has spent most of his life trying to come to terms with that fact."

"And not succeeding, by the looks of it." Lukan watched as Lorenzo threw a dark look at his brother, lips curling up into a pout more suited to a spoiled child than a nobleman. "No love lost there, it seems."

"Not much. They've been feuding for years. They hate each other, but not quite as much as they hate their new stepmother."

"I'll bet. No wonder Lorenzo is pissed off, missing out on a dukedom and then being saddled with a stepmother half his age."

"Yes, it must be so hard being the second son of one of the richest families in the Old Empire."

A small man rode behind the brothers, looking mildly panicked as he struggled to sit upright in his saddle. A golden medallion slapped against his purple robes with every step his horse took. "Who's that?" Lukan asked.

"Artemio, the Lord Chancellor."

"I hope he's better at counting coins than riding horses."

"I've heard he's a decent man," Ashra said, a note of grudging respect in her voice. "The two new hospices that recently opened in the Splinters were apparently his doing."

"A decent man," Lukan echoed, eyes narrowing. "That's certainly not something you'd say of the man riding behind him."

"Prime Inquisitor Fierro." Ashra's tone hardened. "No, it's not."

"He's certainly handling his nerves better than the Pontifex."

Fierro didn't wear the look of a man who was unnerved by the ambassador's impending murder, or his own part in it. He sat ramrod straight in his saddle, face impassive, cigarillo clenched between the hard line of his lips. *Cold bastard, that one.*

"Look at that!" Flea cried.

At first Lukan couldn't see where she was pointing, his gaze sweeping over the pack of attendants, officials, and hangers-on that marched on foot behind the ducal party. They moved in three ordered columns, which disintegrated toward the rear as the people at the back jostled for space, pressing forward even as they glanced nervously over their shoulders.

Lukan's eyes widened. *I don't blame them.*

Two large crimson-scaled lizards followed just a few yards behind, padding forward on their hind legs. Wicked talons crushed the rose petals that lay strewn across the ground, before whiplike tails swept them aside. The beasts' angular heads snapped left and right as their yellow eyes took in the crowds, jaws widening to reveal rows of sharp teeth. Their claws, held before them, twitched as if in anticipation of blood. *No doubt they'd have it,* Lukan mused, *if it wasn't for their riders.* They sat in high-backed saddles, tugging sharply on the reins whenever their mounts took too close an interest in the lines of guards and the crowds beyond. They were no less intimidating than the beasts they rode, adorned in armor of burnished copper scales, their faces concealed by spiked bronzed helmets. Both carried long spears, dark blue feathers pinned just below their triangular points.

"Scaleriders," Lukan said, dredging the name from the depths of his mind. "The elite cavalry of Zar-Ghosa. I forget what the lizards are called, but they're captured as hatchlings and then paired with a rider for life. Apparently they share a special bond and each lizard can only be ridden by its own rider. Some sort of sorcery . . ." He trailed off when he realized that Ashra and Flea were both staring at him.

"How do you know that?" Ashra asked.

"I traveled briefly with a man from Zar-Ghosa. He told me a little about his homeland. He had some good stories, but was a lousy cardplayer."

"Lukan," Flea said, her eyes wide as she pointed again, "what are *those*?"

This time he had no answer—his erstwhile Zar-Ghosan companion hadn't spoken of an animal that might have passed for a pony were it not for the vibrant black and yellow stripes that covered its hide. There were four of the beasts, their powerful muscles rippling as they pulled a large blue chariot, its sides adorned with carved silver wings.

"I have no idea," he replied, his gaze moving to the figure who stood atop the chariot, "but that can only be the Zar-Ghosan ambassador." *She's certainly dressed for the occasion, even if it's not the one she's expecting.*

The ambassador cut a striking figure in pale blue robes embroidered with silver, a shawl of darker blue draped across her chest and right shoulder. Silver also gleamed from the small discs woven into her braided hair, the rings in her ears, and the bracelets on her wrists. Her diadem—also made from silver—was studded with sapphires that flashed in the sun as she waved to the crowds, wearing the smile of a woman who was finally realizing a lifetime's ambition. *If only she knew,* Lukan thought. *If only we'd somehow found a way to get word to her.* The ambassador was flanked by grim-faced guards, while several well-dressed attendants rode behind on a selection of dusky-colored horses. They were followed by three ranks of soldiers, ten to a row, breastplates shining as they marched in perfect unison.

"If they fight as well as they look," Ashra said, "perhaps the ambassador might yet have a chance."

"Not against the Faceless she won't."

"There's Marquetta," Flea said, pointing again. "The arrogant prick." Lukan and Ashra both looked at her. "What?" She shrugged.

"Nothing," Lukan replied, hiding his smile as he turned his gaze to where Saphrona's merchant princes rode behind the Zar-Ghosan delegation in a swirl of colorful silks and glittering jewelry. Their personal guards walked alongside them, armor buffed to a sheen. Lord Marquetta led the contingent of Saphrona's elite citizens from the back of a dappled grey mare, nodding and waving at the crowds, as if the swelling noise were all for him. Six other riders made up his entourage—the rest of the Silken Septet, Lukan guessed, noting Lord Murillo among them. The lesser merchant princes formed their own contingent a short distance behind their more illustrious peers, though they looked no less resplendent—save for a solitary rider at the back.

"Is that . . ." Lukan squinted at the large figure. "Lady's mercy, it *is* him."

"Who?" Ashra asked.

"General Leopold Razin, the big fellow in the fur cloak. Face as red as a smacked arse."

"Friend of yours?"

"We had a brief chat at Lady Valdezar's gala. He tried to bore me to death with his war stories but I escaped." Lukan squinted again. "Is he riding a *donkey*?"

"Crushing it, more like."

"Razin mentioned being involved in a massacre," Lukan said, vaguely recalling the general's words. "Looks like he's going to witness another."

"How do you think they'll do it?" Ashra asked.

"Hmm?"

"The Faceless. How are they going to murder the ambassador?"

"I don't know. We'll see soon enough."

The head of the procession eventually arrived at the steps leading up to the Lady's House. A detachment of constables saluted as the Grand Duke and his young wife stepped down from their carriage. The old man waved away his wife's offer of help, only to stumble against her and end up with his face buried in her cleavage. A ripple of laughter passed through the crowd, followed by a few cheers. The Grand Duke laughed the episode off and strode forward with renewed vigor, only to hesitate at the first step, which took him a good few moments—and the arm of his blushing wife—to climb.

"Lady's mercy," Lukan muttered, as the old man took a similar amount of time to mount the subsequent step. "We'll be here all bloody afternoon at this rate. Hopefully the Faceless charge by the hour and end up costing Marquetta a lot more than just the Sandino Blade."

"What's so special about the blade?" Ashra asked. "I heard it was just an old ceremonial dagger. What do the Faceless want with it?"

"I've been wondering the same thing," Lukan admitted, watching as the Grand Duke reached the fourth step. "The truth is we just don't know much about them. The few historical accounts we have are vague and fragmented. But there's one detail they all agree on."

"What's that?"

"Crystals."

Ashra gave him a blank look.

"Every time the Faceless have appeared across the centuries," Lukan continued, "their appearance has followed the discovery of a certain crystal."

"What sort of crystal?"

"All the records say is that they're purplish black in color. Beyond that, we don't know. My father believed they must have possessed some sort of sorcerous power, or held special meaning for the Faceless." He shrugged. "Whatever the truth, the pattern's always been the same. A crystal is discovered and the Faceless arrive to trade for it."

"They *trade* for it? Trade what?"

"Whatever the owner of the crystal wants. It's said they once paid a fortune to a farmer who dug one up in his field. The man ended up richer than a duke."

"But if the Faceless are as powerful as you say," Ashra replied, her voice edged with doubt, "surely they could just take these crystals by force? Why bother trading for them?"

"Who knows. From what the records tell us, the Faceless only ever use force when provoked into confrontation. That's only happened twice and it didn't end well for the folks who threatened them."

"But they used force against you. That wolf in the catacombs."

"True, but that was at Marquetta's request. He's struck a deal with them—he's promised them the Sandino Blade in return for doing his dirty work. He has no need of coin or riches—"

"So he asked them to commit murders for him instead."

"Right. And in return, he'll give them the Sandino Blade."

"But why do they want the blade?" Flea asked. "That's not a crystal."

"It's not," Lukan agreed, "but they must have their reasons."

"It makes some sort of sense," Ashra admitted. "Not that any of this helps us."

"Probably not," Lukan replied. *Then again . . .* A thought sparked in his mind. *What if . . . what if we somehow—*

An excited murmur passed through the crowd, drawing him from his thoughts. The Grand Duke had nearly reached the top of the steps, his two sons close behind, but the ducal party's slow progress had caused a bottleneck behind them, and what had been an orderly procession was slowly collapsing into a confused mess. Officials and delegates shouted and jostled, horses snorted and stamped, and the constables at the foot of the steps did their best to maintain order as insults flew in all directions. As the Zar-Ghosan delegation pressed in from behind, one of the lizards—perhaps excited by the tumult—sank its fangs into the horse ridden by the Lord Chancellor, Artemio. The horse reared, throwing the Lord Chancellor to the ground, before bolting back down the avenue. Several constables ran over, two attending to the fallen man as the others bellowed something at the lizard's rider, who regarded them silently from the creature's back. Suddenly some of the ambassador's guards arrived, and the two sides engaged in a furious round of shouting and gesticulating, the stricken Lord Chancellor lying dazed at their feet.

"I thought this was meant to be a display of unity," Lukan said dryly, as one of the constables half drew his sword, only for a comrade to push it back into its scabbard. The Grand Duke, meanwhile, had finally reached the top of the steps. The old man raised a trembling hand to the crowd and gave a triumphant wave, seemingly oblivious to the chaos he'd caused behind him. As he hobbled over to where the Pontifex stood, the Grand Duke's retinue was able to climb the steps freely, the clamor and heightened tempers slowly dissipating. Even so, it took some time for the entire procession to form up before the huge doors of the Lady's House. Eventually everyone was in position, though tempers had flared again between several minor functionaries who were packed in around the edges, leading to a couple of embarrassing shoving matches.

A hush fell over the crowd as the Pontifex finally raised his hands, and the knot of anxiety that had been sitting in the pit of Lukan's stomach forced its way into his throat. *This is it.* A glance at Flea revealed similar nerves; the girl's amusement had faded, leaving a solemn expression in its wake—a look that didn't seem right on her young face. Ashra showed no such nerves, her features unreadable as she watched the spectacle below. They listened in silence—along with the entire crowd—as the Pontifex began to speak.

". . . witness this . . . momentous day . . . two great cities . . . in friendship . . ."

"I can't hear what he's saying," Flea complained.

"Doesn't matter," Lukan replied. "It's about to become irrelevant."

The speech continued, only snatches of it reaching them up in the bell tower. Lukan concentrated instead on the dignitaries gathered before the huge doors, searching for any sign of trouble. He saw nothing; the only daggers in sight were the metaphorical ones wielded in the glares of the Grand Duke's sons, as they conducted a furious whispered argument. *We're not seeing the full picture,* Juro had said, and, while he'd been referring to Marquetta's motives for the ambassador's murder, the same could be said of the way the Faceless intended to carry it out. Perhaps they would summon a spectral wolf to tear her apart, or deploy the same method they'd used on Lord Saviola—whatever *that* was—and reduce the ambassador to an ice-coated, blue-lipped corpse. *No,* Lukan thought, *both would raise far too many questions. Marquetta will want something subtle.*

A sudden movement drew his eye—a young man in ceremonial robes was approaching the Pontifex, arms held before him, a shaft resting across the palms of his upturned hands. *The Silver Spear,* Lukan realized, as the weapon's sharp head caught the sunlight. Ribbons fluttered from the shaft in the black and gold of Saphrona and the blue and silver of Zar-Ghosa. The official presented the Phaeron artifact to the Pontifex with a stiff bow. The older man took the spear and held it aloft as he faced the crowd, his face shiny with sweat.

"Behold . . . symbol of unity . . . renew our friendship . . ." Lukan didn't catch the rest of the man's words, but the crowd seemed to appreciate them; a huge roar rolled across the plaza. On another day, this might have been the Pontifex's personal moment of glory. As it was, he forced a pained smile, arm trembling as he held the spear high. *Guilt weighs heavily, doesn't it?* Lukan thought. *I should know.*

The Pontifex lowered the spear and nodded in the direction of the Grand Duke, but if that was an invitation for Saphrona's ruler to step forward it passed unnoticed; the old man remained where he was, idly twirling one end of his mustache. The Lord Chancellor, Artemio—who appeared to have escaped the fall from his horse without serious injury—was forced to whisper in his master's ear. The Grand Duke stiffened and strode toward the Pontifex with what little vigor he had left, which wasn't much judging by how heavily he leaned on his two sons. *Better hold him tightly, boys, lest he topples over and impales himself on that spear.*

The Pontifex bowed deeply as the three men took up position before him, then glanced to where the ambassador stood. This time his nod received an immediate response as the ambassador approached, two of her personal guards shadowing her. *She could have a hundred of them and it wouldn't be enough.* The Pontifex bowed to the Zar-Ghosan—though not as deeply, and he didn't make eye contact. *Hard to look a dead woman in the eyes, isn't it?*

"Now we . . . now we renew . . ." Whether he'd lost his voice from all the shouting, or he was choking on his own hypocrisy, Lukan couldn't be sure, but the Pontifex grimaced and gestured to the official who had handed him the spear. With a fleeting look of panic, the young man turned to the crowd. "Now we renew our ties of friendship," he called, his stronger voice echoing across the plaza. "Our two great cities, joined together for another decade of peace and prosperity, divided by the sea but united in friendship."

As the crowd roared its approval, the Grand Duke stumbled forward like a toddler taking their first steps. He accepted the spear from the Pontifex (who quickly stepped back, as if worried he might lose an eye) and, with as much of a flourish as he could manage, presented the weapon to the ambassador. The Zar-Ghosan accepted the spear with a wide smile—which suddenly turned to a frown. She shuddered, then slumped, her body sagging yet somehow remaining upright, like a puppet hanging slack in its strings.

"This is it," Lukan said, anxiety squeezing him as whispers swept through the crowd. "She'll be dead before she hits the ground."

But the ambassador didn't fall. She shuddered again, then

straightened—as if reinvigorated by an unseen energy. Her frown faded, but her smile didn't return. Instead her features remained blank as she met the Grand Duke's gaze.

And thrust the tip of the spear into the old man's throat.

Silence reigned for a few heartbeats, followed by a collective intake of breath from the crowd as the Grand Duke exhaled his own in a splutter of blood.

"What in the hells . . ." Lukan murmured, staring in disbelief as the old man staggered backward and collapsed to the ground. The Grand Duke's two sons gaped at their father, their shock quickly followed by fury. They both stepped forward, hands that had never drawn a sword in anger making up for that now as they drew their blades—and froze, weapons raised, their bodies twitching even as they remained still, the fury in their expressions changing to confusion, then fear. Other people were rushing forward—guards from both delegations, officials, even a couple of the merchant princes.

Too late.

"Lady's mercy," Lukan whispered as the ambassador stepped over the Grand Duke's body and—with two swift thrusts— opened the throats of his two sons. The men's mouths widened in silent screams as blood gushed from their wounds. They stood still as statues for another few heartbeats and then collapsed at the same time, falling against each other, limbs tangling in an embrace the likes of which they'd never managed in life. As Gaspar and Lorenzo slumped beside their father's corpse, a stunned silence fell across the entire plaza. The figures rushing to help all hesitated, disbelieving eyes flicking between the three bodies and the woman who stood over them, bloody spear still clutched in her hands. The ambassador jolted, as if waking from a daydream, and glanced around in apparent confusion. Her eyes widened at what she saw. She stared open-mouthed at the corpses lying at her feet, then at the bloody spear in her hands. The weapon fell from her fingers, clattering on the stones as she put a hand to her mouth, her face ashen.

No one moved for several heartbeats.

Then the ambassador's guards formed a protective ring around her as the Grand Duke's retinue surged toward them. Swords flashed in the sunlight as both sides squared up, bellowing at each other even as the Lord Chancellor waved his hands and pleaded for calm. The Pontifex, in his haste to escape the impending violence, almost tripped over the young duchess, who had fainted and was now surrounded by panic-stricken attendants. Officials who had earlier been jostling for position now pushed and shoved each other in their haste to escape. Amid the unfolding chaos, Lukan caught sight of Marquetta. The man stood still as his fellow princes fled. Lukan could have sworn he was smiling. *He doesn't just mean to start a war,* he realized, his fingers whitening as he gripped the balcony's edge. *This is a damned coup.* A roar of fury rose from ten thousand throats as the crowd finally found its voice. The two lines of guards holding it back suddenly seemed very thin indeed.

"Marquetta's seizing power," Ashra said calmly, looking sidelong at Lukan. "That's what this is all about. He wants to rule Saphrona."

"I know."

"You said he was going to murder the *ambassador,* not the Grand Duke and his sons."

"I *know.*" Lukan watched as the Duke's retinue and the ambassador's guards continued to shout at each other. Below them in the plaza, the crowd surged and the two lines of guards buckled and then broke. Citizens spilled onto the central avenue, running toward the steps to the Lady's House like hounds baying for blood.

"It's all falling apart," Ashra said, shaking her head. "This is going to turn into a bloodbath."

Lukan barely heard her as his mind reeled with the enormity of what had just happened. *Lady's mercy, I was wrong. I was so, so wrong.* Feeling numb, he turned away from the unfolding chaos and headed for the stairs.

"Lukan," Flea called after him, a note of fear in her voice he'd never heard before. "Where are you going?"

"To get a bloody drink."

"Now is hardly the time—" Ashra started.

"Now is *exactly* the time," he retorted, rounding on her. "It's over. Finished." He slashed at the air with his open hand. "I'm done."

He turned and stormed from the room.

33

AGREEABLE COMPANY

Should never have come to this damned city.

Lukan took a swallow of wine and winced as the events he'd just witnessed flashed through his mind again and again. The ambassador's body shaking as she was possessed—*is that really what happened?*—by the Faceless. The tip of the spear puncturing the Grand Duke's throat. Blood. The Duke's sons stepping forward, swords drawn, only to freeze. *Held by an invisible force.* The point of the spear—the symbol of peace—flickering once, twice. The twins tumbling, bloody wounds in their throats and shock on their faces. The ambassador dropping the spear and staring, stupefied, at the horror she'd wrought.

Lady's mercy, he thought, taking another drink. *Definitely should never have come here.*

Just as the afternoon's events had revealed the truth of Marquetta's plans with shocking clarity, so too had they revealed the hopelessness of Lukan's own actions. To think that he'd strolled into Saphrona believing that the answers he sought were just a whisper or two away. That—as events grew increasingly out of hand—he could somehow foil Marquetta's grand design and free Zandrusa. How foolish those beliefs seemed now. *I'm sorry, Father,* he thought, raising his clay mug. *I did my best—Lady knows I did—but it wasn't enough. It was never going to be enough.* The cup jolted as it touched his lips, spilling wine across the tabletop and shaking him from his thoughts. Ashra sat across from him, her right hand gripping his wrist as she regarded him with narrowed eyes.

"Tell me what happened back there," she said.

"I already told you," he replied wearily, "I don't know."

"But you were in the catacombs. You said—"

"I know what I said," Lukan cut in, anger coiling like a snake. He looked down at the table, recalling again what he'd overheard. "Marquetta said they would strike as planned at the ceremony. The Prime Inquisitor mentioned the ambassador, to which the Pontifex asked how they would commit a murder in front of the whole city." He shrugged. "How was I to know they were referring to the ambassador as the tool, rather than the victim?"

"But what actually *happened*?" Ashra demanded. "The ambassador wasn't in control of her own body. It was like she was drugged, or—"

"They possessed her," Lukan said flatly, recalling the woman's stiff, erratic movements. "The Faceless somehow took control of her body, her very mind. They *made* her do those things."

"But . . . is that even possible?"

"They can travel through portals and summon sorcerous wolves. At this point I'd consider them capable of anything." Lukan nodded at Ashra's hand. "If you don't mind?"

The thief released her hold on his wrist. "So Marquetta has the Faceless murder the Grand Duke and his sons. That leaves Saphrona without a ruler. And with the support of the Pontifex and the Prime Inquisitor—"

"Marquetta can use his influence on the Gilded Council to proclaim himself lord regent, or king, or whatever the hells he wants." Lukan took a swallow of wine, grimacing at the sour taste. "That must be why he murdered Lord Saviola and framed Zandrusa for the crime. He wanted them out of the way."

"Because they would oppose him."

"Exactly. Zandrusa told me herself that she and Saviola were leading a new faction that was starting to gain power on the council. A group of merchant princes that opposed the old traditions and were dedicated to reform. No doubt Marquetta feared they would make things difficult for him."

"So he did away with them." Ashra's lips thinned. "All this murder and scheming, just to satisfy one man's lust for power."

"A tale as old as time. Anyway, it's done now." *And so am I.* Lukan swallowed the rest of his wine and glanced at the bar. *Wonder if there's any gin.* He would have to find it himself; the barkeep had left moments after they'd arrived at the small backstreet tavern. *Celebrations given you a thirst?* the man had asked with a smile as they'd entered. *No,* Lukan had replied, *it was the murder of the Grand Duke and his two sons that did that.* The man's smile had wilted when he'd realized Lukan wasn't joking. Without another word he'd thrown off his apron and disappeared out of the door, leaving his tavern in Lukan's care. *Which suits me just fine.* He stepped behind the bar and eyed the dusty bottles. *There's got to be some gin somewhere . . .*

"Flea should be back by now," Ashra remarked. "She only went to buy an apple."

"*Steal* an apple, you mean." He picked out a bottle, grimaced, and put it back. "I'm sure she's fine, probably talking someone's ear off—"

"What are you doing?"

"What does it look like? Getting another drink."

"Haven't you had enough already?"

"No."

The thief's chair squeaked across the floor as she rose and stalked after him. "We don't have time to waste. We need to plan our next steps."

"I've already got a plan," he replied, nodding at the bottles. He picked one out and examined the label. *Deladrian dandelion wine. Lady's mercy, I'd rather drink a glass of piss.*

"Getting drunk is not going to help us stop Marquetta."

"It's over," Lukan replied, turning to face her. "It's done. Finished. Can't you see that? Marquetta has won. Going up against him now would be like spitting into the face of a storm. Juro was right—we weren't seeing the full picture. Now we are, and it's beyond anything we could have imagined. You can cook up whatever plan you want. Mine is to get drunk and then get the hells out of here. I should never have come here in the first place."

"So that's it? After everything you've done, you're going to walk away?"

"I came to Saphrona to find answers about my father's death. I wasn't counting on getting caught up in a damned conspiracy, or being imprisoned by a crime lord, or being chased by a bloody sorcerous wolf set loose by the *Faceless* . . ." He laughed, shook his head in bewilderment. It all sounded so ludicrous when spoken out loud. *And somehow I'm still alive.* That was perhaps the most surprising thing of all. "Alphonse was right," he added wearily. "He told me to leave the city. I should have listened."

"'Phonse always thinks he knows best. But he doesn't. Not always."

"Well, he was right about this." Lukan turned back to the array of bottles. "Now, if you'll excuse me, I need to find some more . . . agreeable company."

"Seeking solace at the bottom of a bottle," Ashra replied derisively. "I hadn't figured you for a coward."

Lukan tensed, jaw tightening as her last word struck him like a blow, a sharp-edged memory stealing into his mind: the blue spring sky above, the bloodstained cherry blossoms below, Amicia's face between the two. Her eyes wide with shock as she spoke the two words that had haunted him ever since. *You coward.*

The old fury rose inside him.

Lukan spun and hurled the bottle of dandelion wine against a wall. Ashra didn't flinch as it shattered, nor did she back away as Lukan stormed toward her. "I am many things," he said, voice tight with fury. "A disappointment. A failure. Some even call me a murderer, which is a weight I'll always have to bear. But one thing I am *not*"—he stabbed the air with a finger—"is a bloody coward."

Ashra remained silent, green eyes holding his gaze.

"Bad time?" a voice inquired from the doorway.

Lukan glanced over, ready to deliver a sharp retort, only for the words to die on his tongue as he saw Delphina Delastro standing in the tavern's doorway. She was flanked by two of her crew, but it was the small figure standing before her that made Lukan's heart lurch. *Lady's blood* . . . Flea appeared unharmed, the anger in her eyes tempered by the point of Delastro's dagger as it hovered before her throat. Lukan reached for his own blade; the two women flanking Delastro raised small crossbows in response.

"If I wanted you dead," the mercenary leader said, "I'd have shot you both during your little lovers' tiff."

"We're not lovers," Ashra replied, shooting Lukan a sour look that disguised the question glinting in her eyes. *What now?* A question to which Lukan had no answer.

"I'm glad to hear it," Delastro continued in her throaty Talassian accent. "A woman of your talents could do so much better. Yes, I know of you, Lady Midnight. One doesn't have to scratch too deeply beneath the surface of this city to hear your name mentioned."

"You know nothing of me. Who are you, anyway?"

"My name is Delphina Delastro."

"Diamond," Ashra said, her expression darkening. "Marquetta's puppet."

"I am my own woman," Delastro replied curtly. "And from what I've heard, so are you. Which is why I struggle to understand why you've thrown your lot in with this one." She thrust her chin at Lukan. "Especially when you've already got the entire underworld searching for you. I understand the Twice-Crowned King's put quite the price on your head."

"It should be you they're looking for," Ashra shot back. "You're the one who stole the Sandino Blade."

"Yes, I heard you took the fall for our little piece of larceny. I'd apologize, but . . ." Delastro shrugged. "It all worked out rather well for us. Drawing the ire of the King was the last thing Lord Marquetta wanted."

"I should take your head and clear my name."

"You're welcome to try." Delastro's mouth twitched in amusement. "I've heard you're good, but can you throw a blade faster than my two Jewels here can pull their triggers?"

"Maybe not," Ashra replied, drawing a knife from her belt, "but it doesn't matter. I'd rather die than go back to that cell."

"You can put your knife away, Lady Midnight," Delastro replied, smiling thinly. "I've no intention of handing you over to the Twice-Crowned King." Her gaze flicked to Lukan. "Nor you, Gardova. Strange as it might seem, I mean neither of you any harm."

"And yet," Lukan replied, "I find myself staring at two loaded crossbows while you hold a blade to my friend's throat."

"I am first and foremost a woman of business, Master Gardova. I learned a long time ago that the first rule of negotiation is to ensure you have the upper hand. Still, if it will help convince you I come in good faith . . ." She lowered her dagger and gave Flea a shove, sending the girl stumbling forward. Lukan stooped and caught her as she fell.

"You old witch!" Flea snarled, struggling against Lukan's grip as she tried to throw herself at Delastro. He had half a mind to let her go; even the Faceless would shrink from Flea when she was in this sort of mood. Instead, he held her close.

"Cool it," he whispered as she continued to struggle, his relief countered by the two crossbows that were still trained on them. *Clearly Delastro's not willing to give up all her advantages.* Still, the fact that the mercenary leader was willing to release Flea gave him hope that there might be a way out of this encounter that didn't end with him and Ashra being dragged to Marquetta in chains. *Best tread carefully.*

"Let go of me," Flea muttered, falling still. Lukan reluctantly obliged, half expecting the girl to lunge at Delastro, but instead she contented herself with making an obscene gesture. Delastro ignored her, eyes on Lukan. "Does you master know you're here?" he asked her, holding her gaze.

"Lord Marquetta is my client, not my master. And no, he does not. This meeting is none of his concern."

"Even if it involves his enemy?"

"Enemy?" The woman snorted. "You think too highly of yourself,

Gardova. You're nothing more than a loose end that Marquetta would like tidied up."

"Then why haven't you put a bolt in me?"

"Believe me, I'd like nothing more. I lost one of my Jewels in the catacombs thanks to your intrusion."

"Blame the Faceless. It was their wolf who killed him, not me. How's Amethyst anyway?"

"Looking forward to seeing you again."

"I do have my charms."

"So she can stick a blade in your belly."

"Ah. Well, sounds like she recovered from that blow to the head, at least. And the bolt in her leg."

"Amethyst's in good health, all things considered." Delastro's eyes narrowed. "I wonder if the same can be said of Topaz. I do hope you've not mistreated him."

Lady's blood, Lukan thought, recalling the man he'd fought as the Scrivener's house burned. The man whom Juro had extracted information from at the point of a blade, or a burning iron, or however the hells he had done it. *I'd forgotten about him. I don't even know if he's still alive.* "Why do you think we have Topaz?"

"Because no bodies were found in that house once the fire was put out. And an eyewitness saw a man and a child dragging someone— a man, they think—away into the night. My guess is you interrogated Topaz and extracted information from him, which is how you knew about Marquetta's midnight visit to the catacombs. Am I wrong?"

"No."

"Pity," the woman said, lip curling. "I thought I'd taught Topaz better than that."

"You didn't tell Marquetta about him, did you?" Lukan asked. "He would have called off his meeting with the Faceless if he thought his plan was compromised."

"I trusted Topaz to keep his silence." Delastro's lips thinned. "And if he didn't, I trusted my other Jewels to deal with you, should you make an appearance."

"Seems your trust was misplaced," Lukan replied, grinning.

"Where is he?" Delastro asked, ignoring the barb. "Where are you keeping Topaz?"

"I don't know."

"Don't play games with me."

"I'm not," Lukan said truthfully. "Some . . . friends of ours are looking after him. I'm not sure where."

"So he lives? Because if he doesn't . . ." She gestured at the two crossbows.

"He lives," Lukan replied. *I hope.*

"Then name your price for his safe return."

"My price . . . as in coin, you mean?"

"What else?"

Lukan took a breath, his mind racing through the different possibilities—whether Topaz was alive or dead, whether the Scrivener would willingly give him up, how much of the coin she might demand in return—

"Three ducats," Delastro said, sighing as if already bored of the conversation. "How does that sound?"

Three ducats. Even if the Scrivener demanded half, he'd still have more than enough to travel wherever he wanted, leave all this chaos and conspiracy behind him. *I could take a ship to Zar-Ghosa, or one of the ports of the Mourning Sea.* Yet even as he indulged the notion, it faded as a new idea rose in his mind. A realization that maybe, despite everything he'd said to Ashra, there was a way they could stop Marquetta after all. *I should just walk away,* he thought, a wry smile touching his lips. *Just take the money and run.* But he couldn't. Not when there was a chance.

"I don't want coin," he said, meeting Delastro's gaze.

"Then what do you want?"

"The Sandino Blade."

Delastro didn't so much as blink.

"We know Marquetta has it," Lukan continued, "and that he plans to give it to the Faceless as payment for the murders they've committed in his name."

"Maybe he's already given it to them."

"Has he?" Lukan smiled as the mercenary leader remained silent. "I'll hand over Topaz if you give me the Sandino Blade."

"To what end?" Delastro asked, with a flicker of irritation. "Do you honestly think you can stop what Marquetta has set in motion? This city will soon tear itself apart. Let me give you some advice: Take the gold and get the hells out of Saphrona. You are powerless to prevent what is coming."

"Not if you give me the one thing the Faceless want."

"You would put yourself between the Faceless and the object they desire? Don't be a fool, Gardova. They are not to be trifled with. You saw what they unleashed in the catacombs, what they just did to the Grand Duke and his sons—"

"Their blood is on your hands as well."

"I knew nothing of this," Delastro snapped. "I was as surprised as anyone when the Faceless stepped through that portal in the catacombs. If I'd known . . ." She trailed off, jaw tightening. "If I'd known," she continued, more calmly, "I'd never have signed on for this job. I had no idea what forces Marquetta was messing with, or what he wanted that old blade for."

"Yet you stole it anyway. And without the blade, none of this would have happened. Saviola would still be alive. Jelassi wouldn't be in the Ebon Hand." Lukan gestured to Ashra. "Lady Midnight wouldn't be a pariah."

"What's done is done."

"You knew that Marquetta planned to murder the Grand Duke," Lukan continued, his voice rising. "You knew he planned to seize control of the city. You *knew* and yet you still—" He flinched as a crossbow bolt flew past his face, shattering a bottle on the bar behind him.

"The next bolt goes in your throat," Delastro warned.

"Kill me and you'll never get Topaz back."

"Then tell me what you want so we can come to a more amicable arrangement. How about five ducats?"

"I already told you. I want the Sandino Blade."

"Remarkable," Delastro said, shaking her head. "Not content with making enemies of the three most powerful men in the city, not to mention the Twice-Crowned King, you're now intent on crossing the Faceless. How far do you intend to push your luck, Gardova?"

"As far as I have to." *Which is likely to be a damned long way.*

"This will be the death of you."

"Maybe. Give me the blade and we'll find out."

"I can't."

"Can't or won't?"

The mercenary leader looked away, lips pursed, as she considered her answer. *Probably weighing up how much of the truth to tell.* "Marquetta has it under lock and key," she said eventually.

"Where?"

"Somewhere you'll never get hold of it."

"You forget," Lukan said, gesturing at Ashra, "I have the best thief in the city on my side."

"She could be the best thief in the known world and it wouldn't make a difference," Delastro replied. "No one is good enough to break into the vault at the Three Moons Counting House. Not even her."

Ashra's expression remained impassive, but Lukan caught the flash in her eyes. *Doubt.* "Ashra?" he prompted.

"She's right," the thief replied, wincing as if the words tasted bitter. "That's where all the merchant princes keep their wealth. The place is like a fortress, guards everywhere. The vault is said to be protected by some sort of alchemical device, with a door of solid oak banded with iron. Not even I could get in there."

"You see, Gardova?" Delastro said, a note of satisfaction in her voice. "This is a fool's errand—"

"The Faceless," Lukan interrupted, a thought striking him. "Marquetta promised them the blade, but he won't be able to hand it over to them at the counting house—mythical beings appearing out of a portal would raise more than a few eyebrows."

"He'll want to hand the blade over somewhere private," Ashra said, following his line of thought. "Which means he'll need to move it from the vault."

"And if the murder of the Grand Duke and his sons was the final part of their agreement," Lukan continued, "then it's likely to be soon. He won't want to keep the Faceless waiting. They won't stand for it." He looked at Delastro. "Do you know what Marquetta intends?"

"You're wasting your time, Gardova."

Lukan grinned. "That sounds like a yes to me."

"I've never broken a contract or betrayed a client's trust," Delastro replied, an edge returning to her tone. "*Never*. And I'm not going to start now."

"Not even to get Topaz back?"

"I came here to strike a deal. I could have used the girl as a bargaining chip but I released her to show my good faith. I made you a generous offer and all I get in return is your childish belligerence. My patience is wearing thin."

"To be fair, you're the one making demands at the point of a crossbow—"

"Enough!" As the mercenary's face darkened, Lukan thought he'd pushed her too far. He tensed, heart racing, expecting to hear the twang of a crossbow. Instead the woman merely glared at him, but if looks could kill he would have been dead several times over. "I should just put you down and be done with it."

"If you do that you won't get your son back," Flea shouted.

Everyone in the room looked at her.

"Flea," Lukan warned, raising a hand, "just keep quiet—"

"No, don't you see?" the girl demanded, twisting away from Ashra as the thief tried to cover her mouth. "They look the same! They have the same nose and the same pointy chin."

Lukan looked at Delastro, taking in her sharp features and the small scars that were the marks of her profession. He tried to picture Topaz's face, but couldn't recall much beyond an impression of olive skin and dark hair—those, at least, he shared with the mercenary leader, but it was hardly enough to mark them as blood. Delastro, meanwhile, was staring at Flea as if she regretted removing her blade from the girl's throat. Then—as the silence stretched—the woman broke the tension in the most surprising way: she smiled.

"You have sharp eyes, girl," she said, with the faintest trace of amusement. "But you're wrong—Topaz is my nephew, not my son. My profession never lent itself to motherhood." She sighed, as if suddenly weary of the confrontation, and just for a moment Lukan caught a fleeting glimpse of a different woman altogether— someone who had seen too much of a world that had lost its luster some time ago. "The things we do for family, no?"

"Tell me about it," Lukan replied. "Help me get hold of the Sandino Blade and you can have your nephew back."

"Thirty years," Delastro murmured, lips forming a thin line. "Thirty years without ever betraying an employer's trust. I've based my entire reputation on that fact. Now it'll be in ruins. Nothing but dust."

"Is that such a high price to pay for a life?"

"I suppose not. Not when it's blood. But it hurts all the same." She sheathed her blade and took a seat at the table. "Fetch me a drink."

Lukan grinned. "What's your poison?"

"Something rough enough to wash away the bad taste in my mouth."

"Let's see . . ." Lukan pulled the cork from an unmarked bottle and took a sniff. "Hells, this smells like it could wash away pretty much anything." He poured two glasses. "Ashra?" The thief shook her head, her eyes not leaving the two women, who still held their crossbows ready.

"I'll have one," Flea said.

"No you won't." Lukan returned to the table and took a seat opposite Delastro. He pushed her glass across the table and raised his own. "To your health." He grinned again. "That's not something I expected to say when you appeared in the doorway."

"I'd return the favor," the woman replied, mouth twitching

into a grimace, "but I still have half a mind to put a bolt in you once this is all over."

"So much for coming in good faith."

"Enough," Delastro replied, scowling as she raised her glass. "Let's get on with this sordid business. I'll help you obtain the Sandino Blade. In return you'll give Topaz to me—alive and unharmed. Deal?"

"Deal." *If he still lives. And if the Scrivener is willing to hand him over.*

The mercenary held his gaze, searching for any sign of a lie. "Fine," she said eventually, knocking back the liquor in one swallow. "Marquetta's moving the blade tonight. He's having it transported to the ducal palace by carriage, with my own crew providing the escort."

"So you'll have the blade in your possession?"

"Yes, but I can't just hand it over. Marquetta keeps the blade in a Phaeron chest that can only be opened with the right code."

"Which I suppose he didn't share with you."

"His trust in me didn't extend that far."

"Then we'll just take the whole chest. There's got to be a way to open it."

Delastro shook her head. "Won't work. The chest isn't big"— she sketched a rough shape in the air—"but it's unnaturally heavy. Takes four people to lift the damned thing."

"Seven hells," Lukan muttered, pinching the bridge of his nose. *Why does everything have to be so complicated? And why does it always involve the bloody Phaeron.* "Tell me about this code— how does it work?"

"There're five glass panels set in the chest's lid. Each one glows a different color. To open the chest you need to press four of the panels in the correct order. If you get the sequence wrong—"

"Let me guess," Lukan interrupted. "Bad things happen. I've been on the wrong end of a Phaeron relic before." *And hopefully never again.*

"Then you'll know you're playing with fire."

"And all the rest." He took a swallow of liquor. "Is there any-one besides Marquetta who knows the code?"

Delastro drummed her fingers on the tabletop. "Come to think of it, there is. The Pontifex knows it."

Lukan frowned. "So Marquetta didn't trust you, but he trusted that spineless idiot?"

"Marquetta's tongue tends to loosen after he's had a few glasses of wine. He mentioned the Pontifex had somehow discovered the code and delighted in teasing him about it. That ended once Marquetta told him of all the possible ways he might die if he ever shared the secret."

"So if we can somehow get close to him," Lukan mused, "and find a way to get him to talk—"

"Not possible," Delastro said, shaking her head. "The Pontifex is too well guarded."

"I'll take care of that," Ashra replied, her expression thought-ful. "I can get close to him. Make him talk." Her eyes found Lukan. "You have a plan?"

"I'm still working on it," he admitted.

"Then work quickly." Ashra made for the door. "I'm going to pay His Holiness a visit."

34

STEEL AND SILK

"Hello Rosario."

The owner of the Golden Lily bordello jolted in his seat, the tip of his quill slashing across the page of his ledger. "Seven shadows," he snapped, glancing up, "I—" The words died in his throat as he saw Ashra standing by the open window. "You . . ," he breathed, his eyes widening.

"Me," Ashra agreed as she strolled toward his desk.

"But . . . you shouldn't be here!" Rosario spluttered, rising to his feet. "You can't be here!"

"But here I am."

"You—you need to leave. Now!" The ruby ring on the man's right hand flashed red as he punctuated his final word with a jab of a finger. Rosario liked the color red. The silken drapes by the window were red, the rug on the floor was red, and his velvet waistcoat was red. Normally his face was red too, but at this moment it was white, as if the color had drained from his cheeks and into the furnishings. "Now," he repeated, when Ashra didn't reply.

"I only just arrived." The thief slid into the chair opposite his desk.

"But . . . haven't you *heard*?" the man hissed.

"Heard what?"

Rosario gaped at her. "The King! They've put a bounty on your head." His eyes flicked to the window and back to Ashra. "Everyone's looking for you."

"I know."

"So . . . you need to leave! Now! If the King finds out you're here—"

"They won't."

"But my guards—"

"Are useless and wouldn't notice a threat until it punched them in the face. They didn't see me. No one did. Not your guards, your girls, or the gutter rat you pay to watch the street for you. I'm only seen when I want to be."

"You need to leave," Rosario insisted. "If you don't, I'll call my guards—"

"And have them drag me away? I wouldn't. Eyes will see. Tongues will wag." Ashra leaned forward. "Questions will be asked about why I was here in the first place."

The man swallowed and sank back into his chair. "But why *are* you here?"

"I've come to claim that favor you owe me."

"The favor . . . What, *now*?"

"Now."

"But . . . the city's in uproar! The Grand Duke is dead!"

"I know. That's why I'm here."

Rosario stared at her in bewilderment.

"I need that favor," Ashra continued, "and I need it now. The sooner you agree, the sooner I'll be gone. The King will never know I was here."

The man's eyes flicked to the door.

"Don't," she warned.

Rosario slumped against the back of his chair with a sigh. "Fine. What do you want?"

"I need you to send some of your girls to the Pontifex—I know he's one of your customers. And I need to go with them."

"Go with them?"

"Yes. Disguised as one of your girls."

"You . . . you want to be one of my lilies?" The man snorted a laugh. "Have you lost your mind?"

"Make your preparations," Ashra replied, rising from her chair. "Have the carriage ready to leave in half an hour."

"No," Rosario replied, standing as well and drawing himself up to his full height, which wasn't much. "Absolutely not. This is preposterous." His eyes narrowed as he stared at her. "What's your game here?"

"It's no game."

"No." He shook his head. "I won't do it. The Pontifex is one of my most valued customers and I won't risk the reputation of my business by going along with . . . with . . ." He flung his hands up. "Whatever this nonsense of yours is."

"We had an agreement," Ashra replied, a sudden edge in her voice. "You promised me a favor after I stole that medicine for you. The medicine that saved your niece's life."

Rosario had the decency to look abashed. "I haven't forgotten," he said tightly.

"So are you going back on your word?"

"Of course not, I just—Look, there must be something else I can do."

"There isn't. Prepare the carriage."

"No. I won't."

"Yes," Ashra replied, drawing a stiletto, "you will."

Rosario's eyes darted to the blade and back to Ashra. "You wouldn't."

"I would," she lied.

"I'll call the guards."

"You'll be dead before they get through the door."

"You're not that quick."

"Are you willing to take the risk?"

Rosario glared at her and opened his mouth, which formed silent words as his nerve failed him. "Very well," he said, sagging once more into his chair. "I'll prepare the carriage. But . . ." He raised a finger. "If you are going to impersonate one of my lilies, then I insist you at least look the part. The powder room is down the corridor. Madame Estrella will help you prepare. No doubt she'll be delighted at the prospect."

Ashra started toward the door.

"Wait," Rosario said, hurrying after her. "I'll go first and clear the place out. Can't have anyone recognizing you. I'll tell the madame you're a new lily, fresh off a ship from Lady-knows-where." He opened the door and looked back at her. "Stay here. Don't touch anything."

"What do you take me for," Ashra replied. "A thief?"

———

"You?" Madame Estrella said, giving Ashra a scornful look. "Master Rosario wants to send *you* to the Pontifex?"

"No, he doesn't. But I'm going anyway."

"I don't understand."

"You don't need to."

"But you're so . . . *thin*," the woman said, circling Ashra as if inspecting a horse. "There's not a pinch of fat on you—you're all sharp edges. The Pontifex likes his girls with curves—"

"I don't care what His Holiness likes."

"Such a severe jawline," the madame tutted, "with a nose like a blade—though you've got excellent cheekbones, my dear, I'll say that for you." She reached out a hand. "Your hair though, it simply *won't* do—"

Ashra caught her wrist. "Enough. Get out."

Madame Estrella blinked her long eyelashes. "But Master Rosario said to help you . . ."

"I can do it myself."

"You?" The woman hissed a laugh. "Those eyes of yours have never seen a dab of kohl—" She gasped as Ashra tightened her grip.

"I won't ask again."

The madame grimaced as Ashra released her. "Vulgar," she muttered, massaging her wrist. "Utterly vulgar. No doubt the Pontifex will be deeply displeased with you."

"I'm sure he will."

Madame Estrella huffed and departed in a whisper of silk, the heavy scent of her perfume lingering in the air long after she'd slammed the door on her way out. Ashra pulled on a silver silk robe—cool and soft against her skin—and sat down at the dressing table. As she glanced at her reflection in the mirror, she couldn't deny the madame's words—she *was* whip-thin, all angles and edges. She'd inherited much of her physique from her mother, with her rough childhood in the Splinters doing the rest. Growing up in such a place tempered you like steel in a forge, hammering the softness from you before hardening what was left. The madame was wrong about the kohl, though—Ashra had watched her mother paint her face many times before her performances with her dance troupe, and on occasion she had given in to her daughter's pleading for a little kohl around her own eyes. Ashra shook away the memories, forced down the familiar stab of grief as she reached for the wooden kohl stick—and froze as she heard a faint scuffling sound. She turned and glanced around the empty room. Her gaze settled on a divan near the open window.

"You can come out, Flea," she said.

The girl rose from behind the divan, her expression downcast. "Didn't think you'd seen me."

"I didn't. I heard the scuff of your shoes on the floor." She smiled. "Next time, go barefoot." Flea grinned back, her face brightening. Ashra nodded at a nearby stool, its cushion covered in red velvet like everything else in the room. "Come sit with me."

As the girl rushed to oblige, Ashra was reminded just how young she was—about the same age Ashra herself had been when her entire world had turned upside down, tipping her from a life of safety and security into a desperate struggle for survival in the Splinters. She could tell that Flea was also a product of Saphrona's notorious slum—she heard it in the girl's speech, with its clipped vowels and staccato delivery, she saw it in her movement and posture—tense, alert, ready for trouble—and she felt it in the

weight of the girl's gaze, which hinted at experiences buried deep.
Ashra knew all about those.

"They've made Marquetta Lord Protector," Flea said, perching
on the edge of the stool. "I just heard it from a gutter rat."

"That was quick."

"That's what Lukan said."

"How's his plan coming along?"

"He's swearing and pacing a lot."

"Not well, then."

The girl shrugged. "I think he's more worried about your plan.
Do you think it'll work?"

"The fourteenth rule of thievery," Ashra said, dipping the stick
into the small vial of kohl, "is to expect your plan to fail. But yes,
I think it'll work."

"There are rules? Who made them?"

"I did."

"Why?"

"Because all professions have rules. Lukan said you're a pickpocket. You work the plaza? Tell me what rules the merchants
have."

The girl thought for a moment. "They always put their most
valuable item at the front of the stall," she said eventually. "Where
everyone can see it."

"What else?"

"They always demand a higher price than they're prepared to
accept."

"You see? They have rules they follow to help them succeed.
Why should us thieves be any different?"

"I thought we were meant to break the rules."

"We do. Just not our own."

"Will you teach me your rules?"

"Perhaps. Don't want you losing a hand, do we?"

Flea stiffened and covered up the stump of her missing finger.

"Don't be ashamed of your mistakes," Ashra continued, drawing
kohl along her lower eyelid. "Learn from them. That's what I did."

"You—you made mistakes?"

"Of course."

"But you're . . ."

"Lady Midnight, master thief, who never puts a foot wrong? That's just a myth." Seeing the girl's disappointment, she added, "I *am* a master thief. That part is true. But it took me many years to get there. Many mistakes too."

"I heard that you . . ."

"Go on."

"I heard that you weren't born in the Splinters. That you were . . ." Flea hesitated again, as if unsure of the right word.

"Respectable?" Ashra offered, a hint of amusement in her tone.

"Yeah. Like, not a frilly or something, I don't mean that   "

"It's fine. And yes, I suppose we were *respectable,* whatever that means. We lived in a house with a red door in Seven Arches. My father was harbormaster and my mother was a performer. A dancer."

"A dancer? Was she good?"

"The best." Ashra paused in her work, feeling another pang of grief. Ten years now and it never really faded. "Some of my happiest memories are of watching her dance. Such poise. Such grace."

"What happened?" Flea asked softly.

"You tell me," Ashra said, dabbing at her eyes once more. "Lukan said you know all about me."

"Only what I've heard."

"Which is?"

"Well . . ." The girl shifted on her stool. "Your father was killed in a brawl, and not long after that your mother had an accident and . . . and couldn't walk anymore. You ended up in the Splinters and had to steal bread to survive."

"Close enough. It's more accurate than most of the other stories about me. But my father didn't die in a brawl, he was murdered in our home. I was sitting on his knee when they came. Three strangers in masks. My father pushed me to safety and I watched as they stabbed him to death. They closed the front door as they left."

For some reason that detail had always stuck in Ashra's mind: the door closing softly as her father lay gasping on the floor, blood bubbling on his lips. "I never found out who did it, or why. One day I will."

Flea was staring at her with wide eyes. "I'm sorry—"

"Don't be. Emotions make for poor allies, particularly when they're for someone else."

"Is that another rule?"

"It is. The fourth."

"Lukan's father was murdered as well," Flea said, a touch of uncertainty in her voice. "But he wasn't there when it happened."

"So I heard. He was lucky."

"I don't think he would agree."

"Likely not. Your friend doesn't seem to agree with anyone about anything."

"He's not my—" the girl started, only to fall silent, brows furrowed. "What about your mother?" she asked eventually. "Did she really have an accident?"

"Yes," Ashra replied, noting the change in subject. "Barely a few months after my father died she was struck by a passing cart and broke her hip. She couldn't walk, let alone dance. We lost everything and ended up in the Splinters. That's where it all started for me. Where I started stealing to survive. I had no choice."

"Neither did I."

"Of course you didn't. We never do. No one chooses to be a thief; it's something that's thrust upon us. We just have to make the best of it."

"I wish I could be as good as you."

"Who says you won't?"

"Because you've never been caught. I've already been caught once"—Flea held up her left hand, showing her missing finger—"and then Lukan caught me when I tried to steal from him. So that's twice now."

"The punishment for a second offense is the loss of a hand. You still have both of yours."

"Only because Lukan didn't report me to the constables."

"Then it doesn't count."

"But Lukan *caught* me."

"And he ended up paying you to be his eyes and ears in the city. You turned the situation to your advantage. That's the true mark of a good thief."

The girl brightened. "Really?"

"Really." Ashra touched up her eyelids a final time, then examined her handiwork in the mirror. It wasn't perfect—certainly not as good as her mother's work—but it would have to do. "I'm done here," she said, rising from the dresser. "How do I look? Will I pass for one of the Golden Lily's finest?"

"Definitely."

"Liar," she replied good-naturedly. "Madame Estrella was right—my hair's too short, I don't have the curves, and *these*"— she gestured at her chest—"are definitely not big enough."

Flea giggled and rose from her stool. "Shall I tell Lukan you're ready?"

"Yes. And tell him he better have figured out the final part of his plan."

The girl nodded and made for the window, only to pause. "What if the Pontifex won't give you the code?"

"He will. The twelfth rule of thievery."

"What's that?"

Ashra smiled. "People will tell you anything when you've got a blade against their throat."

———

Dusk was falling as the carriage rattled up the wide avenues of Arturo's Rise, passing in and out of the great shadows cast by the seven towers. Ashra had never been so close to them—had never even set foot in this exclusive part of the city at all. She mostly targeted the prosperous merchants and citizens of the Silks, whereas the inhabitants of Arturo's Rise—merchant princes and other notable figures—were all protected by the King's Midnight Charter.

And as much as Ashra found herself increasingly chafing against the secret laws that bound all the Kindred, she'd always been careful not to break them.

Not that it mattered now. The King had decided she'd broken them anyway. In an instant she'd gone from being revered to being—what was the word Lukan had used? A pariah. An outcast among her own people, the myth of Lady Midnight forever tarnished. None of the Kindred would associate with her now; the way Rosario had reacted to her presence was proof enough of that. She ground her teeth as she remembered the smirk on Delastro's face, but the mercenary leader was no more than a puppet. Marquetta had ordered the stealing of the Sandino Blade—he had caused Ashra's downfall, even if he didn't realize it. And now she would do her best to cause his.

But there was far more at stake than her desire for vengeance.

As the carriage had set off from the Golden Lily, Ashra had seen the crowds gathering in the streets, felt the tension building in the air. She heard the cries denouncing Zar-Ghosa, demanding justice for the Grand Duke's death, and she realized then a storm was coming—just as Marquetta knew it would. Just as he *wanted* it to. The merchant prince's framing of the Zar-Ghosan ambassador was not just a way for Marquetta to seize power, but a means to relighting a centuries-old prejudice. Now decades of peace and progress would unravel overnight, and Saphrona's Zar-Ghosan citizens—her mother's people—would be driven from the city they called home. And once again, Saphrona and Zar-Ghosa would go to war. Tens of thousands would die.

Ashra would be damned before she let that happen.

She just wished she didn't need to involve the two courtesans—Clara and Pasha—in her scheme to obtain the code for Marquetta's Phaeron casket. The two women had no idea who she really was—Rosario had made sure they didn't recognize her, just as he'd made sure to smuggle Ashra into the carriage without her being seen. Still, their employer's refusal to explain who Ashra was or why she was joining them had set the two women on edge, and they had spent the journey engaged in a whispered conversation, pausing only to shoot her suspicious glances. Ashra could hardly blame them; she'd feel the same in their position. Ideally she'd have done this alone, but Rosario and Madame Estrella had been right—she barely passed as one of the Golden Lilies, and she needed the cover that Clara and Pasha offered her. When this was over she'd ensure they were well compensated for their trouble—a month's wages should do the trick. Perhaps two months—

She was jolted from her thoughts as the carriage lurched to a halt.

"We're here," Clara stated flatly, giving Ashra a pointed stare. Pasha tugged her gown more tightly around her and sat back, as if hoping the cushion would swallow her. Ashra's first rule of thievery was that calmness was the key to success, but at this moment it wasn't her own state of mind that she was worried about.

"Just stay calm," she murmured, watching as the guard standing before the gates ambled toward the carriage. "Go about your business as normal. I'll be right there with you. This won't take long. We'll be back in the carriage before you know it."

"What won't take long?" Clara hissed. "What are you—"

"What's this?" the guard called out, glancing up at the driver, who sat out of Ashra's view. "His Holiness isn't expecting visitors."

"Master Rosario thought His Holiness might need to relax after a trying day," the driver replied, repeating the line Rosario had given him.

The guard grunted a laugh. "Don't we all. I still can't believe what happened to the Duke . . ." He peered in through the carriage window. Ashra gave what she hoped was a coy smile. Clara blew the man a kiss, causing him to grin. "Open the gate," he called, stepping away.

"Tell us why you're here," Clara demanded as the carriage rolled into the landscaped grounds of the Pontifex's villa. "Who are you? Why'd Rosario send you with us?"

"More a question of why he sent you with me."

"Hells does that mean?"

"All you need to know," Ashra said firmly, holding the woman's gaze, "is that I have business with the Pontifex. All I need *you* to do is to go about your business. Let me take care of the rest. You'll be well paid for your trouble."

Clara's eyes glinted, but it was Pasha who spoke. "How much?"

"Three months' wages," Ashra replied, raising the total from her earlier deliberation. Anything to calm the pair down and keep them quiet. "That good enough for you?"

Their stunned expressions told her it was.

Ashra looked out of the window, leaving them to another of their whispered conversations, and counted the guards patrolling the grounds. The fifteenth rule of thievery: Never neglect your escape route. She was intending to leave in the same manner as she was arriving, but no plan was foolproof. There were eight guards on the grounds, so ten overall if she included the pair on the gate. The Pontifex, like so many of the rich and powerful, had made the mistake of assuming there was safety in numbers. But one vigilant guard was worth five lazy ones. The way these guards meandered along the gravel pathways, cigarillos glowing like fireflies in the gloom as they laughed and chatted, told her they were the latter. Good to know.

Moments later, the carriage drew up before the villa's entrance. Light spilled from the open doorway, illuminating a well-dressed man who wore a flustered expression.

"Who's this?" Ashra asked.

"Armando," Clara replied, with a smirk. "Barbosa's steward. He's got a thing for Pasha."

"He does not," Pasha objected.

"Course he does. You've seen the way he looks at you. The way he walks, trying to hide his stiff cock—"

"Remember what I said," Ashra murmured. "Business as usual."

"This *is* business as usual." Clara opened the carriage door. "Let me do the talking."

"You're not supposed to be here!" Armando said, as the women disembarked from the carriage. "His Holiness is . . ." He trailed off as he caught sight of Pasha.

"Told you," Clara muttered.

"His Holiness is resting," the man continued. "He needs to relax—"

"You idiot, Armando," the courtesan replied wearily, one hand on a hip. "We *are* his relaxation. Just take us to him."

"Please," Pasha added, smiling sweetly.

Armando swallowed. "Yes, well . . . Perhaps you're right. Very well, follow me."

"See?" Clara whispered, nodding at the steward. Ashra smiled. There *was* something odd about the stilted way he walked. Pasha rolled her eyes.

The steward led the way into the villa's entrance hall and, once they were all inside, closed the door. Ashra had expected something grand, but the opulence of it all still managed to surprise her. An exquisitely sculpted marble statue of the Veiled Lady—the one concession to Barbosa's status as a man of the cloth—dominated the center of the hall. The rest of the hall's furnishings looked more like they belonged to a merchant prince. An impressive crystal chandelier hung from the ceiling, while the walls were adorned with elaborate tapestries from Liang-Ti. Ashra had stolen one such tapestry before and knew just how valuable they were. Certainly, such furnishings should have been well beyond the means of a priest, even one of the highest-ranking clergymen in the Old Empire. For all the Pontifex's sermons about the dangers of greed and avarice, it seemed he didn't follow his own teachings. Still, that was hardly surprising. Coin, as the saying went, was the only true god in Saphrona.

"This way," Armando said, leading them up one of the spiraling staircases. "His Holiness is in his quarters. It's been a most trying day." The man didn't look at them as he spoke. He'd barely looked at them at all since they'd entered the villa. Ashra wondered if his awkwardness was due to Pasha's presence, or whether it was embarrassment at serving a Pontifex who, despite his supposed vow of celibacy, enjoyed regular visits from the courtesans of the Golden Lily. Lust was clearly another sin His Holiness condemned from his pulpit, but enjoyed indulging in himself.

They followed the steward around the upper gallery and into a wide corridor decorated with yet more tapestries. Just one of them could feed a family of five in the Splinters for a year or more, yet regularly the Pontifex would urge his flock to give the gift of charity. How much of the coin in his collection bowl even reached the needy? Ashra felt a spark of anger, but forced it down. The fourth rule of thievery: Emotions make for poor allies.

The steward stopped before a door and knocked. At a muffled response from within, he opened the door. "Your Holiness, Master Rosario has seen fit to—"

"I've seen the carriage, Armando, I'm not blind. Send them in."

The steward stepped back and gestured to the doorway, again not making eye contact. Ashra made to step forward, only to hesitate as she felt a touch on her arm: Clara's hand, squeezing gently as her eyes conveyed a message: *Let me*. Ashra nodded, moving aside to let the two women past, and then, drawing a steadying breath, she followed. Armando closed the door behind her.

The Pontifex's quarters were even grander than the entrance hall but, whereas the latter possessed a sense of class, no matter how misguided, the man's bedchamber was ostentatious to the point of being garish, with its velvet cushions and gilt furnishings. It looked more like an upmarket brothel, which, Ashra supposed, was entirely fitting. The man himself stood at the center of the room, dressed in a robe of golden silk that would have put the emperors of old to shame.

"Ah," the Pontifex exclaimed, spreading his arms as he watched them approach, "greetings, my lovelies! What a delightful surprise. Your master knows my moods so well. Clara, always a delight . . . and Pasha, wonderful . . ." His eyes, bright with anticipation, narrowed as they regarded Ashra. "And you, my dear, I don't think I've had the pleasure. Your name is . . ."

"Krissa, my lord," Ashra replied, bobbing her head demurely.

"Oh, I'm no lord," the man tittered in response. "Not yet anyway . . ." His gaze became distant for a moment before he collected himself. "Please," he said, looking Ashra up and down, "*Your Holiness* will do just fine."

"As you wish, Your Holiness," she said, nodding again, but Barbosa was already turning away. Ashra wasn't surprised that the man's interest in her didn't stretch beyond a brief glance— Madame Estrella had been right; she wasn't to his taste. An hour of sitting in the carriage opposite Clara and Pasha, with their full lips, large bosoms, and soft curves, had already given her a good sense of where the Pontifex's tastes lay. She watched as he settled himself on the bed, fighting to keep the disgust from her face. A man who had conspired in the murder of the Grand Duke, who had aided Marquetta in his plot to seize control, and his only concern seemed to be with plumping his pillows. Clara and Pasha disrobed in a rustle of silk and lay down on either side of him, Pasha giggling as the man pawed at her breasts. "Come on, Krissa," Barbosa called, glancing at her. "Don't be shy."

"Yes, join us," Clara said, her singsong tone not matching the wariness in her eyes. Ashra forced a smile and moved purposefully toward the bed, stepping up onto the mattress so she was standing over Barbosa.

"That's better," the man murmured, as Ashra sank down so she was straddling his belly. "Now we just need to remove your gown and—" Ashra slapped his hand away. Clara and Pasha stared at her, their eyes wide. "Oh, wonderful," Barbosa tittered. "I must admit, I wasn't sure why Rosario had chosen you, but he knows I love a little steel beneath the silk."

"So do I," Ashra replied, sliding a stiletto from her sleeve.

"Oh," the Pontifex exclaimed, blinking as the candlelight caught the blade's wicked point. He laughed again, though it seemed forced. "I'm not sure what sort of game this is, but—"

"It's not a game."

"I don't understand . . ."

"It's simple," Ashra said, eliciting a gasp from the man as she pressed the stiletto's point to his throat. "I'm going to ask you some questions. You are going to answer. If you lie to me, you die. If you call for the guards, you die. Understand?"

The man stared at her, dumbfounded.

"Do you understand?" Ashra repeated, exerting a little more pressure on the blade.

"No," the man spluttered, face reddening. "This is . . . You—you can't do this. I'm the *Pontifex*—"

"A title," she sneered. "A word. A *lie*." With a flick of her wrist she slashed his right cheek.

Barbosa gasped, raised a hand to the wound, blinked at the blood coating his fingertips. "You . . . you *cut* me."

"That's for all the children who go hungry while you line your pockets with coin from the collection plate."

The man swallowed, realization finally seeming to dawn in his eyes. "You're not one of Rosario's girls . . ."

"No," Ashra agreed, pressing the stiletto back against his throat. "I'm not."

"Then . . . who are you?"

"I'll be asking the questions."

"But I'm the *Pontifex*," he squealed again.

"No. You're a liar." She twisted the stiletto, eliciting another gasp. "You're a fraud."

"I'm . . . the Lady's Chosen."

"You're a murderer."

Barbosa stilled, his eyes widening. "No, that's a lie—"

"You deny plotting with Marquetta? You deny conspiring to murder the Grand Duke?"

The man's lips quivered. "How do you . . . No, I—I never meant—"

"Save your pleas for your Lady. I'm sure She'll have a few words to say. I can send you to Her right now, if you wish. Always better to admit your guilt than bottling it up."

"No!" the Pontifex squealed. "Please—"

"Tell me the code to Lord Marquetta's Phaeron chest."

"The chest?" The man blinked in confusion. "But why?"

"Tell me."

"No, I—I can't. Marquetta would kill me if I did."

"I'll kill you if you don't."

"Please! Please, I—"

"No. Only the innocent get to beg. Make your choice." Ashra twisted the stiletto again. "Talk to me, or talk to your god."

The Pontifex took a great heaving breath, blinking away tears. And began to talk.

35

THE BLADE ITSELF

The Zar-Ghosan quarter burned.

Fire writhed across the rooftops, casting the narrow streets in a hellish glow. Columns of smoke rose into the night sky, carrying embers up toward the uncaring stars. Sorcery flashed, vivid emerald against the flames, the boom of its detonations like the rolling of distant thunder, only far more ominous.

Lukan could see it all from his vantage point, halfway up the wide, sloping avenue known as Quill Lover's Lane, which wound up and around Borja's Bluff to the ducal palace at its summit. He could hear the screams as well, carrying on the wind, and wished he couldn't.

The Grand Duke and his sons might have been the first casualties of Marquetta's play for power, but it was Saphrona's Zar-Ghosan citizens—both those who had arrived after the war and those who were born in the city later—who were the true victims. *Forty years of peace up in flames,* Lukan thought, as another flash of sorcery illuminated the night. The Twice-Crowned King had claimed there were six pairs of gleamers in the city, and Lukan guessed at least half of them were out there now, enforcing Marquetta's will with their deadly sorceries. *What mindless stupidity.* Not that the violence surprised him; it was inevitable things would turn ugly after the bloodbath in the shadow of the Lady's House. As Ashra prepared for her visit to the Pontifex's villa, Lukan had toured the taverns of the Silks and Seven Arches. The talk had been the same in each establishment—accusations of treachery, whispers of war, angry denunciations of Zar-Ghosa. Much of the talk came from men and women old enough to remember the last war, scarred veterans of that conflict whose prejudices—never fully eradicated—now boiled to the surface. Their audience of younger folk—who had never known war, never held any hostility toward the Zar-Ghosans—nodded along with enthusiasm. Young and old alike toasted the calls for justice and retribution with alcohol, though the emotions that drove them were far stronger.

The rising fury finally exploded into violence at sunset. A mob stormed the Zar-Ghosan embassy in the Silks district and murdered the officials inside before embarking on a rampage through the city, targeting known Zar-Ghosan businesses. By the time the rioters arrived at the edge of the Zar-Ghosan quarter itself, they numbered several hundred strong. The first flames appeared soon afterward, bright orange against the indigo of twilight. Then the screams began. Lukan had seen it all from his vantage point, a different sort of fury gripping him as he stood helplessly, powerless to intervene. Flea had stood at his side, shocked to silence for the second time that day.

By the time the constabulary showed up, supported by at least two pairs of gleamers, it was already too late. *Which was probably the entire point.* Lukan had little doubt that Marquetta had delayed his response as long as possible. Even now, as he watched the flashes of sorcery amid the flames, he half suspected it was targeting innocent citizens rather than the rioters themselves. *And this is just the start.* How many more would die in the days and months to come as Marquetta wielded his newfound power? *We've got to stop him.* In that moment, his desire to free Zandrusa and obtain his father's casket was far from Lukan's mind. As he watched the destruction of the Zar-Ghosan quarter, all he could think about was stopping Marquetta and saving a city that was on the verge of tearing itself apart. He could only hope the desperate plan they'd thrown together that afternoon would work.

Fortune had been on their side so far. Topaz, much to Lukan's relief, was still alive, and the Scrivener had agreed to hand him over to Lukan's care—"a small price to pay," she had said, "if it means I never have to lay eyes on you again, Master Gardova."

Lukan had held his tongue, refraining from telling her the feeling was more than mutual. In any case, he could now hold to his side of the bargain—all he needed was for Delastro to hold to hers and deliver the Sandino Blade into his care. *But even that will be meaningless if Ashra fails to get the code.* He moved to the archway that marked the courtyard's entrance and stole a glance at the avenue beyond. *Where the hells has she got to?*

The great bells of the Lady's House had tolled to mark the tenth hour of the evening some time ago, their peaceful tones at odds with the chaos engulfing the Zar-Ghosan quarter. *She's late.* And something told him the thief was never late; she seemed the kind of person who regarded timing as a virtue, which it undoubtedly was in her line of work. *Which means she's run into trouble, or worse.* He glanced around the small courtyard, wondering if he was in the wrong place, but no—the small fountain in the center was just as she'd described, with its crumbling statue of a man in an old-fashioned suit of armor. Lukan was exactly where he was meant to be, but if Ashra failed to join him before the carriage arrived then it would all be for nothing. *And what if something happens to the carriage?* The journey from the Three Moons Counting House to the ducal palace was little more than a mile, and far from the chaos on the western side of the city. Yet plenty of thieves and opportunists were using the riots as cover for looting and other crimes—he'd been forced to evade several small groups as he made his way to the rendezvous point. Delastro and her crew could surely handle a few armed thugs, but what about twenty? Or thirty?

Lukan cursed under his breath as the plan seemed to tear apart in his mind. There were too many variables, too many things that could easily go wrong. *Can we even trust Delastro? What if this is all part of some ploy?* He wasn't even sure he could fully trust Ashra—after all, he barely knew her. *And what about Flea?* He worried about her most of all. Not with regards to her trustworthiness—on the contrary, she was the only person in the entire city he felt he could rely on. That realization brought a faint smile to his lips. *We've come a long way since the little devil tried to pick my pocket.* No, his concern with Flea was that he'd asked too much of her. The girl had thrown him her familiar withering look when he'd asked her that question earlier, yet he'd thought he'd caught a flicker of uncertainty in her eyes. *And rightly so; this could easily get her killed.* He'd never forgive himself if that proved to be the case. The last thing he wanted was another death on his conscience. *Especially hers.*

Lukan sighed and went back to pacing the courtyard. Even if this all went to plan—even if he managed to get his hands on the Sandino Blade—the hardest part was still to come. And that was something he couldn't plan for, not least because of the nature of who he was going up against—*what* he was going up against. In his mind he saw the portal opening and the three figures emerging, armor steaming from the cold as they moved in unison . . . *Enough. First things first. We don't even need to worry about the Faceless if we can't get hold of the blade.*

The sound of distant hooves drew him from his thoughts. *One rider, coming this way.* He returned to the archway, peering through just as a rider appeared round the curve of the avenue farther down the hill. *Delastro,* he realized, as the streetlamps revealed the mercenary's sharp features. *But where's the rest of her crew?* He felt a flicker of trepidation as he stepped out into the street and raised a hand in greeting. "The carriage?" he prompted, as Delastro vaulted from her saddle and landed lightly in front of him.

"Following behind," the woman replied, glancing around at the tall buildings that lined either side of the avenue. Their windows were mostly dark, but here and there a candle glowed against glass as a scribe or notary worked late even as the city burned. Delastro's eyes found Lukan. "Where's the thief?"

"I don't know. She's not shown yet."

"Yet? What makes you think she'll show at all?"

"She'll be here."

"Well, she better not be long. This city is tearing itself apart."

"I know," Lukan replied, an accusing note in his voice. "I've seen the fires." *The fires your employer started.* Delastro gave him a pointed look, as if sensing his thoughts and daring him to speak them. He decided not to give her the satisfaction. *Besides, now is hardly the time.* "Did you have any problems on the way over here?"

"Nothing we couldn't handle," she replied with a dismissive shrug. "Most of the trouble is farther west, but my scouts reported several mobs moving toward the Silks. Seems every lowlife is out tonight, looking to cause some trouble. It's only a matter of time before one of them heads this way, and I don't plan on being here when they do—understand?"

"We just need to give Ashra some time—"

"I've already played my part, Gardova. You wanted me to bring you the Sandino Blade, and that's exactly what I've done."

As if on cue, the sound of hooves on cobbles rang out, accompanied by the rumbling of wheels. Lukan watched as two riders appeared round the curve of the avenue, crossbows at the ready as they scanned the shadows. The carriage followed behind, the driver hauling on the reins of two horses. A further rider brought up the rear. Delastro was clearly not taking any chances.

"The blade is within," the mercenary said, gesturing at the approaching carriage. "I've fulfilled my part of the bargain. Now it's time for you to fulfill yours. Where is my nephew?"

"I need to see the blade first."

"You don't trust me?"

"No."

"You wound me, Gardova." Delastro spun on her heel. "Follow me."

The carriage juddered to a halt as they approached, the horses snorting and stamping their hooves. Delastro gave a low whistle accompanied by some sharp gestures. One of the riders turned his horse and rode back the way they'd come, while another spurred her mount up the avenue, giving Lukan a glare as she passed him. *Amethyst,* he realized, catching a glimpse of her features. He was in no hurry to cross swords with her again. The rest of Delastro's crew took up positions around the carriage, their eyes constantly searching the shadows for any sign of a threat.

"Let's make this quick," Delastro said as she opened the carriage door.

"We'll need a light—" Lukan began, then fell silent as a soft glow spilled out across the cobbles. He stared in surprise at the interior of the carriage, which was illuminated by a small alchemical globe hanging from the ceiling.

"That good enough for you?" Delastro asked wryly. "The Three Moons Counting House spares no expense."

"So I see." Lukan turned his attention to the object that lay on the floor of the carriage. The chest was smaller than he'd imagined, leaving him room to clamber inside and ease onto one of the cushioned seats. It was forged from a golden-hued metal that gave the subtle impression of movement as light played across its sides, like faint ripples on a lake. *Definitely Phaeron, no doubt about that*. He examined the five small glass panels in the lid. When he reached out a tentative hand the panels lit up, each one a different color. They pulsed softly, as if urging him to press his fingertip to them. *Not bloody likely*. He drew his hand back and the panels darkened again.

"Satisfied?" Delastro asked.

"Not until I get my hands on the blade." *Damn it, Ashra, where are you?*

"Whether you do or not is of no concern to me." The mercenary stood aside as Lukan stepped down from the carriage. "Now tell me where my nephew is."

"How do I even know the blade is in—"

Delastro moved fast; Lukan didn't even manage to finish the sentence before she shoved him up against the side of the carriage, a knife pressed against his throat. "No more games, Gardova," she hissed, the bright alchemical light revealing every nick and scrape on her face. "I've risked my reputation for this pathetic little plan of yours. The blade is in the chest—whether you can get it out is your problem, not mine. Now tell me where my nephew is."

"A few moments. That's all I ask."

"You're in no position to . . ." Delastro trailed off as the sound of hoofbeats echoed up the avenue. The rider she had sent down the slope came racing out of the shadows, his expression grim. "A mob," he called, tugging hard on his mount's reins. "Thirty strong, coming this way."

"Time's up," Delastro said, twisting the knife. "Out with it."

Lukan winced as the steel rasped against his skin. "Topaz is being held at the Soot and Stars, a tavern on the edge of the Smokes."

Delastro turned away and moved to her horse. "Our business is concluded," she called over her shoulder. "I hope for your sake our paths don't cross again."

"How much coin do you want?" Lukan asked.

Delastro paused, one foot in a stirrup. "For what?"

"To stay here until Ashra arrives."

"You heard Garnet. There's a mob coming—"

"I need the blade." *Or all of this has been for nothing.*

Delastro tilted her head, as if regarding him anew. "I'm not sure if you're brave or stupid."

"Just name your price."

"I very much doubt you could afford it."

"Try me."

A series of shouts carried on the wind, followed by the sound of shattering glass.

"Captain," Garnet urged, "we should go—"

Delastro silenced him with a raised hand, brow furrowed in thought. "Fifty ducats," she said, locking eyes with Lukan.

"Thirty."

"Fifty. I don't see any other mercenaries willing to help, do you?"

"You'll protect the carriage until Ashra gets here?"

"We will."

"Done. Fifty ducats."

"How do I know you're good for it?"

You don't. Nor do I, for that matter. He could only hope that if they succeeded in this desperate gamble, someone—Zandrusa perhaps—would cover the payment. *And if we don't, we'll have far bigger problems to worry about. Like being dead.* "Because I've seen what you do to people who break their promises," Lukan replied. "I've no desire to end up like Doctor Vassilis."

"Go back on your word and you'll suffer a worse fate." Delastro mounted her horse and gave a low whistle. "Jewels," she called, "we have work to do."

Lukan watched as Delastro ordered her crew to form a line across the avenue, positioning herself at the center. All of them were on horseback, which would count for something, save for the driver of the carriage, who took up position on the left flank. *She might lack morals,* he thought, as Delastro barked instructions, *but she doesn't lack leadership.* He glanced up as Amethyst returned, ignoring him this time as she rode past and took her place in the line. The mercenaries all listened closely as Delastro ran through whatever plan she had concocted in the moment since accepting Lukan's offer. There were no muttered objections, only solemn nods of assent. If they were all cut from the same cloth as Amethyst, then Lukan had no doubt they'd carry out Delastro's orders to the end. *Still, five mercenaries against a thirty-strong mob drunk on violence and bloodlust . . .* Even with their formidable skills, and the advantage of being on horseback, he doubted it would be enough.

The mob spilled round the curve of the avenue to a chorus of shouting and laughter. There was a hunger to their movements that suggested they'd seen some violence already and were now eager for more. Some of their number carried burning torches; many more swigged from bottles of stolen liquor. Their laughter suggested they didn't give two figs for their duke's murder and instead only cared about taking advantage of the current upheaval to indulge in a little looting and vandalism. *Opportunists, then, drawn to the chaos like moths to a flame. The constabulary must be stretched thin if they've made it this close to the palace.*

The mob slowed as it caught sight of the mercenaries, its unruly

ranks forming up behind a woman who looked incongruous in a
feathered hat and a green velvet jacket—items of clothing, Lukan
guessed, that until very recently had been on display in an upmarket tailor's shop. An uneasy silence fell as both parties regarded
each other. Then the mob's ringleader stepped forward, a steely
glint in her eyes. "Evening, all," she said, tilting her hat in mock
salute. "Quite the night, ain't it?"

"That's close enough," Delastro warned.

The woman stopped and made a show of eyeing the mercenaries.
"You the leader of this sorry lot?"

"I am."

"Then tell them to move aside. We've got business to attend
to. And I ain't talking about the parchment and quills kind." The
ringleader turned and grinned at the mob behind her, which responded with ragged cheers.

"The only thing I'm going to tell them," Delastro said coldly,
"is when to put a bolt in your throat."

The ringleader's grin turned to a scowl. "That sounds like a
threat."

"It's merely a statement. A threat would look like this." Delastro
snapped her fingers and a crossbow string snapped, causing the
woman to jump backward as a bolt struck the cobbles at her feet.
The mob retaliated with a volley of insults and obscene gestures.
The ringleader squared her shoulders, her resolve strengthened by
the anger of the crowd at her back.

"You got some steel, grandma," she said, meeting Delastro's
gaze. "But here's the thing: There's only five of you and"—she
thumbed over her shoulder—"a lot more of us. So you might want
to think carefully before you—"

"Enough!" Delastro barked, voice cracking like a whip. "Let's
get to the point: If you and your rabble leave now, my crew won't
kill you all. Your call."

The mob responded with a fresh volley of insults, only to quiet
as the ringleader motioned for silence. "What's in the carriage?"
she asked.

"None of your business."

"That's where you're wrong." The woman's grin returned. "'Cause from what I can see, that carriage is from the Three Moons Counting House. Which means it's probably carrying something valuable. And *that* is very much my business."

"Last chance. Leave now and no one gets killed."

The woman spat. "I don't take orders from no one, 'specially not some old bitch who thinks she's—"

The bolt struck the ringleader clean in the right eye. Her head snapped backward, her jaw working as if she was trying to give voice to some exclamation of surprise, before her knees buckled and she fell to the cobbles. She twitched once before lying still.

The night itself seemed to hold its breath.

"I warned her," Delastro said coldly, eyeing the mob as she slid another bolt into her crossbow. "She didn't listen. Will you?"

For a moment it seemed they might, as the rioters exchanged uncertain glances. Then an incoherent shout sounded from the rear of the mob, and while the words were lost there was no mistaking the anger behind them. More voices joined the first. Someone hurled a bottle, which smashed on the cobbles no more than a yard from Delastro's horse. Fury bled into the air.

Lukan drew his sword, an old cavalry saber Alphonse had found for him.

With a roar, the mob surged forward.

The thrum of crossbows sounded above the shouting. Five bodies tumbled to the ground. Yet the rioters came on, leaping over their fallen comrades. Lukan's heart raced as the rioters closed the distance, their faces contorted with rage. The mercenaries drew swords, which flashed as the two sides collided, their keen edges slicing through limbs, their sharp points skewering throats. A horse reared, flailing hooves crushing a man's skull. Shouts of fury became screams of terror, and it seemed the mercenaries would drive the mob back. Then one of the Jewels was pulled from their horse, disappearing in the crush of bodies, and a hole appeared in the line as one of their comrades rode to their aid. Two rioters seized the opportunity and darted through the opening, slowing as they saw Lukan standing before them. The men's eyes flicked to the carriage behind him. *Deciding whether the risk is worth the reward,* he thought, as the men shared a look. *Greed will win out. It always does.*

He was proven right as the men charged. They came at him from both sides, only for the attacker on his left to hesitate—something that Lukan might have taken for a deliberate ploy, if it weren't for the gleam of fear in the man's eyes. The other rioter continued his attack, yelling as he took a wild swing with his club. Lukan twisted away and delivered a slash to the man's back as he staggered past, his shout turning to a gasp as he fell to the ground. Lukan advanced on the other man, only to realize it wasn't a man at all, but a boy barely into his teens. The youth dropped his notched axe, which clanged dully on the cobbles.

"P-please," the boy stammered. "I . . . I didn't mean—"

"Get the hells out of here."

The boy turned and fled into the shadows of a nearby alley. Lukan lowered his blade and sucked in a deep breath. He turned back to the fight, only to find that it was already over. Half the rioters lay on the ground, either dead or close to it, while the rest were running for their lives. None of the mercenaries—all of whom had survived—were bothering to give chase. *Can't say I didn't get my money's worth.*

He tensed at the sound of footsteps. *Shit.*

Lukan spun to find the first attacker lurching toward him. The man spat an insult as he raised his club . . . and tripped, falling heavily to the cobbles. Ashra stood behind him, one eyebrow raised at Lukan.

"You took your damned time," he said, sheathing his sword.

Ashra slammed the pommel of her dagger against the man's head, and his body slackened into unconsciousness. "I got delayed," she replied, as if that explained everything. Still, it hardly mattered. Questions could wait for later.

"Do you have the code?"

"Of course. Did you doubt me?"

"No," he admitted. *Though I was starting to wonder.* "And the Pontifex?"

"Is unharmed and won't be saying a word to anyone."

"Are you sure? Because—"

"I'm sure."

The thief moved toward the carriage, making it clear the conversation was over. Lukan climbed in behind her and took the opposite seat.

The chest lay between them.

"Ready?" Lukan asked, watching the thief as she studied the Phaeron object, green eyes moving over the glass panels. "There's no room for error."

"I know."

"So what's the code?"

"Let me concentrate," Ashra replied sharply, eyes not leaving the chest. The panels lit up in their different colors as she reached out, her hand steady. "Blue," she murmured, pressing the corresponding panel. A chime sounded, giving Lukan an uncomfortable flashback to Salazar's as the blue light faded. Nothing else happened.

"One down," he said, relieved.

Ashra gave no indication she'd heard him as she pressed her finger to the red panel. Another chime sounded as the light faded.

Two down. Lukan's mouth was dry, his heart trying to force its way into his throat. *And I'm not even the one touching the panels.* He couldn't help but admire Ashra's poise—her eyes betrayed not a hint of fear, her hand not the faintest of tremors. She pressed the orange panel. "One more," Lukan said as the panel's glow faded. *Lady's mercy, we're actually going to pull this off.*

"Green," Ashra breathed, finger moving toward the panel of the same color. She hesitated, eyes narrowing. "Shit."

"What is it?"

"Green is the last color in the sequence."

Lukan leaned over the casket. "That looks green to me," he

offered, indicating the panel beneath Ashra's hovering finger.
"What's the problem?"

"If this is green, then what color is *that*?" The thief pointed to
the other panel.

"Ah . . . green. A lighter green, but . . ."

"Still green."

"You could argue it's turquoise . . ."

"It's light green."

Damn it, she's right. Lukan sighed and ran a hand through his
hair. "You're sure the Pontifex wasn't more specific?"

"He just said green." Ashra sucked her teeth. "We're going to
have to guess."

Lady's blood. "If we get it wrong—"

"A punishment. I know."

They stared at the casket in silence.

"So which one?" Lukan asked. "Light green or dark?"

"Dark." She reached for the panel.

"Wait."

The thief met his gaze. "For what?"

Lukan swallowed. "Um . . . perhaps I should—"

"Press it for me? How chivalrous of you."

Ashra turned her attention back to the casket and—without
any hesitation—pressed the dark green panel. Lukan held his
breath, bracing himself for the thief's arm to burst into flame, or
dissolve into dust, or any of a dozen horrific scenarios, but instead
a chime sounded—a lower note than the others—and the dark
green light faded. A series of clicks followed, accompanied by a
strange whirring sound. All five of the glass panels started flashing
in unison, then went dark.

"Is it open?" Lukan asked, scarcely able to breathe.

As if in answer, the chest's lid slowly started to rise, hinging
backward to reveal an interior lined with golden silk. And a dagger,
resting on a velvet cushion.

The Sandino Blade.

Lukan couldn't keep the grin from his face. "Now *that*," he said, meeting Ashra's eyes, "was a good call." The thief made no reply, though the shadow of a smile might have flitted across her lips as she reached into the casket and withdrew the dagger. It wasn't much to look at; the blade itself was speckled with rust, the silver hilt and cross guard both tarnished.

"What could the Faceless possibly want with this?" Ashra murmured. The rough-cut gem set in the pommel glinted as she turned the blade over.

"The gem," Lukan said excitedly, "hold it up to the light." The thief obliged, and they both watched as the gem gleamed a purplish black.

"A purple crystal," Ashra said, eyes widening as realization dawned. "Like the kind you said the Faceless always trade for."

"Exactly," Lukan replied, unable to keep the excitement from his voice as a missing piece of Marquetta's plan finally slotted into place. "It's not the blade the Faceless want, it's the crystal set in the pommel." He held out a hand. "May I?" Ashra offered him the blade hilt-first and he took it with an almost reverential air, unable to stop staring at the gem. *One of the fabled purple crystals. I can't believe it.* He pressed a thumb to the crystal, its surface rough and surprisingly cold against his skin. *If only Father could have seen this—*

He flinched as a strange feeling stole over him, the sensation of a presence—timeless and vast—filling his mind. *What in the hells . . .* The taste of copper on his tongue. A keening in his ears, like a thousand screaming voices at the very edge of hearing. And a succession of images, each bleeding into the other: a black tower, a stream of white light, pale tentacles writhing against an iron-grey sky—

Then the presence was gone, as swiftly as it had arrived, leaving Lukan shaking on the carriage seat, a primal fear churning in his gut.

"Lukan?" Ashra ventured. "Are you—"

"Fine," he managed, waving her concern away. "Just a bit of dizziness. Not enough sleep."

The thief's eyes narrowed but she didn't press him further. "We should move."

"Agreed." He clambered down from the carriage to find Delastro standing nearby, cleaning her sword with a cloth. A spatter of blood covered her right cheek.

"So you got the blade, I see," she remarked. Her eyes flicked to Ashra. "Seems you're just as good as they claim."

Ashra remained silent.

"The battle," Lukan said, glancing at the dead bodies and the mercenaries who crouched beside them, rifling through pockets and removing rings. "Are your crew all right?"

"Of course they're all right. This was nothing more than child's play. A slaughter, not a battle." She tossed the rag aside and pointed her blade at Lukan. "You owe me fifty ducats."

"You'll get them. You have my word."

"I don't care for your word, only the coin. I want it deposited at the Brandt and Balinor Banking House in Amberlé—mention my name and they'll make all the necessary arrangements. If the coin isn't in their vault a month from now—"

"Yeah, I know. You'll hunt me down and pin my balls to the wall with a crossbow bolt."

"Something like that." Delastro sheathed her sword. "So, you have the blade. What will you do now?"

"That's none of your concern."

"No, but I must admit to a professional curiosity as to what you intend and how you plan to do it. I take it you still want me to deliver that empty chest to Marquetta? It would be far easier to just leave the carriage here. I can tell him that my crew were attacked by a large mob and we had no choice but to abandon it."

"No. I need you to take the chest to him." *If this crazy plan is to have any chance of working.*

Delastro gave him a searching look. "Fine," she replied, shrugging. "That was what we agreed. I'll see it done."

"And what then? Surely you can't stay at Marquetta's side after this."

"Scared that you might have to cross swords with me, Gardova?"

Hells, yes. Lukan shrugged, forced a smile. "Professional curiosity."

Delastro offered him a lopsided smile of her own. "Mind your own damned business. And try not to get yourself killed before you've paid me that money." She made to turn away, only to pause. "The name of that tavern you gave me. The Soot and Stars . . ."

"That's where Topaz is. I promise."

The mercenary gave him a final, searching look. "Then it seems our business is concluded," she said eventually. "It's been interesting, to say the least." She gave him a brusque nod and turned away. "Jewels, mount up. Let's get this carriage to the palace."

Lukan closed the carriage door and stepped away as one of the mercenaries climbed into the driver's seat and snapped the reins. The two horses snorted and broke into a trot. The other mercenaries took up the same positions as before. *It's all on you now, Flea,* Lukan thought as he watched the carriage move away up the rising avenue. *Don't let us down.* He felt a stab of guilt. *But most of all, stay safe.*

"Let's go," Ashra said.

The thief made for the shadows of a nearby alley. Lukan started after her, only to pause and look up at the palace, looming on the top of the hill above them, blotting out the stars. "We're coming for you, Marquetta," he whispered, hefting the Sandino Blade.

Then he followed Ashra into the darkness.

36

THE RIGHT MOMENT

Colors swam before Flea's eyes.

Bright orange, hints of yellow, flashes of green. She blinked away her tears and just for a moment it all came into focus: the ravenous flames, the flickering sorcery. The Zar-Ghosan quarter burning beneath the stars. Then fresh tears came and it all blurred again. *How could they do this?* she wondered, wiping her eyes with the back of her hand. She'd grown up on the streets, meaning that home was wherever she chose to lay her head, and the Zar-Ghosan quarter had proven safer than most. Countless nights she'd slept there, lulled to sleep by the jingling prayer bells of the red-robed priests as they performed their rituals at dusk. She'd come to know several of the quarter's inhabitants—Misha the baker, who often slipped her a honey cake from her oven, Kalam the carpenter, who had once carved her a horse because he said she reminded him of the daughter he'd lost. But she'd liked Obassa best of all, the kindly beggar who was clearly more than he claimed to be, who always had a smile for her—and, more importantly, a coin or two in return for a favor.

They were all gone now, consumed by the flames.

No, she thought defiantly. *They got out. They didn't die.* Flea clung to the hope even as it flitted away, like the embers rising in the columns of smoke. Even if they had survived, they'd be left with nothing, their homes and livelihoods reduced to ashes. She gritted her teeth so tightly her jaw ached. *None of this was their fault.* But then bad things often happened to people who didn't deserve them—she'd learned that the day her brother left her and never came back. It was a fact of life as tangible as the constant hunger in her belly. She turned and looked up at the palace, rising against the night sky, windows aglow. *It's Marquetta's fault. He did this. All of it.*

Lukan was right, not that she'd ever tell him. Marquetta had to be stopped. She saw that clearly now, even if she hadn't seen it earlier. Before today, he'd seemed like all the other merchant princes—an almost mythical figure who moved in a world far removed from her own. Even after she'd learned of his plot, even after she'd seen it unfold, she hadn't grasped the significance of it all. How did any of this affect her, a pickpocket from the slums? Her life would be the same as before, regardless of who ruled the city.

Now, as she stared at the flames, she realized how wrong she'd been.

"I'll make him pay for this," she whispered, thinking of Misha, Kalam, and Obassa, and all the other Zar-Ghosans who had shown her kindness over the years. "I promise. And when I make a promise, I keep it."

For a fleeting moment, as she crouched atop the archway that spanned the avenue below, she felt less a simple pickpocket and more a spirit of vengeance. Then her resolve faded as her thoughts turned once more to the task ahead. Could she do what Lukan asked of her? She'd told him—with her deflective derision, a mask she'd honed over the years—that of course she could. At the time she'd even believed it. Now, as the knot of fear reasserted itself in the pit of her stomach, she didn't feel nearly so sure.

Flea took a deep breath to calm herself, just as she always did before dipping her fingers into someone's pocket. It wasn't the potential danger, or even the prospect of pain, that worried her. When you grew up on the streets, you lived with both every day of your life. No, what unnerved her was the fear that she might fail. That Lukan's hopes—*her* hopes—of saving the city would die, leaving Marquetta to unleash his evil plans . . . and it would all be her fault. Yet worse even than that was the thought of letting Lukan down.

No one had ever put their trust in Flea the way Lukan had. Not her brother Matteo, when he had told her to keep watch during one of his thieving escapades, not even Obassa when the old man had set her one of his little tasks. Yet somehow Lukan—a man of odd mannerisms whom she'd known for only a short time, and who at first had been nothing more than a target for her nimble fingers—trusted her more than anyone ever had. He'd looked her in the eye earlier that evening and said, "I have faith in you." In that moment Flea had realized that trust freely given was more valuable than any trinket she'd ever stolen. It was an almost physical presence inside her chest, lending her a degree of confidence and pride that she'd never felt before. The thought of losing that, of seeing the disappointment in Lukan's eyes, was more than she could bear. *I won't let you down,* she thought, clenching her fists. *And I won't let the city down.*

The distant sound of hooves striking cobbles cut through her thoughts.

Riders. The carriage is coming.

Flea turned to the muslin-wrapped bundle that sat on the stonework beside her, hands trembling only a little as she untied the loose knot. An acrid scent tickled her nostrils as she unwrapped the gloves that lay within, the muslin cloth stained from the tar-like substance that coated them. Wiggling her fingers, Flea slipped her right hand into the first glove. The fit was looser than she would have liked, but it would have to do. She eased her other hand into the second glove, wrinkling her nose at the smell, which reminded her of the leather tanners on the edge of the Smokes. "I paid an alchemist at the Collegium to develop this substance for me," Ashra had told her. "It looks nasty. Smells worse. But cover some gloves in it and you'll stick to any surface." The master thief had forced a smile. "Even a moving one."

It should have been one of the best moments of Flea's life. Lady Midnight, her hero, trusting her with the secrets of her trade. But Ashra *didn't* trust her—Flea had seen past her smile to the doubt in the woman's eyes, and realized then that Ashra didn't share Lukan's confidence in her. Her suspicion was confirmed later when she overheard the two of them having a heated conversation about the task Lukan had given her. "She's just a child," Ashra had said at one point, her dismissive tone striking Flea like a blow. She hadn't taken the words to heart—she had far too much respect for Ashra to do that—but she couldn't deny that they hurt. Now her desire to prove Lady Midnight wrong was almost as strong as her desperate need to prove Lukan right.

The sound of hooves grew louder, accompanied by the rumbling of the carriage. *I hope this stuff works,* she thought, flexing her hands inside the gloves. She pressed a finger to the stonework, noting with relief how it stuck fast. *Not bad.* With some effort she managed to pull her finger free. *But will it be enough to hold me?* Butterflies danced in her stomach as the first rider appeared farther down the avenue, the carriage following behind.

Flea crept up the incline of the arch, hoping the four riders that accompanied the carriage wouldn't think to look up, or that if they did they'd see nothing but a shadow. The carriage was traveling more quickly than she had anticipated, but there was nothing she could do about that other than get her timing right. Flea turned her back on the approaching riders and moved to the other side of the arch, her heart racing as she peered over the edge at the cobbles some fifteen feet below.

It suddenly seemed a long way down.

It's just like cutting a purse in the plaza, she told herself. *Just got to pick the right moment.* The thought brought a measure of comfort, even if she knew it to be false. Make a mess of an attempted snatch, and you could just turn and run. But if she got this wrong . . . *I can't run with broken legs.*

"Stop it," she hissed, angry at herself. "I can do this. I *have* to." The words helped focus her mind, the fiery determination that had helped her survive so many years on the streets reasserting itself, shoving aside the fear and doubt.

The echo of horses' hooves grew louder.

Flea's breath caught in her throat as the first of the riders passed below her, oblivious to her presence above them. *This is it.* Her heart threatened to burst out of her chest as the rumble of the carriage filled the world, a malevolent presence pressing down on her, stealing her breath. Flea gritted her teeth, not daring to so much as blink. *Any moment now . . .*

The horses drawing the carriage appeared below the archway. Flea jumped.

She saw the carriage beneath her as she fell. It was moving fast. *Too fast.* Fear lanced through her and she opened her mouth to scream, already thinking of the impact of her legs on the cobbles. Her bones shattering. Instead her breath was crushed from her lungs as she struck the roof of the carriage, her woolen knee pads and padded shoes—further gifts from Ashra—dampening the sound of her landing. Flea fell forward, slapping her gloved hands against the smooth roof. She gritted her teeth, expecting to be hurled to the ground; already she could feel her legs sliding to one side.

The gloves held.

Flea grinned, a heady mix of relief and elation flooding through her. She shifted her legs back into position and lay flat against the roof, anchored by her hands. *I'm not safe yet,* she thought, staring at the back of the driver's head. She expected him to turn round and see her, he *must* have heard her landing, but he remained facing forward. Nor did any of the other mercenaries raise any alarm. She could see the nearest one, a woman riding to the left of the carriage, her eyes scanning the surrounding buildings as she sought out potential threats. Flea grinned again. Somehow she'd managed to drop into the midst of one of the most dangerous mercenary companies in the Old Empire, and they didn't have so much as an inkling. *That's the easy part out the way,* she told herself, as the carriage rumbled on up the slope. *But the hard part is still to come.*

Flea's elation quickly faded as her entire world became the carriage roof, her sole purpose to hold on and try to keep her body as low and straight as she could. Tall buildings and side streets flashed past—glimpses of a part of the city she'd heard about but never seen with her own eyes. Quill Lover's Lane, the unofficial name for the wide avenue that led up to the ducal palace at the top of Borja's Bluff, was the heart of law and government: the Inquisition's headquarters was located here, along with the Gilded Council's chambers, the Esteemed Court of the Lady's Law, and dozens of other legal and municipal institutions. Consequently, Quill Lover's Lane was the most highly protected district in the city, even more so than Arturo's Rise. The lawmen and bureaucrats that worked here made for enticing targets, but Flea had never dared to prowl the avenue's mile-long cobbled expanse. She'd heard the rumors, of course, which claimed that any thief caught here was handed over to the Inquisition and never seen again. That, at least, was something she didn't need to worry about tonight. With the city in an uproar and the Zar-Ghosan district ablaze, there wasn't a constable or inquisitor in sight.

Flea almost cried out as the carriage took a sharp turn, flinging her body in the opposite direction. She gritted her teeth as her right leg slipped over the edge of the roof, the muscles in her arms and stomach burning as she hauled herself back into position. She gasped as something twinged in her lower back, trying to ignore the numbing pain as she waited for the hue and cry from the riders. *One of them must have seen me.*

No shout of alarm came.

Flea was forced to endure a few more scares as the carriage wound its way up toward the palace. Every moment seemed like an age; her arms were numb from the effort of trying to keep her body straight, her scrawny muscles tense with the effort. Her breaths came in ragged gasps, thankfully masked by the sound of the horses' hooves and the carriage's rumbling wheels. *I can't do this,* she thought, during one desperate moment when her left hand almost slipped straight out of its glove. *I can't hold on.*

But she did.

Eventually the carriage reached the top of the rise and slowed to a halt before a huge wrought-iron gate. Two stone bats glowered down at her from either side, but Flea only had eyes for the towering building that loomed beyond them. *The Grand Duke's*

palace. She'd only ever seen it from a distance, its domes and tur-
rets seeming somehow insubstantial, as if they were just a figment
of her imagination. Now the palace rose before her, undoubtedly
real and far larger than she could have imagined, its countless
windows glowing against the night. Flea was so awestruck she
barely registered the guard's challenge from beyond the gate, or
Delastro's clipped response. *If only Obassa could see me now,* she
thought, pride pricking her chest. *I'll bet no one from the Splinters
ever made it this close—*

The squeal of iron hinges brought her back, the carriage jolting
as it started forward once more, passing through the gates and
into the palace grounds. Sculpted hedgerows, marble statues, and
paved walkways—all illuminated by the soft light of alchemical
globes—passed before Flea's eyes, yet trepidation replaced her awe
as the palace drew closer. *How am I going to get inside?* She was
no closer to an answer as the carriage finally rumbled to a halt
before the impressive columned entrance. Light spilled across marble steps as the ornate doors opened and a tall, broad-shouldered
man stepped through. He wore the black-and-silver uniform of
the Inquisition, but it was his face—taut, hard angles beneath a
grey widow's peak—that caused Flea's stomach to flip over. *Prime
Inquisitor Fierro.* A boy dressed in fine clothes stood behind the
man, nervously clasping his hands.

"You're late," Fierro drawled in his gravelly voice, speaking
around the cigarillo clamped between his lips. "Lord Marquetta—or
should I say, the Lord *Protector*—expected you over half an hour
ago." He started down the steps, his movements slow and measured. "I always told him he had too much faith in you."

"Save me your bullshit, Fierro," Delastro snapped back. "Half
the damned city's on fire and you're worried about a little delay.
Be grateful we made it here at all, what with all the rioters in the
streets." She cocked her head. "Speaking of which, shouldn't you
be doing something about that?"

"It's all in hand."

"It doesn't look like it."

Fierro's eyes narrowed, cigarillo glowing red. Delastro stared back, unruffled. Flea sensed a sudden tension in the other mercenaries, the rustling of cloth as weapons were readied. The Prime Inquisitor seemed to sense it as well. "Do you have it?" he asked, a cloud of smoke accompanying his words. "The Lord Protector's casket?"

"It's in the carriage."

"Good. Have your crew carry it up to the great hall immediately."

"My crew are mercenaries, not packhorses."

"Your crew are whatever Marquetta wants them to be."

"Not anymore."

"What?"

"We're done. Finished."

"I knew it." Fierro dropped his cigarillo and ground it beneath his boot. "I told Marquetta you wouldn't have the stomach for this."

"Seems like you tell him a lot of things. I wonder why he never listens."

"*Enough,*" Fierro snarled, anger flickering across his face as he pointed at the carriage. "Get that damned casket into the palace. *Now.*"

"Forget it. We're getting out of this city before it devours itself."

"You bloody coward—"

"Save your insults, Fierro. I hope you choke on them. Lady knows it's the least you deserve."

"Says the woman who kills for a living."

"At least I'm honest about my profession." Delastro wheeled her horse round. "Jewels, with me. We ride."

Flea tensed as the driver slid from his seat, but the man didn't notice her as he jumped down from the carriage. One of his comrades offered him a hand and he clambered up onto their horse behind them.

"You'll regret this," Fierro barked. "I'll make sure your reputation is torn to shreds."

The only response he got was the sound of hooves echoing across the palace grounds as the mercenaries spurred their horses back toward the gates. The Prime Inquisitor glared after them, clenching and unclenching his fists in impotent rage. He swore under his breath and turned to the palace entrance. "Boy," he called, snapping his fingers. The boy hurried down the steps, his young face a picture of nerves.

"S-sir?" he warbled, fidgeting with a button on his tunic.

"Never trust a mercenary, boy," Fierro said, opening a silver box and withdrawing another cigarillo. "They'll always be more concerned with saving their own skin than yours."

"Um . . . yes, sir."

The man lit the cigarillo, took a long drag. "What was your name again?" he asked, exhaling a cloud of smoke right into the boy's face.

The boy coughed. "Um, Padran. Sir."

"Then listen closely, *Um* Padran. Go and find Captain Jerima and tell her to bring six of her guards out here. There's a casket in that carriage that needs carrying up to the great hall immediately."

The great hall, Flea thought. *That must be where Marquetta's meeting the Faceless.*

"Um . . . sir?" Padran swallowed nervously. "Captain Jerima is off duty in the evenings. She's probably playing cards in the officers' mess . . ." The boy trailed off as the Prime Inquisitor loomed over him, the hard lines of his face made more severe by anger.

"I don't care whether Jerima is playing cards or sitting on the privy," he growled, flicking ash at the boy. "Find her and bring her here with her men. *Now.*"

"Of—of course," Padran stuttered, as he scuttled back up the steps. "Right away. Sir."

"And Padran?"

The boy paused, looked back.

"If you return without them, I'll slit your throat."

The boy paled, nodded, and fled into the palace.

Flea watched Fierro, looking for any sign that the threat had been a joke. There was none: no suppressed chuckle, no relaxing of his posture. Instead the man paced before the carriage, his movements taut with a barely suppressed rage that Flea suspected was always present, simmering just below his surface. She'd seen plenty of men like the Prime Inquisitor as she'd grown up in the Splinters—men who liked to bully others, who used their anger as both a weapon and a way of disguising their fear. Mostly they met a bloody end. *I hope Fierro does too.*

Her eyes moved to the open palace door and the welcoming glow beyond. *I need to get inside before it closes.* Yet Fierro barred her way, and soon Padran would return with the guards. She looked around, desperately seeking a solution. *Nothing.* Fear squeezed her chest.

Her attention snapped back to Fierro as he suddenly approached the carriage. She tensed, thinking he'd seen her, but instead the man hauled the carriage door open and climbed inside. *Now,* Flea realized. *I've got to go now.* She slipped her hands free from the gloves, which were stuck fast, slid across the roof as quietly as possible, and eased herself off the edge. She dropped down beside the window, hitting the gravel with a soft crunch, and pressed herself against one of the front wheels. Her heart raced as she peered between the horses' legs and eyed the palace entrance. All of a sudden it seemed very far away.

Flea took a deep breath. *Now or never.*

She ran for the door.

37

Still Breathing

How long has it been? Lukan wondered, as he paced back and forth along the alley. *An hour? More? She'll be inside the palace by now.* He paused. *If she found a way in, that is.* He shook his head. *Of course she did. The kid's nothing if not resourceful.* He began pacing again. *But what if she didn't even make it—what if she fell from the carriage?* Images flashed in his mind of Flea lying in the street, limbs splayed and bones broken. *Or worse, what if she's been captured in the palace?* He didn't even want to think what Marquetta would do to her . . .

"Stop pacing," Ashra said.

"What?" Lukan squinted, barely able to make out the shape of the thief where she leaned against a wall, arms folded.

"I said stop pacing. You're like a little boy who needs to piss."

"Sorry. I'm just . . ."

"Nervous."

Lukan swore silently. He did not want to have this conversation again.

"You're nervous about Flea," Ashra pressed.

"Aren't you?" he replied, with more venom than he intended.

"Of course. But it wasn't me who asked this of her."

"You didn't try and talk her out of it."

"Maybe I should have done."

Lukan snorted. "You think she'd have listened? Look, Flea agreed to this. I didn't force her."

"Maybe she felt like she didn't have a choice."

"Of course she did. If she refused, we would have found another way."

"Such as?"

"I don't bloody know . . ." Lukan sucked in a breath, letting his anger cool. "She'll be fine," he continued, trying to reassure himself as much as Ashra. "Flea's tough, she's a survivor—"

"She's eleven years old. A child."

"Try telling her that."

"But if something happens to her—"

"Then I'll regret it for the rest of my life," Lukan snapped. "Trust me, the last thing I want is Flea's death on my conscience. But if we're going to stop Marquetta, we have to take risks. All of us." *And me most of all.* He resumed pacing and this time Ashra made no protest. A moment passed. Then another.

"I hope you're right about this," the thief said eventually.

"About Flea?"

"Flea, the Sandino Blade, Marquetta, the Faceless . . . everything."

"If you have a better plan, I'm all ears."

"I don't. And I'm not questioning your logic or judgment. This plan is the best we've got."

"I sense a *but* coming . . ."

"Just listen, will you?" Ashra demanded, her tone hardening. "In my profession I deal in absolutes. The romantic myth of the thief you see in plays or hear in stories is bullshit. We don't revel in danger or enjoy chancing the odds of the unknown. Instead we examine every angle and possibility. We plot our moves to the smallest detail. Chance and uncertainty are our sworn enemies. And in this plan of yours I'm seeing a lot more of them than I'd like."

"Yeah, you and me both." Lukan sighed. "Ashra, look . . . I'm glad to have you with me and Lady knows we wouldn't have got this far without you, but you've done enough. There's no need for you to risk your life any further. I can handle this on my own."

"Forget it. I'm not walking away. This is my fight as much as it is yours. More, even. And I'll see it through to the end."

Lukan smiled. "Passion before reason."

"What?"

"Don't you remember? It's what the Scrivener said to me this morning. It's always been my weakness, apparently. Perhaps it's yours as well."

"You have it the wrong way round," Ashra replied. "It's reason that brought me here. Not passion."

"Reason?" Lukan echoed. "This plan is . . . well, to call it *unconvincing* would be generous. You mean to say you listened to it and thought, 'Yes, this has a high chance of success, count me in'?"

"Don't be a fool. Of course not. The plan is bad and the odds are worse."

"Then why—"

"Am I here? Because reason tells me that Marquetta must be stopped, and that you—we—are the best chance the city's got. Maybe the only chance. And risking our lives to save thousands of others seems a worthwhile gamble to me. Besides, I won't get a better chance to settle my score with Marquetta."

"Reason before passion," Lukan remarked, with a wry smile that was lost in the darkness. "Doesn't quite have the same ring, does it?"

Ashra made no reply.

Lukan resumed pacing, his thoughts returning to Flea.

"Tell me more about the Faceless," the thief said suddenly, as if to distract him. "I remember my father saying they traveled on some sort of flying ship. But surely that's—"

"Impossible?" Lukan replied. "You'd think. But the most detailed account we have clearly describes the Faceless descending from the sky in a ship forged from metal with black sails. Two of the other records mention it too."

"It seems implausible."

"Trust me, when you've seen what the Faceless can do, a flying ship suddenly doesn't seem so unlikely."

"What else do we know about them?"

"Not much. I've told you most of it already."

"So they appear without warning, trade for these purple crystals, then leave just as quickly," the thief said, recalling Lukan's earlier words during the ceremony. "And they don't use force unless provoked."

"That's what the records suggest," Lukan confirmed. "Oh, and they never speak—instead they're said to communicate by projecting images into the subject's head, though they seem to understand spoken language. I saw Marquetta communicate with them in this fashion. Seemed to give him a bit of a headache."

"But who are the Faceless? *What* are they?"

"I've no idea." He recalled the three masked figures, icy vapor steaming from them as they moved in chilling synchrony. "The records name five of them, but there might be more. They're named for the animals depicted on their armor. I only saw three of them—the Wolf, the Viper, and the Kraken. Whoever they are—*whatever* they are—they're powerful beyond belief, no doubt about that. They travel through portals, for pity's sake."

"So do I."

"Right, but you summon your portals with your Phaeron rings. The Faceless conjured theirs up on their own. And that damned wolf—they summoned that with a snap of their fingers. Even the most powerful gleamers would struggle to perform that kind of sorcery."

"You don't think . . ." Ashra paused. "What if . . . no, it's impossible—"

"I'm starting to think nothing's impossible where the Faceless are concerned," Lukan said dryly. "Go on, speak your mind."

"Fine. What if the Faceless are actually Phaeron who somehow survived the collapse of their civilization?"

"That was a thousand years ago."

"You said yourself the records show the Faceless appearing across centuries."

"True. The last survivors of a lost race, flitting in and out of history." Lukan shrugged. "I mean, I guess it's possible. But . . ."

"But what?"

"The portal the Faceless summoned was different from yours. When you summon yours, you get the glowing Phaeron glyph, right? That didn't happen with the Faceless; theirs manifested in a different way. These little glowing spheres of light that joined together . . ."

"Different sorcery," Ashra said, quick to grasp his meaning.

"Yeah, that's my guess."

A brief silence fell, each of them lost to their own thoughts.

"I still find it strange," the thief said eventually, "that the Faceless trade for these crystals instead of taking them by force. Lowering themselves to murdering on behalf of Marquetta when they could just crush him like a fly and take the blade for themselves."

"It's odd," Lukan agreed, "but like I said, we don't know much about them—there's a reason they faded into myth and became the monsters in children's stories. We don't know the extent of their power or what drives them. Maybe they have, I don't know, some sort of moral code—"

"A moral code?" Ashra snorted. "They set a sorcerous wolf on you, they murdered three—no, *four* people—and you think they have *morals*?"

"Well . . . maybe not," Lukan admitted. "But for some reason conducting a trade seems important to them. Whatever their motives are, they revolve around the crystal. Which means whoever possesses the crystal is in a powerful position. And right now"—he patted the Sandino Blade at his belt—"that's us."

"Let's hope you're right." The thief tilted her head, as if appraising him. "You know a lot about all this. The Faceless, the Phaeron . . ."

"That's what happens when you have an obsessive scholar for a father," Lukan said, unable to keep the bitterness from his voice. "He couldn't get enough of the history of the Phaeron and the myths of the Faceless. And I couldn't help but absorb it all." He sighed. "I came to resent it after my mother died. My father spent more time with his books and scrolls than he did with me. But looking back, maybe that was just how he dealt with his grief."

"You weren't close to your father?"

"No. I was closer to my mother. My father . . . always seemed distracted, as if his mind was elsewhere half the time. When I was younger, he was always good to me. Kind. Generous. That changed after my mother died. I was only eleven and struggling with the emotion of it all. I didn't know how to . . . you know, grieve. I looked to my father for comfort, but it was like he'd changed overnight. He withdrew into himself, became terse and short-tempered—like a completely different person. Shafia, my father's steward, told me it would pass, but as the weeks became months my father only seemed to grow more distant, locking himself away in his study for days at a time. I think he blamed himself for my mother's death, though I've no idea why—the physician said it was a sudden fever that took her. I was only young, but I could sense this . . . *void* growing between us, and I didn't know how to stop it. I guess the fact that I looked like my mother didn't help—same eyes, same color hair . . ."

Lukan trailed off, surprised at how much he'd revealed. He rarely spoke about his father, even with people he knew, but now—standing in the dark with only a thief for company—he found the words almost spilling from his lips. Surprisingly, it felt like a relief to speak them.

"The distance between us only grew as I got older and started getting into trouble. Wine, gambling, women . . ." He shrugged. "Things came to a head when I was kicked out of the Academy for killing Giorgio Castori in a duel. His family, the Castoris, are said to be one of the most powerful families in the Talassian Isles—Giorgio was always boasting about their influence. They demanded compensation, which I told my father not to pay, but he gave in to their demands. They bled us for what was left of our family's fortune and ensured that I became a pariah among Parva's aristocracy. So I left home and have been wandering ever since, trying to find some sort of meaning in my life. Trying and failing."

"But you're still breathing."

"It's not the same as living though, is it?"

"I suppose not."

"I just wish . . ." Lukan shook his head, feeling a fresh jolt of grief. "I wish I'd managed to settle things with him. Make things up with him before he died."

"I know how you feel," Ashra said, a note of sympathy in her voice. "I lost my father when I was young."

"You did?"

"Yes. And not a day passes that I don't wish I could talk to him one more time."

Lukan waited for the thief to elaborate, but it seemed that was all she intended to say. "So these rings of yours," he said, feeling a need to change the subject, "I don't suppose you'd care to share how you came by them?"

"What did 'Phonse tell you?"

"How do you know I asked him?"

"Did you?"

"Um . . . well, yes."

"And?"

"He told me not to ask or he'd have to put a bolt in me."

"There's your answer."

"You don't have a crossbow."

"I can throw a knife just as fast. And I have plenty of those."

"Good. We might need them before the night's out."

They lapsed into silence once more.

When he was sure Ashra wasn't looking—or as sure as he could be in the gloom—Lukan slipped the Sandino Blade from his belt and, holding his breath, pressed a finger to the purple crystal. Nothing. No sense of a colossal, ancient presence. No strange images flitting through his mind like the last time he touched it. He exhaled in relief and removed his finger. *Just exhaustion after all. My own mind playing tricks on me.* It was hardly surprising given all that had happened, all that he'd seen. *I've barely slept properly since I came to this city. And perhaps . . . perhaps the Scrivener was right. Maybe I've been hitting the drink a little too hard. Not that I'd ever admit that to her—*

"This is taking too long," Ashra said, interrupting Lukan's

thoughts and drawing his mind back to more pressing concerns. "I hope Flea is all right."

"I'm sure," he replied, with a confidence he didn't feel, "that she's fine."

———

Miaow.

"Shut up," Flea hissed at the cat. The animal purred in response and rubbed itself against her legs. She sighed. "Stupid thing," she whispered, giving it a quick scratch behind the ears. She'd crossed paths with the tabby cat in a hallway after scampering up a grand, spiraling staircase, and it had followed her as she'd snuck through a series of rooms. At first she'd tolerated its company, finding it soothing to her nerves, and had named it Velmatica after the villainess from her favorite story. But now the damned animal wouldn't leave her alone. Worse, it wouldn't keep quiet.

Miaow.

"Enough!" she hissed, raising a finger. The cat blinked its large green eyes at her. Flea turned back to the doorway and peered through into the corridor beyond. *Looks clear . . . but which way should I go?* The palace had so far proven to be a labyrinth of richly appointed rooms, hallways, and passages, and the sheer opulence of it all—not to mention its confusing layout—had set her mind reeling. Now, as she scanned this new corridor, she felt a sneaking feeling she'd seen it before.

Miiiaaaooow.

"I said *enough*!" Flea shoved the cat away with her foot as it tried to weave between her legs. Velmatica slid across the polished floor tiles on her backside, then turned and hissed, green eyes sparkling with fury. "I'm sorry," Flea whispered, feeling absurdly guilty, "but you can't come with me." The cat fixed her with the sort of withering stare that cats reserve for people who have disappointed them, before slinking off toward a vase that stood on a table at the center of the room. Relieved—and a little sad to see Velmatica go—Flea turned her attention back to the corridor. *I need to find some stairs.* The Prime Inquisitor had told Delastro to carry the chest *up* to the great hall, so Flea guessed the hall was upstairs somewhere. Her task was to get as close to it as possible and then find a safe place to activate Ashra's ring. Without being captured, of course.

Crash.

Flea whirled, heart in her mouth. Her eyes were drawn first to the vase, which now lay in several pieces on the floor, then to Velmatica, who stood on the table. As they locked gazes, Flea could have sworn she saw a glint of satisfaction in the feline's green eyes. *Stupid cat.* She turned back to the door and listened intently.

Silence, save for her own breaths.

"What was that for?" she whispered, scowling at Velmatica. "Are you trying to get me caught?" The cat ignored her as it settled on the table and licked its paws. Then it tensed, ears pricking, before hopping down from the table and bolting toward the other doorway, on the far side of the room. "Thanks," Flea muttered as the cat disappeared, "leave me to clean up your mess . . ." She trailed off, fear lancing through her.

Voices.

Flea's instinct was to run, just as Velmatica had done, just as she herself always did when a purse-snatch went sideways—disappear into the chaos of the market and lose herself amid its familiar stalls. *But this isn't the market.* There was nothing at all familiar about this strange world of wooden paneling, gilt mirrors, and velvet drapes. *And there's far fewer places to hide.*

The voices grew louder, footsteps echoing just beyond the door.

Do something. She glanced around the room and her gaze settled on a statue in one corner. The marble base looked just about wide enough to conceal her. *If they don't look too closely.* Flea was moving before the thought had slipped from her mind. She squeezed in behind the statue just as two guards entered, their short swords drawn. They paused as they saw the smashed vase.

"What in the hells—" one of them started, only to be interrupted by a familiar sound.

Miaow.

Velmatica was back. Flea couldn't see the cat from where she crouched, though she could imagine the slinking form of the animal as she sashayed into the room.

"It's just that bloody cat again," the other guard said, sheathing her sword. "That's the third time this month it's broken something."

"Probably does it on purpose," her male companion agreed. "Little devil."

"Maybe you should file a report."

The man grunted a laugh. "Sure. As if the new Lord Protector's going to care about a broken vase when half the bloody city's on fire."

"I'm not sure he even cares about the fire. Took him long enough to send the gleamers in to deal with the riots." The woman approached a window close to Flea's hiding place. "Lady's blood, it's still going strong. That'll burn all night."

Flea didn't dare to breathe. If the woman so much as glanced to her left, she'd see her instantly, crouched behind the statue's base. She was so close that the girl could see the embossed details on her leather armor.

"Yeah, well I'm bloody glad we're in here and not down there," the man replied.

"Can't argue with that."

"They reckon there's going to be a war. Blood for blood. That's what all the rioting is about. They say the Grand Duke's death can't go unpunished."

"Who says?" the woman asked, a scornful note in her voice. She turned away from the window. "Your drinking companions don't know shit."

Flea sagged with relief as the guard moved away.

"Almiro says," the man replied, a touch defensively. "He should know; he fought in the last war."

"Almiro's a senile old fool and you know it. The Grand Duke only kept him on out of sentiment, and now he's gone I expect

Almiro will be pensioned off— Hey, what the hells are *you* doing, kid?"

Flea's heart lurched; for a moment she thought she'd been discovered. Then a high, tremulous voice sounded.

"I . . . I . . ."

"Lady's mercy," the man breathed. "Between sneaking cats and stuttering boys, I'd almost rather face the riots and fires. Spit it out, kid."

"Um, of course . . ."

The boy from earlier, Flea realized, recognizing his voice. *What's he doing here?* She resisted an urge to steal a glance round the statue.

"I'm sorry to, um, interrupt—" the boy continued.

"You already have," the woman retorted, though there was a touch of amusement in her tone. "Padran, isn't it? What do you want?"

"I'm looking for Captain Jerima." Flea imagined Padran anxiously wringing his hands, as he'd done earlier on the palace steps. "I can't find her—"

"She's probably in the guardroom, playing cards."

"I already looked there."

"Well, in that case she's probably enjoying a little private time with that woman from the kitchens. Best leave her alone." The two guards shared a laugh.

"But it—it's urgent!" Padran squealed, his voice rising even higher.

"Seven shadows," the man sighed. "*What's* urgent?"

"There's a carriage out the front, with a chest that needs carrying up to the great hall—"

"I don't suppose it's a chest full of liquor, by any chance?"

The guards laughed again.

"I-I don't know! But the Prime Inquisitor is out there, and he said it's important."

"The *Prime Inquisitor*?" the man spluttered. "Damn it, boy, why didn't you say so . . ."

"I tried to, but—"

"Let's go," the woman said to her companion. "Best not keep Fierro waiting. This might be important." The two guards left the room, their footsteps receding down the corridor. Flea allowed herself a sigh of relief, which died on her lips as she realized Padran hadn't followed them out; she listened as his softer footsteps moved across the room. One of the couches creaked. *He's sitting down,* she realized, frustration welling inside her. *I'm trapped.*

"Hello, kitty," the boy said, before making that silly kissing noise that Flea had heard people make when trying to attract a cat's attention. Any hope she had that Velmatica might spurn Padran's overtures was dashed when she heard the feline's loud purrs. *Stupid animal.* She had an important mission to carry out, and here she was, stuck behind a statue while a boy petted a cat . . . *A boy who works here at the palace,* she thought suddenly. *Who must know where the great hall is.*

Flea snuck a look round the statue.

Padran was sitting with his back to her as he stroked the cat, which had jumped onto his lap.

Flea crept out from her hiding place, drawing her dagger as she tiptoed toward the boy. Padran remained oblivious as he petted Velmatica, and it was only when the animal hissed at Flea that the boy realized something was amiss. The cat sprang from his lap as Flea placed her blade against his neck. "Don't move," she whispered.

Padran froze, save for his lower lip, which trembled. "I . . . Please—"

"Shut up," Flea cut in, trying to sound menacing despite her racing heart, hoping the boy didn't notice how the dagger twitched in her shaking hand. It occurred to her that she was just as scared as Padran. The realization stung, strengthening her resolve. "Listen to me," she continued, "I need to find a quiet room somewhere. A room where no one goes. Somewhere near the great hall." She wet her lips nervously. "Do you know one?"

"I—I . . . yes, I know a place—"

"How far is it?"

"Not—not far . . ."

"Then take me there. Now."

"But . . . but . . ." The boy's breathing was fast and ragged. "All—all right. But . . . why?"

"Best you don't know." That was the truth; as annoying as she found the boy, with his nervous mannerisms and squeaky, posh voice, Flea didn't want him getting in any trouble. "You're going to take me there by the quickest route, and if anyone challenges us you'll tell them we're working under Marquetta's—I mean the Lord Protector's orders. Got it?"

"Yes," the boy squeaked, meek as a mouse, and Flea scowled with disdain. *He wouldn't last long in the Splinters.* "Then let's go," she replied, lowering her blade.

Padran turned slowly, as if afraid of what he might find. He blinked in surprise. "You're . . . a *girl*—" He fell silent as Flea raised her blade once more.

"And you're an idiot."

He swallowed. "I-I'm sorry."

Flea sighed, shook her head. "Just . . . stop apologizing for everything." She gestured at the door with her knife. "Lead the way."

———————

It's gone wrong. Flea's in trouble. Lukan was pacing again, unable to help himself. This time Ashra hadn't tried to stop him, and he sensed that the thief shared his worry. *It's all my fault. What was I thinking? I should never have asked this of her—*

"Lukan."

"I can't help it," he replied, exasperated. "I just . . . I think something's happened to Flea."

"Lukan, it's not—"

"It *is* my fault. I should never have sent her in there."

"Will you stop wallowing in self-pity and *look at me*."

Lukan turned to the thief. "What is . . ." He trailed off, his mouth dropping open.

Ashra arched an eyebrow, her features illuminated by the golden glow of her ring. "You were saying?"

"She did it," Lukan breathed, relief coursing through him.

"We don't know that," Ashra cautioned. "Someone might have taken my ring from her. There's every chance we'll tumble out the other side and find a load of crossbows pointed at us."

"Wouldn't be the first time," Lukan replied wryly.

Ashra pressed her thumb to the ring, rubbing its surface in a circular motion. Lukan's pulse quickened as the familiar glyph appeared in the air before them, bathing the alley in golden light. The symbol dissolved the same way as before, the resulting sparks forming a glowing ring. The air within began to stir, rippling like the surface of a lake.

"You ready?" Ashra asked.

"To try and strike a deal with the Faceless, who could kill us with a flick of their wrists?" He forced a grin. "Of course." He stepped toward the portal, felt the hairs on his arms rising. He hesitated, trying to force down the fear that was clawing its way into his throat—the terrible knowledge of what was to come. *Pure, grasping cold . . .*

"Want me to hold your hand?" Ashra asked.

"Oh, would you?"

The thief snorted, pushing past him and striding toward the portal.

Lukan took a deep breath and followed.

38

LOOSE THREADS

Lukan's last thought as he stepped into the portal was that perhaps he might find the experience easier this time—and that he might remember something of the journey from one place to another.

He was proven wrong on both counts.

Just like before, the transition was abrupt and disorienting—one moment he was following Ashra into the rippling air, the next he was shivering on a hard floor. Nor was the cold any less forgiving this time round; he shook uncontrollably, gasping as he tried to draw breath into lungs that felt like they were encased in ice. *Lady's blood* . . . He was distantly aware of someone wrapping something round his shoulders. He tried to rise, only to fall back, coughing as dust tickled the back of his throat.

"Get it . . . off," he managed, trying to push the fabric away. He felt a pressure on his arm and looked up, blinking to clear his vision. Flea's face swam into focus, her mouth forming words that Lukan couldn't hear over the distant roar in his ears. "What?" he croaked.

The girl raised a finger to her lips. *Quiet.*

It all came back to Lukan then—where they were, what they had come to do. What he had asked *Flea* to do. The realization that she had succeeded brought a relief that drove the cold from his limbs. "You're all right," he whispered, reaching out a shaking arm to her. The girl rolled her eyes and batted his arm away, then threw the old tapestry she was holding over his head. Lukan coughed again as he pushed it away, grinning despite himself. *Yeah, she's definitely all right.* Still shivering, he managed to push himself up off the floor and looked around the small room. Ashra was sitting nearby, rubbing warmth back into her arms. She gave him an almost imperceptible nod. Lukan's grin faded as he caught sight of the figure standing in one corner—a small boy, eyes wide and mouth agape, holding a lantern in one hand. "Who the hells is that?" he asked, raising a trembling finger.

Flea glanced at the boy. "That's Padran." The boy didn't react to his name, just continued to stare as if he couldn't comprehend what he'd just seen. Lukan could hardly blame him. "He works here at the palace," Flea continued. "He guided me to these rooms."

"Nice of him."

"Well, I did put a blade to his throat."

"I bet you did."

"I had no choice," Flea insisted. "Could hardly use the ring in a room with guards everywhere, could I?" She lowered her voice to a whisper. "Though I do feel a bit bad. Padran's all right for a frilly."

"And the chest?"

"Delastro refused to carry it into the palace. She told the Prime Inquisitor they were leaving the city and then they rode away."

"The Jewels have gone?" Lukan asked, sharing a look with Ashra.

Flea nodded. "Fierro told Padran to fetch the captain of the guard—"

"Captain Jerima," Padran blurted, suddenly finding his voice. His eyes widened in panic. "She—she—that is to say, the Prime Inquisitor told me there's a chest that needs to be moved. He said if I didn't return with the captain as quickly as possible he'd slit my throat—"

"Don't worry about the Prime Inquisitor," Lukan cut in. "If our plan works out you won't need to worry about that bastard ever again."

"Plan?" Padran echoed, glancing round at them. "What plan? Who . . . who are you?"

"I already told you," Flea hissed, waving her blade at the boy. "Better you don't know."

"We need to move," Ashra said, rising to her feet. "Chances are the chest has already been delivered to Marquetta. If he realizes the blade's gone—"

"Let's hope he doesn't," Lukan replied.

"Even so, if he meets with the Faceless before we get there—"

"Then we miss our chance. I know. Can we stop worrying about everything that might go wrong?"

"Preparation is a thief's secret weapon," Ashra said coolly.

"Yeah, well, throwing caution to the wind is mine," Lukan snapped back. "Which is exactly what's called for right now."

"Are you two *done*?" Flea demanded, a look of disgust on her face. "I didn't risk my skin so you two could ruin everything."

"She's right," Ashra said, giving Lukan a sharp look. "We're wasting time."

"Agreed," he replied, ignoring her stare. "Flea, where are we?"

"In some old rooms near the great hall," the girl said, her voice softening. "That's where Marquetta is right now. There's a door round here somewhere that leads to it. Right, Padran?"

The boy didn't reply; instead he just stared at Lukan with wide eyes, mouth slightly gape.

"Hey," Flea said, snapping her fingers.

Padran blinked at her. "She—she mentioned the Faceless," the boy stammered, glancing at Ashra. "She said—"

"How many times do I have to tell you?" Flea growled, pointing her dagger at him.

"Padran," Lukan said, raising a placating hand in Flea's direction. "Just tell us how to get to the great hall."

"There's a secret passage," the boy replied, wringing his hands. "I—I found it last winter. By accident, I mean. It's that way." He pointed to a darkened doorway on one side of the room.

"Can you show us?"

The boy nodded.

A moment passed.

"Go on then," Flea snapped.

The boy jumped. "Oh. Um, this way. Please."

"Idiot," the girl murmured.

"Great work," Lukan told her as the three of them followed Padran. "I knew you could handle it."

The girl dodged his attempt to clap her shoulder.

"Lukan's right," Ashra said dryly. "For once."

"It was nothing," the girl replied, shrugging as she handed Ashra's ring back to the thief, though Lukan thought he saw the hint of a grin beneath her scowl. "Anyway, that's the first part done."

"Let's not get ahead of ourselves," Ashra cautioned. "There's a long way to go."

They walked on in silence.

———

"I—I think this is the one," Padran ventured, picking at a loose thread on one of his cuffs.

"You said that about the last room," Lukan replied.

"Yes, but . . . I feel sure this time—"

"You said *that* as well," Ashra pointed out.

"I know, but . . . I just have a feeling . . ."

Lukan suppressed a sigh. He certainly didn't have a feeling—this room, as far as he could see, looked just like all the others, full of old furniture concealed by yellowed sheets, with layers of thick dust covering every surface. *How many have we passed through now?* He'd lost count; the place was a bloody warren, and their progress was slow as Padran searched every room for whatever he was looking for. The boy had stubbornly refused to be drawn on what exactly that was, perhaps fearing his usefulness would be compromised, and so they'd been forced to trail after him as he scampered from room to room. Padran had been convinced that each of the last three rooms had been the right one, but with each disappointment Lukan had felt his own patience wear a little thinner. *We're running out of time.* The others knew it too; he could see it in the tight line of Ashra's mouth, in the glares that Flea threw at Padran with each admission of failure. If this new room offered up no reward, he would have no choice but to force an explanation from the boy. *With the point of a blade if necessary.* He winced at the thought.

"This is it," Padran said excitedly, running toward a section of wood paneling that looked no different to the many others they'd seen.

"Are you sure?" Lukan asked, doubtful. "I don't see any door . . ."

"Wouldn't be a secret door if you could *see* it," Flea retorted, rolling her eyes.

"Right. So what are we looking for?"

"That sconce," Padran said, hopping from foot to foot, as if sensing his salvation was at hand. "Pull it down!"

Lukan grasped the iron sconce and did as the boy instructed. It moved more easily than he expected, sliding downward before stopping with a loud click. A section of the wood paneling swung open, revealing nothing but darkness beyond.

"Third time's a charm," Lukan murmured, taking the lantern from the boy and holding it up to reveal a secret passage, its bare stone walls and dusty floor leading to a door covered in cobwebs. "How'd you discover this, Padran?"

"Um, well . . ." The boy clasped his hands, shifting awkwardly. "One of the cats came in here, and I was trying to find it, and there was this spider—a really big one, with eyes on stalks, and—"

"Never mind," Lukan cut in, glancing back at the passage. "So that door opens into the great hall?"

"Yes."

"Whereabouts?"

"Um, about halfway down the lower gallery."

"Perfect." *This plan might just work after all.* He patted the boy's shoulder. "You've been a great help to us, Padran."

The boy sagged with relief. "So . . . you're not going to hurt me?"

"Hurt you?" Lukan replied, catching Ashra's inquiring look and responding with a subtle nod. "Of course not."

"So . . . um, can I get back to my duties now?"

"No."

The boy blinked. "But . . . I-I don't understand . . ."

Flea understood, her eyes widening in alarm. "Don't hurt him!" she cried, as Ashra stepped up behind the boy and clamped a damp cloth over his face.

"Says the girl who threatened him with a blade," Lukan said wryly, as Padran struggled and quickly went limp in Ashra's arms.

"I was never going to *hurt* him," Flea protested.

"He'll be fine," Ashra replied, laying the unconscious boy gently on the floor. "He'll wake up in an hour with a bad headache, nothing more than that."

"But what about Fierro? He said he'd slit Padran's throat."

"He won't if he's in chains," Lukan replied. "Padran's safe here for now. We'll leave the lantern for him."

Flea nodded, seemingly mollified. "All right."

"Let's get moving." He checked that the Sandino Blade was secure in his belt. *Can't turn up late to the party without the showpiece. Not when it's the only thing that might keep us alive.* "You know the plan?"

"Yeah," Flea replied, pulling a face. "And it stinks."

"It's got us this far."

"*I* got us this far."

Ashra cleared her throat.

"Ashra *and* I got us this far," Flea corrected.

"Then I guess it's up to me to end this."

"You ready?" Ashra asked.

"I'm not sure I'll ever be ready," Lukan replied, feeling a stab of fear. "In a few moments I could be a steaming lump of meat, or a pile of dust—"

"If you're lucky, maybe they'll just turn you into a frog," Flea offered. "Or a fat, horned toad."

"Either would be an improvement," Ashra put in.

"They can turn me into whatever the hells they want," Lukan retorted, managing a smile, "as long as I'm far away from the pair of you. Now *quiet*."

He led the way into the passage, lantern held aloft, his heart beating faster with every step. *This is it now. No going back.* Ashra and Flea followed silently behind, the absence of conversation forcing his mind back to the matter at hand. Flea was right, the plan stank worse than a week-old corpse left out in the sun, but it was the only shot they had. A desperate gamble to save the city, where the price of failure was death. *Or perhaps something even worse.*

The door at the end of the passage might have been a secret entrance to the great hall, but there was nothing secretive about its operation, a tarnished bronze handle glinting as Lukan approached. He handed the lantern to Flea and gripped the handle, heart now hammering in his chest. He pressed his ear to the door but heard nothing beyond. "Ready?" he whispered over his shoulder.

"Ready," Ashra replied, cool as ever. Flea merely nodded, her face set with determination. Lukan felt a sudden urge to pull her close, this fiery girl who had tried to pick his pocket back in the Plaza of Silver and Spice. He'd known her for little more than a week, but it felt as if she'd been at his side far longer, teasing him and testing the limits of his patience. *Not to mention saving my life twice—*

"Lukan," Flea hissed.

He blinked. "What?"

"Why are you staring at me?"

"Oh . . . sorry." The urge to embrace the girl faded—he'd only get a punch in the face for his trouble, and the last thing he needed before confronting the Faceless was a bleeding nose. "All right," he said, taking a deep breath. "Here goes. Remember the plan." He turned the handle and pulled the door open, expecting a squeal from a rusty hinge. Instead the door opened silently.

Light spilled through from beyond, revealing a polished floor and marble columns set at regular intervals. *Looks like Padran was right. This has to be the great hall.* He glanced around, expecting to see guards reacting with alarm to his presence, but the immediate area was deserted. A voice sounded from deeper in the hall, somewhere to his left. He couldn't see the speaker, nor make out the words, but there was no mistaking their cadence and intonation.

"He's here," he whispered, glancing over his shoulder. "Marquetta is . . ." He frowned at Ashra. "Where's Flea?"

"Taking the lantern back to Padran. You said we'd leave it with him."

"Right." He felt a flicker of guilt for leaving the boy alone and unconscious, but forced it aside. "Listen," he continued, taking advantage of Flea's absence, "if this goes wrong—"

"I'm to get Flea out of here. I know."

"It's just that . . . if something happens to me, I worry she'll do something stupid."

"You mean like trying to save your life again?"

"Something like—wait, she told you about that?"

"Of course. She seemed rather pleased about it."

"I'll bet she bloody is. I was hoping she'd keep it to herself."

"The girl's got a mind of her own."

"Yeah, that's what I'm worried about—"

"What are you worried about?" Flea whispered as she rejoined them. Lukan hadn't heard her approach, could barely even see her in the darkness of the passage.

"Oh, you know. Being turned into a horned toad or something."

"Are they there?" the girl asked, trepidation edging her voice. "The Faceless?"

"Let's find out."

Lukan slipped through the door and crept across to the nearest column, Ashra and Flea following behind. A glance to his right revealed the great hall's doors, which were closed and unattended. *Can't have any guards witnessing their Lord Protector's treachery.* The voices sounded again to his left, drawing his gaze to a huge window at the far end of the hall, the glass reflecting the light of a hundred candles. Banners hung on either side, the black bat of Saphrona on its gold background, along with the personal standard of the late Grand Duke. Marquetta hadn't found time to replace the latter with his own symbol, but he lounged on the throne beneath the window all the same. Lukan's expression hardened as he watched the Lord Protector smiling as he spoke, uncaring as to the havoc that his plotting had unleashed upon the city. Still, at least he wasn't wearing the look of a man who had learned his most valuable possession had been stolen. *He doesn't know about the blade,* Lukan realized, with a smile of his own. That meant the Faceless hadn't already arrived to claim their prize. *We're just in time.*

His gaze moved to a figure standing before the throne. *The Pontifex.* The man was clearly a bundle of nerves. He fidgeted with his rings, with the buttons on his gown, with the amulet round his neck. *Guilt at his involvement?* Lukan wondered, as the man dabbed sweat from his forehead with a silken handkerchief. *Or terror at being stuck between two fates?* A fresh cut on his cheek was no doubt Ashra's handiwork, though Lukan still had no idea how she had obtained the code from the man and bought his silence at the same time. Whatever the thief's method, it seemed to have worked. *Two of the players are here,* Lukan thought, *but where's the third?*

As if in answer, the doors to the hall creaked open and the Prime Inquisitor strode through, customary cigarillo clamped between his lips, which were drawn in a scowl. Several guards struggled along behind him, red faces shining with sweat as they strained beneath the weight of the Phaeron chest.

"Apologies for the delay, my lord," Fierro called out as he approached the throne. "It seems the efficiency of the palace guard is not what it could be." He threw a glare at the guards, who struggled along in his wake.

"No matter, Fierro," Marquetta replied, waving the apology away. "Our guests have not yet arrived." He gestured at the floor to one side of the throne. "Leave it there."

"You heard the Lord Protector," Fierro barked. "Quickly!"

With a final effort, the guards set the chest down.

"Now get out," the Prime Inquisitor added, flicking ash from his cigarillo.

The guards didn't need to be told twice. Fierro followed them to the doors, which he then slammed shut and slid a bar across.

"Excellent work, Fierro," Marquetta said as the Prime Inquisitor stalked back toward the throne, not so much as glancing at the column where Lukan, Flea, and Ashra hid. "Now, if you wouldn't mind fetching our dear friend . . ."

Fierro disappeared into the shadows in one corner of the hall and reappeared with a body slung over his shoulder, which he unceremoniously dumped before the throne. *Artemio,* Lukan realized, as the figure struggled to sit up. The last time he'd seen the Lord Chancellor had been in the chaos following the Grand Duke's assassination, as the small man pleaded for calm. Now he was gagged and tied, blood seeping from a cut on his head.

"Artemio," Marquetta said brightly, leaning forward. "How kind of you to join us. I only wish the circumstances were different. You should be standing here with Barbosa and Fierro, but instead you're trussed up like a hog for the roasting spit. What a shame you refused my offer. We could have been allies, but no— you just had to stick to those morals of yours." He shook his head in mock sadness. "Such a pity. I could have used your skills in the days ahead. I'll need every last copper if I'm to restore Saphrona's glory and give the Zar-Ghosans a bloody reminder of our superiority. You're good at raising coin, Artemio, I'll give you that, but you've always spent it in the wrong ways. Charitable works, donations to the poor . . ." Marquetta spat the last word as if it tasted foul. "Those wretches already bleed the Lady's coffers dry, as our esteemed friend here can attest. Isn't that right, Your Holiness?"

The Pontifex stiffened. "Ah . . . yes. Quite right, my lord."

"So you see," Marquetta continued smoothly, "there simply isn't any room for *charity*. Nor weakness. This city has forgotten its own glorious past, when strength of arms was a virtue, when our power cast a shadow that the Zar-Ghosans cowered beneath. Such a time can come again, but not with a simpering weakling like the Grand Duke on the throne. Not with upstarts on the council who would see even more of our wealth given away to the poor. No, Saphrona needs strong men to restore its former glory. Men of means, but more importantly men of vision. Men who won't flinch, who have the courage to do what needs to be done . . . What was that, Artemio?" He looked to the Prime Inquisitor. "Fierro, it seems our dear friend has something to say. If you would be so kind . . ."

Fierro strolled toward the Lord Chancellor, exhaling a cloud of smoke. "Cry for help," he said, speaking around his cigarillo, "and I'll open your throat here and now." With one sharp tug he pulled the gag from the man's mouth.

"You were saying, Artemio?" Marquetta prompted, eyes alight with amusement.

The small man pushed himself onto his knees and looked the Lord Protector in the eyes. "You can kill me," he said, his voice calm and measured, "just as you've killed all the others. But it will do you no good. You can't kill what this city has become, what it represents."

"And what's that?" Fierro sneered, blowing a cloud of smoke in the Lord Chancellor's face.

"Hope," the man replied, unflinching. "Peace. Prosperity. Progress. You think your vision for this city—this vision of might and conquest—is born of loyalty to Saphrona. Love, even. But it's not. It's born from fear, from a desperate need to reforge the world into a vision that you don't feel threatened by—"

"That's enough," Marquetta said airily, gesturing at Fierro.

"You can't kill hope," Artemio shouted, before the Prime Inquisitor shoved the gag back in his mouth.

"That's where you're wrong. I can kill who or whatever I want." Marquetta paused and glanced to his right, where a glowing scarlet orb had materialized in the air. "As you are about to witness," he added, his smile widening. "What marvelous timing . . ."

"Look," Flea whispered. "Over there—"

"I see it," Lukan replied, swallowing his fear as the purple and green orbs appeared, joining the first in the familiar circular motion.

Fierro and the Pontifex both backed away, as they had done the first time in the catacombs. Artemio simply stared with wide eyes as the orbs began to move more quickly, blurring into the ring of white light. Flea shifted uneasily beside Lukan as the portal expanded, her face pale even though she'd seen it all before. He took her hand as the air contorted, lightning flickering across its roiling surface. For once the girl didn't try to shove him away. Ashra watched in silence, her mouth a tight line; as unfamiliar as this sorcery might have been to her, she was no stranger to portals.

Yet even she couldn't help but gasp at what came through.

The lightning flickered around the first armored shape to emerge, icy vapor steaming from ornate crimson plate edged with silver. *The Wolf*, Lukan realized, his stomach lurching. *Leading the way, just like last time*. The figure's cloak of liquid shadow swirled, as if catching an otherworldly breeze, garnet eyes in the wolf-shaped pauldrons flashing as they caught the candlelight. The Kraken appeared next in its familiar armor of purple and bronze, followed by the Viper in plate mail of green and gold. The three figures stood in a row as the portal closed silently behind them. Then they stepped forward in unison, their synchronicity just as unnerving as Lukan remembered. He took a deep breath, trying to slow his racing heart.

"When I was a boy," Marquetta said, adopting a conversational tone, "one of my aunts owned a tapestry that depicted an ancient battle, the name of which I forget. It was a beautiful piece of work, truly wonderful."

The Faceless approached Artemio, their strides measured and imbued with dread purpose. The Lord Chancellor remained still, staring at them in horror.

"My aunt also had a cat," Marquetta continued, "and one day the cat managed to get into the room where the tapestry hung. The little monster must have found a loose thread, because by the time my aunt's butler chanced upon the scene the tapestry had been ruined."

The Faceless halted before Artemio.

"Even though I was just a child, I understood the moral of the story. That no matter how meticulous your work, it only takes one loose thread for it to all unravel." Marquetta smiled coldly. "My problem is that I don't just have one loose thread. I have three."

His words hung in the air for several heartbeats.

"Three," Fierro echoed, his brow creasing.

"No," the Pontifex said weakly, for once grasping the situation more quickly than the Prime Inquisitor. "Lord Protector, please . . . I—I've always been loyal—"

"You *fool*," Fierro cut in, spitting the word around his cigarillo. "He's not referring to us." The glance he threw at Marquetta suggested he lacked the conviction of his words.

The Faceless moved as one, shadow cloaks swirling around their armored forms as they strode past the trembling form of Artemio.

"Marquetta?" Fierro asked, hand moving to his sword as he took a step back. "What's happening here?"

"It's ironic," Marquetta mused, "that a man whose profession requires him to seek out the truth cannot see it at the time of his own death."

The Prime Inquisitor's face darkened. "You . . . you would betray me? You *coward*."

"Peace, Fierro. Show some dignity."

"I'll have your bastard head," the Prime Inquisitor barked, steel rasping as he drew his sword.

"No," Lukan murmured. *I need Marquetta alive.*

As Fierro lunged at the Lord Protector, the Kraken raised one gauntleted hand, and what Lukan could think of only as a *tentacle* of black energy shot through the air, wrapping itself round the Prime Inquisitor's sword arm. The man's cigarillo fell from his lips as he was wrenched backward. He hit the floor hard but regained his feet quickly, sword still in hand, murder flashing in his eyes. "Think you can take me?" he snarled at the Faceless, who stood in a silent line before him. The Kraken jerked its hand and the tentacle released the Prime Inquisitor. He staggered and lashed out at the tentacle with his sword, only for the blade to pass straight through as if slicing smoke.

"Cowards!" Fierro barked, backing away. "Hiding behind your masks and sorcery . . . Face me with a blade, damn you!"

The Faceless exchanged sightless glances. The Wolf then stepped forward, raising a fist. A corona of scarlet energy flickered around its gauntleted fingers, solidifying into the shape of a crystalline sword that glowed with a crimson light. Fierro bellowed and leaped at the armored figure, which parried his savage cut with ease. Light flashed as their blades came together and the Prime Inquisitor's sword shattered, fragments of steel skittering away across the tiles. Fierro bared his teeth—the last act of defiance from a cornered animal—and hurled his sword hilt at the Wolf. It struck the figure full on the helm, but didn't slow its advance. The Prime Inquisitor turned and ran for the doors as his courage failed him.

He didn't make it more than a few paces.

With an action that appeared almost lazy, the Wolf hurled its crystalline blade through the air. The spinning sword took the fleeing man square in the back, sending him to the floor, where he twitched and gasped and bled and—after several heartbeats—died.

"Lady's blood," Ashra whispered. "The Scrivener was right. This is madness. We can't fight them."

"We won't need to," Lukan replied, trying to keep the fear from his voice. "Not if I'm right about this."

"And if you're not?"

"Then pray to the Lady for divine intervention."

"That doesn't appear to be working too well for His Holiness."

The Pontifex had fallen to his knees, trembling arms raised as his lips moved in what Lukan suspected was the first sincere prayer he'd offered in years—perhaps ever.

It did him no good.

The Kraken's black tentacle shot toward the man and seized him by the throat. His eyes bulged, bright with panic, as he tried to free himself. His grasping, bejeweled fingers closed on empty air.

"Peace, Barbosa," Marquetta called out, raising a hand. "There is no truer sacrifice than dying in service to an ideal greater than oneself."

The Pontifex's face was turning purple, spittle foaming on his lips.

"You have my deepest thanks," Marquetta continued. "Cherish it, for I'm sure it's more than you'll receive from the Lady when you stand before Her."

Barbosa's eyes glazed over, his body slackening. The black tentacle disappeared like ink dissolving in water and the Pontifex toppled to the floor, where he lay unmoving in a puddle of silken robes.

"Good riddance," Ashra murmured. "That was a better death than he deserved."

Marquetta rose from his throne and approached Artemio, not giving the Pontifex's corpse so much as a glance as he passed. "My dear Lord Chancellor," he said, spreading his arms, "do you think me cruel? Do you fear you will suffer a similar fate at the hands of the Faceless? Well, worry not. I won't let them kill you." He stood before the man and drew a knife from his belt. "I intend to indulge in that little pleasure myself." The Lord Protector raised the blade, only to freeze, grimacing in apparent pain. "Yes," he hissed through gritted teeth, raising a hand toward the Faceless. "I-I haven't forgotten . . . the payment. Of course . . . Let me fetch it for you."

The Lord Protector staggered as whatever telepathic hold the Faceless had over him withdrew. Straightening, he sheathed his dagger and started toward the Phaeron chest.

"This is it," Lukan whispered, his throat dry. "Stay here, both of you. If this goes wrong, then run. Get the hells away from here."

"I'll come with you," Ashra replied, drawing her stiletto.

"No. I have to do this alone."

"Lukan," Flea said, as he started to move away.

"What?"

The girl balled her fist and drove it into his thigh. "Don't die," she told him, her gaze fierce.

He forced a grin. "I'll try not to."

With those last words—and a deep breath to try to slow his pounding heart—Lukan stepped round the column and strode toward Marquetta and the Faceless with as much conviction as he could muster. It wasn't easy, deliberately walking toward mythical beings who wielded power far beyond his comprehension, but he found strength in the knowledge that there was no other way, and in knowing that he was—for once—doing the right thing. *Just a shame it's probably going to get me killed.* He gritted his teeth as the Faceless turned at his approach, feeling the weight of their collective gaze almost as a physical force. He expected the Wolf to summon another crystalline blade, or the Kraken to hurl a black tentacle at him. Perhaps the Viper would even get in on the act.

Instead the armored figures appeared unmoved by his presence.

The same couldn't be said for Artemio. The man stared at him, wide eyes pleading. It would have taken only a moment to cut him free, but Lukan ignored him and pressed on. The situation was on enough of a knife-edge as it was, and he couldn't risk complicating it any further.

The Faceless remained still as Lukan drew close to the throne, as if intrigued by his presence and curious as to his intent. The Lord Protector, by contrast, hadn't even registered his arrival, absorbed as he was in the act of entering the correct code on the Phaeron chest.

"It has been an honor doing business with you," Marquetta said, pressing the final panel with an unnecessary flourish. The panels flashed their respective colors, a series of clicks sounding as the chest unlocked and the lid began to rise. "And now here's the Sandino Blade, just as I . . ."

Marquetta's jaw dropped as he stared at the empty interior.

"Looking for this?" Lukan said, drawing the blade from his belt.

Marquetta's head snapped up, his face darkening with fury. "Master Gardova," he replied, quickly recovering his composure as he stood. "Once again you surprise me with your stupidity.

Don't you realize that stealing from the Lord Protector is punishable by death? Not a pleasant one, I might add."

"The same is true of people who cross the Faceless."

Marquetta glanced at the three armored figures, though his smile remained in place.

"I must confess," he continued, moving to stand beside the throne, "a certain curiosity as to how you were able to steal my property. Perhaps you would enlighten me."

"You could have asked the Pontifex, if you hadn't already murdered him."

"Ah, Barbosa," the Lord Protector murmured, his gaze moving to the man's corpse in its puddle of silks. "For a man of the Lady, it was faith he lacked most of all."

"Or you could have asked Delastro," Lukan continued, enjoying the way Marquetta's eyes narrowed at the mention of the mercenary's name. "If she were here, of course. Though I understand she and her crew have already left the city."

"Then more fool them," Marquetta snapped, his mask of cool disdain slipping. "I offered her a fortune and she willingly signed up for it. What could a pauper like you possibly have offered that would change her mind?"

"Blood." Lukan managed a smile. "Sometimes it's more valuable than gold."

"Oh, I'd certainly pay a lot to see you bleeding out before me. But fortunately I get that for free." Marquetta turned to the Faceless. "You see this man?" he demanded, jabbing a finger at Lukan. "He has the Sandino Blade—the crystal I promised you. Kill him and take what is rightfully yours."

The Faceless remained still.

"Take it!" Marquetta shouted. "Kill him!"

The Wolf broke rank and started toward Lukan with slow, purposeful movements. Lukan swallowed his fear and held his ground. *They never use force to take a crystal.* He raised the blade, the purple gem glinting in the candlelight. *Let's see if that's true.*

The Wolf continued to advance. As it passed by the Prime

Inquisitor's corpse, it effortlessly pulled the crystalline sword from the man's back. Blood dripped to the polished floor.

"I wish to discuss a trade," Lukan called out, unable to keep the tremor from his voice. "Agree to my terms and this blade is yours."

The Wolf raised its sword as it approached, closing the distance between them to ten paces. Nine. Eight.

I was wrong, Lukan thought, terror gripping him as he backed away. He glanced toward the secret doorway, saw Flea and Ashra watching with horror from behind the pillar. *Too far.* He'd make it only a few steps before the crystalline sword cut him down.

"Lukan!" Flea cried, Ashra hauling the girl back as she tried to come to his aid.

"Go!" Lukan yelled, waving frantically. "Get the hells out of here!" He turned back to the Wolf, who still advanced in silence. *It's all been for nothing,* he thought, lowering the Sandino Blade, hopelessness stealing over him. *It's finished.* He didn't bother drawing his own sword; there seemed little point. *Better just to get this over with—*

Lukan gasped as he felt something shift inside his skull, a cold presence that stole the breath from his lungs. He fell to his knees, gritting his teeth as icy fingers seemed to grasp at his very thoughts. He shuddered, instinctively trying to fight back, to resist the intruding force. Suddenly an image formed in his mind: an old willow tree, its low-hanging branches reaching out across the sun-dappled surface of a river. Dragonflies hovered amid the reeds at the river's edge, iridescent wings flashing in the sunlight. *The river at the bottom of the orchard.* It had been his favorite place as a child, where he'd whiled away lazy summer days, and where—when he was older—he had brooded on his relationship with his father. A place of comfort he'd not thought about for years. *So why am I thinking about it now?*

Realization dawned as the image faded.

I didn't think of it. The Faceless placed the image in my mind. Lady's mercy, they can see my memories. And they picked this one to show me—but why? To demonstrate their power? Lukan winced as the cold intensified, as if in denial. *No . . . then maybe they hope to calm me, to reassure me they mean no harm.* The cold lessened in confirmation.

Lukan looked up to find the Wolf standing before him.

"I understand," he said, rising to his feet and staring at where the eye slits should have been on the figure's featureless helm. "You want to talk to me."

A pulse of ice shot through his mind in clear response. *Yes.*

"Then speak. I'm listening."

An image of the Sandino Blade formed in his mind, followed by a series of others—a pile of gems, a chest of gold, a bundle of silks. As the last image faded, another pulse flared. A question.

"You're asking me what I want in return for the blade. The crystal."

Another pulse of ice.

Lady's blood, Lukan thought, exhilaration pushing out his fear. *The stories are true. They won't take a crystal by force . . .*

The pulse came again, stronger this time.

"All right," Lukan replied, raising a hand. "I hear you. And I'll give you the crystal, but I don't want gold or gems in return—"

"No," Marquetta shouted, snatching up his cane from where it stood propped against the throne. "This man's a thief . . . I demand you kill him and take what is rightfully yours!"

"You're a fine one to talk," Lukan shot back, "given you had Delastro steal the crystal from Lord Sandino."

"That old fool had no idea of what he possessed, he didn't deserve to have it." Marquetta slashed the air with his cane. "Kill him!" he urged again, glancing at the Kraken and the Viper. "I *order* you to kill him."

None of the Faceless moved.

"What I want," Lukan continued, addressing the Wolf, "is proof of your dealings with this man." He pointed the blade at Marquetta, who glared back with naked fury. "Proof of the crimes—um, the *acts* that you carried out on this man's behalf.

Proof that you killed Lord Saviola, that you possessed the Zar-Ghosan ambassador to kill the Grand Duke and his two sons. Proof of everything. Can you do that?" *Because if you can't, this has all been for nothing—*

"You insolent wretch," Marquetta spat, twisting his cane's handle and pulling away the casing to reveal a long, thin blade. He hurled the casing aside as he stormed toward Lukan. "You think to use *my* crystal as a bargaining tool against me?"

"Can you do that?" Lukan repeated, keeping his gaze on the Wolf.

A single icy pulse. *Yes.*

Lukan grinned at Marquetta. "Looks like I just did."

The Lord Protector lunged at him with surprising speed, the point of his blade not nearly as sharp as the rage in his eyes. Lukan twisted away from the thrust and drew his own sword.

He needn't have bothered.

The Kraken raised a hand, and a black tentacle shot through the air, wrapping around Marquetta and hauling him backward. The Lord Protector hit the floor hard, breath exploding from his lungs as his blade skittered away across the tiles.

Ice pulsed in Lukan's mind and he turned back to the Wolf. The armored figure's left arm was outstretched, a small object—oval in shape and black as jet—resting in its palm. Tentatively Lukan reached out, only to jerk his hand back as two icy pulses flared. *No.* He watched as the Wolf brought the object close to its helm. For several heartbeats nothing happened; then golden light flared round the object, before fading as quickly as it had come. When the Wolf lowered its hand again, Lukan saw a glowing golden symbol etched into the surface of the oval. *What in the hells just happened? What even is this thing?* He opened his mouth to ask the question, only to realize that the Wolf had heard his thought as if he'd spoken it aloud. The armored figure pressed a finger to the glowing symbol.

The golden light returned, radiating up from the object in a shimmering prism. At first Lukan saw nothing within the light, save what looked like sparkling motes of dust. Then an image formed: Marquetta, gesturing as he spoke to the three Faceless. Lukan flinched as he heard the Lord Protector's voice, loud and clear.

". . . so you can do it then? You can possess, ah, *control* the ambassador as if she were a puppet? Because I need her to kill the Grand Duke, you understand. My whole design pivots around that detail . . ."

Lukan looked at Marquetta, who was sitting on the floor, tentacle still wrapped around him, his mouth hanging open in disbelief as he listened to his own voice sounding from the black object. The prism of light flickered, showing another scene.

". . . needs to look like Saviola was murdered, you understand? I need the blame to fall on Lady Jelassi . . ."

Memories, Lukan realized, a shiver inching up his spine. *The Wolf has placed its memories of the Faceless's dealings with Marquetta in that object.* How the Wolf had done so, or how the object even worked, Lukan couldn't begin to guess. It didn't matter—this was all the proof he needed. *And if anyone doubts what happened here tonight,* he thought, looking to Artemio, who was watching events through wide eyes, *they only need to ask the Lord Chancellor. Poor bastard's had a front-row seat.*

A pulse of ice drew his gaze back to the Wolf.

"I accept your offer," he told the armored figure.

"No," Marquetta groaned from the floor. "The crystal is mine . . . you can't do this—"

"Just watch me," Lukan replied, as the Wolf pressed the black oval into his free hand. The object was warm to the touch, golden symbol still glowing. In return he held out the Sandino Blade, which the armored figure took without hesitation.

Three icy pulses flashed through his mind. *Goodbye.* The Wolf began to turn away.

"Wait!" Lukan called, stepping forward. "What are these crystals? Why do you seek them?" He knew he was taking a risk, pushing his luck further than he had any right to, but he couldn't let this opportunity pass by. As the Wolf regarded him, he half expected the figure to raise its crystalline sword to punish him for his insolence.

Instead, an image formed in his mind: a vast city, black towers rearing up against the sky. *Phaeron towers,* he realized, *they look just like the Ebon Hand. Lady's blood, this is a Phaeron city* . . .

The image faded, to be replaced by another: a cavernous room with a huge purple crystal at its center. The crystal rested in a metal cradle, with some sort of tendrils attached to its smooth, faceted surface. A bright glow pulsed in its depths like a heartbeat, illuminating several humanoid figures as they fought beside the crystal. *Lady's blood, are they Phaeron?* The staccato light lent the scene a dreamlike quality, offering only glimpses of the struggle. One of the figures broke free from the melee and threw themselves at the gem, a spherical object held in their outstretched hand.

A blinding light as the crystal shattered . . .

Another scene followed, a landscape that Lukan had never seen, but had heard so much about—a scarred, shadow-haunted landscape where the ruins of black towers cowered beneath a bruised sky. *The Grey Lands* . . . *Seven shadows, the theories were right—it was some sort of sorcerous cataclysm that destroyed the Phaeron.*

The image faded from his mind. Lukan realized he'd been holding his breath and sucked in a lungful of air, his mind racing through the implications of what he'd just seen—the end of the Phaeron civilization, if he was correct, and the creation of the Grey Lands. Yet what was the purpose of the huge gem, and what had the fighting been about? *The purple crystals,* he realized, *they're shards from the huge gem. But what do the Faceless want with them?* So many questions, yet there was one that surged to the front of his thoughts. "Are you," he managed, pointing a shaking finger at the Wolf, "are you . . . Phaeron?"

A single icy pulse. *No.*

Lady's blood, they're something else entirely. "Then—then what are—"

Lukan gasped as three pulses flashed through his mind, severing whatever link he shared with the Faceless. He staggered, feeling suddenly dizzy. The Wolf turned away and strode back toward its companions.

"I'll let you keep that secret," Lukan murmured as the three glowing orbs appeared in the corner of the hall, a new portal materializing within moments. The Wolf and the Viper started toward it, leaving the Kraken standing over Marquetta. The Lord Protector gasped as the black tentacle tightened around his chest.

"Please," Lukan said, appealing to the Kraken with a raised hand. "I need him alive. Though if you could perhaps leave him unconscious . . ."

The Kraken flicked its wrist and the black tentacle snapped out, hurling Marquetta across the hall. The Lord Protector's cry was cut short as he slammed into the base of a pillar and crumpled to the floor.

"Yeah," Lukan said, lowering his hand. "That'll do it."

The Kraken rejoined the two other Faceless, the three of them standing before the portal as the violet lightning flickered across its churning expanse. One by one they stepped through—the Viper first, then the Kraken, lastly the Wolf.

The portal closed behind them.

It's over. Lukan sank to his knees, exhaustion sweeping over him. He stared at the black oval in his hand, golden symbol aglow. *Oh Father, how you would have loved to see this . . .*

The hall doors boomed as something struck them from the other side, accompanied by the faint clamor of raised voices.

Ah, the palace guard with the fashionable late entrance.

"Lukan!"

He looked up to find Flea running toward him, and barely had time to stand before the girl threw herself at him.

"I'm fine," he said, as she hugged him tightly. "I'm all right."

"I can't believe your stupid plan worked," she replied, grinning as she pulled away.

He managed a weak smile in return. "That makes two of us."

"Three," Ashra said as she joined them.

The hall doors boomed again.

"Yeah, well I couldn't have done this without either of you."

"Let's save the backslapping for later," the thief replied, drawing her stiletto. "I'll cut Artemio free. Hopefully he'll be able to explain this damned mess to the guards." As Ashra set about slicing through the Lord Chancellor's bonds, Lukan approached Marquetta, Flea trailing behind him.

"Is he dead?" the girl asked.

I bloody hope not. "No," he replied, relieved to find a faint pulse below his fingers as he pressed them to the man's neck. "But when he wakes up he'll damn well wish he were."

Boom. The hall doors flew open and a group of guards charged through, swords drawn, led by a short, stout woman whose shoulders bore golden epaulettes. "Don't move!" she bellowed at Ashra. "Drop your weapons and . . . and . . ." She trailed off, her wide eyes moving to the dead bodies of the Pontifex and Prime Inquisitor, and then to where Lukan and Flea crouched over Marquetta.

"I can honestly say," Lukan said, raising a hand as he stood, "that this is not what it looks like."

"Seize them!" the woman bellowed, regaining her composure.

Ashra tore the gag from Artemio's mouth.

"Stop!" the Lord Chancellor cried out, lurching to his feet and staggering toward the guards, waving his hands like a madman. "Lower your weapons!"

"Lord Chancellor?" the woman asked, now completely befuddled. "The Lord Protector told us not to enter under any circumstances, but we heard shouting, and I thought—"

"The Lord Protector," Artemio interrupted, "is a murderer and a traitor."

"A . . . *murderer*? I-I don't understand."

"Neither do I, Captain, but trust me on this: Lower your weapons."

The woman and her fellow guards exchanged baffled looks but did as asked.

"Marquetta is guilty of the Grand Duke's murder," Artemio continued, his voice firm and measured, "as well as those of his sons, and Pontifex Barbosa and Prime Inquisitor Fierro. He would have murdered me too, if it weren't for the intervention of this fellow here"—he gestured at Lukan—"and his two friends. I owe them my life."

"You're . . . sure about this, Lord Chancellor?" the captain asked, her tone one of disbelief. "You're saying the Lord Protector murdered the Grand Duke—"

"And his sons," Lukan cut in, already growing tired of the conversation. "And those two sacks of shit over there, who were in on the entire conspiracy until Marquetta decided they were expendable. Oh, and he also had the Faceless murder Lord Saviola so he could frame Zandrusa—ah, Lady Jelassi—for the crime."

The captain stared at Lukan, utterly lost for words.

Lukan grinned at her. "I can prove it," he added, holding up the black oval. "All of it."

"Please," Artemio interjected. "Captain . . . ?"

The woman straightened, a little of her resolve returning. "Jerima, sir."

"Captain Jerima, please send word to the Inquisition," the Lord Chancellor continued, in the manner of someone used to dealing with crises—though Lukan doubted that the man had had to deal with anything quite like this before. "And summon all members of the Gilded Council. We need to show the merchant princes the full extent of their Lord Protector's treachery."

The captain glanced at Lukan, at the dead bodies, at the unconscious form of Marquetta, and clearly decided that she wasn't paid enough to deal with this sort of shit. "Fetch the Inquisition," she ordered one of her guards, before issuing the others a series of instructions. They all saluted and disappeared back through the doors.

"It's done," the captain said, turning back to Artemio. "While we wait, perhaps you could tell me what in the hells happened here."

"Oh, we can do better than that," Lukan said, pressing his thumb to the golden symbol on the oval. "We can show you."

39

PROFESSIONAL CURIOSITY

It had been only a few days since Lukan had last stood in the atrium of Zandrusa's villa, yet it seemed like a lifetime had passed. Even so, the place was just as he remembered it: colorful birds flitting between the small trees, sunlight flashing on the waters of the fountain. The only thing missing was Magellis, the traitor who for years had posed as Zandrusa's steward. *And a fat lot of good that did him.* Magellis had been rewarded with a slit throat courtesy of Delastro's blade, and for all Lukan knew his corpse still lay down in the catacombs, rats gnawing at his bones. As for his real master, Marquetta, the former merchant prince was chained up in the Ebon Hand—apparently in the same cell that Zandrusa had occupied. *Which is no less than he deserves.*

It was over.

Marquetta's treachery had been revealed, Saphrona saved, Zandrusa's innocence proven.

And yet, as Lukan sat in the sunlight, he couldn't shake the unease that lingered at the back of his mind. He shivered despite the warmth. *It's just tiredness,* he told himself, stifling a sudden yawn. Three days had passed since he'd thwarted Marquetta's plans, and they'd been nothing if not exhausting, filled with endless interrogations from a series of inquisitors who all seemed determined to exonerate their leader—and institution—of any involvement in Marquetta's conspiracy. They grilled him for hours at a time, denying him food and water and rest, repeatedly trying to tear his story apart at the seams—not least the parts involving the Faceless.

Lukan could hardly blame them; even to him his tale of murders and mercenaries, spectral wolves and purple crystals sounded like the ravings of a lunatic. Yet the black oval, as strange an artifact as it was, backed up his story, projecting the Wolf's memories in golden light every time he pressed the glowing symbol. More importantly, so did Artemio. The Lord Chancellor confirmed every detail of what had unfolded in the palace's great hall, leaving Lukan grateful that Marquetta hadn't slit his throat when he'd had the chance. Even so, it was the word of another man that ultimately convinced Lukan's interrogators that he was telling the truth.

The Pontifex, it transpired, hadn't died at the hands of the Faceless. Whether it was his fleshy neck that had saved him from the Kraken's black tentacle, or the Lady looking out for Her wayward disciple (highly unlikely, in Lukan's opinion), he had instead fallen unconscious and remained that way for nearly two days. When he finally awoke and learned that Marquetta was in chains, he had confessed to his role in the conspiracy and begged for clemency, claiming he had been forced into it. Whatever the truth, it was enough for the Inquisition to finally denounce Marquetta as a traitor and murderer, and admit their own leader's involvement in his plot. Lukan had heard the news earlier that morning, when an inquisitor had informed him—along with Flea and Ashra—that their confinement to a suite of rooms in the palace was over, and they were free to go.

"Probably best if you leave the city," the inquisitor had said, giving Lukan a dark look—still mistrusting, even now. Despite everything Lukan had done.

"Trust me," Lukan had replied, giving the man a friendly slap on the shoulder, "I fully intend to."

Yet as keen as he was to leave Saphrona, he couldn't. Not yet. *Not until I've got what I came all this way for . . .*

"Lukan Gardova." The voice was smooth and rich.

"Zandrusa," Lukan replied, turning to find the merchant prince standing beneath an arch. "Though I suppose I should call you Lady Jelassi now."

"Please," the woman said, smiling as she stepped forward. "Zandrusa is fine. You've more than earned that right." She offered her hand.

"You look well," Lukan replied, accepting the handshake. The woman's grip was firm.

"I feel it," the merchant prince replied, her eyes bright with newfound vigor. "Funny what a taste of freedom can do for you." Her appearance was a far cry from that of the woman Lukan had met for the first time in the depths of the Ebon Hand; she had swapped filthy rags for a high-collared brocaded tunic fastened by silver buttons. "Still, I can't deny that after sitting through a four-hour council meeting the novelty has already worn off a little." She gestured to a pair of wicker chairs. "Shall we?"

"Has the council decided Marquetta's fate?" Lukan asked as they sat.

"Not yet," Zandrusa replied, smile fading. "Many things have changed since I was last a free woman, but the workings of the Gilded Council most certainly have not."

"What's the delay? Surely no one is claiming Marquetta's innocent?"

"No, nothing as crass as that—the council has unanimously accepted his guilt. The extraordinary evidence you provided has more than proven that. Unsurprisingly, some of my fellow merchant princes had trouble believing the role that the Faceless played, but fortunately Artemio's account corroborated your version of events and so they had little choice but to accept it. Even so, there are those among my peers who argue for clemency to be shown to Marquetta."

Lukan snorted. "The man's a murderer. A traitor."

"He is, but his bloodline is old and his name still commands respect."

"Even after all he's done?"

"The old families have always protected their own. No doubt to some of my fellow councillors, Lord Marquetta's only crime was getting caught. There are many of them who share his vision for Saphrona, even if they might balk at his methods. Old men clinging to older prejudices."

"Like Lord Murillo."

"Indeed." Zandrusa's eyes glazed over, as if she was seeing the walls of her cell once again. "When we spoke back in the Ebon Hand, I told you it must have been Murillo who was behind it all, since he made no attempt to hide the fact that he loathed me and my ideas. But Marquetta . . . he always seemed so genial, despite our differences. I suppose evil is at its most powerful when it wears a smile and smells of rose water."

"Marquetta was afraid of you, wasn't he?"

"Of course he was. Men like him are afraid of anything that threatens their view of the world and their sense of where they belong in it. As the first Zar-Ghosan to sit on the Gilded Council, I represented everything he and his allies feared, everything they despised. They wanted to turn back time, to re-create a world where Saphrona reigned supreme and Zar-Ghosa cowered beneath its might. A world that made them feel safe, for small-minded men are easily scared by progress, by change. No doubt the growing support for my various reforms only made them fear me even more."

"Which is why Marquetta had Saviola murdered and framed you for the crime—he wanted you both out of the way."

"Indeed. He knew we would oppose his elevation to Lord Protector and that, even if we couldn't prevent it, we would be a thorn in the side of his ambitions for Saphrona." Zandrusa's expression hardened. "And we would have been, mark my words. We would have fought against his prejudices and imperialistic ambitions every step of the way. That's why he knew he had to have us dealt with. We were a threat. Marquetta was many things, but he wasn't stupid. Far from it, in fact. His plot was ingenious, though I find myself wondering . . . How did he contact the Faceless in the first place?"

"I'm not sure he even did," Lukan replied. "In the records, the Faceless have always shown up whenever one of the purple crystals was discovered. Maybe they can sense them somehow . . ." He trailed off as he recalled the visions he had seen when he pressed his finger to the gem in the pommel of the Sandino Blade: the black tower, the stream of white light, the pale tentacles in the sky—and the sensation that had gripped him, a sense of a vast, timeless presence . . .

"Well, I've no doubt our inquisitors will learn the truth from him in time—Lukan, are you well?"

He jolted and the memory faded away. "Fine," he said, forcing a smile. "So what will happen to him now?"

"My fellow councillors will argue for another day or two, no doubt, but Marquetta *will* go to the Bone Pit. Have no doubt. In years past he might have been able to avoid such a fate, but change is coming to the Gilded Council—slowly, but it's coming. He'll get what he deserves."

"I doubt he'll face that monster with the same courage you did."

"It is my hope that in the future no one will ever have to face that creature again. It's a barbaric practice that belongs in the past, along with so much else. But right now we have more pressing matters to attend to."

"I can imagine. I saw what happened to the Zar-Ghosan quarter."

"An unspeakable tragedy." A shadow passed across Zandrusa's face. "My people have lost our home in this city. The whole district lies in ashes and needs to be completely rebuilt. Then there's the matter of Zar-Ghosa itself. When the Queen learns that her ambassador was not the aggressor but a victim in all this, she will demand compensation as a matter of honor, and my people are nothing if not stubborn."

"I heard the ambassador survived the chaos in the plaza."

"She did, thank Llalu. Fortunately, from what I'm told, it seems calm heads prevailed and she was arrested rather than being cut down on the spot, which is a mercy. Her death would have made things much more complicated. Fortunately, she's already on her way home, bearing a letter for her queen written by my own hand. The Zar-Ghosan quarter may have gone up in flames but the peace treaty between Saphrona and Zar-Ghosa need not follow suit. It *must* not. Another war benefits no one."

"Try telling that to the crowd I saw in a tavern last night. They seemed rather keen on spilling Zar-Ghosan blood."

"Emotions are still running high," Zandrusa acknowledged with a nod. "And we must quickly find a way to explain to our citizens that all this blood and chaos was Marquetta's doing, not some Zar-Ghosan plot. I worry about further violence . . ." She waved her own words away, her smile returning. "Look at me, loading all my problems on to you. My apologies."

"If there's anything I can do to assist you—"

"Oh, you've done more than enough already, Lukan. Saphrona owes you a considerable debt. As do I."

"Yeah, well . . . I had some help."

"Yes, I hoped to meet these friends of yours—Flea and Ashra, correct? They didn't come with you?"

"Flea's with your gardener. I'm afraid she had more interest in your fishpond than in you."

Zandrusa laughed. "And Ashra? Who the inquisitors would surely have imprisoned if they had so much as an inkling as to who, or what, she really is."

"You know?"

"Of course. I used to be a smuggler, after all. But don't worry, my lips are sealed. The Inquisition will never find out that one of the heroes who saved the city is also one of its finest thieves."

"*The* finest, apparently. And I've seen nothing to make me doubt that claim."

"I've heard stories about her. They say she can walk through walls . . ."

Lukan remained silent. He'd managed to keep Ashra's secret during his various interrogations, and he wasn't about to reveal it now, not even to a former smuggler. He merely smiled instead.

Zandrusa laughed again. "Very well, keep your secrets. It's a shame not to make her acquaintance, I would have liked to thank her in person."

"She disappeared after we were released," Lukan replied, remembering the thief's hasty departure and brusque goodbye, though she had consented to giving Flea a hug. "I'm not sure where she is." *Keeping her head down, most likely.*

"Well," Zandrusa continued, "as I said, the city owes you a debt—all three of you. As do I. A debt I can never hope to repay."

"Talking of debts, there's the matter of Delastro's payment . . ."

"I've already seen to it," the merchant prince said, her lips thinning at the mention of the mercenary leader's name. "While it pains me to pay such a large sum to someone complicit in Marquetta's conspiracy, a deal's a deal. You can rest assured she will get her money." Zandrusa waved her hand as if fanning away a noxious odor. "I can only hope my debt to you can be paid as easily."

"It can," Lukan replied. "I can't speak for Flea or Ashra, but all *I* want from you is the casket my father left for me."

"And you shall have it," the merchant prince replied, brows knitting. "But surely there is more I can offer you—gold, or perhaps—"

"There's more important causes that need your gold. I just want my father's casket."

"You're a good man, Lukan Gardova."

"I try to be."

Zandrusa glanced at the arches to her left and snapped her fingers. "Valestia, if you would . . ." A well-dressed young woman, her dark hair tied back in a single braid, entered the courtyard, carrying a silver tray. "My new steward," the merchant prince added, her smile rueful. "Who I'm sure will prove far more loyal than the last."

"And far less willing to put up with your mess," the woman replied good-naturedly. "When your business is concluded here, perhaps my lady will consider tidying the desk in her study."

"I regret hiring her already," Zandrusa whispered theatrically, behind a raised hand.

Lukan barely heard the exchange and was almost oblivious to the smile Valestia offered him as she held out the tray. On another day, under different circumstances, he would have met her deep brown eyes and returned the smile—might have even tried his luck with a touch of flirting.

Instead he could only stare at the small casket on the tray. He could tell at a glance that it was Phaeron; it had that peculiar quality of *otherness* that all such items possessed. It was forged from an alloy that had a peculiar green tint, though the embellishments at each corner appeared to be made from gold—occasionally the Phaeron had lowered themselves to working with materials that humankind would later treasure. A single glass panel was set in the middle of the curved lid. *Well, Father,* Lukan thought, with a sense of anticipation, *let's see what surprise you have for me from beyond the grave.* He took the casket and thanked Valestia, who bowed and swept away in a rustle of silk. "So you're sure you don't know what's in here?" he asked Zandrusa, turning the casket over in his hands. "My father never said?"

"Not a word."

"And you've never tried to open it?"

"Of course I've *tried*," Zandrusa replied, with a smile. "I used to be a smuggler, remember? Call it . . . professional curiosity."

"But you never managed to get it open?"

"No. As I said, it'll open for you alone."

"You're lucky it didn't set you on fire." *Or something worse.*

"No risk, no reward." Zandrusa gestured at the box, eyes bright with anticipation. "Come on then, let's have at it. If the damned thing sets *you* on fire, you have my word I'll throw you in the fountain."

"And if it bursts my eyeballs?" Lukan asked, smiling to hide his nerves. "Or melts my flesh?"

Zandrusa laughed. "We'll cross that bridge when we come to it."

"Fine, but you might have to carry me."

Lukan pressed his thumb to the glass panel, his heart leaping into his throat.

There was no fire. No ice, no disease, no insects crawling under his skin. Only a soft chime as the panel glowed gold. Relieved, Lukan removed his finger. The lid rose silently of its own accord. Zandrusa leaned in and joined him in peering at the solitary object that lay in the padded interior of the casket.

"A key," Lukan breathed. *What in the hells . . .*

Tentatively he picked it up, wary of more Phaeron trickery, but the key seemed to have been made by human hands, forged from cast iron that gave it a solid weight as it lay across his palm. Its handle was shaped like a B and bore two gems, a garnet and an amethyst, one set in each half of the letter.

"A key," he repeated, anger bleeding into his voice. "I've come all this way, risked my life several times . . . Lady's blood, I helped prevent a *war,* and all I get in return is a bloody *key*—"

"That's not just any key," Zandrusa said, her tone curious. "The motif is that of the Blackfire Bank in Korslakov. The most secure vault in the Old Empire, if you believe the rumors. Not to mention the bank's own claims—"

"Korslakov?" Lukan cut in, shaking his head in bewilderment as he turned the key over in his hands. "But my father doesn't— *didn't* have any interests in Korslakov. He never mentioned it. I didn't think he'd ever been there."

"This would suggest otherwise." Zandrusa sat back, her expression thoughtful. "It seems there's something in the vault of the Blackfire Bank that your father wants you to have."

"Like what?"

The merchant prince shrugged. "Who can say? Your father was ever a man of mystery."

"Don't I just know it," Lukan replied, biting the words out as he tightened his fist round the key's shaft. *First the letter, now the key. Mysteries upon mysteries.* In that moment he wanted nothing more than to hurl the key into the fountain and leave it there to rust. Instead he swallowed his growing anger.

"To Korslakov, then," he said, without enthusiasm.

"It'll be an adventure," Zandrusa said with a grin, spreading her hands. "A chance to see the City of Spires, and all the wonders within. I envy you, Lukan."

"It'll be a long trip," Lukan replied, recalling the map of the Old Empire that hung in his father's study, with Korslakov nestled in the far north, surrounded by mountains and the sprawling Winterglade Woods. He could still recall the legend scrawled in the empty space beyond the Wolfclaw Mountains north of the city. *These be the unmapped lands of men that look like beasts and beasts that walk like men.* Even now it sent a faint chill down his spine.

"You'll travel by ship, the fastest I can find," Zandrusa said, snapping her fingers. "Let me handle the details. It's the least I can do for you."

"I appreciate it," Lukan replied, his mind still on Korslakov. He stared at the key, gems glinting in the light. *What the hells has Father been keeping in this vault? What could possibly be so important? And why leave the key without so much as a note of explanation . . .*

"And now," Zandrusa said, rising to her feet with a deep sigh, "I'm afraid I must leave you. Council business waits on no woman. We have a city to set to rights."

"Can we talk again?" Lukan asked, standing with her. "I would know more of your friendship with my father."

"Of course." Zandrusa grinned. "I'll tell you the tale of how we met. Phaeron ruins, a swarm of angry guards, a desperate escape . . . It was quite the adventure."

"Adventure?" Lukan echoed, his brow furrowing. "We *are* talking about Conrad Gardova? A man of letters who could barely find the way out of his own study?"

"The one and same." The merchant prince laughed. "Conrad was quite the adventurer in his day. Though . . ." Her expression turned rueful. "I sense he changed a lot after your mother died."

"He did."

"I'm sorry to hear that." Zandrusa's smile returned. "We'll talk more later. For now, enjoy my villa and treat it as your own. I'll see you this evening." She bowed and made to leave.

"One more thing."

"Of course," Zandrusa replied, turning back. "You only have to name it."

"I don't suppose you've got a bottle of Parvan Red in the cellar?"

40

THREE'S COMPANY

"I thought you said your father was a sco . . ." Flea frowned, trying to find the right word. "A sholar."

"Scholar," Lukan corrected. "He was."

"But he was also some sort of explorer?"

"Apparently. Before I was born."

"So he explored ruins and stuff?"

"Seems that way."

"Looking for what? Treasure?"

"I guess." *Though I suspect my father's idea of treasure ran beyond gold and silver.*

"And he never told you about this?"

"No."

"Why not?"

Why indeed. Zandrusa's tales—told to Lukan over a bottle of excellent Parvan Red—had sparked countless questions about the father he thought he'd known, but why Conrad Gardova had kept his past a secret was the one question he pondered the most. Lukan had spent his entire life believing his father was no more than a nobleman scholar who rarely left the confines of his study, so the revelation that in a former life he had been some sort of dashing adventurer had come as something of a surprise. *And that's putting it mildly.* It felt like the world had shifted beneath his feet, as if he'd become untethered from a truth that had always secured him, and the ropes that still held him fast were now woven from doubt instead of certainty. *What further secrets did you hide from me, Father?* he wondered, reaching for the key that now hung on a chain about his neck. *What awaits me in this vault in Korslakov?*

If he was honest with himself (which he rarely was, especially when brutally hungover), the copious amount of wine he'd sunk the night before probably wasn't helping his newfound sense of disorientation. Yet he'd needed the alcohol to offset the shock of hearing Zandrusa describe his distant, bookish father as a rapier-wielding plunderer of Phaeron ruins. The two—no, *three*—tumblers of Parvan Bronze he'd downed after the merchant prince had retired to bed, however, were admittedly a bit of an overindulgence. *I'm certainly paying for them now.* He winced at the ache behind his eyes, which wasn't helped by the clamor of the waterfront. Despite the early hour, Saphrona's docks were already busy with laborers hefting crates, bleary-eyed mariners spilling out of taverns, and customs officers yawning as they squinted at their ledgers.

"So what do you . . ."

Flea's words were drowned out by a tattooed sailor enthusiastically hammering at a ship's rail.

"Lady's blood," Lukan muttered, gritting his teeth as each strike of the hammer sent a jolt of pain through his temple. "I think that last nail needs another hit," he shouted, as the sailor momentarily paused in her work. She flicked him an obscene gesture and went back to her hammering.

"What's up with you this morning?" Flea asked as they moved away. "You're grouchier than an old tomcat."

"Don't you bloody start. It's too early for your bullsh—"

"It's just after sixth bell. It's not *that* early."

"Any time before eleventh bell is too early. Best you remember that."

"Or you'll what?"

"Chuck you in the damned sea and let the lion sharks have you. But knowing you, you'll just talk their bloody fins off."

"I know why you're grumpy," the girl teased, cracking a grin.

"I'm not grumpy, I'm hungover."

"You're all grouchy because Va-les-tia"—the girl spoke the steward's name in a singsong voice, tilting her head as she did so— "refused your invitation to join you in your bedchamber last night."

"Oh, for the love of . . . you heard that?"

"Yep."

"You were supposed to be asleep."

"Spying on you was more fun."

"You little . . ." The girl easily evaded his half-hearted swipe, her grin still intact. "Anyway," Lukan continued, "she didn't refuse, she . . . politely declined."

"She took your bottle away and said she'd smash it over your head if you said another word."

"That counts as polite in my book."

"You are *such* an idiot."

"I know." Truth was, trying to talk the steward into bed definitely *had* been a mistake—even if her lips had held a curl of amusement as she'd snatched the bottle from him. He glanced at Flea. *But am I about to make a greater mistake?* "Flea," he said, trying for a more serious tone, "are you sure about this?"

The girl sighed, rolled her eyes. "We've been over this more times than a beggar over a corpse."

"I know, I just want to be sure that . . . *you're* sure. About this."

"I'm sure."

"It's just that Saphrona is your home—"

"I already told you," the girl cut in, eyes narrowed in annoyance. "There's nothing for me here. My brother is gone, I lost friends in the fire . . ."

"That old rogue Obassa is still alive."

"Yeah, but what am I gonna do—run errands for him until I'm dead?" She shook her head, lips pressed together. "I want more than that."

"I understand, Flea. I get it. But . . . well, my path could be a dangerous one. I have no idea what awaits me in Korslakov."

"All the more reason for me to come with you. Who else is gonna watch your back?"

"It'll be a tough journey. Three weeks by sea. You've not even been on a ship before."

"Do you want me to come or not?" the girl demanded.

"Yes," Lukan replied, raising his hands in a calming gesture, "I do."

The girl chewed her lip. "Swear?"

"I swear." And he meant it. As infuriating as Flea could be, he'd realized he would be glad of her company. Besides, she *had* saved his life twice now—not that she needed reminding, of course. Whatever awaited him in the City of Spires, he felt strangely reassured that he would face it with Flea at his side. *A skinny eleven-year-old with a sharp knife and sharper tongue. Who would have thought it.* They made a peculiar pairing, but he couldn't deny it worked. Somehow.

The girl looked him dead in the eye, as if searching for a lie. "Good," she said, brightening. "Let's get going then." As they continued along the waterfront, she added, "I wish Ashra was coming with us."

I bloody don't. After three days of confinement in their palace rooms, with Ashra prowling about and glaring daggers at anyone who so much as breathed, he had been glad to see the back of the thief—and he was certain the feeling was mutual. He doubted they could survive another hour in each other's company, let alone three weeks in the cramped confines of a ship. *I'd rather go up against the Faceless again.* "Hmm," he replied.

"What do you mean, *hmm*?"

"I mean . . ." He shrugged. "Ashra has her own path. Anyway, she wouldn't want to come with us."

"But how do you know?"

"Because," a familiar voice said from behind them, "men always think they know best."

It can't be. Lukan turned and blinked at the sight of the figure standing before them. *Lady's mercy . . .*

"Ashra!" Flea cried, springing toward the thief, who wore the faintest of smiles.

"Hello, little one," she murmured, returning the girl's enthusiastic hug.

"Thought we'd seen the last of you," Lukan said.

"I had some business to take care of," Ashra replied, glancing around warily, her posture tense, alert. "And I needed to make sure that Alphonse was okay."

"And?"

"He's fine. Lying low."

"Good. And you?"

"I need to leave the city for a while." She glanced around again. "It's not safe for me here. Not with the King turning the place upside down looking for me."

"Is it just me," Lukan said, "or do I sense the words 'can I come with you' sliding toward this conversation?"

"I thought," the thief replied, face impassive, "that perhaps you could use my help in Korslakov." She shrugged. "It also happens to be about as far from the King as I'll ever get."

"Yes!" Flea exclaimed, hopping on the spot. "Come with us!"

"Hold on," Lukan said, frowning. "How do you know we're going to Korslakov?"

"I visited Zandrusa last night and asked what your plans were."

"You visited her . . ."

"Well, I broke in."

"Of course you did."

"She was very understanding. And she told me about the key."

"That was kind of her," Lukan muttered.

"So how about it? You think you could use my help?" Ashra held his gaze, her expression impassive, but he sensed a vulnerability behind her mask. *A fear I might say no.*

And there was a part of him that wanted to do just that—after all, the three days they'd spent cooped up together had hardly been a bundle of laughs. Was he really prepared for three weeks of sharp comments and judging glances? Yet he couldn't deny Ashra's skills or the strength of her character. She was smart, daring, and stubborn as the hells. *And she uses portals to literally walk through walls. Who wouldn't want her on their side?* He glanced at Flea, saw the hope shining in her eyes. That sealed it. "I'm sure we could find a use for you," he told Ashra, a wry smile on his lips.

"So we're agreed, then?" the thief asked, her relief evident, the tension seeming to leave her shoulders. "I'll come with you to Korslakov?"

"If you're sure . . ."

"I'm sure."

"Then let's get going."

"Yessss," Flea exclaimed, punching the air, as they started walking. "An adventure!"

"Let's see if you still feel the same when you're throwing your guts up on the ship," Lukan replied.

"Maybe I won't."

"You've never been on a ship, kid. Trust me, you'll be decorating the walls with your insides in no time."

"Yeah, well if I *am* sick I'll make sure I puke all over *you*."

"Charming."

"Are you two going to argue all the way to Korslakov?" Ashra asked warily.

Lukan grinned. "There's still time to back out."

"Don't tempt me." The thief slipped a stiletto from her belt, twirled it in her fingers. "Still, if it gets too much, I can always remove your tongue."

"*My* tongue? What about Flea's?"

"You'd have me harm a girl?" Ashra pursed her lips. "Who do you think I am?"

I really have no idea. Hopefully by the time they arrived in Korslakov he would have an answer to that question. *Or a vague idea, at least.*

"What was the pier number again?" Flea asked.

"Fifty-four," Ashra replied.

"Of course Zandrusa told you," Lukan said dryly. "Don't suppose she mentioned the ship's name?"

"No, but she did say it would serve our purpose well enough."

"Well, as long as it's better than the wreck I arrived on—"

"This is it!" Flea interjected, pointing at a faded sign nailed to a pillar. "Pier fifty-four."

A queasy sense of unease settled in Lukan's gut as his gaze wandered over the ship's expanse, taking in the tarnished fittings and splintering timbers. *Lady's blood, it can't be . . .*

"Friend Lekaan!" Grabulli called down from the railing, doffing his battered hat in greeting. "Welcome! I'm so pleased to be making your acquaintance again."

"I wish I could say the same," Lukan muttered.

"You know this man?" Ashra asked.

"You could say that. The last time we met he threatened to throw me overboard."

"Why?"

"Because I had the audacity to suggest that I pay the fee we'd agreed, and not a copper more."

"You really do bring out the worst in people, don't you?"

"Must be my good looks."

"Or your subtle charm." The thief started toward the gangplank. "Don't worry," she added over her shoulder, "I won't let the bad man throw you to the sharks."

"Much obliged," Lukan muttered, ushering Flea on board. Yet as he followed them onto the *Sunfish,* up toward the widespread arms and gold-toothed grin of Graziano Grabulli, he couldn't help but smile. *Perhaps bringing Ashra along wasn't such a bad idea after all.*

ACKNOWLEDGMENTS

I was fifteen when I started to pursue the dream of writing a fantasy novel and becoming a published author. I'm now forty and that dream, elusive for so many years, has finally been realized. It's been a long road. But no road is long in good company, as the Turkish proverb goes. And I've been blessed with some amazing company on this journey.

I therefore offer a tip of the hat, a raise of the glass, and my deepest thanks to the following people.

My parents, Liz and Ian, for their love and support over the years, and for insisting on weekly childhood visits to the library, which opened doors to worlds far beyond the woods and fields of home.

My brothers, Matthew and Richard, for keeping me grounded ("You're not writing *another* book about wizards?"), and for all the fun, banter, and arguments over *Settlers of Catan*. Thanks, fellas.

Ian O'Connor, my old friend from way back when, for the winter nights playing *Quake* and the summer days when we faced down hordes of monsters armed with nothing more than bamboo poles. And for reading the first chapter I ever wrote and encouraging me to write more.

Mark Newton for the lazy Buxton days, the countless emails and chats over the years, and for reading an endless succession of first chapters. (You'll get your wolfmen. Patience!)

The LiveJournal crew from the late aughts who tolerated my excessive navel-gazing about whatever book I was working on at the time. I've forgotten most of your names, but not your enthusiasm and the encouragement you gave me. Thank you.

Sara King, editor of the now-defunct zine *Aberrant Dreams*, who rejected a short story of mine many years ago, but whose kind words and encouragement kept me going through the lean years. I hope this book has proven you right.

Paul Kearney, who kindly read a chapter of mine a long time ago, and whose blunt feedback ("This is better than I expected.") provided a valuable confidence boost. Those words from a writer of such quality meant a lot.

Anne C. Perry—former agent, current editor, longtime friend—for working tirelessly on my behalf, for improving this book immeasurably, and for making a long-held dream a reality. I owe you more than I can say. (Also, thanks for all the Oreos.) Thanks too to Gaby Puleston-Vaudrey and everyone else at Quercus for all their efforts on my behalf.

Hillary Sames for her enthusiasm, brilliant editorial notes, and for helping this book shine all the brighter.

Jacqui Lewis and Terry McGarry for their heroic efforts in the copyediting trenches, where they bravely faced down the horrors of my grammar, punctuation, and complete lack of regard for the story's timeline.

Jeff Brown for his superb cover art and for being a pleasure to work with.

The other three-quarters of the Garlic Club—Jared, Paul, and Mike—for years of fun and, um, garlic-fueled frolics. Cheers guys.

Jenni and Nazia for the cat videos, the memes, and for all their support and enthusiasm.

Stephanie Stein, Sanaa Ali-Virani, Devi Pillai, and everyone at Tor for giving *The Silverblood Promise* a home in the U.S., and for all their passion and hard work.

Finally, my deepest thanks of all to my partner, Emma Swift, for enduring my endless complaints with saintlike patience, for always being a source of sound advice, and for lending me some of her belief when I had lost all my own. This book would not exist without her, and this little world I've created was blessed to have her at my side as it took shape. Love always.

Oh, there's one final thank-you to give—to you, dear reader, whoever you are, for taking a chance on *The Silverblood Promise* and for reading this far. I put my heart and soul into this book, and I truly hope you enjoyed it. (And if you're doing that weird thing that I also do, of reading the acknowledgments before the book, then I hope you *do* enjoy the read!)

Right, I think that's it. The sun's shining as I write this, on a warm day in late spring, but we'll all need heavy coats for where we're going next. In Korslakov, the City of Spires, the snow has already begun to fall.

James Logan
London
28 May 2023

About the Author

ELLA KEMP

James Logan was born in the southeast of England, where he grew up on a diet of Commodore 64 computer games, Fighting Fantasy gamebooks, and classic '80s cartoons, which left him with a love of all things fantastical. He lives in London and works in publishing. *The Silverblood Promise* is his first novel.

jamesloganauthor.com
Instagram: @jamesloganauthor